THE SIMON & SCHUSTER YOUNG READERS'

THESAURUS

BY GEORGE BEAL

Published by Wanderer Books
A Division of Simon & Schuster, Inc.
Simon & Schuster Building
1230 Avenue of the Americas
New York, New York 10020

Manufactured in Spain

Wanderer and colophon are registered
trademarks of Simon & Schuster, Inc.

Also available in
Julian Messner Library Edition

10   9   8   7   6   5   4

ISBN: 0-671-50816-4

Introduction

HOW THIS BOOK IS ARRANGED

1. SYNONYMS

This book is arranged alphabetically in normal dictionary style, and these alphabetical words are called entries. Following each entry are a number of words which have a similar, or closely related meaning. These words are called synonyms. English words do not have *exact* synonyms, although some words are very close in meaning to others. The word *fast*, for instance, means almost the same as *quick*, but the two words cannot always be interchanged. One can speak of a "fast car", or of a "fast train", but we do not say "quick car" or "quick train", since these expressions sound odd and awkward. So, in selecting synonyms, remember that they should be used with care.

Some entries in the book have more than one meaning. Take the word *hand*, for instance. It can mean the appendage with four fingers at the end of our arms; we can also talk of "farm hands"—meaning farm laborers; we can also ask someone to give us a "hand" in doing a job; or we can "hand" someone an object they may require.

Within each entry, every meaning is numbered and followed by an abbreviation to show whether the words are nouns, verbs, pronouns, adjectives, adverbs, conjunctions or prepositions. In the case of the example quoted above, *hand*, with its four meanings, is a noun in three cases and a verb in the last.

From quill pen . . .   *to hand press.*

2. ANTONYMS

In addition to synonyms, the book also shows antonyms. An antonym is a word which represents the opposite meaning to that of the entry word. For example, an antonym of *quick* could be *slow*, *sluggish*, or *tardy*. In this book, all the entries are numbered within each letter of the alphabet. In other words, all the entries beginning with A are numbered from A1 to A186, from B1 to B187, and so on. Antonyms are indicated by reference to these numbers. In the case of *quick*, for instance, we find the numbers S270, S271, T27 and O25 following the definitions. If we check these in the main list of entries, we find that S270 refers to *slow*, S271 to *sluggish*, T27 to *tardy*, and O25 to *obtuse*. The second definition of *quick* gives "active, nimble, agile, sprightly", meaning "quick-witted". An antonym for this is *obtuse*, meaning "dull-witted".

In some cases, where meanings are obscure, an example of the use of the word is given in an example sentence.

From typesetter and typewriter . . .

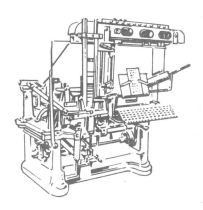

3. FURTHER SYNONYMS

Further synonyms may be found by referring to words shown in *italics*. If we look up *rigid*, for example, we find the synonyms are "*stiff*, inflexible, unbending". Now if we look further under *stiff*, we find the further words "firm, solid", which could, under certain circumstances, also be used for *rigid*. In fact, all words shown can be checked against others in the body of the book, where other possible synonyms or antonyms may be found.

4. ADDITIONAL WORDS

In a book of this size, it is not possible to include every possible variation of each word as a main entry. Where a related word can be shown, it is included at the end of the entry. There is, for instance, an entry for *wealth*, but no main entry for *wealthy*, which can be found under the entry for *wealth*.

5. HOMONYMS

Lastly, the book also shows homonyms. A homonym is a word which has the same *sound* as another, but which has a different meaning, and usually a different spelling. For instance, *right*, *rite*, *write*, and *wright* all sound the same, but have quite different meanings. Homonyms are printed at the end of an entry in CAPITAL letters.

to word processor.

KEY TO THE ENTRIES

Here is a specimen entry from the book:

C418 **correct** 1. *adj.* faultless, exact, precise, *accurate*, true (E126, F59, I93, I127, W121) 2. *v.* rectify, amend, set right (E123) *n.* **correction** (E127) *n.* **correctness** (M187).

The entry is the word *correct*, which has the reference number C418. The first meaning, numbered 1, gives *correct* as an adjective, followed by five synonyms. The word *accurate*, shown in italics, can be looked up for further synonyms. The figures in brackets (E126, F59, and so on) refer to antonyms, which will be found under the reference numbers. The second meaning, which shows *correct* as a verb, gives three synonyms, and a further reference to an antonym. Extra words related to *correct* are the nouns *correction* and *correctness* both of which have synonym references.

ABBREVIATIONS

adj.	adjective
adv.	adverb
conj.	conjunction
n.	noun
n.pl.	plural noun
prep.	preposition
pron.	pronoun
v.	verb
colloq.	colloquial

An abbey church being built.

A   a

A1 **abandon** *v.* 1. *leave*, desert, forsake 2. surrender, give up (C114, C125) *adj.* **abandoned.**

A2 **abbey** *n. church*, priory.

A3 **abbreviate** *v. shorten*, condense, reduce (A107).

A4 **abdicate** *v. resign*, surrender, renounce (U103).

A5 **ability** *n. skill*, capacity (I91).

A6 **able** *adj.* capable, fit, qualified, clever (I120, U4).

A7 **abnormal** *adj.* unusual, peculiar, odd (A181, U102).

A8 **aboard** *prep.* on board.

A9 **abolish** *v.* end, *cancel*, wipe out (K2, R219).

A10 **abominable** *adj.* nasty, unpleasant (A55, N57) *v.* **abominate.**

A11 **about** *prep.* 1. *concerning*, regarding 2. near, around.

A12 **above** *prep.* over, aloft, higher than (B55, U22, U25).

A13 **abridge** *v.* shorten, abbreviate, *condense* (A107, E215).

A14 **abroad** *adv.* overseas, away (H149).

A15 **abrupt** *adj.* 1. sudden, hasty, curt, blunt 2. steep (G113).

A16 **absent** *adj.* away, missing, lacking (P360) *v.* be absent (A172) *n.* **absence** (P359).

A17 **absolute** *adj. complete*, perfect, ideal (P60) *adv.* **absolutely** (P140).

A18 **absorb** *v.* swallow, consume, monopolize (D208).

A19 **abstain** *v.* give up, refrain, renounce (I151).

A20 **absurd** *adj.* foolish, silly, ridiculous (S127).

A21 **abundant** *adj.* plentiful, profuse, lavish (S52) *n.* **abundance** (S54).

A22 **abuse** *v.* misuse, mistreat, hurt (R204).

A23 **accelerate** *v.* hasten, hurry, quicken (S270).

A24 **accent** *n.* stress, emphasis.

A25 **accept** *v.* receive, admit, *take* (D50, R114, R129, R166).

A26 **access** *n.* entrance, admission, approach (E191).

A27 **accident** *n.* mishap, disaster, *calamity adj.* **accidental** (D83).

A28 **acclaim** *v.* praise, applaud, approve, *cheer* (D101).

A29 **accommodate** *v.* house, oblige, assist.

A30 **accompany** *v.* escort, follow (D126).

A31 **accomplice** *n.* partner, helper (O69).

A32 **accomplish** *v.* do, complete, *achieve*, finish (A171, F15).

A33 **accord** 1. *v.* agree, consent, *allow* 2. *n.* harmony, agreement (C386, D217, S503).

A34 **account** *n.* 1. report, story 2. ledger, record, invoice.

A35 **accumulate** *v.* gather, collect, grow, pile.

A36 **accurate** *adj. correct*, exact, precise (E126, M188, W121).

A37 **accuse** *v. blame*, charge, denounce (A42).

A38 **accustomed** *adj.* used to, usual (U5).

A

A39 **ache** *(ake)* *v.* hurt, be sore, throb (C239).

A40 **achieve** *v. accomplish,* reach, complete, do (F15).

A41 **acquire** *v.* obtain, gain, get (L142).

A42 **acquit** *v.* set free, release, excuse, forgive, pardon (A37, C309, S128).

A43 **act** 1. *v.* behave, work, operate, perform 2. *n. deed,* action, feat 3. *n.* law.

A44 **action** *n.* 1. movement, act, behavior 2. *battle,* combat.

A45 **active** *adj.* live, agile, nimble, alert (D35, I94, S244).

A46 **actual** *adj. real,* true, genuine, certain (I25, M291).

A47 **acute** *adj.* sharp, keen, astute, shrewd (O25).

A48 **adapt** *v.* adjust, suit, fit, *modify.*

A49 **add** *v.* increase, sum up, total, join, unite (D57, S543). .

A50 **address** 1. *n.* location, home, abode 2. *v.* speak to, talk to, greet, hail (I13).

A51 **adequate** *adj.* enough, sufficient, capable (I95).

A52 **adhere** *v.* stick, cling, hold, *attach* (S130).

A53 **adjacent** *adj.* near, next to, close to, touching (A119, D251).

A54 **adjust** *v.* 1. set, regulate, change, alter, *adapt* 2. get used to; *Mary has adjusted to her new home.*

A55 **admire** *v.* esteem, respect, regard (D135) *adj.* admirable (H61) *n.* **admiration** (C369).

A56 **admit** *v.* 1. confess, own up (D104) 2. let in, permit (B20).

A57 **ado** *n.* trouble, fuss, bother, stir (T173).

A58 **adopt** *v.* 1. take care of, foster 2. assume, affect (D206); *He adopted a fighting attitude.*

A59 **adore** *v.* love, *admire,* worship, honor (L119).

A60 **adorn** *v.* decorate, beautify, ornament (D72, D226).

Makeup and jewels adorn the face.

A61 **adult** 1. *adj.* mature, ripe 2. *n.* a grown-up (C131, I164, M158, Y10).

A62 **advance** *v. proceed,* progress, approach (R71, R226).

A63 **advantage** *n.* gain, benefit, profit (D195, H23).

A64 **adventure** *n.* exploit, experience, enterprise.

A65 **adverse** *adj.* hostile, unlucky, unfavorable, *contrary* (L159).

A66 **advice** *n.* guidance, counsel, tip.

A67 **affable** *adj.* civil, *cordial,* courteous, obliging (U44).

A68 **affect** *v.* influence, impress, alter.

A69 **affection** *n.* liking, devotion, tenderness, warmth (S368) *adj.* **affectionate.**

A70 **afford** *v.* be able to pay, give, support.

A71 **afraid** *adj. fearful,* timid,

frightened, scared (B110, V6).

A72 **after** *prep. behind,* afterward, following, later (B47).

A73 **again** *adv.* anew, often, once more.

A74 **against** *prep.* opposed to, facing, opposite to, close up.

A75 **aged** *adj.* old, elderly, *ancient*, feeble (Y9).

A76 **agent** *n.* representative, operator, delegate (O69).

A77 **aggravate** *v.* 1. make worse, intensify, exaggerate (M194); *His illness was aggravated by hunger.* 2. exasperate, irritate, *annoy* (S322).

A78 **aghast** *adj.* shocked, amazed, appalled, startled (C15).

A79 **agitate** *v.* shake, jar, excite, rouse (C15).

A80 **agony** *n.* pain, torment, torture, suffering (C239).

A81 **agree** *v.* assent, *consent*, settle (D196, D249) *n.* **agreement** (C324, D245).

A82 **agreeable** *adj.* friendly, pleasing, welcome (B41, C379).

A83 **aid** *v.* help, assist, support, relieve (F181, O20).

A84 **aim** 1. *v.* point, direct, level 2. *n.* purpose, goal.

A85 **aisle** *n.* passage, opening, corridor. ISLE

A86 **alarm** *v.* frighten, scare, terrify, startle (C239).

A87 **alert** *adj.* agile, nimble, watchful, lively (D333).

A88 **alien** 1. *adj.* foreign, strange 2. *n.* foreigner, stranger (N14).

A89 **alike** *adj.* similar, same, like, identical (D169, U59).

A90 **alive** *adj.* active, live, living, alert (D35, E221, I98).

A91 **allot** *v.* allocate, divide, deal out (W88).

A92 **allow** *v. permit*, let, grant, approve (B16, D104, P418).

A93 **ally** 1. *n.* friend, helper, *colleague* (E70, O60) 2. *v.* unite, combine, join.

A94 **almost** *adv.* nearly, somewhat.

A95 **alone** *adj.* solitary, lonely, *lone*, desolate.

A96 **aloud** *adv.* loudly, audibly, noisily.   ALLOWED

A97 **alter** *v. change*, vary, modify, adjust (P362).   ALTAR

A98 **alternative** *n.* choice, selection.

A99 **altogether** *adv.* entirely, completely, quite.

A100 **always** *adv.* forever, eternally.

A101 **amaze** *v.* astound, *astonish*, surprise (B120).

A102 **ambition** *n.* desire, drive, enthusiasm, aspiration.

A103 **amend** *v.* correct, rectify, *revise*, improve.

A104 **amiable** *adj.* friendly, good-natured, obliging (C490, P112).

A105 **amount** *n.* quantity, measure, sum, whole.

A106 **ample** *adj. abundant*, plentiful, liberal (S52).

A107 **amplify** *v.* 1. enlarge, extend, expand (C523) 2. make loud (M266).

A108 **amuse** *v.* divert, entertain, please (B120).

ANCESTOR

A109 ancestor *n.* forebear, forefather, predecessor.

A110 ancient (ayn-*shent*) adj. antique, old, aged (C520, M206, O52).

A111 anger *n.* ire, rage, fury, indignation, wrath (C15).

A112 angle *n.* 1. corner, edge 2. point of view, position.

A113 anguish *n.* agony, *pain,* suffering, misery (C239).

A114 announce *v. proclaim,* publish, declare (C291).

A115 annoy *v. vex,* irk, bother, irritate (C239, O8, P249).

A116 answer *v.* respond, *reply,* retort (A153, D92, I203, Q22).

A117 anticipate *v. expect,* foresee, forecast, hope for *adj.* **anticipated** (U37).

A118 anxious *adj.* worried, *concerned,* careful, fearful (C15, C319, C402).

A119 apart *adv.* separately, alone, away (A53).

A120 aperture *n. hole,* cleft, gap, opening.

A121 apologize *v.* regret, ask pardon, be sorry (B139).

A122 appall *v. shock,* alarm, frighten, terrify (C239).

A123 apparent *adj.* obvious, plain, *evident,* clear (S104).

A124 appeal *v.* plead, pray, implore, beg, ask.

A125 appear *v. seem,* look, emerge, arise, *arrive* (D198, V14).

A126 appease *v.* pacify, *calm,* satisfy, allay (E90, P458).

A127 appetite *n.* craving, hunger, desire.

A128 applaud *v.* cheer, praise, *clap,* approve of (C82, C128).

A129 appliance *n.* machine, apparatus, instrument, tool.

A130 apply *v. use,* employ, utilize, avail.

A131 appoint *v.* name, designate, choose, *select,* pick (D237).

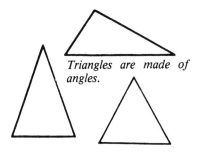

Triangles are made of angles.

A132 appreciate *v.* understand, prize, value (D22, D113, D151).

A133 approach *v.* go near, draw near, *advance* (A182).

A134 appropriate 1. *adj.* fitting, proper, suitable 2. *v. adopt,* employ; *The council's funds were appropriated for road improvement.*

A135 approve *v.* like, endorse, applaud, *commend* (C82, D201) *n.* approbation (C369), approval (R68, V48).

A136 approximate *adj.* near, rough, inexact (P339).

A137 ardent *adj.* eager, passionate, enthusiastic, keen (C402).

A138 area *n.* district, region, territory.

A139 argue (arg-*yoo*) v. debate, dispute, disagree (A81, C307).

A140 arid *adj. dry,* barren, parched (D11, M210, W53).

A141 **arise** v. *rise,* get up, emerge, appear (S226).

A142 **army** n. military force, troops, legions.

A143 **arouse** v. awaken, *wake,* stir, excite (C15).

A144 **arrange** v. order, organize, place, group, plan (D261).

A145 **array** 1. v. dress, clothe, attire, adorn 2. n. arrangement, *order,* display (D239).

A146 **arrest** v. stop, stay, check, capture, catch (R136).

A147 **arrive** v. come, reach, attain (D105, L56).

A148 **arrogant** adj. proud, haughty, disdainful (B31, M105, U9).

A149 **artful** adj. wily, crafty, *cunning,* tricky, sly (N4).

A150 **artificial** adj. synthetic, unreal, unnatural (R57).

A151 **ascend** v. rise, arise, mount, soar, *climb,* go up (D123, F24) n. **ascent** (F24).

A152 **ashamed** adj. embarrassed, abashed, shamefaced (A148).

A153 **ask** v. *request,* inquire, question (A116).

A154 **aspect** n. look, appearance, outlook, view.

A155 **aspire** v. yearn for, aim, desire, long for.

A156 **assault** v. attack, charge, assail (D64).

A157 **assemble** v. meet, collect, *gather* (D241, S57, U29).

A158 **assent** v. agree, consent, *approve* (D249, O5).

A159 **assert** v. declare, affirm, maintain, say (D104).

A160 **assign** v. appoint, allot, allocate.

A161 **assist** v. help, aid, support, sustain (H127).

A162 **assorted** adj. mixed, various, varied.

A163 **assume** v. 1. suppose, presume, suspect 2. adopt, take on; *He assumed a false mustache as a disguise.*

A164 **assure** v. pledge, promise, certify (D104).

A165 **astonish** v. surprise, astound, amaze (B120).

A166 **astute** adj. *shrewd,* crafty, cunning, keen (D333).

A167 **athletic** adj. strong, muscular, brawny, robust (P475).

A168 **attach** v. fasten, fix, affix, *connect* (D145, D213).

A169 **attack** v. *assault,* set upon, charge (D64, P447).

A170 **attain** v. accomplish, *reach,* acquire, achieve (M182).

A171 **attempt** v. try, seek, endeavor, struggle (A32, A40).

A172 **attend** v. be present, frequent, go to, visit, pay attention (A16) adj. **attentive** (I100, L105).

A173 **attire** 1. n. clothes, costume, garments 2. v. dress, clothe, equip.

A174 **attitude** n. pose, position, disposition.

A175 **attract** v. draw, pull, invite, enchant, allure (R172).

A176 **attractive** adj. charming, fascinating, appealing, lovely, *beautiful,* pretty (F259, U1).

A177 **authority** n. *command,* rule, permission, power.

A

A178 **avail** *v.* use, benefit, help, profit.

A179 **available** *adj.* obtainable, accessible, ready, convenient.

A180 **avenge** *v.* punish, revenge (P50).

A181 **average** *adj.* normal, usual, ordinary (A7, R153).

A182 **avoid** *v.* escape, shun, elude, avert (A133, E59, F4).

A183 **award** *n.* prize, reward, payment, medal.

A184 **aware** *adj. conscious,* informed, knowing (I12, U10).

A185 **awe** *n.* fear, respect, wonder, dread (C369).

A186 **awkward** *adj. clumsy,* inept, cumbersome (C388, G110) *n.* **awkwardness** (P273).

B b

B1 **babble** *v.* chatter, prattle, gabble.

B2 **baby** *n.* toddler, infant.

B3 **back** *adj.* rear, hind (F267).

B4 **background** *n.* 1. setting, framework 2. training, experience.

B5 **backward** *adj.* 1. dull, slow, retarded, sluggish 2. behind (F221).

B6 **bad** *adj.* evil, wicked, sinful, naughty, rotten, spoiled (G98, R259).

B7 **badge** *n.* symbol, emblem, crest.

B8 **baffle** *v.* puzzle, bewilder, confuse, mystify (A83).

B9 **bag** *n.* sack, case, pouch.

B10 **bait** 1. *n.* lure, snare 2. *v.* entice, entrap 3. *v.* heckle, tease, pester. BATE

B11 **bake** *v.* cook, dry, roast, harden.

B12 **balance** 1. *n.* steadiness 2. *v.* weigh, steady.

B13 **bald** *adj.* hairless, bare (H9).

B14 **balk** *v.* 1. foil, *baffle* 2. balk at, hesitate, stop.

B15 **ball** *n.* 1. sphere, globe 2. party.

B16 **ban** *v.* forbid, prohibit, outlaw (A92).

B17 **band** *n.* 1. strip, stripe, ribbon, *belt* 2. *group,* society, body, gang. BANNED

B18 **bandit** *n.* brigand, outlaw, robber, thief.

B19 **bang** *v.* hit, strike, *boom.*

B20 **banish** *v. exile,* deport, expel, dismiss (A56).

B21 **bank** 1. *n.* embankment, shore, coast 2. *n.* countinghouse 3. *v.* save (D205).

B22 **bar** 1. *v.* prevent, stop, block (A83) 2. *n. barrier,* barricade 3. *n.* pub, counter.

B23 **bare** *adj.* 1. naked, nude, unclothed 2. plain, empty, barren. BEAR

B24 **bargain** *n.* deal, agreement, contract, something cheap.

B25 **bark** 1. *v. bay,* howl, yap, yelp 2. *n.* tree covering.

B26 **barren** *adj.* unfruitful, sterile, *bare* (F88, F273, P420). BARON

B27 **barrier** *n.* bar, barricade, fence, wall, obstacle.

B28 **barter** *v.* trade, exchange, swap.

B29 **base** 1. *n. bottom,* stand, foundation (S561, T140) 2. *v.* found, establish; *Many films are based on fact.* 3. *adj.* low, vile, *bad; Cruelty to animals is a base act.* 4. *adj.* cheap, worthless. BASS

B30 **basement** *n.* cellar, vault.

B31 **bashful** *adj.* timid, *shy,* modest, coy (A148, B110).

B32 **basic** *adj.* fundamental, main (I108).

B33 **batter** *v. beat,* pound, pummel, hit.

B34 **battle** *n. & v.* fight, combat, contest, war, struggle.

B35 **bay** 1. *n.* inlet, gulf, bight 2. *v.* yelp, *bark.* BEY

B36 **beach** *n.* shore, sands, *coast,* seaside. BEECH

B37 **bead** *n. ball, bubble.*

B38 **beam** 1. *n.* girder, joist, truss 2. *n.* ray, gleam 3. *v.* shine, flash, glow.

B39 **bear** 1. *v.* carry, convey, transport 2. *v.* suffer, endure, stand, tolerate *adj.* **bearable** (I234, I270) 3. *n.* animal.

B40 **bearing** *n.* 1. manner, posture, conduct; *The man walked with a soldierly bearing.* 2. direction, course, position. BARING

B41 **beastly** *adj.* bestial, brutal, brutish (A82).

B42 **beat** *v.* 1. pound, strike, hit, batter 2. defeat, conquer 3. throb, pulsate. BEET

B43 **beautiful** *adj.* lovely, *pretty,* fair, attractive (H119, P234, U1).

B44 **beauty** *n. charm,* loveliness, grace.

B45 **become** *v.* grow, change, come to be.

B46 **becoming** *adj.* 1. *pretty,* graceful, neat 2. suitable, fit, proper (U1).

B47 **before** 1. *adv.* earlier, previously 2. *prep.* in front of, preceding (A72, B52).

B48 **beg** *v.* 1. entreat, beseech, implore 2. scrounge, cadge.

B49 **begin** *v. start,* commence (C74, D216, F126, H17).

B50 **beginning** *n.* start, origin, opening, commencement (D140, E62, F121, L29).

B51 **behavior** *n.* conduct, manners, deportment.

B52 **behind** *prep. after,* at the back of, following (B47).

B53 **believe** *v.* have faith, *accept,* trust, suppose (D291).

B54 **belong** (to) *v.* 1. be owned by, be the property of 2. be a member of, be part of.

B55 **below** *prep.* under, beneath, underneath (A12).

B56 **belt** *n.* strip, strap, band, zone.

A bench.

B57 **bench** *n.* seat, form, trestle, table.

B58 **bend** *v.* curve, bow, turn, fold.

B59 **benefit** *v. & n.* aid, help, profit (D195, H44, H211, I196).

B60 **besides** 1. *adv.* too, also, yet, further 2. *prep.* in addition to, except.

B61 **best** *adj.* finest, tiptop, first-rate, excellent.

B62 **bet** *v. gamble,* wager.

B63 **betray** *v.* mislead, be treacherous, *delude* (P447, S172).

B64 **better** *adj. superior,* preferable, greater.

B65 **beware** *v.* be careful, guard against.

B66 **bewilder** *v.* mystify, *perplex,* puzzle, confuse (C173).

B67 **beyond** *prep.* on the far side, later than, past, *after.*

B68 **bias** *n.* prejudice, sway, tendency *adj.* **biased** (F19, I47, J44, U11).

B69 **bid** *v.* 1. command, order, enjoin 2. *offer,* tender, propose.

B70 **big** *adj. large,* great, important (D183, L111, S276, W45).

B71 **bill** *n.* 1. beak, nib 2. invoice, account 3. draft of law.

B72 **bin** *n. box,* container, tub.

B73 **bind** *v.* tie, fasten, *attach,* join, link.

B74 **birth** *n.* beginning, start of life, creation, start (D40).
BERTH

B75 **bit** *n.* small piece, scrap, speck, particle.

B76 **bite** *v.* gnaw, *chew,* nip.
BIGHT

B77 **biting** *adj.* cutting, crisp, *keen,* incisive.

B78 **bitter** *adj.* acrid, harsh, acid, *sour,* sharp (B81, S611).

B79 **black** *adj.* dark, dusky, murky (R295).

B80 **blame** *n. fault,* guilt, responsibility (C471, F206).

B81 **bland** *adj. smooth,* kind, tasteless, insipid (B78, P473, S511).

B82 **blank** *adj.* void, empty, *vacant.*

B83 **blast** 1. *n.* explosion, eruption 2. *v.* blow up.

B84 **blaze** *v. flame,* flare, glow, *burn.*

B85 **bleach** *v.* whiten, blanch (D22).

B86 **bleak** *adj.* cheerless, *dismal,* dreary, bare, barren (C124).

B87 **blemish** *n.* stain, spot, defect, speck, blot, flaw.

B88 **blend** *v.* mix, merge, *mingle,* combine (S130)).

B89 **bless** *v.* praise, glorify, exalt (C521, D10) *n.* **blessing** boon (C10, C65, D203).

B90 **blight** *n.* disease, mildew, sickness.

B91 **blind** *adj.* 1. sightless, unseeing 2. unaware, thoughtless, ignorant (A184); *He was blind to his son's faults.*

B92 **blink** *v.* wink, flicker, twinkle.

B93 **bliss** *n. happiness,* joy, rapture (M174).

B94 **block** *v.* obstruct, *bar,* impede, hinder (A83). BLOC

B95 **bloom** *v.* flourish, flower, thrive, blossom (D43).

B96 **blot** *n.* stain, blemish.

B97 **blow** *n.* rap, tap, smack, slap, cuff, clout, buffet.

B98 **blue** *adj.* 1. azure, sky colored, sapphire 2. sad, glum, depressed (C124). BLEW

B99 **bluff** 1. *v. deceive,* trick, delude 2. *n.* fraud, fake, deceit

3. *adj.* outspoken, *blunt.*

B100 **blunder** 1. *n.* mistake, error 2. *v. bungle.*

B101 **blunt** *adj.* 1. *dull,* obtuse, unsharp 2. brusque, curt, bluff, gruff, abrupt (F123, P123, S161).

B102 **blur** *v. obscure,* dim, smear, confuse (C173).

B103 **blush** *v.* redden, flush, glow.

B104 **board** 1. *n.* plank 2. *n.* committee, *council* 3. *v.* embark.   BORED

B105 **boast** *v.* brag, crow.

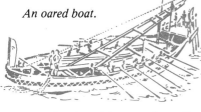

An oared boat.

B106 **boat** *n.* ship, vessel, craft.

B107 **body** *n.* 1. corpse, carcass 2. group, collection, crowd.

B108 **boil** *v.* seethe, simmer, stew, foam.

B109 **boisterous** *adj.* roaring, loud, stormy, lively (C15).

B110 **bold** *adj.* brave, courageous, unafraid, fearless, valiant, daring, reckless (A71, B31, D98, R223).

B111 **bolt** 1. *n.* bar, rod 2. *v.* secure, *lock,* close 3. *v.* flee, run away.

B112 **bond** *n.* 1. band, tie, rope, fastening 2. security, guarantee, promise.

B113 **bonny** *adj.* handsome, beautiful, *fair,* pretty (U1).

B114 **bonus** *n.* award, premium, *reward,* gift.

B115 **boom** 1. *v.* thunder, roar 2. *n.* spar, *beam,* pole.

B116 **boon** *n.* favor, benefit, blessing, windfall (C10, C65).

B117 **boost** *v.* lift, raise, elevate, hoist, increase, expand.

B118 **booty** *n.* spoils, loot, plunder, prize.

B119 **border** *n.* 1. margin, verge, edge, *rim,* brink 2. frontier, *boundary.*

B120 **bore** *v.* 1. perforate, drill, puncture 2. tire, weary (A101, A108, E100, I253) *adj.* **boring** (E75, I78, I254).   BOAR

B121 **borrow** *v.* take, receive as a loan (L67, L118).

B122 **bosh** *n.* nonsense, trash, twaddle.

B123 **boss** *n.* manager, director, employer (E54).

B124 **botch** *v.* mend, patch, bungle.

B125 **bother** *v. worry,* harass, harry, pester, tease, annoy, irritate, vex (C239).

B126 **bottom** *n.* 1. *base,* ground, depths, underside 2. buttocks, behind, rear, butt.

B127 **bough** (rhymes with *cow*) *n.* branch, limb, shoot.   BOW

B128 **bounce** *v.* spring, recoil, rebound.

B129 **bound** 1. *v.* jump, *leap,* spring, vault 2. *adj.* tied 3. *n.* boundary, *limit.*

B130 **boundary** *n.* bound, *border,* frontier.

B131 **bounty** *n.* present, gift, bonus, *reward,* generosity.

B132 **bow** (rhymes with *cow*) *v. bend,* stoop, yield, submit. BOUGH

B133 **bow** (rhymes with *go*) *n*. curve, bend.

B134 **bowl** *n*. beaker, dish, basin. BOLE BOLL

B135 **box** 1. *v*. strike, hit, smite, punch 2. *n*. crate, *case,* carton, bin.

B136 **boy** *n*. lad, youth, youngster (G57). BUOY

B137 **brace** 1. *v. support,* sustain, prop, bolster 2. *n*. bracket, strut.

B138 **bracing** *adj*. invigorating, strengthening, stimulating.

B139 **brag** *v. boast,* crow, swagger (A121).

B140 **braid** *v*. plait, intertwine, interlace, twine. BRAYED

B141 **branch** *n. bough,* limb, shoot 2. subdivision.

B142 **brand** *n*. mark, stamp, label, tag.

B143 **brandish** *v*. flourish, wave, shake.

B144 **brave** 1. *adj*. courageous, unafraid, gallant, valiant, heroic, *bold* (C451) 2. *v*. defy, dare, challenge.

B145 **brawl** *n*. quarrel, wrangle, *squabble,* fight, riot.

B146 **brawny** *adj*. muscular, sinewy, *sturdy,* athletic, strong (F134).

B147 **break** *v*. crack, burst, snap, shatter, rupture, *smash* (M120). BRAKE

B148 **breathe** *v*. emit, exhale, inhale.

B149 **breed** 1. *n*. kind, species, race, sort 2. *v*. rear, bring up, raise.

B150 **bribe** *v*. lure, entice, *corrupt,* buy off.

A bow.

B151 **brief** *adj*. short, concise, pithy, terse (I258).

B152 **bright** (rhymes with *bite*) *adj*. 1. brilliant, radiant, luminous (D180) 2. clever, keen, intelligent (D333) 3. cheerful, happy, lively (G79) *v*. **brighten** (D22, E12, T30).

B153 **brilliant** *adj*. 1. bright, sparkling, glittering 2. alert, intelligent, gifted (D333).

B154 **brim** *n*. rim, edge, brink, *border.*

B155 **bring** *v. fetch,* carry, take, convey, get.

B156 **brink** *n*. edge, *border,* margin, verge, brow.

B157 **brisk** *adj*. nimble, agile, spry, lively, quick (I156, S270).

B158 **brittle** *adj*. crisp, *fragile,* weak, breakable (F152).

B159 **broad** *adj*. wide, large, expansive (N10).

B160 **brood** *v*. think about, ponder, dwell upon. BREWED

B161 **brook** *n*. stream, rivulet, creek.

B162 **brow** *n*. forehead, brink, border, *edge.*

B163 **bruise** *(brooze) v*. crush, break, injure, squash. BREWS

B164 **brusque** *adj*. rude, rough, blunt, gruff (B81, P280).

B165 **brutal** *adj*. beastly, cruel, mean, savage (G42).

B166 **bubble** *n.* blister, blob, foam, froth.

B167 **buckle** 1. *n.* clasp, fastening 2. *v. bend,* twist, curve.

B168 **bud** *n.* sprout, shoot, germ.

B169 **budge** *v.* stir, move, go, shift.

B170 **build** (rhymes with *milled*) *v.* construct, erect, assemble (D93). BILLED

B171 **bulky** *adj.* massive, huge, large, *clumsy* (D84).

B172 **bully** 1. *n.* tyrant, ruffian, brute, thug 2. *v.* force, *coerce* (C8, C216).

B173 **bump** *v.* clash, collide, *bang,* strike.

B174 **bumper** 1. *adj.* large, generous, brimming 2. *n.* fender, guard.

B175 **bunch** *n.* bundle, bale, batch, cluster.

B176 **bundle** *n.* package, pack, parcel, roll, bunch.

B177 **bungle** *v.* botch, fumble, muff, *blunder,* spoil (M31).

B178 **burden** *n.* 1. load, weight, pack 2. worry, trial, trouble (C351).

B179 **burglar** *n.* thief, robber.

B180 **burly** *adj.* stout, lusty, *brawny,* bulky (F237).

B181 **burn** *v.* scorch, char, sear, singe, *blaze,* flame, scald.

B182 **burst** *v.* break, crack, snap, explode.

B183 **bury** *v.* hide, conceal, place in ground. BERRY

B184 **business** *n.* 1. work, occupation, trade, industry, profession, job 2. firm, company.

B185 **bustle** *v.* fuss, stir about, rush, hurry.

B186 **busy** *(bizzy) adj.* active, occupied, working, employed (I9, S102, S244).

B187 **buy** *v.* purchase, obtain, get, *acquire* (S121). BY BYE

C c

C1 **cab** *n.* taxi, taxicab, driver's compartment.

C2 **cabin** *n.* 1. compartment, berth 2. *hut,* hovel, shack, shed.

C3 **cabinet** *n.* 1. cupboard, case 2. boudoir, closet 3. ministry, *council,* committee.

C4 **cable** *n.* rope, wire, line.

C5 **cackle** *v.* giggle, titter, snigger, cluck, quack.

C6 **café** *n.* restaurant, bar, coffee, coffeehouse.

C7 **cage** *v.* imprison, shut up (F246).

C8 **cajole** *v. coax,* wheedle, flatter, persuade (B172, C263).

C9 **cake** 1. *n.* bun, tart, pastry 2. *v.* harden, solidify.

C10 **calamity** *n. disaster,* misfortune, mishap, distress (B89, B116).

C11 **calculate** *v.* reckon, compute, *count.*

C12 **call** *v.* 1. *cry,* exclaim, shout 2. name, term, christen 3. summon, invite, send for (D237).

C

C13 **calling** *n.* occupation, profession, *business,* job.

C14 **callous** *adj.* unfeeling, hard, insensitive (T60).

C15 **calm** 1. *adj.* still, tranquil, placid, quiet (A78) 2. *v.* soothe (A143) 3. *n.* tranquility (C253).

C16 **camouflage** *n.* disguise, covering.

C17 **can** *n.* container, tin.

C18 **cancel** *v.* 1. delete, obliterate, erase 2. *abolish,* put off, annul.

C19 **candid** *adj. frank,* honest, open, fair, just (B68, C513).

C20 **candidate** *n.* applicant, claimant, nominee.

C21 **canny** *adj.* clever, artful, skillful.

C22 **canopy** *n.* awning, *cover,* shelter.

C23 **cap** *n.* 1. headgear, *cover,* lid 2. top, peak, *crown,* head.

C24 **capable** *adj. able,* competent, clever, skillful (I103).

C25 **capacity** *n.* 1. *ability,* cleverness, skill (I91) 2. content, volume.

C26 **cape** *n.* 1. headland, promontory 2. cloak.

C27 **caper** *v.* hop, skip, jump, *bound,* gambol, dance.

C28 **capital** 1. *n.* chief city 2. *n.* cash, money, wealth 3. *n.* large letter 4. *adj.* good, excellent.

C29 **capsize** *v.* upset, overturn, tip up.

C30 **capsule** *n.* case, envelope, shell, sheath, pod.

C31 **captain** *n.* commander, leader, chief, skipper.

C32 **caption** *n.* title, description, heading.

C33 **captivate** *v. charm,* fascinate, enchant, bewitch.

C34 **captive** *n.* prisoner, hostage.

C35 **capture** *v.* seize, take prisoner, arrest, *catch,* trap, grab (R136).

C36 **car** *n.* vehicle, motorcar, carriage, automobile.

C37 **carcass** *n.* body, corpse.

C38 **card** *n.* cardboard, sheet, ticket, stiff paper.

C39 **care** 1. *n.* anxiety, *concern,* worry 2. *n.* caution, heed, regard; *Take care when you cross the road.* 3. *n.* charge, custody, protection 4. *v.* mind, look after (N32).

C40 **career** 1. *n.* job, profession, occupation 2. *v.* sweep, rush, move quickly.

C41 **careful** *adj.* watchful, *cautious,* attentive, discreet (C42, I60, I96, I124, R36).

C42 **careless** *adj.* heedless, thoughtless, neglectful, rash, unconcerned, sloppy (C41, C71, F301) *n.* **carelessness** (C70, P332).

C43 **caress** *v.* fondle, cuddle, *pet,* embrace, hug, kiss, stroke (C116).

C44 **cargo** *n.* load, burden, freight.

C45 **carnival** *n.* fair, fête, festival.

C46 **carol** *n.* song, hymn, ditty, chorus.

C47 **carp** 1. *v.* find fault, *criticize* 2. *n.* fish.

C48 **carriage** *n.* vehicle, conveyance, *coach,* cab.

C49 **carry** *v.* convey, bear, transport, support.

C

C50 **cart** *n. wagon,* vehicle, wheelbarrow, van.

C51 **carve** *v.* sculpture, chisel, cut, form, *shape,* whittle, engrave, slice.

C52 **cascade** *n.* waterfall, cataract, fall.

C53 **case** *n.* 1. covering, sheath, capsule, *box* 2. lawsuit, action, occurrence, instance.

C54 **cash** *n.* money, bank notes, currency.   CACHE

C55 **cashier** 1. *n.* moneyer, money-changer 2. *v.* discharge, dismiss; *The officer was cashiered.*

C56 **casino** *n.* clubhouse, dance hall, gaming house.

C57 **cask** *n.* keg, barrel.

C58 **cast** 1. *v.* throw, fling, hurl, pitch, toss 2. *n.* mold, form, shape 3. *n.* troupe, players, actors.   CASTE

C59 **castaway** *n.* outcast, shipwrecked person.

C60 **castle** *n.* 1. palace, fortress, château 2. rook (chess).

C61 **casual** *adj.* 1. accidental, *chance,* occasional 2. informal (F209).

C62 **casualty** *n.* misfortune, accident, mischance.

C63 **catalog** *n.* list, register, roll, record.

C64 **cataract** *n.* 1. waterfall 2. sight obstruction.

C65 **catastrophe** *n.* disaster, misfortune, mishap, calamity (B89).

C66 **catch** *v.* grasp, seize, snatch, clutch, *arrest,* capture (M182, R136).

C67 **catching** *adj.* infectious, contagious.

C68 **category** *n. class,* head, division, rank, sort, kind.

C69 **cause** 1. *n.* origin, reason, source 2. *n.* undertaking, enterprise 3. *v.* produce, create, originate, bring about; *His speech caused the crowd to cheer.* (R217).   CAWS

C70 **caution** *n.* 1. wariness, heed, care (C42) 2. warning, *advice.*

C71 **cautious** *adj. prudent,* wary, careful, watchful (C42, F189, R36).

A French château or castle.

C72 **cave** *n.* cavern, den, grotto, hole.

C73 **cavity** *n.* hollow, empty space, void.

C74 **cease** *v.* stop, desist, *end,* leave off, terminate, finish (S432).

C75 **celebrate** *v.* praise, extol, honor, observe (G136, M256).

C76 **celebrity** *n.* person of note, notable, dignitary, hero.

C77 **cell** *n.* room, apartment, den, cubicle.   SELL

C

C78 **cellar** *n.* basement, vault, crypt. SELLER

C79 **cement** 1. *v.* unite, stick, join, attach 2. *n.* mortar, adhesive.

C80 **cemetery** *n.* graveyard, churchyard, burial ground.

C81 **censor** *n.* inspector, critic, examiner. CENSER

C82 **censure** *v.* blame, reproach, *chide,* criticize (A128, A135, C244, F206).

C83 **center** *n.* middle, heart (E15).

C84 **central** *adj.* middle, inner, main, chief.

C85 **ceremony** *n.* rite, ritual, form, solemnity, pomp, service *adj.* **ceremonious** (I180).

C86 **certain** *adj.* 1. *sure,* assured, confident, unfailing, positive (D292, D330, P331, Q23) 2. *particular,* special; *A certain man had come to visit. n.* **certainty** (C97, S600).

C87 **certainly** *adv.* surely, absolutely, plainly, positively.

C88 **certificate** *n.* testimonial, document, voucher.

C89 **chafe** *v.* rub, irritate, vex, annoy (S322).

C90 **chaff** 1. *n.* husks, refuse 2. *v.* ridicule, mock, jeer, scoff.

C91 **chain** *n.* fetter, shackle, link, *bond.*

C92 **chair** *n.* seat, bench, stool.

C93 **chairman** *n.* presiding officer, speaker (also **chair, chairwoman, chairperson**).

C94 **challenge** *v.* defy, *dare,* brave, threaten.

C95 **chamber** *n.* room, apartment, hall, cell, cavity.

C96 **champion** *n.* defender, *hero,* protector, victor, winner.

C97 **chance** *n. opportunity,* possibility, accident, fate, fortune, luck, risk (C86).

C98 **change** *v.* vary, modify, make different, replace, exchange, barter, substitute, *alter* (E69) *adj.* **changeable** (S447).

C99 **channel** *n.* passage, canal, duct, trough, gutter, groove.

C100 **chant** *v. sing,* warble, carol, intone, recite.

C101 **chaos (kay-***oss***)** *n.* disorder, confusion, turmoil *adj.* **chaotic** (C341).

C102 **chap** 1. *n.* boy, youth, *fellow* 2. *v.* crack, split, cleave; *The cold weather had chapped her lips.*

C103 **chapter** *n.* 1. section of book 2. society branch 3. period of time, episode.

C104 **char** *v.* burn, scorch, singe.

C105 **character** *n.* 1. mark, figure, sign, symbol, letter 2. qualities, disposition, reputation; *The prime minister was a man of character.* 3. actor, performer.

C106 **characteristic** *n.*

A rocking chair and an antique chair.

C107 **charge** 1. *n*. price, *cost* 2. *v*. attack, *assault* (R226) 3. *v*. *accuse, blame*.

C108 **charitable** *adj*. kind, liberal, generous, considerate (M92).

C109 **charity** *n*. kindness, love, goodness, good nature.

C110 **charm** 1. *v*. fascinate, *enchant,* delight, attract (R172) 2. *n*. trinket, amulet, talisman.

C111 **charming** *adj*. fascinating, enchanting, bewitching (R187).

C112 **chart** *n*. map, plan, diagram.

C113 **charter** 1. *n*. right, privilege, deed 2. *v*. hire, let.

C114 **chase** *v*. pursue, hunt, track, run after, follow (A1).

C115 **chaste** *adj*. pure, virtuous, innocent, modest (C423, W17).
CHASED

C116 **chastise** *v*. punish, whip, flog, *beat* (C43).

C117 **chat** *v*. prattle, chatter, babble, gossip, talk.

C118 **chatter** *v*. talk, chat, gossip, prattle.

C119 **cheap** *adj*. low-priced, inexpensive, paltry, inferior (C426, D39, E197, P336, P377, S119, S563).

C120 **cheat** 1. *v. swindle,* deceive, defraud 2. *n*. impostor, trickster, rogue, knave.

C121 **check** *v*. restrain, curb, hinder, obstruct, stop, halt (A62, C375).

C122 **cheek** *n*. 1. impertinence, impudence 2. side of face.

C123 **cheer** *v*. 1. *applaud,* clap, salute, shout, yell (H132) 2. comfort, encourage (D114).

C124 **cheerful** *adj*. glad, lively, joyful, happy, jolly, merry (B86, B98, D214, D235, D281, F207, G79).

C125 **cherish** *v*. care for, support, hold dear, treasure (A1).

C126 **chest** *n*. 1. breast, trunk, torso, bosom 2. *box,* case, trunk, coffer.

C127 **chew** *v*. bite, gnaw, munch, masticate.

C128 **chide** *v*. rebuke, scold, blame, reprove (A128).

C129 **chief** 1. *adj*. leading, principal, *main,* head (M158) 2. *n*. leader, chieftain, commander, head, boss.

C130 **chiefly** *adv*. mostly, mainly, principally, especially.

C131 **child** *n*. infant, baby, boy, girl, youngster (A61).

C132 **chilly** *adj*. cold, cool, brisk (H176) *n*. & *v*. **chill** (H88).

C133 **chime** *v*. harmonize, accord, ring, peal.

C134 **chink** *n*. opening, *gap,* crack, cranny, crevice.

C135 **chip** 1. *n*. flake, fragment, slice 2. *v*. hew, cut, splinter.

C136 **chit** *n*. voucher, note, slip, memo.

C137 **chivalrous** *adj*. gallant, adventurous, *valiant,* noble.

C138 **chirp** *v*. tweet, twitter, warble, cheep.

C139 **choice** 1. *n*. selection, pick 2. *adj*. select, exquisite, rare, fine.

C140 **choke** *v*. suffocate, *stifle,* smother, strangle, gasp.

C

C141 **choose** *v.* select, elect, prefer, pick out. CHEWS

C142 **chop** *v.* cut, slice, hew, cleave, mince.

C143 **chorus (kaw-***rus***)** *n.* choir, refrain, tune, melody, song.

C144 **chronic** *adj.* constant, continuing, persistent.

C145 **chubby** *adj.* plump, buxom, round, stocky (S238).

C146 **chuck** *v.* throw, pitch, hurl, toss.

C147 **chuckle** *v.* giggle, titter, laugh.

C148 **chum** *n. friend,* mate, pal, companion, comrade.

C149 **chump** *n.* log, chunk.

C150 **chunk** *n.* lump, piece, log, mass.

C151 **church** *n.* chapel, temple, house of worship.

C152 **churlish** *adj.* rude, harsh, *brusque,* impolite (C165, G6).

C153 **churn** 1. *n.* milk container 2. *v.* agitate, jostle, upset, foam.

C154 **cipher** *n.* 1. nothing, zero, nought 2. secret code.

C155 **circle** *n.* 1. ring, loop. disk 2. class, company, group, set.

C156 **circuit** *n.* revolution, orbit, circle, tour, journey.

C157 **circular** 1. *adj.* round, spherical 2. *n.* leaflet, advertisement, handbill.

C158 **circulate** *v.* spread, distribute, publish, broadcast, move around.

C159 **circumstances** *n.* situation, condition, position.

C160 **cistern** *n.* tank, reservoir.

C161 **citadel** *n.* fortress, castle, stronghold.

C162 **cite** *v.* quote, name, refer, mention, bring forward. SIGHT SITE

C163 **citizen** *n.* inhabitant, resident, dweller, townsman.

C164 **city** *n.* town, capital, metropolis.

C165 **civil** *adj.* 1. public, municipal (M147) 2. polite, courteous, refined, obliging (C152, C496).

C166 **civilization** *n.* culture, society, refinement *adj.* **civilized** (S41, U14).

C167 **claim** *v.* demand, require, ask, *assert,* declare (W8).

C168 **clammy** *adj.* slimy, sticky, cold and damp.

C169 **clamor** *n.* noise, hullabaloo, hubbub, uproar, din (S211).

C170 **clamp** *v.* fasten, secure, cramp.

C171 **clan** *n.* tribe, race, family, clique, set, group.

C172 **clap** *v. applaud,* cheer, acclaim, slap.

C173 **clarify** *v.* purify, clear, make clear, explain (B66, B102).

C174 **clash** *v.* 1. collide, crash 2. disagree, conflict, oppose.

C175 **clasp** 1. *v. grasp,* grip, clutch, hug 2. *n.* hook, catch, pin, brooch, buckle.

C176 **class** *n.* 1. rank, order, grade, set, species 2. form, set.

C177 **classical** *adj.* standard, model, master, elegant, polished, refined.

C178 **classify** *v.* arrange, class, sort, order, categorize.

C179 **clatter** *n.* rattle, clash, noise, din.

C180 **claw** *n.* nail, talon, hook.

C181 **clean** 1. *adj.* unstained, unspotted, unsoiled, pure, clear (D193, F120, I90) 2. *v.* cleanse, purify, scrub, wash (D69, S418) *n.* **cleanliness** (D192, F119) *v.* **cleanse** (D69, I166, P282).

C182 **clear** *adj.* 1. transparent, bright, light (F18, H72) 2. free, unobstructed 3. unquestionable, evident (I147, O15) 4. musical, silvery (H137) 5. *v.* free, loose, remove.

C183 **cleave** *v.* 1. separate, divide, split 2. stick, hold, be attached, cling.

C184 **cleft** *n.* crevice, chink, fissure, break.

C185 **clemency** *n.* mercy, lenience, mildness.

C186 **clench** *v.* grasp, *clutch,* seize.

C187 **clerk** *n.* office worker, shop assistant.

C188 **clever** *adj. skillful,* apt, ingenious, smart, quick, expert (D3, D102, D334).

C189 **client** *n.* customer, patron.

C190 **cliff** *n.* precipice, crag, headland.

C191 **climate** *n.* weather, clime.

C192 **climb** *v.* clamber, scramble, ascend, surmount (F24) CLIME

C193 **cling** *v.* adhere, stick, hold, embrace, clasp.

C194 **clip** 1. *v.* cut, prune, trim, snip 2. *n. clasp,* fastener.

C195 **clique** *n.* group, set, clan, crowd. CLICK

C196 **cloak** *n.* mantle, wrap, coat.

C197 **clock** *n.* watch, chronometer, timepiece.

C198 **clod** *n.* 1. lump, chunk 2. dolt, dunce, oaf.

C199 **clog** 1. *v. obstruct,* choke, hinder, stop up 2. *n.* wooden shoe, sabot.

C200 **close** (rhymes with *nose*) 1. *v.* shut, fasten, lock (O63) 2. *v.* end, cease, finish, stop (I194) 3. (rhymes with *dose*) *adj.* near, adjacent (F41, R160) 4. *adj.* uncomfortable, stuffy 5. *adj.* mean, stingy.

C201 **closet** *n.* cupboard, cabinet.

C202 **cloth** *n.* material, fabric.

C203 **clothe** *v.* dress, *attire,* wrap, cover *adj.* **clothed** (B23).

C204 **cloudy** *adj.* murky, obscure, dim, blurred, (F19).

C205 **clown** *n.* buffoon, fool, harlequin, jester, dunce, dolt.

C206 **club** *n.* 1. cudgel, bludgeon, stick 2. *society,* company, set.

C207 **clue** *n.* evidence, hint, guide. CLEW

C208 **clumsy** *adj.* awkward, unwieldy, blundering, inept (D74, G110, H27, S234) *n.* **clumsiness** (F6, S235).

Clowns.

C209 **cluster** *n.* clump, bunch, group, collection.

C210 **clutch** *v.* grasp, *grip,* clasp, clench, seize, grab.

C211 **clutter** *n.* mess, disorder, disarray.

C212 **coach** 1. *n.* bus, vehicle, carriage 2. *v.* instruct, train, drill.

A stagecoach.

C213 **coarse** *adj.* 1. rough, crude, impure, unpurified (F123, R105) 2. rude, vulgar, indelicate (D5, E31). COURSE

C214 **coast** *n.* shore, beach, seacoast, seaside.

C215 **coat** *n.* jacket, wrap, covering, layer.

C216 **coax** *v.* wheedle, *cajole,* flatter, persuade (B172, C219, F192, O8). COKES

C217 **cock** *n.* 1. male bird, chanticleer, rooster 2. tap.

C218 **coddle** *v.* humor, pamper, indulge, fondle.

C219 **coerce** *v.* force, compel, drive (C8, C216).

C220 **coffer** *n.* chest, box, casket, trunk. COUGHER

C221 **coil** *v.* wind, twist, loop.

C222 **coin** *n.* 1. money, cash 2. invent, devise, create; *Many new words have been coined this year.*

C223 **coincidence** *n.* chance, harmony, accident (P235).

C224 **cold** *adj.* chilly, bleak, raw, arctic, icy, wintry, frigid, freezing (F111, H176, W21) *n.* **coldness** (A69).

C225 **collapse** 1. *v.* fall, drop, subside, break down (R91) 2. *n.* downfall, failure, breakdown.

C226 **collar** *n.* neckband, ring, belt, band.

C227 **colleague** *n.* partner, helper, associate, companion, ally (O69).

C228 **collect** *v. gather,* assemble, bring together, muster, accumulate, amass (D241, D258, S57).

C229 **collection** *n.* group, cluster, gathering, hoard, store, pile.

C230 **college** *n.* school, university, institute.

C231 **collide** *v.* clash, crash, smash together.

C232 **color** *n.* hue, tint, tinge, shade, pigment.

C233 **colossal** *adj.* gigantic, huge, monstrous, immense, enormous, vast (T125).

C234 **column** *n.* 1. pillar, post, line, row 2. article, feature.

C235 **combat** *v.* fight, oppose, resist, *battle.*

C236 **combine** *v. unite,* join, mix, blend, connect.

C237 **come** *v.* approach, *advance,* arrive, reach (D105, G93, L56).

C238 **comedy** *n.* farce, slapstick, burlesque, wit (T166).

C239 **comfort** 1. *v.* console, cheer, gladden, encourage, soothe (A39, A86, B125, T146, W102) 2. *n.* rest, relief, ease, enjoyment, peace (A113, P13) *adj.* **comfortable** (U15, U33).

C240 **comic, comical** *adj.* funny, droll, farcical, laughable, humorous (S4, T167).

C241 **command** 1. *v.* lead, rule, govern, control 2. *n.* order, direction, commandment, decree.

C242 **commemorate** *v.* honor, celebrate, remember, observe.

C243 **commence** *v.* start, *begin,* open, originate (F127, T64).

C244 **commend** *v.* recommend, *praise*, applaud (B80, C82, C486, D101).

C245 **comment** *n. remark,* observation, note.

C246 **commerce** *n.* business, dealing, *trade*, exchange, marketing.

C247 **commission** *n.* 1. allowance, fee, compensation 2. board, committee.

C248 **commit** *v.* perform, enact, do, promise, pledge.

C249 **committee** *n.* council, board, commission, group.

C250 **commodity** *n.* product, goods, merchandise.

C251 **common** 1. *adj.* public, general, usual, frequent, habitual, customary, ordinary, vulgar (E176, I182, P103, R34, U16, U52, U86) 2. *n.* field, park, green.

C252 **commonplace** *adj.* trite, stale, ordinary, *common,* hackneyed (E48, E225, F3, M64, P184, R153, U86).

C253 **commotion** *n.* disturbance, turmoil, disorder, bustle, upheaval, fuss, noise (C15).

C254 **communicate** *v.* inform, impart, give, disclose, reveal, declare (C291).

C255 **community** *n.* association, society, group, town, village.

C256 **commuter** *n.* passenger, traveler.

C257 **compact** 1. *adj.* close, dense, firm, *solid,* compressed 2. *n.* agreement, contract, pact.

C258 **companion** *n.* comrade, partner, associate, mate, fellow, friend.

C259 **company** *n.* group, party, fellowship, society, firm, partnership, *business*.

C260 **compare** *v.* liken, match, contrast *adj.* **comparable** (I118).

C261 **compartment** *n.* division, section, part.

C262 **compassion** *n.* pity, sympathy, tenderness, kindness *adj.* **compassionate** (C497).

C263 **compel** *v.* force, oblige, coerce, drive, impel (C8, C216).

C264 **compensate** *v.* recompense, remunerate, reimburse, reward, counterbalance, make up for.

C265 **compete** *v.* rival, oppose, *contest,* contend.

C266 **competent** *adj.* able, capable, qualified, suitable, fit (I120).

C267 **competition** *n.* contest, rivalry, tournament, match.

C268 **compile** *v.* write, prepare, compose, draw up, select.

C

C269 **complacent** *adj.* pleased, satisfied, gratified, contented, *smug*.

C270 **complain** *v.* grumble, find fault, moan, groan, murmur, lament, protest (R130).

C271 **complaint** *n.* 1. grumbling, lamentation, accusation 2. malady, disease, ailment.

C272 **complement** *v.* add to, supply, complete, supplement. COMPLIMENT

C273 **complete** 1. *v.* finish, *perfect,* accomplish, achieve, end, conclude 2. *adj.* total, whole, completed (D68, I55, I121, P60).

C274 **complex** 1. *adj.* complicated, tangled, intricate (S215) 2. *n.* network, organization; *A new factory complex was built on the edge of town.*

C275 **complicate** *v.* involve, entangle, confuse, mix up *adj.* **complicated** (S215).

C276 **compliment** *v.* praise, commend, flatter, congratulate (G51, I237, O117, S299) *adj.* **complimentary** (D122). COMPLEMENT

C277 **comply** (with) *v.* observe, consent to, yield to, satisfy, agree to, fulfill (R114).

C278 **compose** *v.* 1. write, create, invent, *comprise* 2. quell, calm, *pacify* (P168).

C279 **composure** *n.* calm, calmness, self-possession *adj.* **composed** (F240).

C280 **compound** 1. *v.* mix, mingle, intermix, blend, combine 2. *adj.* complicated, *complex* 3. *n.* mixture, composition; *Lemonade is a compound of lemons and water.*

C281 **comprehend** *v. understand,* grasp, see, perceive (M191) *adj.* **comprehensible** (I122).

C282 **comprehensive** *adj.* extensive, wide, broad, full, complete (P60).

C283 **compress** *v.* squeeze, force, press, make brief, abbreviate, *condense,* abridge (E192).

C284 **comprise** *v.* include, enclose, embrace, contain, constitute, consist of (E175).

C285 **compromise** *v.* 1. adjust, agree, settle, come to an understanding 2. endanger, imperil, jeopardize; *Fred's career was compromised by his poor English.*

C286 **compulsory** *adj.* obligatory, necessary, enforced, unavoidable (O77, V87).

C287 **compute** *v.* reckon, calculate, estimate, count.

C288 **computer** *n.* calculator, word processor, microprocessor.

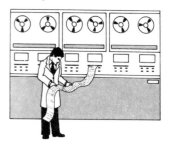

Electronic computer, 1946.

C289 **comrade** *n. companion,* associate, mate, chum, friend, pal (E70).

C290 **concave** *adj.* hollow, hollowed, scooped (C394).

C291 **conceal** *v. hide,* secrete, cover, screen, bury, cover up (A114, C254, D148, D211, D220, D242, I179, R229, S384, U20).

C292 **concede** (*con*-seed) *v.* surrender, yield, grant, give up, admit (C378, D104).

C293 **conceited** *adj.* vain, egotistical, opinionated, *arrogant,* proud, smug (M207) *n.* **conceit** (M208).

C294 **conceive** *v.* create, devise, contrive, plan, invent, imagine.

C295 **concentrate** *v.* 1. condense, reduce, boil down 2. focus, centralize, engross (D256).

C296 **concept** *n.* idea, notion, opinion, thought, theory.

C297 **concern** 1. *v.* affect, interest, touch, regard 2. *v.* trouble, disturb, disquiet 3. *n.* matter, affair, consequence; *My taste in music is no concern of yours.* 3. *n.* firm, *business,* company *adj.* **concerned** (I141).

C298 **concerning** *prep.* respecting, regarding, about.

C299 **concert** *n.* performance, recital.

C300 **concerted** *adj.* joint, together, united.

C301 **conciliate** *v.* pacify, *appease,* reconcile, win over.

C302 **concise** *adj.* brief, *short,* summary, terse, pithy, condensed.

C303 **conclude** *v.* 1. end, *finish,* terminate, close 2. determine, judge, presume, understand *n.* **conclusion**.

C304 **concoct** *v.* devise, plan, contrive, design, invent.

C305 **concord** *n.* agreement, friendship, peace, harmony (D217, F97).

C306 **concrete** 1. *n.* cement 2. *adj.* firm, solid, real, definite.

C307 **concur** *v.* agree, coincide, harmonize, combine (A139, D245) *n.* **concurrence** (O6).

C308 **concussion** *n.* shaking, agitation, clash, shock.

C309 **condemn** *v.* blame, disapprove, denounce, criticize, sentence, pronounce guilty, judge, convict (A42, P50).

C310 **condense** *v.* compress, concentrate, compact, press together, reduce, *abbreviate,* abridge (E84).

C311 **condition** *n.* situation, case, state, plight, *predicament.*

C312 **condone** *v.* pardon, forgive, overlook (P474).

C313 **conduct** 1. (*kon-***duct**) *v.* manage, lead, *direct,* guide, escort 2. (**kon**-*duct*) *n.* behavior, manners, actions.

C314 **confederation** *n.* league, coalition, alliance, union.

C315 **confer** *v.* 1. bestow, give, grant 2. discuss, converse, consult.

C316 **conference** *n.* interview, meeting, council, consultation.

C317 **confess** *v.* admit, concede, own up, acknowledge (D104).

C318 **confide** *v.* trust, entrust, disclose, reveal, divulge, declare (D260).

C319 **confident** *adj.* assured, certain, sure, positive (A118, S200, T119).

C320 **confidential** *adj.* secret, private, intimate.

C321 **confine** *v.* restrain, shut up, imprison, limit, restrict (D88, L82) *adj.* **confined** (S338).

C322 **confirm** *v.* verify, assure, establish, strengthen (R170).

C323 **confiscate** *v.* take, seize, *appropriate,* distrain.

C324 **conflict** 1. *n.* struggle, fight, battle (A81) 2. *v.* clash, interfere, oppose, contend.

C325 **conform** *v.* comply, agree, harmonize, tally, correspond, obey (R67).

C326 **confound** *v.* perplex, *bewilder,* embarrass, mystify.

C327 **confront** *v.* face, oppose, threaten (A182).

C328 **confuse** *v.* puzzle, mystify, bewilder, disorder, disarrange, disturb, mislead (C173, D207, D253, E85) *adj.* **confused** (C182).

C329 **congenial** *adj.* favorable, agreeable, suited, friendly (D197).

C330 **congested** *adj.* crowded, blocked, full, thick (E55).

C331 **congratulate** *v.* praise, compliment, acclaim, honor.

C332 **congregate** *v.* convene, gather, meet, assemble (D241).

C333 **congress** *n.* meeting, council, conference.

C334 **conjecture** *n.* guess, theory, supposition.

C335 **conjurer** *n.* magician, juggler, wizard.

C336 **connect** *v.* join, unite, combine, couple, link (D145, D213, S142, S373).

C337 **conquer** *v.* overcome, overthrow, *defeat,* beat, vanquish, succeed, win (S593).

C338 **conquest** *n.* triumph, victory.

C339 **conscientious** *adj. honest,* diligent, scrupulous, fair, painstaking (C42).

C340 **conscious** *adj.* alive, awake, alert, *aware,* sensible (D37, I208, U10, U17).

C341 **consecutive** *adj.* successive, uninterrupted, continuous (C101).

C342 **consent** 1. *v.* agree, *assent,* concur, yield (D97) 2. *n.* agreement, approval, permission.

C343 **consequence** *n.* effect, result, outcome.

C344 **conservative** *adj.* cautious, opposed to change, careful, moderate (R79).

C345 **conserve** *v.* preserve, save, keep, protect, maintain (E196).

C346 **consider** *v.* examine, study, contemplate, ponder (P70).

C347 **considerable** *adj.* not small, not little, worthwhile.

C348 **considerate** *adj.* thoughtful, patient, polite (I124).

C349 **consist** *v. comprise,* constitute, compose, contain.

C350 **consistent** *adj.* compatible, harmonious, suitable (I119, I125).

C351 **consolation** *n.* solace, comfort, sympathy (B178).

C352 **consort** *n.* companion,

A building being constructed.

partner, associate, husband, wife, spouse.

C353 **conspicuous** *adj.* noticeable, plain, clear, visible, apparent, prominent (I213).

C354 **conspiracy** *n.* plot, intrigue, scheme.

C355 **constant** *adj.* 1. faithful, true, devoted, loyal (F102) 2. fixed, unchanging, stable, permanent (E125, I259, V18).

C356 **consternation** *n.* alarm, amazement, terror, horror, fright, dismay.

C357 **constitute** *v.* set up, establish, create, form, compose (D250).

C358 **constitution** *n.* 1. formation, organization, law, code 2. temperament, health, spirit; *Cold weather is not good for her constitution.*

C359 **constrain** *v.* 1. *compel,* force, drive, oblige, coerce, urge (E103) 2. confine, restrain, hold, curb (R136).

C360 **constrict** *v.* cramp, contract, compress.

C361 **construct** *v.* build, erect, raise, fabricate (D93).

C362 **consult** *v. confer,* seek advise, discuss.

C363 **consume** *v.* 1. use up, use, devour, eat 2. destroy, exhaust.

C364 **contact** *n.* touch, connection, union, junction.

C365 **contagious** *adj.* infectious, catching.

C366 **contain** *v.* include, embody, *comprise,* hold, consist of.

C367 **contaminate** *v.* defile, pollute, corrupt, *taint,* infect, poison.

C368 **contemplate** *v.* consider, ponder, study, think about, survey.

C369 **contempt** *n.* disdain, scorn, mockery, derision (A55, A135, A185, E137).

C370 **contend** *v.* 1. strive, struggle, combat, fight, dispute (S593) 2. *maintain,* assert, affirm, claim.

C371 **content** 1. *v.* satisfy, appease 2. *adj.* satisfied, happy, pleased 3. *n.* satisfaction (D215).

C372 **contest** 1. *n. dispute,* debate, controversy, quarrel, competition, rivalry 2. *v.* argue, oppose, dispute.

C373 **context** *n.* treatment, composition, matter.

C374 **continual** *adj.* incessant, endless, perpetual, eternal (I259, I300).

C375 **continue** *v.* endure, last, stay, persist, carry on (P94, S479, S599, V21).

C376 **contort** *v.* twist, writhe, distort, deform.

C377 **contract** 1. (*kon-*tract) *v.* shorten, lessen, diminish, shrink (E84, E192, L69, S384, S500) 2. *v.* get, take, acquire, take in 3. (kon-*tract*) *n.* agreement, bargain, treaty, pact.

C378 **contradict** *v.* deny, dispute, oppose, challenge (C292).

C379 **contrary** *adj.* opposed, opposite, perverse, disagreeable, stubborn (A82).

C380 **contrast** 1. *n.* opposition, difference (A81) 2. *v.* distinguish, differ.

C381 **contribute** *v.* give, grant, bestow, supply, donate (W88).

C382 **contribution** *n.* gift, donation, offering.

C383 **contrite** *adj.* repentant, *humble,* penitent, sorry.

C384 **contrive** *v. devise,* plan, design, invent, form, scheme, plot.

C385 **control** 1. *v.* direct, manage, *regulate,* rule 2. *n.* command, mastery, direction.

C386 **controversy** *n.* dispute, debate, discussion, argument, quarrel (A33, A81).

C387 **convene** *v.* meet, assemble, muster, congregate.

Open fire cooking.

C388 **convenient** *adj.* fit, suitable, proper, appropriate, suited (A186) *n.* **convenience** (D195).

C389 **convent** *n.* monastery, abbey, priory, nunnery.

C390 **convention** *n.* 1. assembly, meeting 2. custom, practice *adj.* **conventional** (I180, Q17, U18).

C391 **converge** *v.* meet, unite, join (S130).

C392 **conversation** *n.* talk, chat, discussion.

C393 **convert** *v.* change, transform, reverse, turn, alter.

C394 **convex** *adj.* protuberant, rounding (C290).

C395 **convey** *v.* carry, bear, bring, transmit, transport.

C396 **conveyance** *n. carriage,* vehicle, car.

C397 **convict** 1. (*kon-*vict) *v.* find guilty, sentence 2. (kon-*vict*) *n.* prisoner, criminal, felon.

C398 **convince** *v.* satisfy, persuade, prove.

C399 **convoy** *n.* escort, guard, attendant.

C400 **convulse** *v.* agitate, shake, disturb.

C401 **cook** *v.* prepare (food), heat, fry, grill, roast, boil, broil, stew, simmer *adj.* **cooked** (R48).

C402 **cool** *adj.* 1. *cold,* frigid, chilly (F111, H176, W21) 2. calm, quiet, collected, composed (A118, A137, P74, V25) *n.* **coolness** (H88, Z2).

C403 **coop** *v.* confine, cage, imprison.

C404 **cooperate** *v.* work together, collaborate, unite, combine (O71) *n.* **cooperation** (O73).

C405 **cope** (with) *v.* deal with, endure, manage.

C406 **copious** *adj.* abundant, plentiful, *ample,* profuse, rich (S52).

C407 **copper** *n.* coin, cauldron, policeman (slang), penny (slang).

C408 **copse** *n.* thicket, coppice, grove.

C409 **copy** *v.* imitate, transcribe, reproduce, *duplicate.*

C410 **cord** *n.* string, line, rope, braid. CHORD

C411 **cordial** 1. *adj. hearty,* warm, ardent, affectionate, earnest, sincere 2. *n.* liqueur, fruit juice.

C412 **core** *n.* center, heart, kernel. CORPS

C413 **corn** *n.* grain, maize, cereal 2. callus.

C414 **corner** *n.* angle, bend, elbow, nook, recess, niche.

C415 **coronation** *n.* crowning.

C416 **corpse** *n.* body, carcass.

C417 **corpulent** *adj.* fleshy, *fat,* stout, portly, plump, rotund (T84).

C418 **correct** 1. *adj.* faultless, exact, precise, *accurate,* true (E126, F59, I93, I127, W121) 2. *v.* rectify, amend, set right (E123) *n.* **correction** (E127) *n.* **correctness** (M187).

C419 **correspond** *v.* agree, suit, fit, answer, write letters, communicate.

C420 **corridor** *n.* gallery, passage, hall, hallway.

C421 **corroborate** *v.* strengthen, *confirm,* establish, support.

C422 **corrode** *v.* eat away, erode, wear away.

C423 **corrupt** 1. *adj. dishonest,* wicked, evil, crooked, shady (C115, H151, M231, U92) 2. *v.* bribe, entice, deprave *n.* **corruption** (G100).

C424 **corsair** *n.* pirate, buccaneer, sea-rover.

C425 **cost** *n.* 1. *price,* charge, expense, outlay, value 2. sacrifice, damage, suffering; *Nelson's bravery was performed at the cost of an eye.*

C426 **costly** *adj.* expensive, dear, rich, sumptuous (C119, I159).

C427 **costume** *n.* dress, uniform, livery.

C428 **cot** *n.* 1. bed 2. cottage, hut.

C429 **cottage** *n.* hut, cabin, lodge (C60, P20).

C430 **couch** *n.* settee, bed, sofa.

C431 **council** *n.* assembly, meeting, congress, conference, committee. COUNSEL

C432 **counsel** *n.* 1. advocate, barrister, lawyer, attorney 2. advice, opinion, suggestion. COUNCIL

C433 **count** *v.* calculate, number, *reckon,* estimate.

C434 **counter** 1. *n.* disk, chip, token, coin 2. *n.* bench, table, board 3. *adv.* contrary, against.

C435 **counteract** *v.* oppose, contravene, resist, hinder, *thwart,* annul (A83).

C436 **counterfeit** *adj.* forged, fake, bogus, *spurious* (G43, R57, V7).

C437 **countless** *adj.* innumerable, many, endless, unlimited (F99).

C438 **country** 1. *n.* nation, state, fatherland 2. *adj.* rural, rustic (T158).

C439 **couple** *n.* pair, brace, two, married pair.

C440 **coupon** *n.* ticket, certificate, card, slip.

C441 **courage** *n.* bravery, *valor,* gallantry, fearlessness, pluck, boldness, resolution (F63) *adj.* **courageous** (C451, F64).

C442 **course** *n.* 1. route, way, track, road 2. advance, progress, passage. COARSE

C443 **court** 1. *n.* courtyard, square, yard 2. *n.* tribunal 3. *v.* flatter, coddle, woo, make love to.

C444 **courteous** *adj.* polite, civil, affable, respectful (I59, I66, I87, I218, R313, U19).

C445 **courtesy** *n.* politeness, civility, respect.

C446 **cove** *n.* inlet, bay, bight.

C447 **covenant** *n.* agreement, bargain, contract, treaty, pledge.

C448 **cover** *v.* 1. conceal, hide, secrete, mask (D242) 2. include, embrace, comprise; *The school course covers Latin as well as French.* 3. screen, disguise, cloak (S506, U20).

C449 **covet** *v.* desire, long for, hanker after (D135).

C450 **cow** 1. *v.* frighten, overawe 2. *n.* female ox.

C451 **coward** *n.* weakling, dastard, shirker, sneak (H114) *adj.* **cowardly** (B110, B144, D29, F65, G6, H115) *n.* **cowardice** (C441, P260, P459, V9) COWERED

C452 **cower** *v.* crouch, cringe, stoop (D19).

C453 **coy** *adj.* modest, shy, bashful, timid (B110).

C454 **crack** 1. *v.* break, split, chop, snap 2. *n.* cleft, chink, fissure, *crevice.*

C455 **cracker** *n.* biscuit, wafer, firework.

C456 **craft** *n.* 1. skill, ability, *talent,* expertise 2. trade, art, handicraft, occupation 3. cunning, guile, deceit.

C457 **cram** *v.* stuff, gorge, glut, fill, ram, press.

C458 **cramp** 1. *n.* pain, spasm 2. *v.* restrict, restrain *adj.* **cramped** (S338).

C459 **crank** *n.* 1. a turning handle 2. grouchy person.

C460 **cranny** *n.* cleft, crack, fissure, nook.

C461 **crash** *v.* shatter, splinter, smash.

C462 **crass** *adj.* gross, coarse, thick, raw, stupid.

C463 **crate** *n.* *box,* container, hamper, case.

C464 **crave** *v.* entreat, beg, implore, desire, hunger for (R166).

C465 **crawl** *v.* creep, inch along, dawdle.

C466 **crazy** *adj.* insane, mad, lunatic (R40, S24).

C467 **crease** *n.* fold, pleat, wrinkle, furrow.

C468 **create** *v.* originate, bring

into being, produce, make, form (D143, O11) *n.* **creation** (D144).

C469 **creature** *n.* animal, being, person, brute.

C470 **credible** *adj.* believable, trustworthy, reliable (I129).

C471 **credit** *n.* 1. merit, honor, praise (B80) 2. belief, trust, faith 3. reputation, esteem, regard 4. *v.* place to the credit (as money).

C472 **creed** *n.* belief, faith, dogma.

C473 **creek** *n.* inlet, cove, bay, rivulet. CREAK

C474 **creep** *v.* crawl, steal, glide, cringe.

C475 **crestfallen** *adj.* discouraged, dejected, depressed.

C476 **crevice** *n. fissure,* chink, gap, cleft, crack.

C477 **crew** *n.* company, band, gang, party, crowd.

C478 **crib** 1. *n.* manger, bin 2. *v.* pilfer, purloin, *steal.*

C479 **crime** *n.* felony, *sin,* wrongdoing, offense.

C480 **criminal** 1. *adj.* illegal, unlawful 2. *n.* felon, culprit, crook, *convict.*

C481 **cringe** *v.* crouch, fawn, sneak, draw back, cower.

C482 **cripple** 1. *v.* maim, make lame, disable 2. *n.* invalid, disabled person.

C483 **crisis** *n.* emergency, critical time, climax.

C484 **criterion** *n.* standard, test, basis.

C485 **critical** *adj.* 1. disapproving, carping, faultfinding (F142) 2. dangerous, hazardous, risky 3. crucial, decisive, important; *The girl's condition was critical during her illness.*

C486 **criticize** *v.* scold, judge, censor (A128, C244) *n.* **criticism** (P325).

C487 **crony** *n.* chum, pal, *friend,* partner.

C488 **crooked** *adj.* 1. bent, curved, distorted 2. dishonest, unfair, criminal (D189, S486).

C489 **crop** 1. *n. harvest* 2. *v.* gather, pluck, browse, cut, lop.

C490 **cross** *v.* 1. traverse, go over, intersect 2. mingle, interbreed 3. thwart, hinder, obstruct 4. *adj.* fretful, peevish, testy (A104).

C491 **crouch** *v.* squat, stoop, cower, cringe (S427).

C492 **crow** 1. *v.* boast, brag, bluster 2. *n.* raven, jackdaw, bird with black feathers.

C493 **crowd** *n.* throng, multitude, host, herd, horde, mob *adj.* **crowded** (D131).

C494 **crown** *n.* 1. coronet, tiara, circlet 2. head, skull 3. top, summit, crest.

A market square cross.

D

C495 **crucial** *adj.* severe, trying, searching, decisive.

C496 **crude** *adj.* raw, uncooked, *coarse,* immature, unripe (C165, E31).

C497 **cruel** *adj. brutal,* inhuman, merciless, ruthless, savage, ferocious (C262, H195) *n.* **cruelty** (M129, P227).

C498 **cruise** *v.* voyage, rove, sail. CREWS

C499 **crumb** *n.* particle, bit, fragment.

C500 **crumble** *v.* crush, fall to pieces, disintegrate.

C501 **crumple** *v.* wrinkle, rumple, crease.

C502 **crush** *v.* compress, squeeze, *break,* smash, overpower, conquer.

C503 **cry** *v.* 1. exclaim, call, shout 2. *weep,* sob, shed tears (L35).

C504 **cuddle** *v.* embrace, *hug,* fondle, snuggle.

C505 **cue** *n.* 1. hint, suggestion, catchword 2. rod for billiards. QUEUE

C506 **cull** *v.* select, choose, pick, gather.

C507 **culminate** *v.* end, terminate, reach highest point.

C508 **culprit** *n.* offender, *criminal,* felon.

C509 **cult** *n.* 1. worship, homage, sect, group 2. fashion, fad, craze.

C510 **cultivate** *v.* 1. till, farm, work 2. refine, improve, educate *n.* **cultivated** (S41).

C511 **culture** *n.* civilization, refinement, breeding *adj.* **cultured** (P384).

C512 **cumbersome** *adj.* unwieldy, *clumsy,* awkward, troublesome.

C513 **cunning** *adj.* crafty, artful, sly, wily, shrewd (C19, I186, S215).

C514 **cup** *n.* chalice, beaker, bowl, mug, vessel.

C515 **cupboard** *n.* cabinet, closet for dishes.

C516 **curb** *v.* restrain, check, control (E60).

C517 **cure** 1. *n.* remedy, antidote, treatment 2. *v.* heal, restore, preserve.

C518 **curious** *adj.* 1. strange, unusual, unique, peculiar, odd 2. inquisitive, prying, peering, nosy.

C519 **curl** *n.* coil, curve, twist.

C520 **current** 1. *adj.* present, common, general (A110, O19) 2. tide, course, stream. CURRANT

C521 **curse** 1. *v.* denounce, damn, condemn, swear (B89) 2. *n.* oath, malediction *adj.* **cursed** (F219).

C522 **curt** *adj.* short, brief, terse, rude, tart.

C523 **curtail** *v. shorten,* abridge, cut short (A107).

C524 **curve** *n. bend,* twist, turn.

C525 **cushion** *n.* pillow, bolster, support.

C526 **custom** *n.* habit, usage, *fashion,* practice, rule.

C527 **customer** *n.* purchaser, buyer, patron, client.

C528 **cut** *v.* 1. gash, wound, hurt 2. sever, slice, cleave 3. chop, lop, crop 4. reduce, decrease.

D

C529 **cute** *adj*. 1. delightful, charming, appealing, dainty 2. clever, smart, shrewd.

C530 **cycle** *n*. 1. period, circle, revolution 2. bicycle etc.

C531 **cynical** *adj*. sarcastic, mocking, sneering, scornful.

D d

D1 **dab** 1. *n*. strike, slap 2. *n*. flounder (fish), small flatfish 3. *v*. touch lightly or quickly.

D2 **dabble** *v*. 1. sprinkle, wet, spatter 2. tamper, *meddle, trifle*.

D3 **daft** *adj*. stupid, *silly, foolish* (C188).

D4 **dagger** *n*. dirk, stiletto, blade, knife.

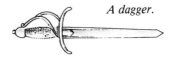

A dagger.

D5 **dainty** *adj*. delicate, elegant, neat (C213).

D6 **dale** *n*. vale, valley, dell, glen (H125).

D7 **dally** *v*. trifle, waste time (H216).

D8 **damage** *n*. injury, harm, mischief, loss.

D9 **dame** *n*. mistress, matron, lady, madam.

D10 **damn** *v*. condemn, curse, find guilty (B89).

D11 **damp** 1. *adj. moist*, humid, dank, wet (D329) 2. *v*. moisten, dampen (A140).

D12 **damsel** *n*. maiden, girl, maid, lass.

D13 **dance** *v*. & *n*. caper, frisk, hop, waltz.

D14 **dandy** 1. *n*. fop, swell, beau, dude 2. *adj*. great, good.

D15 **danger** *n*. risk, *peril*, jeopardy, hazard (S8).

D16 **dangerous** *adj*. perilous, hazardous, unsafe, risky (H46, S6).

D17 **dangle** *v*. swing, hang loosely, sway.

D18 **dank** *adj*. moist, wet, damp.

D19 **dare** *v*. defy, *challenge* (C452).

D20 **daring** *adj*. bold, adventurous, fearless, *brave* (A71).

D21 **dark** *adj*. dusky, shady, overcast, shadowy, murky (B152, F19, L90, P22, R6, S565).

D22 **darken** *v*. grow dark, shade, obscure, blacken (B85, B152, I20, L90).

D23 **darling** *n. dear*, pet, beloved, precious.

D24 **dart** 1. *v*. shoot, emit, run, hurry 2. *n*. arrow, missile.

D25 **dash** *v*. 1. rush, run, scurry 2. smash, strike, break.

D26 **date** *n*. 1. time, era, age 2. fruit *adj*. **dated** (R74).

D27 **daub** *v*. smear, plaster, cover, soil.

D28 **daunt** *v*. frighten, intimidate, cow, dishearten (E60).

D29 **dauntless** *adj*. fearless, intrepid, gallant, valiant (C451).

D30 **dawdle** *v*. lag, linger, idle, fritter (H210, R2, S49).

D31 **dawn** *n.* sunrise, daybreak (D343, E146).

D32 **day** *n.* daytime, daylight (N53).

D32 **daze** *v.* dazzle, blind, bewilder, confuse, stun. DAYS

D34 **dazzle** *v.* 1. daze, astonish, *bewilder,* surprise 2. shine, glow, glare.

D35 **dead** *adj.* 1. lifeless, breathless, deceased (A45, A90, L112) 2. dull, flat, inert (A90).

D36 **deadly** *adj.* fatal, mortal, murderous, lethal.

D37 **deaf** *adj.* unhearing, heedless, regardless (A184, C340).

D38 **deal** *v.* 1. distribute, allot, divide 2. trade, do business, traffic.

D39 **dear** *adj.* 1. costly, expensive, high-priced (C119, I159) 2. *darling,* beloved, loved. DEER

D40 **death** *n.* decease, demise, dying (B74, L88).

D41 **debate** *n.* discussion, disputation, *dispute,* argument (A81).

D42 **debt** *n.* due, obligation, liability.

D43 **decay** *v.* rot, spoil, decompose, *perish* (B95).

D44 **deceive** *v.* cheat, delude, *dupe,* fool, hoax.

D45 **decent** *adj. proper,* becoming, fit, seemly, respectable (I134, S157).

D46 **deception** *n.* treachery, trickery, deceit.

D47 **decide** *v.* determine, conclude, settle, choose (H116) *adj.* **decided** (I136).

D48 **decision** *n.* conclusion, judgment, settlement.

D49 **declare** *v.* affirm, say, state, *assert* (D104, I65).

D50 **decline** 1. *v.* refuse, reject, avoid, deteriorate (A25, F168, P444) 2. *n.* slope, incline, descent.

D51 **decompose** *v. rot,* decay, putrefy, molder, break up.

D52 **decorate** *v. adorn,* ornament, paint, beautify (D61).

Decorated brick smokestacks.

D53 **decoy** 1. *n. lure,* bait 2. *v.* allure, lure, entice, tempt (G166).

D54 **decrease** *v.* lessen, diminish, *dwindle,* wane (E84, G155, I128, M13, M268, R270, W34).

D55 **decree** *n.* order, edict, law.

D56 **dedicate** *v.* devote, hallow, consecrate.

D57 **deduct** *v.* subtract, withdraw, remove, take away (A49).

D58 **deed** *n.* 1. act, action, performance, *feat,* achievement 2. contract, policy, title.

D59 **deem** *v.* judge, think, consider, believe.

D60 **deep** *adj.* 1. *low,* profound (S154, S570) 2. absorbed, wise.

D61 **deface** *v.* mar, spoil, disfigure, soil (A60, D52).

D62 **defeat** *v.* overthrow, overcome, *conquer,* beat (T210,

V56) *n.* **defeat.**

D63 **defect** 1. *n.* flaw, blemish, *fault,* weakness 2. *v.* desert, abandon, leave *adj.* **defective** (F145).

D64 **defend** *v.* guard, shield, protect, support (A156, A169) *adj.* **defensive** (O41).

D65 **defense** *n.* protection, guard, bulwark.

D66 **defer** *v.* postpone, delay, put off.

D67 **defiant** *adj.* bold, daring, courageous, obstinate.

D68 **deficient** *adj.* lacking, defective, insufficient (C273, S571) *n.* **deficiency** (G88).

D69 **defile** *v.* soil, dirty, stain, tarnish, debase (C181).

D70 **define** *v.* explain, describe, clarify, interpret.

D71 **definite** *adj.* precise, *certain,* fixed (G35, H72, I136, R23) *adv.* **definitely** (P140).

D72 **deform** *v.* disfigure, distort, mar, make ugly (A60).

D73 **defraud** *v.* cheat, trick, dupe, deceive, hoodwink.

D74 **deft** *adj.* skillful, clever, apt, expert (C208).

D75 **defy** *v.* resist, challenge, disobey, disregard (S534).

D76 **degrade** *v.* disgrace, dishonor, demote, reduce (D153).

D77 **degree** *n.* 1. step, stage, extent, standard 2. award, grade, honor.

D78 **deign** *v.* condescend, stoop, descend, grant.

D79 **dejected** *adj.* depressed, dispirited, discouraged, downcast, *sad* (C124).

D80 **delay** *v.* defer, *postpone,* put off, hold up (A62, Q27).

D81 **delegate** 1. *n.* representative, deputy 2. *v.* authorize, appoint, nominate.

D82 **delete** *v.* erase, remove, blot out, *cancel* (A49).

D83 **deliberate** 1. *adj.* wary, cautious, careful, planned (A27, H30, I89, S376, S549) 2. *v.* reflect, ponder, consider, think.

D84 **delicate** *adj.* dainty, soft, mild, frail, tender (R281).

D85 **delicious** *adj.* luscious, palatable, tasty (U65).

D86 **delight** *n.* joy, gladness, pleasure, ecstasy (D229, M174, O40, P13).

D87 **delightful** *adj.* charming, enchanting, ravishing, pleasant (D197, H166, H167).

D88 **deliver** *v.* 1. transfer, hand over, convey 2. set free, release (C321).

D89 **delude** *v.* deceive, mislead, cheat, dupe (G166).

D90 **deluge** *n.* flood, downpour, rush, inundation.

D91 **delusion** *n.* trick, illusion, deception.

D92 **demand** *v.* ask, inquire, want, request (A116, E107, W8).

D93 **demolish** *v.* destroy, overthrow, ruin, raze (B170, C361, E121).

D94 **demon** *n.* devil, fiend, evil spirit, goblin.

D95 **demonstrate** *v.* prove, establish, show, exhibit.

D96 **demote** *v.* degrade, downgrade, reduce (P424).

D97 **demur** *v.* hesitate, pause, stop, waver (C342).

D

D98 **demure** *adj. coy,* modest, bashful, shy (B110).

D99 **den** *n.* haunt, retreat, cave.

D100 **denote** *v.* signify, mean, indicate, imply.

D101 **denounce** *v.* condemn, blame, censure, *accuse* (A28, C244, E178, V63).

D102 **dense** *adj.* 1. close, *compact,* thick, crowded (S344, V85) 2. stupid, dull, foolish (C188). DENTS

D103 **dent** *n.* nick, depression, indent, notch.

D104 **deny** *v.* contradict, *refute,* renounce, dispute, refuse (A159, C292, C317, C322, D49, D56, I151, L74, O42, O146, R189) *n.* **denial** (O42).

D105 **depart** *v.* go, *start,* set out, leave (A147, C237, R150, S446, T31, W6).

D106 **department** *n.* part, portion, section.

D107 **depend** (on) *v.* rely upon, rely, trust, confide *adj.* **dependent** (I138).

D108 **depict** *v.* paint, sketch, portray, describe.

D109 **deplorable** *adj.* pitiable, sad, regrettable, distressing (D257).

D110 **deposit** 1. *v.* lay, lay down, put, place 2. *n.* store, hoard, pledge (W86).

D111 **depot (dep-***owe***)** *n.* store, storehouse, warehouse, station.

D112 **deprave** *v. corrupt,* pollute, demoralize (I83).

D113 **depreciate** *v.* disparage, undervalue, reduce, (A132).

D114 **depress** *v. discourage,* dishearten, deject, sadden (C123, E188, H84, R240, S466) *adj.* **depressed** (E28, O135).

D115 **depression** *n.* 1. dejection, sadness, gloom 2. cavity, hollow, dent 3. recession, hard times.

D116 **deprive** *v.* divest, strip, rob (E68, P455).

D117 **depth** *n.* deepness, profundity (H97).

D118 **deputy** *n.* envoy, agent, representative, delegate.

D119 **derelict** 1. *adj.* forsaken, abandoned, left, dilapidated 2. *n.* destitute person 3. *n.* abandoned property.

D120 **deride** *v.* ridiculous, laugh at, mock, *jeer* (R204).

D121 **derive** *v.* draw, receive, obtain, get, deduce.

D122 **derogatory** *adj.* belittling, *offensive,* disparaging, insulting (C276).

D123 **descend** *v. fall,* sink, drop, go down, climb down (A151, M253, R270, S47) *n.* **descendant** (A109, F195) *n.* **descent** (R270).

D124 **describe** *v.* characterize, define, picture, trace.

D125 **description** *n.* explanation, narrative, report.

D126 **desert (dez-***ert***)** 1. *n.* wasteland, wilderness 2. *adj.* wild, desolate, barren 3. (*dez-ert*) *v.* forsake, leave, quit (A30). DESSERT

D127 **deserve** *v.* merit, be worthy of, be entitled to, earn (F203).

D128 **design** 1. *v.* plan, *devise,* concoct 2. *n.* pattern, drawing, sketch, outline *adj.* **designed** (H30).

D129 **desire** 1. *n.* need, longing, craving, wish 2. *v.* wish, *crave, lust after,* want (D151).

D130 **desk** *n.* table, board, stand, counter.

D131 **desolate** *adj. solitary,* deserted, empty, lonely (C493).

D132 **despair** *v.* lose hope, give up (H161) *adj.* **despairing** (H162).

D133 **desperate** *adj.* hopeless, despondent, despairing, reckless (C15).

D134 **despicable** *adj.* contemptible, mean, *base,* worthless (A55).

D135 **despise** *v.* scorn, spurn, *disdain* (A55, C449, R234).

D136 **despite** *prep.* notwithstanding, in spite of, regardless of.

D137 **despoil** *v.* plunder, rob, loot.

D138 **despondent** *adj.* melancholy, dejected, *sad* (J33, S25).

D139 **despot** *n.* autocrat, dictator, tyrant, oppressor.

D140 **destination** *n.* goal, end, objective (B50).

D141 **destiny** *n.* lot, doom, fortune, fate.

D142 **destitute** *adj.* needy, poor, penniless, (W38).

D143 **destroy** *v.* demolish, *ruin,* raze, kill, finish (C468, M24, M120, R169).

D144 **destruction** *n.* demolition, ruin, havoc (B50, C468).

D145 **detach** *v.* separate, sever, divide (A168, C336, F132).

D146 **detail** *n.* part, portion, feature, item.

D147 **detain** *v.* stay, *delay,* retain, stop, keep back (D208).

D148 **detect** *v.* discover, expose, ascertain, find out (C291).

D149 **deter** *v.* restrain, hinder, discourage, prevent (E103, I51).

D150 **determine** *v.* 1. decide, settle, adjust 2. certify, check, find out (W33).

D151 **detest** *v.* hate, abominate, loathe (A55, A59, D129, L151, W103).

D152 **devastate** *v.* ravage, pillage, plunder, sack, destroy.

D153 **develop** *v.* 1. grow, expand, flourish, mature (D76) 2. reveal, disclose.

D154 **deviate** *v.* digress, diverge, turn aside, err (C375).

D155 **device** *n.* machine, instrument, contrivance, invention, scheme, plan.

D156 **devil** *n.* demon, Satan, Lucifer, goblin.

D157 **devise** *v.* contrive, invent, create, plan.

D158 **devoid** *adj.* vacant, empty, destitute (F281).

D159 **devote** *v.* dedicate, give, assign, apply (R146).

D160 **devoted** *adj.* attached, loving, affectionate, *ardent* (U39).

Deserts of the world.

39

D161 **devour** v. gorge, eat greedily, gulp.

D162 **devout** adj. religious, pious, holy, saintly.

D163 **diagram** n. drawing, sketch, design, plan.

D164 **dial** n. face, clock, meter.

The dial of an electricity meter.

D165 **dialect** n. language, tongue, speech, accent.

D166 **dictate** v. speak, utter, direct, order, decree.

D167 **die** v. expire, decease, depart, wither, perish (F168, L112, S596). DYE

D168 **difference** n. contrast, diversity, variation, disagreement (A33, C223) v. **differ** (A81, S555).

D169 **different** adj. distinct, separate, unalike, unlike (A89, I4, L91, S19, S213).

D170 **difficult** adj. hard, arduous, laborious, complicated, complex (E7, S215) n. **difficulty** (E6, F6).

D171 **dig** v. excavate, delve, scoop, burrow.

D172 **digest** 1. v. absorb, assimilate, master 2. v. summarize, arrange, systematize 3. n. summary, synopsis.

D173 **digit** n. symbol, figure, number, numeral, finger, toe.

D174 **dignified** adj. stately, noble, *majestic,* grave.

D175 **dignity** n. majesty, importance, distinction, bearing.

D176 **dilapidated** adj. decayed, ruined, shabby.

D177 **dilemma** n. *quandary,* predicament.

D178 **diligent** adj. hardworking, industrious, active, busy (I94) n. **diligence** (I149).

D179 **dilute** v. weaken, thin, reduce, water down.

D180 **dim** adj. faint, shadowy, unclear, vague, pale (B152, R6).

D181 **dimension** n. extent, measure, size.

D182 **diminish** v. *lessen,* decrease, reduce, shrink (A77, E80, E84, I128, M13, S587, S612).

D183 **diminutive** adj. little, *small,* tiny, puny (B70, E88, L26).

D184 **din** n. *noise,* uproar, clamor, racket (Q28).

D185 **dingy** adj. soiled, sullied, dull, dusky (B152).

D186 **dip** v. *immerse,* plunge, douse, wet.

D187 **diplomat** n. ambassador, negotiator, emissary, envoy.

D188 **dire** adj. dreadful, dismal, fearful, shocking. DYER

D189 **direct** 1. adj. *straight,* unswerving, plain, frank (C488, D232, I143, M287, R301, S449, U24) 2. v. command, order, instruct 3. v. aim, point, show.

D190 **direction** n. 1. way, course, bearing 2. control, guidance.

D191 **director** n. manager,

D192 **dirt** *n.* soil, filth, muck, grime (C181).

D193 **dirty** *adj.* unclean, foul, filthy, soiled (C181, I30, P479, S379).

D194 **disable** *v.* cripple, weaken, enfeeble, paralyze *adj.* **disabled** (F131).

D195 **disadvantage** *n.* drawback, *handicap,* harm, inconvenience (A63, B59, C388).

D196 **disagree** *v.* differ, *dispute,* quarrel, argue, oppose (A81, A158, C307).

D197 **disagreeable** *adj.* unpleasant, *offensive,* distasteful (A82, A104, C329, D87, H47, P248).

D198 **disappear** *v. vanish,* fade, dissolve, cease (A125, E45).

D199 **disappoint** *v.* frustrate, balk, foil, dissatisfy, fail (P249).

D200 **disappointment** *n.* frustration, failure, unfulfillment, dissatisfaction.

D201 **disapprove** *v.* condemn, censure, dislike, *reject* (A28, A135, F60) *n.* **disapproval.**

D202 **disarm** *v.* disable, weaken, render powerless.

D203 **disaster** *n. mishap,* calamity, mischance, misfortune, catastrophe (B89).

D204 **disbelief** *n. doubt,* distrust, rejection (F21) *v.* **disbelieve** (B53).

D205 **disburse** *v.* spend, pay out (B21, S42).

D206 **discard** *v. reject,* throw away, get rid of, scrap (A58, E53, K2).

D207 **discern** *v.* see, *perceive,* discover, behold, distinguish (C328).

D208 **discharge** *v.* 1. *emit,* expel, eject (A18) 2. unload 3. dismiss, let go (A131, D147).

D209 **disciple** *n.* follower, supporter, pupil, student (L47).

D210 **discipline** *n.* training, practice, control (C42).

D211 **disclose** *v.* uncover, expose, *reveal,* show, betray (C291, D228).

D212 **disconcert** *v.* frustrate, defeat, *balk,* upset (C15).

D213 **disconnect** *v.* separate, disjoin, *sever,* detach (A167, B73, C336).

D214 **disconsolate** *adj.* cheerless, *forlorn,* desolate, melancholy (C124).

D215 **discontent** *n.* dissatisfaction, uneasiness, restlessness (C371) *adj.* **discontented** (C371).

D216 **discontinue** *v.* stop, *cease,* interrupt (B49, E135, M19).

D217 **discord** *n.* disagreement, strife, conflict (A33, A81, C305, H48, P98, U54) *adj.* **discordant** (H47, M110, S611).

D218 **discount** *n.* rebate, deduction, reduction, allowance.

D219 **discourage** *v.* dishearten, *depress,* deject (E60, I150, I174, P163, R66, T133, U97) *n.* **discouragement** (I105).

D220 **discover** *v. reveal,* find, learn, find out (C291, M179).

D221 **discreet** *adj. prudent,* cautious, wise, considerate, tactful (C42, I144). DISCRETE

D222 **discriminate** *v.* distinguish, judge, set apart *adj.* **discriminating**.

D223 **discuss** *v. debate,* deliberate, talk over, consider *n.* **discussion**.

D224 **disdain** *n. scorn,* contempt, arrogance (C346, E112, H96, P392).

D225 **disease** *n.* illness, sickness, malady, ailment, complaint.

D226 **disfigure** *v.* deform, deface, injure, blemish (A60).

D227 **disgrace** *n.* disfavor, *shame,* dishonor, infamy, scandal (H153, V30).

D228 **disguise** *v.* conceal, mask, cloak, hide, camouflage (D211, D242).

D229 **disgust** 1. *n.* dislike, distaste, nausea, loathing (D86, R147) 2. *v.* sicken, displease, offend, revolt (A55).

D230 **dish** *n.* 1. platter, plate, bowl, container 2. food, meal, course.

Radio telescope dishes.

D231 **disheveled** *adj.* untidy, disordered, muddled, loose (N26).

D232 **dishonest** *adj.* fraudulent, crooked, false, corrupt (D189, F215, F239, H151, M231, R259, R260)

n. **dishonesty** (G100, H152).

D233 **disintegrate** *v.* crumble, break up, separate, decay.

D234 **dislike** *v.* disapprove, hate, *loathe* (A55, A59, E82, L91, R147) *adj.* **disliked** (P289).

D235 **dismal** *adj.* cheerless, gloomy, dark, dull (C124, G60).

D236 **dismay** *n.* terror, fright, dread, horror.

D237 **dismiss** *v.* send away, discharge, release, discard (A131, C12, E53, R219, S562).

D238 **disobey** *v.* disregard, transgress, neglect, ignore (O4) *adj.* **disobedient** (O3).

D239 **disorder** *n.* confusion, disarray, disturbance, turmoil (A145, O86, R123) *adj.* **disorderly** (O87).

D240 **dispense** *v.* distribute, allot, administer *adj.* **dispensable** (I145).

D241 **disperse** *v. scatter,* separate, diffuse (A157, C228, C332, F161, G26, R17, S480).

D242 **display** 1. *v.* exhibit, *show,* parade, show off (C291, C448, D228, H118).

D243 **dispose** *v. arrange,* order, regulate, settle, dispose (of), sell, get rid of.

D244 **disposition** *n. temper,* nature, temperament, character.

D245 **dispute** 1. *n.* debate, argument, quarrel (A81) 2. *v.* argue, discuss, bicker (C292, C307).

D246 **disregard** *v.* overlook, *ignore,* neglect, disobey (C346, H96, L104, O18, S109).

D247 **disreputable** *adj.* vulgar, mean, base, discreditable *n.*

disrepute (F30, I240).

D248 **dissect** *v*. cut, examine, analyze, scrutinize.

D249 **dissent** *v*. *disagree,* differ (A81, A158).

D250 **dissolve** *v*. 1. liquefy, melt (H38) 2. terminate, break up.

D251 **distance** *n*. space, length, extent, remoteness (V52) *adj*. **distant** (A53, I32).

D252 **distinct** *adj*. separate, *different,* definite, clear (F18, I147).

D253 **distinguish** *v*. detect, *perceive,* discern, divine (C328).

D254 **distinguished** *adj*. *famous,* noted, eminent, celebrated.

D255 **distort** *v*. deform, twist, pervert, misrepresent.

D256 **distract** *v*. *divert,* confuse, bewilder (C295).

D257 **distress** *n*. pain, agony, anguish, *trouble,* danger *adj*. **distressed, distressing**.

D258 **distribute** *v*. deal out, dispense, allocate, divide, apportion (A157, C228).

D259 **district** *n*. region, area, quarter, territory, section.

D260 **distrust** *v*. *doubt,* suspect, disbelieve (C318, R149, T220) *n*. **distrust** (F21).

D261 **disturb** *v*. annoy, ruffle, *vex,* trouble (A54, A144, C15, P3).

D262 **disturbance** *n*. *disorder,* commotion, tumult, riot *adj*. **disturbed** (C15, P99, R212, S133, T173).

D263 **dive** *v*. plunge, jump, drop, fall.

D264 **diverse** *adj*. different, assorted, varying (S213).

D265 **divert** *v*. 1. deflect, turn away, *distract* 2. amuse, entertain, please.

D266 **divide** *v*. separate, sever, disunite, share (J21, M195, U53) *adj*. **divided** (J22).

D267 **divine** 1. *adj*. godlike, heavenly, holy 2. *adj*. delightful, excellent 3. *v*. predict, foretell.

D268 **division** *n*. portion, partition, compartment.

D269 **divorce** *v*. separate, disjoin, part, disunite, annul (M57).

D270 **divulge** *v*. *disclose,* reveal, expose, release (C291).

D271 **dizzy** *adj*. giddy, unsteady, staggering, heedless.

D272 **do** *v*. 1. perform, act, execute 2. complete, finish 3. cheat, hoax, swindle (U29).

D273 **docile** *adj*. meek, mild, obedient, willing, *tame* (I57).

D274 **dock** 1. *n*. wharf, pier 2. *v*. clip, cut short, shorten.

D275 **doctor** *n*. physician, surgeon, learned man or woman.

D276 **doctrine** *n*. dogma, tenet, opinion, principle, creed.

D277 **document** *n*. paper, certificate, record, writ.

D278 **dodge** *v*. avoid, *evade,* elude, quibble.

D279 **dogged** *adj*. sullen, morose, sour, *stubborn,* obstinate.

D280 **dole** *n*. allotment, grant, share.

D281 **doleful** *adj*. sad, sorrowful, woeful, *dismal* (M134).

D282 domestic *adj.* homely, homelike, tame, native.

D283 dominant *adj.* ruling, predominating, commanding (S535).

D284 dominate *v.* rule, control, oversee, command, lead.

D285 donation *n.* gift, gratuity, dole, present.

D286 doom *n.* fate, destiny, lot, death, ruin.

D296 downhearted *adj.* dejected, sad, *gloomy,* glum, downcast.

D297 downright *adj.* plain, simple, sheer, thorough, positive.

D298 doze *v. sleep,* slumber, nap (W9).

D299 drab *adj. dull,* dingy, flat, dreary.

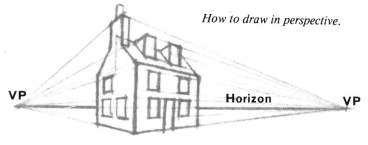

How to draw in perspective.

D287 door *n.* entrance, gateway, opening, portal.

D288 dose *n.* draft, portion, quantity.

D289 dot *n.* point, mark, speck, spot.

D290 double *adj.* twice, twofold, dual, coupled.

D291 doubt (rhymes with *out*) *v.* mistrust, *suspect,* question (B53).

D292 doubtful *adj.* uncertain, *dubious,* undecided (C86, E155) *adv.* **doubtfully** (C87).

D293 dowdy *adj.* slovenly, *shabby,* awkward (F48, S277, S390).

D294 downcast *adj. sad,* dejected, unhappy, crestfallen (J33).

D295 downfall *n.* ruin, *failure,* defeat, destruction (R270).

D300 draft *n.* drawing, sketch, plan.

D301 drag *v.* pull, *haul,* draw, tug, tow.

D302 drain 1. *v.* empty, draw off, exhaust (A18) 2. *n.* sewer, duct, channel.

D303 drastic *adj. severe,* powerful, extreme (M205).

D304 draw *v.* 1. pull, drag, haul, tug (P432) 2. sketch, trace 3. entice, attract 4. suck in, inhale.

D305 drawback *n.* disadvantage, fault, defect (A63).

D306 drawing *n.* picture, sketch, outline, plan.

D307 dread *n. fear,* apprehension, awe, terror.

D308 dreadful *adj.* terrible, horrible, *dire,* awful.

D309 **dream** *n.* reverie, fancy, fantasy (R58).

D310 **dreary** *adj.* gloomy, *dismal,* cheerless, dark, lonely (C124).

D311 **drench** *v.* saturate, soak, steep, flood.

D312 **dress** 1. *n.* frock, skirt, robe, gown 2. *n.* clothes, costume, habit, apparel 3. *v.* clothe, attire, don (U30).

D313 **drift** *v.* float, wander, stray, cruise.

D314 **drill** *v.* 1. pierce, perforate 2. train, exercise, teach.

D315 **drink** *v.* imbibe, swallow, sip, quaff.

D316 **drip** *v.* trickle, dribble.

D317 **drive** *v.* 1. *propel,* send, impel, hurl 2. control, operate, direct.

D318 **drivel** *n.* 1. *nonsense,* twaddle, rubbish 2. *v.* dribble, slaver.

D319 **drizzle** *v.* rain, shower, spray.

D320 **droll** *adj. comic,* funny, ludicrous, laughable.

D321 **drone** 1. *n.* idler, sluggard 2. *n.* male bee 3. *v.* hum, buzz.

D322 **droop** *v.* wilt, wither, fade, hang, *sag.*

D323 **drop** 1. *v. fall,* tumble 2. *v.* lower, let fall 3. *n.* globule, droplet.

D324 **drown** *v.* sink, submerge, suffocate in water.

D325 **drowsy** *adj.* sleepy, dozy, tired.

D326 **drudge** *n.* slave, servant, toiler, plodder.

D327 **drug** 1. *n.* medicine, potion, remedy 2. *n.* narcotic 3. *v.* stupefy, deaden.

D328 **drunk** *adj.* intoxicated, inebriated (S304).

D329 **dry** *adj.* 1. *arid,* waterless, parched, thirsty (D11, H199, M210, M211, S37, W53) 2. boring, *tedious,* uninteresting 3. *v.* make dry (S37) *n.* **dryness** (M212).

D330 **dubious (dew-*bee-us*)** *adj.* doubtful, uncertain, *suspect* (C86).

D331 **duck** 1. *n.* water bird 2. *v.* dive, plunge, immerse.

D332 **due** *adj.* 1. owed, owing, to be paid 2. proper, fit, suitable 3. expected; *The ship was due in port later that day.* DEW

D333 **dull** *adj.* 1. stupid, slow, obtuse (A87, A90, B152, B153, C188, I243) 2. tedious, boring (I254) 3. unsharp (S161) *n.* **dullness** (S176).

D334 **dumb** *adj.* 1. mute, speechless, silent 2. stupid, silly, dense.

D335 **dummy** *n.* puppet, doll, figure, form.

D336 **dump** *n.* pile, heap, tip.

D337 **dunce** *n.* simpleton, fool, dullard, blockhead, ignoramus (G40).

D338 **dungeon** *n. prison,* cell, jail, keep.

D339 **dupe** *v. cheat,* deceive, trick.

D340 **duplicate** *n.* copy, double, repeat.

D341 **durable** *adj.* permanent, lasting, stable, *firm* (P144).

D342 **duration** *n.* time, span, period, term.

E

D343 **dusk** *n.* twilight, sunset, evening, nightfall, gloom (D31).

D344 **duty** *n.* 1. *task,* obligation, responsibility 2. tax, toll, custom; *There is duty to pay on that watch.*

D345 **dwarf** *n.* pygmy, runt, midget (G49).

D346 **dwell** *v.* live, *reside,* inhabit, stay.

D347 **dwindle** *v. diminish,* decrease, lessen, wane.

D348 **dye** *n.* tint, color, stain, tinge. DIE

E · e

E1 **eager** *adj.* avid, desirous, enthusiastic, intent, keen, fervent, *ardent* (H11, R148).

E2 **early** *adj.* soon, recent, forward, premature (L30, T27).

E3 **earn** *v.* gain, deserve, get, acquire, win, merit (S360). URN

E4 **earnest** *adj.* determined, ardent, eager, serious (F158, H11).

E5 **earth** *n.* 1. world, globe, orb, planet 2. soil, dirt, ground, land.

E6 **ease** *n.* 1. rest, repose, quiet, contentment 2. facility, readiness (A39, A80, E23, P13).

E7 **easy** *adj.* 1. *simple,* effortless, not difficult (D170, H37, I298, L3, S462) 2. comfortable, quiet, satisfied.

E8 **eat** *v.* 1. chew, swallow, gobble, gorge, consume, dine 2. corrode, wear; *That old sword is eaten away with rust.*

E9 **ebb** *v.* decline, decrease, wane, recede, retreat (F170, S587).

E10 **eccentric** *adj.* abnormal, odd, whimsical, *peculiar,* quirkish (N67).

E11 **echo** *v.* resound, reverberate, imitate.

E12 **eclipse** *v.* darken, obscure, dim, blot out.

E13 **economical** *adj.* saving, sparing, *thrifty,* frugal (L38).

E14 **ecstasy** *n.* delight, rapture, joy, *pleasure.*

E15 **edge** *n.* border, *brim,* brink, margin, rim, verge.

E16 **edible** *adj.* eatable, wholesome.

E17 **edict** *n.* command, order, decree, law.

E18 **edit** *v.* 1. revise, correct, alter 2. direct (a periodical), publish.

E19 **educate** *v.* train, *teach,* instruct *adj.* **educated** (I12, I18).

E20 **eerie** *adj.* fearful, strange, weird.

E21 **effect** 1. *v.* cause, produce, realize 2. *n.* result, consequence, outcome *adj.* **effective** (I153, I154).

E22 **efficient** *adj.* skillful, *competent,* able, clever, useful (I154).

E23 **effort** *n.* attempt, endeavor, struggle, strain (E6).

E24 **eject** *v. emit,* discharge, expel, throw out.

E25 **elaborate** *adj.* complicated, decorated, ornate (S215).

E26 **elapse** *v.* lapse, pass, go.

E27 **elastic** *adj.* springy,

flexible, pliable (R261).

E28 **elated** *adj.* excited, cheery, proud (C475).

E29 **elect** *v.* choose, select, pick, vote for.

E30 **electrify** *v.* rouse, thrill, excite, astonish.

E31 **elegant** *adj. graceful,* fine, superior, refined (C496).

E32 **elementary** *adj.* primary, basic, simple.

E33 **elevate** *v.* raise, lift, exalt.

E34 **eligible** *adj.* desirable, preferable, qualified, fit (U67).

E35 **eliminate** *v.* remove, omit, expel, exclude, get rid of (I114).

E36 **elongate** *v.* lengthen, *extend,* stretch (S185).

E37 **elope** *v.* abscond, run away, leave.

E38 **eloquent** *adj.* fluent, impassioned, impressive.

E39 **elude** *v.* evade, escape, *avoid,* shun.

E40 **embarrass** *v.* humiliate, harass, distress, vex, *shame.*

E41 **emblem** *n.* symbol, sign, badge, mark, device.

E42 **embody** *v.* include, comprise, embrace, contain.

E43 **embrace** *v.* 1. *hug,* clasp 2. include, contain, enclose.

E44 **embroider** *v.* decorate, stitch, ornament, embellish.

E45 **emerge** *v.* appear, come out, issue (D198).

E46 **emergency** *n.* urgency, crisis, predicament, *dilemma.*

E47 **emigrate** *v.* migrate, remove, depart, leave.

E48 **eminent** *adj.* high, lofty, elevated, distinguished, celebrated (C252).

E49 **emit** *v. eject,* discharge, expel, exhale (I189).

E50 **emotion** *n.* feeling, passion, sentiment *adj.* **emotional** (I48).

E51 **emphasis (em-***fa-***sis)** *n. stress,* importance, accent.

E52 **emphatic** *adj.* strong, forceful, definite, decided, positive (L42).

E53 **employ** *v.* 1. use, apply 2. engage, hire, contract, enlist (D237) *adj.* **employed** (U34).

E54 **employee** *n.* worker, servant, wage earner (B123).

E55 **empty** 1. *adj.* vacant, void, unoccupied, bare, unfilled (F281) 2. *v.* drain, exhaust, discharge, clear (F116, R175).

E56 **enable** *v.* empower, qualify, allow, sanction (P374).

E57 **enchant** *v. charm,* captivate, fascinate, bewitch (B120).

E58 **enclose** *v.* surround, envelop, cover, wrap, shut in.

E59 **encounter** 1. *n.* meeting, clash, collision 2. *v.* confront, face, *meet* (E39, E143).

E60 **encourage** *v.* hearten, *inspire,* support, embolden, foster (C516, D28, D149, D219, F276, I269, M119, P418, R68, T106).

E61 **encroach** *v.* trespass, intrude, infringe.

E62 **end** 1. *n.* limit, extremity, boundary 2. *n.* aim, purpose, object (B50, O93, O120, T96) 3. *v. finish,* terminate, conclude (B49, C243, C375, I194, S432).

E63 **endanger** *v.* risk, imperil, jeopardize (P447) *adj.* **endangered** (S106).

E64 **endear** *v*. charm, win, captivate.

E65 **endeavor** *v. try,* attempt, strive, aim.

E66 **endless** *adj.* boundless, limitless, *infinite,* continuous, everlasting.

E67 **endorse** *v*. confirm, sign, guarantee, sanction (O71).

E68 **endow** *v*. enrich, give, bestow, confer, invest.

E69 **endure** *v*. 1. *bear,* sustain, support, suffer, tolerate (F156) 2. remain, continue, persist *n*. **endurable** (I234, I270).

E70 **enemy** *n. foe,* opponent, adversary, antagonist (A93, C289, F255, P19).

E71 **energetic** *adj. vigorous,* active, strong, effective (L20).

E72 **energy** *n*. force, *power,* might, efficiency, strength.

E73 **enforce** *v. compel,* force, make, require, urge.

E74 **engage** *v*. 1. occupy, involve, busy 2. betroth, pledge (in marriage) 3. employ, hire (D237); *The boss has engaged a new secretary.*

E75 **engaging** *adj.* attractive, captivating, charming.

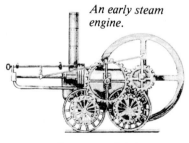

An early steam engine.

E76 **engine** *n. machine,* motor, instrument, device, implement.

E77 **engrave** *v*. carve, cut, chisel, grave, impress.

E78 **engross** *v*. absorb, engage, occupy.

E79 **engulf** *v*. absorb, swallow up, flood.

E80 **enhance** *v. improve,* increase, enrich (D182).

E81 **enigma** *n*. puzzle, riddle, mystery, problem.

E82 **enjoy** *v. like,* relish, appreciate, delight in (D234).

E83 **enjoyment** *n. pleasure,* gratification, satisfaction.

E84 **enlarge** *v*. amplify, expand, increase, *magnify,* extend (C377, D182).

E85 **enlighten** *v. inform,* instruct, teach, educate.

E86 **enlist** *v*. enroll, register, enter, embark.

E87 **enmity** *n*. animosity, antagonism, *hatred,* hostility, rancor (L151).

E88 **enormous** *adj.* huge, monstrous, *immense,* gigantic, vast, stupendous (S259, T125).

E89 **enough** *adj.* sufficient, abundant, *ample,* adequate (I95, I235).

E90 **enrage** *v*. madden, infuriate, *inflame,* anger.

E91 **enrapture** *v. enchant,* entrance, delight.

E92 **enrich** *v*. adorn, embellish, endow, ornament (I73).

E93 **enroll** *v*. enlist, register, engage.

E94 **enslave** *v*. overpower, master, dominate (F246).

E95 **ensue** *v*. follow, succeed, come after, result.

E96 **ensure** *v*. assure, secure,

determine, make certain.

E97 **entangle** v. entrap, catch, ensnare, tangle, perplex.

E98 **enter** v. go into, invade, *penetrate* (L56).

E99 **enterprise** n. 1. undertaking, adventure, *project,* venture 2. energy, courage, boldness.

E100 **entertain** v. amuse, please, cheer, divert (B120).

E101 **enthusiasm** n. ardor, *zeal,* eagerness.

E102 **enthusiast** n. fan, fanatic, zealot, devotee, supporter *adj.* **enthusiastic** (H11).

E103 **entice** v. attract, *tempt,* coax, cajole, lure (D149).

E104 **entire** adj. *whole,* complete, full, intact (P60) n. **entirety** (P59).

E105 **entitle** v. 1. call, christen, dub, style 2. give a right to, empower.

E106 **entrance** 1. (**en**-*truns*) n. entry, way in, gate, *access* 2. (*in*-**trans**) v. charm, enchant, delight, fascinate (E191).

E107 **entreat** v. *beg,* crave, beseech, implore, plead (D92).

E108 **entry** n. entrance, access, passage, record, note (E191).

E109 **envelop** v. enfold, wrap, fold, surround, encircle, cover.

E110 **environment** n. surroundings, neighborhood, atmosphere.

E111 **envoy** n. minister, ambassador, diplomat.

E112 **envy** n. jealousy, covetousness, malice (D224).

E113 **episode** n. occurrence, incident, happening, event.

E114 **equal** adj. 1. like, alike, *same* 2. even, regular (U35) 3. adequate, fit, sufficient; *Sarah's efforts were equal to the occasion.*

E115 **equip** v. furnish, provide, arm, supply.

E116 **equipment** n. apparatus, baggage, furniture, gear, outfit.

E117 **equivalent** adj. equal, synonymous, interchangeable, same (U35).

E118 **era** n. age, date, period, epoch, time.

E119 **eradicate** v. *destroy,* exterminate, annihilate (I229).

E120 **erase** v. obliterate, cancel, remove, expunge, rub out (I206).

E121 **erect** 1. v. *build,* construct, raise (D93) 2. adj. upright, standing, vertical.

E122 **erode** v. consume, corrode, destroy, eat away.

E123 **err** v. mistake, blunder, misjudge, sin, lapse (C418).

E124 **errand** n. message, mission, task, job.

E125 **erratic** adj. irregular, changeable, eccentric (R140).

E126 **erroneous** adj. *false,* incorrect, inexact, wrong (C418).

E127 **error** n. mistake, *blunder,* fallacy, offense, sin.

E128 **erupt** v. eject, emit, cast forth.

E129 **escape** v. evade, elude, *flee,* abscond, avoid.

E130 **escort** 1. n. convoy, guard, conductor, guide 2. v. attend, accompany, lead.

E131 **especially** adv. particularly, specially, peculiarly, unusually.

E

E132 **essay** *n.* article, study, paper, thesis.

E133 **essence** *n.* 1. nature, substance, character 2. extract, odor, perfume.

E134 **essential** *adj. vital,* necessary, important, basic (I108).

E135 **establish** *v. found,* originate, fix, settle, set up (A9).

E136 **estate** *n.* land, property, fortune.

E137 **esteem** 1. *v. admire,* like, value, prize 2. *n.* respect, reverence, regard (S72).

E138 **estimate** 1. *v.* value, appraise, *reckon* 2. *n.* valuation, calculation.

E139 **etch** *v.* engrave, corrode, draw.

E140 **eternal** *adj.* everlasting, endless, ceaseless (T54).

E141 **etiquette** *n.* manners, breeding, decorum, form.

E142 **evacuate** *v.* make empty, quit, leave, abandon (O32).

E143 **evade** *v. elude,* escape, dodge, shun (F4).

E144 **evaporate** *v.* vaporize, vanish, disappear, fade.

E145 **even** 1. *adj.* smooth, level, flat (I300, U36) 2. *adj.* equal, calm, steady 3. *adv.* yet, still.

E146 **evening** *n.* nightfall, dusk, twilight (M237).

E147 **event** *n.* occurrence, *incident,* happening.

E148 **eventually** *adv.* at last, finally, ultimately.

E149 **ever** *adv.* always, evermore, forever.

E150 **everlasting** *adj.* endless, *perpetual,* ceaseless, eternal (T54).

E151 **every** *adj.* each, all.

E152 **everyday** *adj. common,* ordinary, customary, usual (M163, P103, R34, U86).

E153 **evict** *v. expel,* dispossess, dismiss.

E154 **evidence** *n.* proof, testimony, witness, facts.

E155 **evident** *adj.* plain, clear, apparent, obvious (I161).

E156 **evil** *adj.* bad, *wicked,* sinful, harmful, unhappy (G98, G100, R259).

E157 **evolve** *v.* develop, grow, expand, open.

E158 **exact** *adj. precise,* accurate, correct (I93).

E159 **exaggerate** *v. magnify,* overstate, enlarge, amplify (D182).

E160 **examination** *n.* test, inspection, inquiry, scrutiny.

E161 **examine** *v. inspect,* check, scrutinize, investigate.

E162 **example** *n.* sample, model, pattern, instance.

E163 **exasperate** *v.* irritate, provoke, aggravate, *annoy.*

E164 **excavate** *v.* hollow, scoop out, dig, burrow.

E165 **exceed** *v.* surpass, excel, outdo, beat.

E166 **excel** *v.* exceed, outdo, surpass.

E167 **excellent** *adj.* superior, *fine,* admirable, choice (P287).

E168 **except** *prep.* excepting, excluding, but.

E169 **exceptional** *adj.* unusual, rare, extraordinary, *remarkable* (C252).

E170 **excess** *adj*. 1. remaining, left over, surplus (S344) 2. intemperate, *abundant,* extravagant.

E171 **excessive** *adj*. 1. extravagant, enormous, *superfluous* 2. immoderate, intemperate (M205).

E172 **exchange** 1. *v*. barter, trade, swap 2. *n*. trade, dealing, interchange.

E173 **excite** *v*. arouse, awaken, provoke, *stimulate* (P3) *adj*. **excitable** (P87), **excited** (P2), **exciting** (T47).

E174 **exclaim** *v*. cry out, call, shout, declare.

E175 **exclude** *v*. bar, debar, shut out, prohibit (C284, E43, E58, I114).

E176 **exclusive** *adj*. choice, limited, restricted (C251).

E177 **excursion** *n*. *journey,* trip, expedition, outing.

E178 **excuse** 1. *v*. pardon, *forgive* (D101) 2. *v*. exempt, free, release 3. *n*. reason, plea, apology *adj*. **excusable** (I158).

E179 **execute** *v*. 1. accomplish, do, carry out 2. kill, put to death.

An execution by guillotine.

E180 **executive** 1. *adj*. managing, directing 2. *n*. official, manager, director.

E181 **exempt** 1. *v*. free, release, let off 2. *adj*. free, excused.

E182 **exercise** 1. *n*. *practice,* training, use 2. *v*. practice, train.

E183 **exert** *v*. strain, strive, struggle, utilize *n*. **exertion**.

E184 **exhale** *v*. breathe out, emit (I189, I223).

E185 **exhaust** *v*. 1. expend, use up, drain 2. weaken, tire, wear out (R109).

E186 **exhibit** 1. *v*. show, *display,* present (H118) 2. *n*. exhibition.

E187 **exhibition** *n*. display, show, exposition, performance.

E188 **exhilarate** *v*. cheer, enliven, gladden, invigorate (D114, T128).

E189 **exile** *v*. banish, *expel,* cast out.

E190 **exist** *v*. be, live, subsist, survive.

E191 **exit** *n*. way out, egress, door, gate (A26, E98, E108).

E192 **expand** *v*. *extend,* stretch, enlarge, increase, swell (A13, C283, C310, C377, L72).

E193 **expect** *v*. *anticipate,* await, look for, hope *adj*. **expectant** (U37, U42).

E194 **expedition** *n*. 1. journey, *trip,* voyage, undertaking 2. haste, speed, quickness.

E195 **expel** *v*. eject, remove, drive out, banish, exile (I291).

E196 **expend** *v*. spend, use, consume, exhaust (C345) *n*. **expenditure** (I117, R232).

E197 **expensive** *adj. dear,* costly, high-priced (C119, I159).

E198 **experience** 1. *n.* knowledge, practice, skill 2. *n.* sensation, feeling, adventure 3. *v.* feel, endure, suffer; *We experienced some cold weather.*

E199 **experienced** *adj.* practiced, qualified, skilled, expert (I160, R48, U81).

E200 **experiment** 1. *n.* trial, *test,* examination, research 2. *v.* test, try, observe, examine.

E201 **expert** 1. *n.* master, *authority,* specialist 2. *adj.* skillful, experienced, clever (I160, U80).

E202 **expire** *v.* 1. cease, close, *stop,* end 2. die (T99).

E203 **explain** *v.* define, interpret, clarify, simplify *adj.* **explainable** (I219).

E204 **explanation** *n.* solution, description, definition.

E205 **explicit** *adj. clear,* plain, positive, express (I63).

E206 **explode** *v.* burst, detonate, blow up, go off.

E207 **exploit** 1. *n.* act, *deed,* feat, achievement 2. *v.* use unfairly, utilize.

E208 **explore** *v.* examine, scrutinize, investigate, search.

E209 **explosion** *n.* detonation, blast, burst.

E210 **export** *v.* send abroad, send out (I67).

E211 **expose** *v.* uncover, bare, disclose, *reveal* (C448, E109, S172).

E212 **express** 1. *v.* speak, utter, state 2. *v.* squeeze out 3. *adj.* fast, speedy, nonstop.

E213 **expression** *n.* 1. phrase, term, statement 2. look, aspect; *Mary had an amused expression on her face.*

E214 **exquisite** *adj.* excellent, delicate, precious, perfect, exact.

E215 **extend** *v.* stretch, reach out, *expand,* lengthen (A3, A13, C283, C310, C377).

E216 **extensive** *adj.* wide, large, broad, vast (N10).

E217 **extent** *n.* degree, amount, volume, size.

E218 **exterior** 1. *n.* outside, outer surface 2. *adj.* outward, external, outer (I256).

E219 **exterminate** *v. destroy,* annihilate, eliminate, abolish.

E220 **external** *adj.* outside, outward, exterior (I260).

E221 **extinct** *adj.* dead, defunct, finished, ended, vanished (A90).

E222 **extinguish** *v.* put out, smother, suppress (I11, K9).

E223 **extra** *adj.* additional, supplementary, spare.

E224 **extract** 1. *v.* pull out, withdraw, remove (I195, I210) 2. *n.* quotation, passage 3. *n.* essence; *Her new perfume was an extract of violets.*

E225 **extraordinary** *adj. unusual,* remarkable, uncommon, rare (A181, O88, U102).

E226 **extravagant** *adj. lavish,* spendthrift, wasteful, excessive (E13).

E227 **extreme** 1. *adj.* outermost, utmost, farthest, radical (M205, T52) 2. *n.* end, extremity, limit.

F f

F1 **fable** *n.* story, *tale,* myth, legend, parable, fiction.

F2 **fabric** *n.* cloth, textile, material.

F3 **fabulous** *adj.* amazing, remarkable, unbelievable, incredible, legendary (R57).

F4 **face** 1. *n.* front, visage, countenance 2. *n.* look, appearance, expression 3. *v.* meet, confront, encounter (S198).

Faces.

F5 **facetious** *adj.* witty, jocular, humorous.

F6 **facility** *n.* 1. ability, ease, expertness, knack 2. convenience, appliance, resource.

F7 **fact** *n.* certainty, truth, deed, reality (F25, F103, L61).

F8 **faction** *n.* clique, combination, party, gang.

F9 **factor** *n.* constituent, element, part, ingredient.

F10 **factory** *n.* plant, works, manufactory.

F11 **faculty** *n.* power, capability, ability, cleverness.

F12 **fad** *n.* craze, *fashion,* rage, vogue.

F13 **fade** *v.* discolor, bleach, *pale,* weaken, wither.

F14 **fag** 1. *v.* droop, tire, weary 2. *n.* drudge, menial, slave.

F15 **fail** *v.* miss, miscarry, be unsuccessful (A32, A40, F280, M31, P444, S544, S590, S596, T210).

F16 **failing** *n.* *defect,* fault, shortcoming, error.

F17 **failure** *n.* collapse, breakdown, default, bankruptcy (S545).

F18 **faint** 1. *v.* *swoon,* collapse, become unconscious 2. *adj.* weak, dim, feeble, indistinct FEINT

F19 **fair** 1. *adj.* just, reasonable, frank, unbiased (I271, U38) 2. *adj.* average, mediocre 3. *adj.* attractive, beautiful 4. *adj.* blonde, light, white 5. adj. sunny, bright 6. *n.* fete, festival, market, exhibition *n.* **fairness** (B68).

F20 **fairy** *n.* elf, pixie, sprite.

F21 **faith** *n.* 1. belief, *trust,* confidence (D204, T188) 2. creed, religion, belief, doctrine.

F22 **faithful** *adj.* 1. trustworthy, loyal, true, devoted (T186, U39, U85) 2. exact, accurate, strict.

F23 **fake** 1. *adj.* false, *counterfeit* (A46, G43, V7) 2. *n.* forgery, imitation, fraud.

F24 **fall** 1. *v.* drop, descend, sink, plunge (R270) 2. *v.* die, perish 3. *v.* decrease, diminish (I128) 4. *n.* descent, decline, collapse 5. *n.* waterfall 6. *n.* autumn.

F

F25 **fallacy** *n.* deceit, deception, illusion, error.

F26 **fallow** *adj.* uncultivated, untilled, neglected.

F27 **false** *adj.* 1. untrue, incorrect (G43, R57, T217) 2. dishonest, disloyal, treacherous (F22, S219) 3. fake, artificial, counterfeit (G43, R57).

F28 **falsehood** *n.* untruth, *lie,* fib (T222).

F29 **falter** *v.* hesitate, waver, be undecided, stammer.

F30 **fame** *n.* reputation, repute, celebrity, glory, honor.

F31 **familiar** *adj.* 1. intimate, close, friendly (S490) 2. common, well-known, conversant, well acquainted.

F32 **family** *n.* relatives, ancestors, clan, tribe, household.

F33 **famine** *n.* death, scarcity, starvation, want (G88).

F34 **famished** *adj.* ravenous, starving, hungry.

F35 **famous** *adj.* celebrated, renowned, distinguished, eminent, well-known (O15).

F36 **fan** 1. *v.* agitate, rouse 2. *v.* cool, refresh, ventilate 3. *n.* admirer, follower, enthusiast.

F37 **fanatic** *n.* zealot, enthusiast, devotee.

F38 **fancy** 1. *n.* imagination, idea, notion 2. *v.* imagine, suppose 3. *v.* like, wish, desire 4. *adj.* ornate, elegant (U6).

F39 **fang** *n.* tusk, tooth.

F40 **fantastic** *adj.* imaginary, bizarre, incredible, unreal (R57).

F41 **far** *adj.* distant, remote (C200).

F42 **farce** *n. comedy,* burlesque, parody, skit (T166).

F43 **fare** *n.* 1. charge, ticket money, fee, price 2. food, provisions, rations. FAIR

F44 **farewell** *n.* goodbye, adieu, leave.

F45 **farm** *v.* till, cultivate, grow.

Farming—ancient and modern.

F46 **fascinate** *v. charm,* enchant, enrapture, attract (R172) *adj.* **fascinating** (M221).

F47 **fashion** 1. *n.* mode, style, *vogue,* custom 2. *n.* way, manner 3. *v.* form, shape, make; *The sculptor fashioned a statue from stone.*

F48 **fashionable** *adj.* modish, stylish, smart, customary (O19).

F49 **fast** 1. *adj.* swift, quick (L136, S270, S271) 2. *adj.* firm, immovable, fixed; *His foot was caught fast in the trap.* 3. *adj.* steadfast, constant 4. *adv.* swiftly, quickly 5. *v.* starve, go hungry (F67).

F50 **fasten** *v. secure,* bind, tie, attach, fix (R136) *adj.* **fastened** (L137).

F51 **fat** 1. *adj. plump,* stout, fleshy (L51, S256, S260, T84) 2. *adj.* thick 3. *n.* grease, oil.

F52 **fatal** *adj.* deadly, lethal, mortal, disastrous.

F53 **fate** *n.* destination, fortune, luck.

F54 **fatherly** *adj.* paternal, tender, protective *n.* **father** (M245).

F55 **fathom** *v.* understand, penetrate, reach.

F56 **fatigue** *n.* weariness, lassitude, tiredness.

F57 **fatuous** *adj.* foolish, idiotic, silly, absurd (S127).

F58 **fault** *n.* 1. defect, blemish, flaw 2. misdeed, blame, offense, error (M133).

F59 **faulty** *adj.* bad, defective, damaged (P135).

F60 **favor** 1. *n.* kindness, benefit, good deed 2. *v. prefer,* approve *adj.* **favorable** (A65).

F61 **favorite** 1. *n.* darling, dear, pet 2. *adj.* preferred, liked, esteemed.

F62 **fawn** *v.* crouch, cringe, kneel, stoop, flatter. FAUN

F63 **fear** 1. *n.* fright, dread, terror, alarm 2. *v.* be afraid, *dread* (C441).

F64 **fearful** *adj. afraid,* timid, nervous, cowardly, apprehensive (F65, P261, U21, V6).

F65 **fearless** *adj.* courageous, bold, intrepid, *brave* (A71, F64).

F66 **feasible** *adj.* practicable, possible, workable (I74).

F67 **feast** 1. *n.* banquet, treat, entertainment, festival (F49).

F68 **feat** *n.* act, *deed,* exploit, trick, achievement. FEET

F69 **feature** 1. *n.* outline, characteristic, trait; *Mountains are a feature of the American West.* 2. *v.* promote, headline, star; *Movie stars are often featured in newspapers.*

F70 **fee** *n.* charge, payment, reward, compensation.

F71 **feeble** *adj. weak,* frail, infirm, powerless, dim (H10, H42, R281, R319, S511) *n.* **feebleness** (E72).

F72 **feed** 1. *v.* nourish, sustain, nurture, satisfy (S434) 2. *n.* fodder, provender.

F73 **feel** *v.* touch, handle, grasp, experience, suffer.

F74 **feeling** *n.* sensation, emotion, sentiment, sympathy.

F75 **feign** *v.* pretend, sham, simulate. FAIN

F76 **feint** *n.* pretense, trick, dodge, mock attack. FAINT

F77 **felicity** *n.* bliss, happiness, blessedness, joy.

F78 **fell** *v.* cut down, hew, knock down.

F79 **fellow** *n.* companion, comrade, chap, mate, guy.

F80 **fellowship** *n.* brotherhood, partnership, communion.

F81 **felon** *n.* culprit, criminal, outlaw, convict.

F82 **female** *adj.* feminine, womanly, ladylike (M26, M65).

F83 **fen** *n.* marsh, swamp, bog, moor.

F84 **fence** 1. *n.* barrier, rail, paling, hedge 2. *v.* evade, shuffle; *The politician fenced the question, avoiding direct reply.* 3. *v.* defend, defend with a sword.

Fiddles.

F85 fend *v.* 1. repel, deflect, deter 2. cope, look after.

F86 ferocious *adj.* wild, fierce, savage, barbarous, cruel (G42).

F87 ferret 1. *v.* search, hunt, find out 2. *n.* polecat, weasel.

F88 fertile *adj. fruitful,* abundant, plentiful, productive (B26, F274).

F89 fervent *adj. ardent,* earnest, eager, zealous.

F90 festival *n.* feast, holiday, anniversary, celebration.

F91 festive *adj. jovial,* joyous, gay, merry.

F92 fetch *v.* bring, carry, convey, go and get.

F93 fetching *adj.* attractive, pleasing, charming, fascinating.

F94 fete *n.* festival, holiday, carnival, gala.

F95 fetish *n.* charm, talisman, superstition.

F96 fetter *n. & v.* shackle, chain, manacle.

F97 feud *n.* quarrel, dispute, fight, squabble.

F98 fever *n.* sickness, illness, excitement, heat, flush.

F99 few *adj.* not many, very little, rare, scanty (C437, I201, L145, M47, S143) *adj.* **fewer** (M235).

F100 fiasco (*fee*-**ass**-koh) *n.* disaster, failure, calamity, farce.

F101 fib *n. lie,* falsehood, untruth (T222).

F102 fickle *adj.* wavering, changeable, capricious, unstable (C355).

F103 fiction *n. story,* fable, novel, fantasy, invention (F7).

F104 fiddle 1. *n.* violin 2. *v.* trifle, dawdle, idle, waste time.

F105 fidelity *n.* 1. faithfulness, devotion, loyalty 2. accuracy, precision.

F106 fidget *v.* chafe, twitch, worry, fret, fuss, squirm.

F107 field *n.* land, plot, ground, tract, meadow.

F108 fiend *n.* demon, *devil,* monster, ogre.

F109 fiendish *adj.* devilish, diabolical, infernal, cruel.

F110 fierce *adj. savage,* ferocious, furious, wild (G42).

F111 fiery *adj.* hot, heated, glowing, fervent (C402).

F112 fight 1. *n.* combat, struggle, battle, conflict, war 2. *v.* combat, battle, strive, struggle (S534).

F113 figure 1. *n.* form, shape, outline, pattern 2. *n.* number, digit, emblem 3. *v.* calculate.

F114 filch *v.* pilfer, purloin, steal, crib, thieve.

F115 file 1. *n.* column, line, row 2. *n.* rasp, grinder 3. *n.* index, list, folder 4. *v.* sort, classify, arrange.

F116 fill *v.* load, pack, replenish, stuff (D302, E142) *adj.* **filled** (B82, E55).

F117 film *n.* 1. coating, skin, veil, layer 2. spool.

F118 filter *v.* strain, percolate, ooze, sift, separate. PHILTER

F119 filth *n.* dirt, nastiness, foulness, muck (C181).

F120 filthy *adj.* dirty, nasty, foul, unclean, vile.

F121 **final** *adj.* last, latest, ultimate, closing, terminal (I193).

F122 **find** *v.* discover, come upon, meet with (L142, M179).

FINED

F123 **fine** 1. *adj.* excellent, admirable, select 2. *adj.* little, thin, minute (C213) 3. *n.* penalty, punishment, forfeit.

F124 **finery** *n.* decorations, ornaments, trinkets, trappings.

F125 **finger** 1. *n.* digit 2. *v.* handle, touch.

F126 **finish** 1. *v.* accomplish, *end,* terminate, close 2. *n.* polish, gloss, refinement (B49, B50, C243, C375, O63, S432) *adj.* **finished** (I121).

F127 **fire** *n.* combustion, blaze, burning.

F128 **firm** 1. *adj.* fixed, *fast,* rigid, stiff (F134, F155, L42, L136) 2. *adj.* steadfast, strong, robust 3. *n.* company, business, concern.

F129 **first** *adj.* foremost, leading, chief, principal, earliest (F121, L29, U2).

F130 **fissure** *n.* cleft, crevice, chink, crack, cranny. FISHER

F131 **fit** 1. *v.* adapt, adjust, suit 2. *v.* equip, supply 3. *adj.* competent, right, suitable (I120) 4. *adj.* well, healthy (D194, I14, U40) 5. *n.* spasm, paroxysm, stroke.

F132 **fix** 1. *v.* connect, tie, *fasten,* attach 2. *v.* mend, repair 3. *v.* establish, settle (A97) 4. *n.* predicament, dilemma, plight *adj.* **fixed** (M200, T54).

F133 **flabbergasted** *adj.* dumbfounded, astounded, surprised, nonplussed.

F134 **flabby** *adj.* soft, yielding, *limp,* lax (B146, F128, M276).

F135 **flag** 1. *v.* droop, languish, tire 2. *n.* pennant, banner, standard.

F136 **flake** *n. scale,* chip, splinter, sliver, slice.

F137 **flame** *n.* blaze, fire.

F138 **flap** *v.* wave, flutter, vibrate.

F139 **flare** *v.* flame, blaze, glow, flash. FLAIR

F140 **flash** 1. *v.* glare, gleam, spark, glitter 2. *n.* second, instant.

F141 **flat** 1. *adj.* level, horizontal, even, smooth (U36) 2. *adj.* dull, lifeless; *His story was not received well, because it was flat and uninteresting.*

F142 **flatter** *v.* humor, *praise,* compliment, cajole (S259) *adj.* **flattering** (C485).

F143 **flavor** *n. taste,* savor, relish, tang, seasoning.

F144 **flaw** *n. blemish,* spot, defect, imperfection, fault *adj.* **flawed** (F145, P135).

F145 **flawless** *adj. perfect,* whole, complete, unblemished (F59, F144).

F146 **fleck** *n.* spot, streak, speck, speckle, freckle.

F147 **flee** *v.* fly, *run,* escape, abscond, run away (A62, C107).

FLEA

F148 **fleece** *v.* 1. clip, shear 2. rob, strip, plunder.

F149 **fleet** 1. *n.* flotilla, navy, squadron, armada 2. *adj.* swift, rapid, quick, nimble.

F150 **fleeting** *adj.* brief, temporary, passing (L29).

F151 **flesh** *n.* meat, body.

F152 **flexible** *adj. pliable,* pliant, elastic, supple (B158, I176, S514).

F153 **flicker** *v.* waver, fluster, twinkle.

F154 **flight** *n.* 1. flying, soaring 2. departure, leaving, exodus.

F155 **flimsy** *adj.* slight, weak, feeble, *fragile* (S526).

F156 **flinch** *v. shrink,* withdraw, wince, cower.

F157 **fling** *v.* throw, cast, toss, pitch.

F158 **flippant** *adj. pert,* impertinent, forward, bold, frivolous (S135).

F159 **flit** *v.* fly, glide, skim, flutter.

F160 **float** *v.* keep afloat, swim, waft, drift, sail (S226).

F161 **flock** 1. *n.* collection (of sheep), group, gathering, congregation 2. *v.* herd, crowd, gather (S57).

F162 **flog** *v. beat,* whip, lash, thrash.

F163 **flood** 1. *n.* deluge, inundation, overflow 2. *v.* flow, drench.

F164 **floor** *n.* ground, pavement, deck, story.

F165 **flop** *v.* 1. slump, drop, fall, *droop,* sag 2. fail, lose, founder.

F166 **flounce** 1. *v.* fling, jerk, toss 2. *n.* frill, furbelow.

F167 **flounder** 1. *v.* struggle, wallow, tumble 2. *n.* flatfish.

F168 **flourish** *v.* 1. *prosper,* succeed, grow, develop 2.

brandish, *wave* (D43, F13).

F169 **flout** *v.* insult, mock, ridicule, taunt, be contemptuous (R204).

F170 **flow** *v.* stream, run, pour, glide, gush (E9).   FLOE

F171 **flower** *n.* blossom, bloom.   FLOUR

Fools.

F172 **fluent** *adj.* 1. flowing, gliding, liquid 2. articulate, eloquent, voluble.

F173 **fluid** *n.* liquid, liquor, water.

F174 **flush** 1. *v.* redden, color, blush 2. *adj.* level, even, flat *adj.* **flushed** (P22).

F175 **fluster** *v.* excite, agitate, bustle, *confuse.*

F176 **flutter** 1. *v.* hover, *flap,* quiver, ruffle 2. *n.* agitation, confusion.

F177 **fly** 1. *v.* glide, soar, hover, float, sail 2. *v.* flee, run away 3. *n.* winged insect.

F178 **foam** *n.* bubble, froth, lather.

F179 **foe** *n. enemy,* adversary, opponent (A93, F255).

F180 **fog** *n*. mist, haze, cloud.

F181 **foil** 1. *v*. outwit, defeat, baffle, *thwart* (A83) 2. *n*. film, flake, leaf 3. *n*. sword, rapier.

F182 **fold** 1. *v*. bend, double, crease 2. *n*. enclosure, pen (U41). FOALED

F183 **follow** *v*. 1. succeed, ensue, come next 2. pursue, chase 3. obey, heed (G166, L46) *n*. **follower** (G166, L47) *adj*. **following** (P375).

F184 **folly** *n*. foolishness, stupidity, absurdity, *nonsense* (S126).

F185 **fond** *adj*. loving, liking, *tender,* affectionate.

F186 **fondle** *v*. *caress,* coddle, pet, cuddle (W54).

F187 **food** *n*. nourishment, nutriment, bread, meat, provisions, fare, rations.

F188 **fool** 1. *n*. idiot, dunce, ninny, nincompoop (S10) 2. *n*. jester, buffoon, clown 3. *v*. deceive, cheat, trick, dupe.

F189 **foolhardy** *adj*. *rash,* reckless, daring, bold (C71).

F190 **foolish** *adj*. senseless, *silly,* stupid, daft (P461, S127, W81).

F191 **forbid** *v*. *prohibit,* ban, disallow, hinder, veto (A92, B69, E56, L84, P148) *adj*. **forbidding** (I292).

F192 **force** 1. *n*. *power,* strength, might, energy, vigor 2. *n*. army, troop, squadron 3. *v*. compel, coerce, push *adj*. **forced** (V87).

F193 **fore** *adj*. front, face, leading, first (B3, R63). FOR, FOUR

F194 **forecast** *v*. foretell, predict, foresee.

F195 **forefather** *n*. ancestor, predecessor, forebear.

F196 **forehead** *n*. brow, front.

F197 **foreign** *adj*. alien, strange, exotic, outlandish.

F198 **foreman** *n*. overseer, superintendent, master, supervisor, boss.

F199 **foremost** *adj*. *first,* leading, advanced, principal.

F200 **foresight** *n*. forethought, prudence, *precaution,* caution.

F201 **forest** *n*. wood, woodland, grove.

F202 **foretell** *v*. *predict,* prophesy, forecast.

F203 **forfeit** 1. *v*. lose, renounce, *relinquish* 2. *n*. penalty, fine, loss (A41, E3).

F204 **forge** *v*. 1. construct, make, invent 2. fake, counterfeit, falsify.

F205 **forget** *v*. overlook, think no more of, lose sight of (L53, R70, R85, R155) *n*. **forgetfulness** (M118) *adj*. **forgettable** (M116).

F206 **forgive** *v*. *pardon,* excuse, absolve (A180, R231) *n*. **forgiveness** (R231) *adj*. **forgiving** (S458, V64).

F207 **forlorn** *adj*. miserable, desolate, hopeless, *wretched* (C124).

F208 **form** *n*. 1. shape, figure, mold 2. kind, sort, system, style; *Her exercise took the form of a game.* 3. manner, method, mode 4. *v*. mold, shape, contrive.

F209 **formal** *adj*. 1. orderly, regular, conventional 2.

dignified, punctilious, precise (C61, I180).

F210 **former** *adj. previous,* prior, earlier, past (F303).

F211 **formidable** *adj.* appalling, fearful, alarming, terrific, dangerous, difficult (E7).

F212 **forsake** *v.* leave, *quit,* desert, abandon.

F213 **fort** *n.* castle, fortress, citadel, stronghold.

F214 **forth** *adv.* forward, onward, out, abroad, ahead.

F215 **forthright** *adj. frank,* outspoken, direct, candid.

F216 **forthwith** *adv.* immediately, directly, instantly.

F217 **fortify** *v.* strengthen, brace, *reinforce.*

F218 **fortitude** *n.* endurance, *courage,* strength, patience.

F219 **fortunate** *adj. lucky,* happy, favorable, advantageous, successful (U43, U61, W114).

F220 **fortune** *n.* 1. *luck,* chance, fate 2. wealth, riches, affluence (M175).

F221 **forward** 1. *adv.* onward, in advance, ahead 2. *adj.* bold, arrogant, brazen (B5, T119) FOREWORD

F222 **foster** *v.* promote, patronize, favor, cherish, support, nurse, nourish.

F223 **foul** *adj.* 1. impure, *nasty,* dirty, filthy (P479) 2. base, scandalous, vile, wicked 3. stormy, rainy, cloudy. FOWL

F224 **found** *v.* 1. establish, set up, originate 2. discovered (L144).

F225 **foundation** *n.* base, ground, establishment.

F226 **foundling** *n.* waif, orphan.

F227 **foundry** *n.* forge, smithy, smelter, crucible.

F228 **fountain** *n.* spring, well, source, stream.

F229 **fowl** *n.* poultry. FOUL

F230 **foxy** *adj.* artful, wily, cunning, crafty, sly.

F231 **fracas** *n.* uproar, quarrel, *brawl.*

F232 **fraction** *n.* part, portion, fragment, piece.

F233 **fracture** *n. break,* crack, rupture, cleft.

F234 **fragile** *adj.* brittle, frail, *weak,* delicate (S511).

F235 **fragment** *n.* scrap, piece, remnant, chip (W65).

F236 **fragrant** *adj.* perfumed, sweet scented, aromatic, spicy.

F237 **frail** *adj.* fragile, brittle, *weak,* feeble, delicate (B180, H42, M144, S526) *n.* **frailty** (S497).

F238 **frame** *n.* 1. framework, form, carcass 2. surround, edging, border, mount.

F239 **frank** *adj. sincere,* open, candid, honest, direct (I214).

F240 **frantic** *adj.* furious, *wild,* raving, frenzied, hysterical.

F241 **fraternity** *n.* brotherhood, society, company, circle.

F242 **fraud** *n.* deceit, deception, trickery, *swindle* (H152).

F243 **fraudulent** *adj.* dishonest, false, tricky, cheating (H151).

F244 **fray** 1. *n.* battle, fight, conflict 2. *v.* wear, rub, chafe.

F245 **freak** *n.* monstrosity, abnormality, fancy.

F246 **free** 1. *adj.* unrestricted, liberated, independent 2. *adj.* loose, lax, untied 3. *adj.* gratuitous, gratis, complimentary 4. *v.* acquit, dismiss, *release* (A146, C7, C35, C66, C321, F50, I79, R215, R216, S106, S583).

F247 **freedom** *n. liberty,* independence, emancipation.

F248 **freeze** *v.* chill, congeal, benumb, refrigerate, solidify (H88, M188, T77) *adj.* **freezing** (H176). FREES, FRIEZE

F249 **freight** *n.* load, cargo, burden, shipment.

F250 **frenzy** *n.* madness, *rage,* fury, insanity, lunacy, mania, excitement.

F251 **frequent** 1. *adj. often,* common, everyday, customary (I182, O28) 2. *v.* haunt, visit often, resort *adv.* **frequently** (S118).

F252 **fresh** *adj.* 1. *new,* unused, sweet, not stale (O52, S421) 2. vigorous, healthy 3. unsalted.

F253 **fret** 1. *v.* worry, grieve, fume, fuss 2. *n.* openwork (ornament).

F254 **friction** *n.* 1. rubbing, grating, abrasion 2. tension, disagreement, wrangling.

F255 **friend** *n.* ally, associate, companion, *comrade,* mate, chum, pal (E70, F179, R273, S491).

F256 **friendly** *adj. amiable,* kind, affectionate, amicable (H175, U44) *n.* **friendship** (E87).

F257 **fright** *n.* alarm, terror, dismay, panic, *fear.*

F258 **frighten** *v.* alarm, terrify, *scare,* shock.

F259 **frightful** *adj. fearful,* dreadful, awful, dire, alarming.

F260 **frigid** *adj.* icy, cold, stiff, aloof (G39).

F261 **frill** *n.* ruffle, edging, gathering, border, flounce.

F262 **fringe** *n.* edge, border, hem, trimming.

F263 **frisky** *adj.* playful, *lively,* sportive, frolicsome.

F264 **fritter** 1. *v.* waste, dawdle, idle 2. *n.* batter cake.

F265 **frivolous** *adj.* shallow, silly, trivial, trifling, *foolish,* facetious (S135, S304, S313).

F266 **frolic** *v.* gambol, frisk, *play,* romp.

F267 **front** *n.* forehead, brow, face, facade, forepart (B3, H126, P307, R63).

F268 **frontier** *n. border,* boundary, limit.

F269 **frosty** *adj.* wintry, cold, cool, frigid, *chilly* (W21).

F270 **froth** *n. foam,* lather, spume, spray, scum.

F271 **frown** *v. scowl,* pout, look stern (S281).

F272 **frugal** *adj. thrifty,* sparing, careful, stingy (E226).

F273 **fruitful** *adj.* prolific, *fertile,* plentiful, abundant (F274).

F274 **fruitless** *adj. useless,* unavailing, futile, sterile, barren (F273).

F275 **frumpish** *adj.* inelegant, graceless, prim, drab, *dowdy,* unfashionable (F48).

F276 **frustrate** *v.* defeat, balk, *foil,* baffle, discourage (G124).

F277 **fry** 1. *v.* sauté, cook with fat 2. *n.* small fishes.

F278 **fuel** *n.* combustibles (wood, coal, gas, oil).

F279 **fugitive** *n.* deserter, runaway, refugee, escaper.

F280 **fulfill** *v.* complete, realize, *accomplish,* perform, finish (F15).

F281 **full** *adj.* filled, *complete,* entire (E55, H146, H205, V84).

F282 **fulsome** *adj.* gross, excessive, sickening, nauseous.

F283 **fumble** *v.* blunder, grope, feel, *bungle,* mishandle.

F284 **fume** 1. *n.* smoke, vapor, steam, gas 2. *v.* rage, rave, storm, flare up.

F285 **fun** *n.* amusement, pleasure, sport, merriment, gaiety.

F286 **function** 1. *n.* ceremony, business, performance; *A function at the hotel was a business conference.* 2. *n.* purpose, use, exercise; *Answering questions is one of the functions of a computer.* 3. *v.* work, *operate,* act.

F287 **fund** *n.* money, capital, assets, supply.

F288 **fundamental** *adj.* essential, *primary,* basic, radical (I108).

F289 **funeral** *n.* burial, cremation, interment, mourning.

F290 **funk** *n.* fear, *terror,* fright.

F291 **funny** *adj.* 1. *comical,* amusing, humorous, laughable (S135) 2. odd, strange, curious.

F292 **furious** *adj.* frantic, raging, infuriated, angry, stormy (C15).

F293 **furnish** *v.* 1. supply, provide, give; *Furnished with charcoal and paper, the art class set to work.* 2. equip, outfit.

F294 **furrow** *n.* channel, groove, trench, wrinkle, seam.

F295 **further** *adj.* 1. additional, more 2. more remote (O22).

F296 **furthermore** *adv.* moreover, besides, also, too.

F297 **furtive** *adj. stealthy,* secret, sly, surreptitious.

F298 **fury** *n.* rage, *anger,* frenzy, madness, wrath, fierceness, ferocity (C15).

F299 **fuse** *v.* melt, liquefy, blend, intermingle, join.

F300 **fuss** 1. *n.* ado, bustle, worry, flurry 2. *v. bother,* pester, fret.

F301 **fussy** *adj.* fidgety, choosy, finicky, bustling (C61).

F302 **futile** *adj. useless,* pointless, frivolous, worthless, profitless, idle.

F303 **future** *adj.* coming, to come, hereafter, tomorrow, imminent, prospective (P76).

G g

G1 **gabble** *v.* chatter, prattle, babble, jabber.

G2 **gadget** *n. appliance,* contraption, instrument, device.

G3 **gag** 1. *v.* silence, stifle, muzzle 2. *v.* retch, choke 3. *n.* joke, jest.

G4 **gain** 1. *v.* get, *acquire,* obtain, earn, win (F203, L143) 2.

n. increase, profit, addition (S3).

G5 **gale** *n.* wind, storm, tempest, hurricane.

G6 **gallant** *adj.* 1. *brave,* valiant, courageous (C451) 2. noble, chivalrous, courteous.

G7 **gallery** *n.* passage, balcony, arcade, corridor.

G8 **gallop** *v.* ride, canter, hurry, scamper, run.

G9 **gamble** *v.* risk, wager, bet, game, chance. GAMBOL

G10 **gambol** *v.* frisk, *frolic,* dance, play, caper. GAMBLE

G11 **game** 1. *n. match,* contest, competition, play, sport, amusement 2. *adj.* courageous, brave, fearless.

G12 **gammon** *n.* ham, bacon.

G13 **gang** *n.* crew, *band,* party, clique, ring.

G14 **gangster** *n.* criminal, evildoer, hoodlum.

G15 **gap** *n. cleft,* crevice, opening, space, interval.

G16 **gape** *v.* yawn, stare, open, gaze.

G17 **garb** *n. dress,* clothes, attire, costume.

G18 **garbage** *n.* rubbish, offal, refuse, remains, waste.

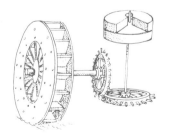

Gear mechanism.

G19 **garish** *adj.* flashy, gaudy, showy, *tawdry,* loud.

G20 **garland** *n.* wreath, crown, chaplet.

G21 **garment** *n.* dress, frock, coat, robe.

G22 **garnish** *v.* adorn, beautify, decorate.

G23 **gash** *v.* cut, wound, slash.

G24 **gasp** *v.* puff, pant, blow, choke, wheeze.

G25 **gate** *n.* door, entrance, portico. GAIT

G26 **gather** *v.* 1. collect, *assemble,* muster, accumulate (D241, S57) 2. infer, deduce, conclude.

G27 **gathering** *n. meeting,* collection, assembly, company.

G28 **gaudy** *adj. garish,* tawdry, flashy, vulgar (M207).

G29 **gauge** (rhymes with *rage*) 1. *n.* measure, instrument, meter 2. *v.* judge, estimate, appraise. GAGE

G30 **gaunt** *adj. haggard,* lean, thin, skinny, spare.

G31 **gay** *adj.* merry, bright, lively, *cheerful,* jolly (G126).

G32 **gaze** *v.* stare, *gape,* regard, look intently.

G33 **gear** *n.* 1. mechanism, cog, rigging 2. equipment, accessories, harness 3. (slang) clothes.

G34 **gem** *n.* jewel, precious stone, treasure.

G35 **general** 1. *adj.* universal, common, usual 2. *adj.* vague, indefinite, inexact (I148, S350) 3. *n.* commander in chief.

G36 **generally** *adv.* commonly, usually, ordinarily.

G

G37 **generation** *n*. 1. family, breed, offspring 2. creation, production.

G38 **generous** *adj*. unselfish, kind, liberal, charitable (G131, M92, P57, S120, S468).

G39 **genial** *adj*. agreeable, cheerful, hearty, merry (S588).

G40 **genius** *n*. 1. ability, sagacity, talent 2. master, prodigy, sage (D337, I7).

G41 **genteel** *adj*. polite, civil, elegant, gentlemanly (C251, U19).

G42 **gentle** *adj*. mild, moderate, bland, kind (B165, F86, F110, H53, P226, V66) *n*. **gentleman** (L8, R284, R316, S48, S73).

G43 **genuine** *adj*. 1. authentic, real, true, actual (A150, C436, F23, F27, S393) 2. sincere, unaffected, frank.

G44 **germ** *n*. seed, embryo, nucleus, origin, microbe.

G45 **gesture** *n*. action, signal, sign, movement.

G46 **get** *v*. 1. gain, obtain, win, earn, procure 2. bring, fetch, carry 3. prepare, make ready 4. become, go 5. arrive, reach, win.

G47 **ghastly** *adj*. dismal, hideous, grisly, horrible.

G48 **ghost** *n*. specter, phantom, shade, spirit, spook *adj*. **ghostly**.

G49 **giant** 1. *n*. monster, colossus, ogre 2. *adj*. huge, *enormous,* gigantic, vast (M155).

G50 **gibberish** *n*. nonsense, drivel, rubbish, balderdash.

G51 **gibe** *v*. sneer, scoff, *jeer,* taunt (C276).

G52 **giddy** *adj*. *dizzy,* unsteady, reeling, flighty, careless (S417).

G53 **gift** *n*. 1. present, offering, donation, contribution 2. talent, ability, genius.

G54 **gigantic** *adj*. giant, *huge,* enormous (M161).

G55 **giggle** *n*. & *v*. snigger, laugh, cackle, titter.

G56 **gingerly** *adv*. cautiously, carefully, tenderly, daintily.

G57 **girl** *n*. female, lass, miss, damsel, maiden (B136) *adj*. **girlish**.

G58 **gist** *n*. essence, pith, substance, point, kernel.

G59 **give** *v*. 1. bestow, supply, provide, grant, present 2. communicate, emit, issue, utter; *Sally gave us a song at the party*. 3. produce, yield; *This climate gives us two crops a year*. 4. recede, give way 5. surrender, sacrifice (R73, T10).

G60 **glad** *adj*. pleased, *happy,* delighted, cheerful, joyful (U47).

G61 **gladden** *v*. *delight,* cheer, make glad, elate.

G62 **glamor** *n*. charm, enchantment, allure, attraction.

G63 **glance** *v*. *glimpse,* look, dart, peep.

G64 **glare** 1. *v*. glower, *scowl,* stare 2. *n*. dazzle, shine, glow, glitter.

G65 **glass** *n*. tumbler, beaker, goblet.

G66 **glaze** *v*. burnish, polish, gloss, shine, varnish.

G67 **gleam** *n*. & *v*. beam, glimmer, sparkle, flash, glow.

G68 **glee** *n*. *fun,* jollity, cheer, merriment, mirth (M108).

G69 **glen** *n.* valley, vale, dale, dell.

G70 **glib** *adj.* smooth, fluent, voluble, talkative, slick.

G71 **glide** *v.* flow, soar, skim.

G72 **glimmer** 1. *v.* shimmer, shine, glitter 2. *n.* inkling, hint.

G73 **glimpse** *n. glance,* sight, look, view (S92).

G74 **glisten** *v.* glitter, sparkle, shine, glimmer.

G75 **glitter** *v.* sparkle, glitter, scintillate, flash.

G76 **gloat** *v.* exult, triumph, revel, glory.

G77 **globe** *n.* sphere, ball, orb, world, earth *adj.* **global**.

G78 **gloom** *n.* 1. sadness, dejection, depression 2. darkness, cloud, dullness, shadow (H33, J32, M166).

G79 **gloomy** *adj.* 1. dismal, cheerless, unhappy, depressed, sad, glum, melancholy (C124, G60, J25, M134) 2. dark, dim, dusky, dreary.

G80 **glorify** *v.* adore, bless, worship, praise, celebrate.

G81 **glorious** *adj.* 1. *splendid,* grand, magnificent, supreme, distinguished, celebrated, renowned, famous (I163).

G82 **glory** *n.* honor, renown, fame, praise, splendor, grandeur.

G83 **glossy** *adj.* smooth, shiny, lustrous, glazed.

G84 **glow** *v. & n. shine,* gleam, glimmer, blaze.

G85 **glower** *v.* stare, *scowl,* glare, frown.

G86 **glue** *v.* stick, paste, bind.

G87 **glum** *adj.* gloomy, *sullen,* moody, morose, sour (J31).

G88 **glut** *n.* surplus, surfeit, excess (F33).

G89 **glutton** *n.* gobbler, gourmand, gourmandizer.

G90 **gnarled** *adj.* knotty, twisted, contorted.

G91 **gnash** *v.* crunch, grind, snap.

G92 **gnaw** *v.* bite, chew, grind, nibble.

G93 **go** *v.* 1. advance, depart, pass, proceed, travel, walk (C237, R150, S446) 2. become, get to be 3. operate, work, function; *This car goes well.*

G94 **goal** *n.* object, destination, *aim,* end, purpose, target.

G95 **gobble** *v.* devour, *eat,* bolt, gulp, gorge.

G96 **God** *n.* Jehovah, Lord, the Creator, the Maker, the Deity, the Father, the Almighty.

G97 **golden** *adj.* bright, shining, yellow, precious, favorable, splendid.

G98 **good** 1. *adj.* excellent, admirable, fine (B6) 2. *adj.* well-behaved, virtuous, upright, obedient (M169) 3. *adj.* suitable, fit, proper, able; *This radio is good for another five years.* 4. *adj.* kind, benevolent, friendly, generous 5. real, genuine, authentic 6. *adj.* agreeable, pleasant 7. *n.* benefit, advantage, profit (I14).

G99 **goodbye** *n. & interj.* farewell, adieu, cheerio, so long (H100).

G100 **goodness** *n.* excellence, honesty, morality, *virtue,* benevolence, value (S217).

G

G101 **goods** *n.* belongings, property, wares, merchandise.
G102 **gorge** 1. *n.* ravine, defile, pass 2. *v.* devour, stuff, gulp, swallow (F49).
G103 **gorgeous** *adj.* splendid, magnificent, *beautiful,* ravishing, dazzling, superb (U1).
G104 **gossip** 1. *v.* tattle, chatter, rumor 2. *n.* scandal, hearsay.
G105 **govern** *v. rule,* control, manage, regulate, command.
G106 **government** *n.* command, control, administration, state, authority, parliament, council.
G107 **gown** *n.* dress, frock, robe, garment.
G108 **grab** *v.* snatch, clutch, seize, grip, grasp.
G109 **grace** *n.* 1. elegance, polish, refinement, *beauty,* symmetry 2. clemency, mercy, pardon, forgiveness.
G110 **graceful** *adj. beautiful,* comely, elegant (U45).
G111 **gracious** *adj. courteous,* friendly, kindly, polite (I66).
G112 **grade** *n.* 1. degree, class, category, brand, stage 2. slope, gradient, incline.
G113 **gradual** *adj.* slow, continuous, little by little (A15).
G114 **graft** 1. *v.* join, splice, transplant 2. *n.* corruption, bribery.
G115 **grain** *n.* 1. particle, atom, scrap, bit 2. corn, cereals, seed 3. wood texture.
G116 **grand** *adj.* stately, lordly, royal, *majestic,* magnificent (M101).
G117 **grant** *v.* 1. *allow,* award, allot, bestow, convey 2. permit, consent, let (W88).
G118 **graphic** *adj.* vivid, lifelike, descriptive.
G119 **grapple** *v.* catch, seize, *clasp,* clutch.
G120 **grasp** 1. *v.* clasp, catch, *clutch,* grip 2. *n.* understanding, comprehension.
G121 **grasping** *adj.* greedy, avaricious, miserly.
G122 **grate** 1. *v.* grind, *rub,* scrape, scratch 2. *v.* annoy, irritate 3. *n.* fireplace. GREAT
G123 **grateful** *adj.* thankful, gratifying, indebted (U46).
G124 **gratify** *v. please,* satisfy, delight, fulfill (D199, M242).
G125 **gratitude** *n.* thankfulness, appreciation, indebtedness.
G126 **grave** 1. *adj.* sober, *serious,* thoughtful, solemn 2. *adj.* important, essential (U50) 3. *n.* tomb, vault.
G127 **gravity** *n.* 1. importance, seriousness 2. gravitation, force.
G128 **graze** *v.* 1. feed, pasture, eat grass 2. scrape, rub, contact, brush. GRAYS
G129 **grease** *n.* fat, oil, lubrication.
G130 **great** *adj.* 1. big, large, vast, huge, immense 2. important, considerable, remarkable (T211) 3. chief, leading, main *adj.* **greatest** (L55). GRATE
G131 **greedy** *adj. selfish,* avaricious, *grasping, ravenous.*
G132 **green** 1. *adj.* blooming, verdant, fresh, unripe 2. *adj.* inexperienced, untrained, new.
G133 **greet** *v.* accost, address, welcome, meet.

G134 **grief** *n. sorrow,* regret, distress, woe, sadness, heartache (J32).

G135 **grievance** *n. complaint,* injustice, wrong, objection.

G136 **grieve** *v.* sorrow, *mourn,* lament, suffer, distress, sadden, agonize, hurt (R130).

G137 **grievous** *adj.* dreadful, *severe,* terrible, atrocious, distressing, deplorable.

G138 **grim** *adj.* 1. *stern,* harsh, severe 2. frightful, horrible, appalling, grisly.

G139 **grime** *n. dirt,* filth, soot, smut.

G140 **grin** *v. smile,* smirk, beam.

G141 **grind** *v.* 1. grate, powder, crush, crumble 2. sharpen, whet, file.

G142 **grip** *v.* grasp, *clutch,* clasp, hold.

G143 **grisly** *adj.* frightful, horrid, hideous, dreadful, grim.

G144 **grit** *n.* 1. gravel, sand, pebbles 2. courage, pluck, perseverance.

G145 **groan** *v.* moan, wail, howl, whine, complain.

GROWN

G146 **groom** 1. *n.* servant, valet, waiter, bridegroom 2. *v.* tidy, clean, preen, tend.

G147 **groove** *n.* channel, *furrow,* rut.

G148 **grope** *v.* feel, fumble, touch.

G149 **gross** *adj.* 1. dense, *thick* 2. coarse, *vulgar,* crude 3. shameful, outrageous (D84).

G150 **grotesque** *adj. fantastic,* fanciful, bizarre, queer, odd.

G151 **ground** *n.* 1. earth, soil, turf 2. base, foundation.

Sowing seeds on the ground.

G152 **grounds** *n.* 1. estate, garden 2. sediment, dregs 3. cause, basis, reasons.

G153 **group** *n.* collection, *set,* bunch, cluster.

G154 **grovel** *v.* creep, crawl, *cringe,* fawn, cower.

G155 **grow** *v.* 1. *develop,* enlarge, expand (S194) 2. germinate, sprout.

G156 **growl** *v.* snarl, grumble, complain.

G157 **growth** *n. increase,* expansion, extension.

G158 **grudge** *n.* dislike, ill will, spite, *malice adj.* **grudging** (G123).

G159 **gruff** *adj. blunt,* brusque, grumpy, churlish, bluff.

G160 **grumble** *v. complain,* growl, mutter, protest.

G161 **grunt** *v.* snort, groan.

G162 **guarantee** *n.* warranty, assurance, pledge, surety.

G163 **guard** 1. *v. protect,* defend, watch, shield 2. *n.* sentry, sentinel, watchman, conductor.

G164 **guess** *v.* surmise, *conjecture,* reckon, assume.

G165 **guest** *n.* visitor, caller (H173). GUESSED

G166 **guide** 1. *v.* conduct, *lead,* pilot, steer (M180) 2. *n.* leader, pilot, director.

G167 **guild** *n.* society, association, union, fellowship.

G168 **guilty** *adj.* criminal, wicked, wrong, responsible.

G169 **guise** *n.* appearance, aspect, dress, form. GUYS

G170 **gulf** *n.* 1. bay, inlet 2. abyss, chasm, opening.

G171 **gulp** *v.* swallow, devour, bolt.

G172 **gun** *n.* firearm, weapon, pistol, rifle, revolver, cannon.

G173 **gurgle** *v.* babble, burble, chortle, chuckle.

G174 **gush** *v.* rush, *spout,* spurt, flow.

G175 **gust** *n. blast,* squall, wind.

G176 **gutter** *n. channel,* conduit, groove, drain, sewer.

G177 **guttural** *adj.* deep, gruff, *hoarse,* throaty.

H   h

H1 **habit** *n.* 1. mannerism, trait, idiosyncrasy, addiction 2. *custom,* practice, usage 3. apparel, clothes.

H2 **habitation** *n.* abode, dwelling, lodging, quarters.

H3 **hack** 1. *v.* cut, *hew,* chop 2. *n.* hireling, mercenary.

H4 **hackneyed** *adj. common,* much used, stale, threadbare.

H5 **hag** *n.* ugly old woman, virago, vixen, shrew, fury, crone, witch.

H6 **haggard** *adj.* gaunt, lean, spare, raw, drawn.

H7 **haggle** *v.* bargain, argue, worry, stickle.

H8 **hail** 1. *v.* salute, *greet,* welcome, accost 2. *n.* sleet, storm, rain. HALE

H9 **hairy** *adj.* hirsute, bristly, bushy, shaggy, woolly (B13).

H10 **hale** *adj. healthy,* robust, sound, strong, well (F71). HAIL

Hair style.

H11 **halfhearted** *adj.* 1. *indifferent,* lukewarm, unconcerned (E102) 2. irresolute, undecided, uncertain.

H12 **half-witted** *adj.* dull, *stupid,* stolid, foolish, silly.

H13 **hall** *n.* passage, chamber, corridor, entrance, vestibule, auditorium. HAUL

H14 **hallow** *v.* sanctify, consecrate, dedicate.

H15 **hallucination** *n.* illusion, delusion, *dream,* vision.

H16 **halo** *n.* ring, circle, aureole, glory.

H17 **halt** 1. *v. stop,* hold up, pull up, cease (S432) 2. *n.* stop, station, end *adj.* **halting** (F172).

H18 **halve** v. divide, dissect, split, share, bisect.

H19 **hammer** 1. v. forge, beat, pound, drive 2. n. mallet.

H20 **hammock** n. hanging bed, swing.

H21 **hamper** 1. n. basket, crate, box, creel 2. v. hinder, restrain, impede, thwart (H102).

H22 **hand** 1. n. palm, fist, fingers 2. n. laborer, craftsman, helper, employee 3. n. participation, share, support; *Give us a hand to put up the tent.* 4. v. give, transmit, pass.

H23 **handicap** 1. n. hindrance, disadvantage, *burden,* impediment 2. v. hinder, hamper, disable (A63).

H24 **handicraft** n. occupation, pastime, trade, art, craft.

H25 **handle** 1. n. haft, stock, knob, hilt 2. v. touch, feel 3. v. manage, wield, manipulate.

H26 **handsome** adj. 1. graceful, good-looking, attractive, elegant (U1) 2. considerable, ample, generous; *Tom inherited a handsome share of his father's estate.* HANSOM

H27 **handy** adj. 1. adroit, *skillful,* clever, dexterous, helpful (C208) 2. convenient, nearby, close.

H28 **hang** v. 1. *suspend,* dangle, droop, depend, sag 2. execute, lynch.

H29 **hanker** v. *desire,* covet, yearn, crave.

H30 **haphazard** adj. chance, *random,* aimless, (T89).

H31 **hapless** adj. ill-fated, *unlucky,* wretched (L159).

H32 **happen** v. take place, *occur,* befall, chance.

H33 **happiness** n. delight, enjoyment, *joy,* pleasure, bliss, blessedness (G78, S327, T215, W93).

H34 **happy** adj. joyful, gay, *cheerful,* blissful, pleased, contented, glad (D294, D296, G79, M108, M173, M227, M257, S4, S319, U47, W114).

H35 **harass** v. worry, plague, molest, *disturb,* torment (S322).

H36 **harbor** 1. n. anchorage, port, haven, dock 2. v. give shelter, protect, shield.

H37 **hard** adj. 1. firm, *solid,* compact, rigid (S308) 2. *difficult,* puzzling, intricate 3. laborious, tiring, arduous 4. unkind, cruel, unfeeling, *stern.*

H38 **harden** v. become hard, solidify, fortify (D250, M112).

H39 **hardhearted** adj. *cruel,* unfeeling, merciless, pitiless, hard (T60).

H40 **hardly** adv. scarcely, barely, narrowly, just (O49).

H41 **hardship** n. toil, fatigue, weariness, suffering, *trouble,* difficulty.

H42 **hardy** adj. strong, *robust,* firm, healthy, bold, intrepid, brave (F234, F237).

H43 **hark** v. *listen,* heed.

H44 **harm** 1. n. injury, *hurt,* damage 2. n. evil, wrong, wickedness 3. v. hurt, mistreat, injure (B59) adj. **harmed** (I239).

H45 **harmful** adj. injurious, noxious, mischievous (H46).

H46 **harmless** adj. innocent, gentle, innocuous, inoffensive (F86, F110, H45, P149, P275).

H47 harmonious *adj.* 1. *melodious,* tuneful, musical (D217) 2. cordial, friendly.

H48 harmony *n.* accord, concord, agreement (C324, C386, D217).

H49 harness *n.* equipment, tackle, bridle, yoke.

H50 harp 1. *v.* repeat, reiterate, dwell on 2. *n.* lyre.

H51 harrow 1. *v.* torment, torture, wound, *distress* (S322) 2. *n.* plow, rake.

H52 harry *v* 1. pillage, plunder, raid, rob 2. *worry,* annoy, vex.

H53 harsh *adj. coarse,* rough, grating, discordant, stern, severe, rude, churlish (M127, S611) *n.* **harshness** (C262).

H54 harvest 1. *n. crop,* produce, yield 2. *v.* gather, reap, pick.

H55 haste *n. hurry,* speed, rush, flurry, muddle.

H56 hasty *adj.* 1. *quick,* swift, rapid, fleet, fast, brisk (S270) 2. irritable, touchy, testy, rash.

H57 hat *n.* cap, headgear, bonnet, helmet, hood.

H58 hatch 1. *v.* incubate, breed 2. *v. devise,* scheme, concoct 3. *n.* door, trap, opening.

H59 hatchet *n.* ax, tomahawk, halberd.

H60 hate *v. loathe,* detest, abhor, despise, dislike (A55, L91, L151).

H61 hateful *adj.* malevolent, malign, *horrid,* detestable, vile.

H62 hatred *n.* hate, *enmity,* hostility, animosity, loathing (L151).

H63 haughty *adj.* arrogant, disdainful, proud (H196, U7).

H64 haul *v. pull,* tug, draw, tow (P487). HALL

H65 haunt 1. *v. frequent,* inhabit 2. *n.* resort, retreat, den.

H66 have 1. hold, *possess,* own, keep 2. get, gain, obtain, take, acquire (W16).

H67 haven *n.* port, harbor, shelter, refuge.

H68 havoc *n.* destruction, *ruin,* damage, carnage.

H69 hawk 1. *n.* falcon, kestrel 2. *n.* trowel 3. *v.* sell, vend, peddle.

H70 hay *n.* fodder, silage, grass. HEY

H71 hazard 1. *n.* chance, *risk,* peril, jeopardy 2. *v.* venture, offer, gamble.

H72 haze *n.* mist, *fog,* dimness, murk *adj.* **hazy.** HAYS

H73 head *n.* 1. brain, skull, crown 2. top, summit, acme 3. chief, leader, principal, director.

H74 headquarters *n.* main center, base, HQ.

H75 headstrong *adj.* obstinate, *stubborn,* dogged, self-willed.

Hats for heads.

H76 headway *n.* leeway, room, progress, improvement.

H77 heady *adj.* rash, impetuous, exciting, strong.

H78 heal *v.* cure, remedy, restore (I196, M242, W107). HEEL HE'LL

H79 **healthy** *adj.* hale, hearty, well, *robust,* wholesome (I14, I146, I173, M234, S201, U48).

H80 **heap** *n.* pile, mass, collection, stack, load.

H81 **hear** *v.* listen, heed, hearken, give ear to.   HERE

H82 **hearsay** *n.* rumor, gossip.

H83 **heart** *n.* 1. center, interior, core 2. courage, spirit 3. sympathy, kindness, warmth.

H84 **hearten** *v.* encourage, cheer, stimulate, comfort (D114).

H85 **hearth** *n.* fireplace, hearthstone, fireside.

H86 **heartless** *adj.* cruel, unfeeling, pitiless, merciless (H195).

H87 **hearty** *adj.* sincere, true, eager, strong, sound (I214).

H88 **heat** 1. *n.* warmth, excitement, fervor, fever (C224) 2. *v.* warm, make hot, cook (C402).

H89 **heathen** *n.* pagan, infidel, idolator, unbeliever.

H90 **heave** *v.* *lift,* hoist, raise, pull, push.

H91 **heaven** *n.* sky, firmament, paradise, bliss (H98).

H92 **heavenly** *adj.* *divine,* angelic, rapturous, ecstatic, blissful, wonderful (H99, I170).

H93 **heavy** *adj.* weighty, bulky, hefty, ponderous (L90, S256).

H94 **hectic** *adj.* feverish, hot, heated, *active,* excited (C15).

H95 **hedge** 1. *v.* evade, dodge, *avoid,* obstruct 2. *n.* fence, barrier, hedgerow.

H96 **heed** *v.* *regard,* notice, obey, listen to (D246, I13) *adj.* **heedful** (I96, O12, R79, W17).

H97 **height** *n.* 1. altitude, elevation, hill, mountain (D117) 2. tallness, stature.

H98 **hell** *n.* hades, inferno, infernal regions (H91).

H99 **hellish** *adj.* diabolical, fiendish, devilish (H92).

H100 **hello** *interj.* greetings, salutations (G99).

H101 **helmet** *n.* helm, casque.

H102 **help** *v.* 1. aid, assist, serve (H21, H23, H127, I50, O22, T106) 2. succor, save 3. avoid, prevent, deter; *She couldn't help laughing. n.* **help** (H128, O73).

H103 **helpful** *adj.* useful, beneficial, profitable (U101).

H104 **helpless** *adj.* weak, feeble, powerless, disabled.

H105 **hem** *n.* edge, border, margin.

H106 **hence** *adv.* therefore, henceforth, from this source.

H107 **herald** *n.* messenger, crier, harbinger, forerunner.

H108 **herb** *n.* plant, flavoring, spice, seasoning.

H109 **herd** *n.* pack, *flock,* crowd, collection, drove. HEARD

H110 **here** *adv.* in this place, thither, at present.   HEAR

H111 **heresy** *n.* error, unorthodoxy, misbelief, dissent.

H112 **heritage** *n.* inheritance, bequest, legacy, portion.

H113 **hermit** *n.* recluse, solitary, ascetic.

H114 **hero** *n.* brave person, champion, idol, favorite (C451, V61).

H115 **heroic** *adj.* *brave,* valiant, bold, daring, gallant.

H

H116 **hesitate** v. pause, delay, *demur,* waver, doubt (D47, R201) *adj.* **hesitating** (F172).

H117 **hew** v. cut, chop, hack, cleave, split. HUE

H118 **hide** 1. v. *conceal,* cover, screen, mask, cloak (D220, D242, D270, R229) *adj.* **hidden** (M36, O26, V72). HIED

H119 **hideous** *adj. ugly,* frightful, appalling, dreadful, ghastly (L152).

H120 **high** *adj.* 1. lofty, elevated, tall (L153) 2. eminent, superior, prominent, great 3. acute, shrill, sharp 4. dear, expensive *adj.* **higher** (I169).

H121 **highly** *adj.* very, extremely, exceedingly.

H122 **highway** n. road, street, thoroughfare.

H123 **hike** v. *walk,* tramp, ramble, trek.

H124 **hilarious** *adj.* happy, jovial, merry, mirthful, cheerful.

H125 **hill** n. height, hillock, knoll, mound, elevation (D6, V8) *adj.* **hilly** (F141).

H126 **hind** 1. *adj.* back, *rear,* posterior (F267) 2. *n.* female deer.

H127 **hinder** v. prevent, *obstruct,* impede, stop, hamper, thwart (A83, A161, E60, H102, L74, S581, S602).

H128 **hindrance** n. *obstacle,* stop, obstruction, restraint (H102).

H129 **hinge** 1. v. turn, depend, hang, rely 2. *n.* pivot, axis.

H130 **hint** v. intimate, insinuate, *suggest,* mention.

H131 **hire** v. rent, lease, let, charter, employ. HIGHER

H132 **hiss** v. 1. deride, scorn, *ridicule,* boo, disapprove 2. fizz, whistle, whizz, buzz, spit.

H133 **history** n. chronicle, record, story, account, memoir *adj.* **historical** (L62, M291).

H134 **hit** 1. v. strike, beat, smite, collide (M182) 2. v. attain, win, accomplish, discover 3. n. stroke, blow 4. n. success, chance, venture.

H135 **hitch** 1. v. *fasten,* tie, attach 2. n. obstacle, snag.

H136 **hoard** v. save, *store,* accumulate, amass (S360). HORDE

H137 **hoarse** *adj.* husky, *raucous,* harsh, rough, grating (C182). HORSE

H138 **hoax** n. fraud, cheat, deception, practical joke, *trick.*

H139 **hobble** v. 1. *limp,* totter, stagger, falter 2. fetter, shackle.

H140 **hobby** n. pastime, amusement, *recreation* (P410).

H141 **hog** 1. n. pig, swine 2. v. monopolize.

H142 **hoist** 1. v. *lift,* raise, heave 2. n. crane, lift, derrick.

H143 **hold** 1. v. *grasp,* clutch, grip (R136) 2. v. *possess,* have, keep, retain 3. v. *contain,* admit 4. n. cargo store 5. n. fort, castle. HOLED

H144 **hole** n. *aperture,* opening, cavity, hollow, cave. WHOLE

H145 **holiday** n. leave, vacation, anniversary, festival.

H146 **hollow** 1. *adj. empty,* vacant (S315) 2. *adj.* false, insincere 3. *n.* depression, hole 4. *v.* dig, scoop.

H147 **holy** *adj. sacred,* blessed, hallowed, consecrated, pious, devout.   WHOLLY

H148 **homage** *n.* loyalty, fidelity, respect, honor.

H149 **home** *n.* 1. dwelling, house, residence 2. family, fireside, hearth 3. institution, hospice (A14).

H150 **homely** *adj.* 1. domestic, simple, comfortable 2. plain, unattractive, ugly.

H151 **honest (on-***est***)** *adj. upright,* virtuous, genuine, reputable, sincere, frank, moral (C423, D232, F243, S174, U24, U66).

H152 **honesty** *n. integrity,* uprightness, sincerity, fairness, frankness (D46, F242).

H153 **honor** 1. *n.* respect, regard, esteem, distinction 2. *n.* repute, fame, glory, reputation (D227, S156) 3. *v.* revere, respect (A22).

H154 **honorable** *adj.* 1. illustrious, famed 2. *honest,* just, fair (I163).

H155 **hood** *n.* cowl, cover, veil.

H156 **hoodwink** *v.* deceive, *cheat,* dupe, trick.

A child's hoop.

H157 **hook** *n.* catch, clasp, hasp, fastener, hanger, crook.

H158 **hoop** *n.* ring, circlet, band, circle.   WHOOP

H159 **hoot** *v.* shout, cry, *yell,* howl, screech.

H160 **hop** *v.* & *n. jump,* leap, spring, skip, caper.

H161 **hope** 1. *n.* expectancy, longing, anticipation 2. *v.* anticipate, desire, wish for (D132).

H162 **hopeful** *adj.* confident, expectant, *optimistic* (H163).

H163 **hopeless** *adj.* despairing, downcast, forlorn, helpless (H162) *n.* **hopelessness** (H161).

H164 **horizontal** *adj.* flat, *level,* straight, even, (P150, U92, V43).

H165 **horn** *n.* 1. bone, antler, prong 2. trumpet.

H166 **horrible** *adj.* horrid, frightful, *terrible,* dreadful (W96).

H167 **horrid** *adj.* frightful, alarming, horrifying, *fearful,* hideous (D87).

H168 **horror** *n.* dread, awe, terror, *dismay,* loathing.

H169 **horse** *n.* steed, charger, mount, stallion, mare, filly, colt, pony.   HOARSE

H170 **hose** *n.* 1. tubing, pipe 2. stockings, socks.   HOES

H171 **hospitable** *adj.* bountiful, open, generous, *friendly,* welcoming (U44).

H172 **hospital** *n.* infirmary, sanatorium, clinic.

H173 **host** *n.* 1. landlord, entertainer, innkeeper (G165) 2. throng, swarm, army, legion.

H174 **hostel** *n.* inn, hotel, boardinghouse.

H175 **hostile** *adj.* unfriendly, antagonistic, adverse, opposed (F256, H171).

H176 **hot** *adj.* 1. burning, fiery, scorching, blazing (C224) 2. *pungent,* piquant, sharp, peppery 3. excitable, violent.

H177 **hotel** *n.* inn, tavern, hostel, guest house, motel, hostelry, public house, pub.

H178 **hound** 1. *n.* dog, hunting dog 2. *v.* incite, urge, spur 3. *v.* persecute, harry, pursue.

H179 **house** 1. *n. home,* dwelling, residence, building 2. *v.* shelter, protect, lodge.

H180 **household** *n.* family, house, home.

H181 **hovel** *n.* hut, *shack,* cabin, mean home (P20).

H182 **hover** *v.* flutter, *fly,* float.

H183 **how** *adv.* in what manner, in what way.

H184 **however** 1. *adv.* in whatever manner 2. *conj.* yet, still, nevertheless, but, though, notwithstanding.

H185 **howl** *v. & n.* cry, *yell,* wail, lament, roar.

H186 **hub** *n.* nave, center, middle, core.

H187 **hubbub** *n.* uproar, *clamor,* din, racket, disorder, turmoil (Q28).

H188 **huddle** *v.* crowd, gather, cluster, bunch, throng (S57).

H189 **hue** *n. color,* tint, tinge, shade, tone, complexion. HEW

H190 **huff** *n.* rage, passion, tiff, angry mood.

H191 **hug** *v.* clasp, embrace, enfold, squeeze.

H192 **huge** *adj.* vast, *enormous,* immense, colossal, gigantic (L111, M161, S259, T125, W45).

H193 **hum** *v. & n.* buzz, drone, murmur.

H194 **human** *adj.* like mankind, of man, of people, sympathetic (I191).

H195 **humane** *adj.* kind, benevolent, thoughtful, tender, sympathetic, good (C497, R334).

H196 **humble** *adj.* meek, modest, lowly, unassuming, *simple,* unpretentious (H63, O128, P370, P452, S569, V5) *n.* **humbleness** (P379).

H197 **humbug** *n.* hypocrisy, cant, quackery, trickery, imposture, swindle.

H198 **humdrum** *adj.* dull, boring, tiresome, *monotonous* (I254, S125).

H199 **humid** *adj.* wet, moist, damp, dank, muggy (D329).

H200 **humiliate** *v. shame,* embarrass, mortify, degrade.

H201 **humor** 1. *n.* temper, mood, state of mind 2. *n.* fun, comedy, amusement, wit 3. *v.* indulge, gratify, pamper; *The natives were hostile, so we had to humor them.*

H202 **humorous** *adj. funny,* amusing, witty, comic, facetious (S135).   HUMERUS

H203 **hump** *n.* bump, ridge, bulge, mound.

H204 **hunch** *n.* 1. bump, hump, bunch, lump 2. suspicion, impression, feeling, notion.

H205 **hungry** *adj.* famishing, starving.

H206 **hunt** *v.* 1. chase, pursue, track 2. *search,* seek, look, probe.

H207 **hurdle** *n.* 1. *fence,* picket, barrier 2. obstacle, hazard, handicap.

H208 **hurl** *v. throw,* cast, fling, pitch, toss.

H209 **hurricane** *n.* tornado, cyclone, typhoon, gale.

H210 **hurry** 1. *v.* hasten, *run,* rush, speed, race (D30, L9, L98, S40) 2. *v.* urge, drive, push forward 3. *n.* haste, dispatch, quickness.

H211 **hurt** 1. *v.* injure, *harm,* damage, mar, impair, wound (B59) 2. *v.* grieve, upset, distress 3. *n.* injury, damage, mischief.

H212 **husband** 1. *n.* spouse, married man 2. *v.* save, economize, store, hoard.

H213 **hush** *v. & n. silence,* quiet, mute, still.

H214 **husk** *n.* rind, bark, hull.

H215 **husky** 1. *adj.* hoarse, grating, rough, harsh 2. *adj.* sturdy, powerful, rugged.

H216 **hustle** *v.* 1. jostle, push, elbow 2. speed, hasten, urge (D7).

H217 **hut** *n.* cabin, *shed,* shanty, shack, cottage.

H218 **hymn** *n.* song, psalm, song of praise.   HIM

H219 **hypnotize** *v.* mesmerize,

Hunting to the hounds.

entrance, fascinate, charm.

H220 **hypocrite** *n.* deceiver, impostor, pretender, cheat, humbug *adj.* **hypocritical**.

H221 **hysterical** *adj.* frenzied, raging, delirious, wild.

I i

I1 **ice** 1. *n.* frozen water, ice cream 2. *v.* freeze, congeal, chill, frost *adj.* **icy** (H176).

I2 **idea** *n. notion,* thought, opinion, belief, fancy, plan.

I3 **ideal** 1. *adj.* complete, *perfect,* supreme 2. *n.* example, model, goal, aim.

I4 **identical** *adj. same,* alike, selfsame, one and the same, indistinguishable (D169).

I5 **identify** *v.* know, *recognize,* distinguish, tell.

I6 **identity** *n.* sameness, existence, personality, character, individuality.

I7 **idiot** *n.* imbecile, *fool,* moron, booby, simpleton (G40).

I8 **idiotic** *adj. foolish,* silly, fatuous, stupid, senseless.

I9 **idle** *adj.* 1. *lazy,* indolent, sluggish (A45) 2. unemployed, unoccupied, inactive.   IDOL

I10 **idol** *n.* 1. deity, god, image, statue 2. favorite, pet, darling.

I11 **ignite** *v. kindle,* set fire to, burn, fire, light (E222).

I12 **ignorant** *adj.* 1. uneducated, unlettered, untrained, illiterate 2. unaware, uninformed (F31, L54, L107) *n.* **ignoramus** (S63).

I

I13 **ignore** v. disregard, neglect, overlook, snub (A25, A50, C346, H96, R83, R220, S109).

I14 **ill** adj. 1. sick, ailing, unwell, indisposed 2. bad, evil, naughty, cross, surly (W52).

I15 **illegal** adj. unlawful, illicit, unlicensed, forbidden (L40, L60).

I16 **illegible** adj. unreadable, indecipherable, unintelligible, obscure (L63).

I17 **illegitimate** adj. unlawful, illicit, improper, spurious (L65).

I18 **illiterate** adj. unlettered, ignorant, unlearned, uneducated (L54, L107).

I19 **illness** n. disease, sickness, ailment, complaint.

I20 **illuminate** v. 1. light, illumine, light up, brighten (D22) 2. explain, clarify, enlighten.

I21 **illusion** n. delusion, deception, fallacy, fantasy, vision (R58).

I22 **illustrate** v. 1. picture, portray, decorate, depict 2. explain, show, demonstrate.

I23 **illustration** n. picture, diagram, photograph, example.

I24 **image** n. 1. likeness, figure, picture, resemblance 2. idol, statue.

I25 **imaginary** adj. fanciful, unreal, illusory, supposed, hypothetical (R57).

I26 **imagination** n. fancy, idea, supposition, vision, conception, originality (R58).

I27 **imagine** v. 1. conceive, fancy, picture, envisage 2. believe, suppose, assume.

I28 **imbecile** n. fool, idiot, moron (G40).

I29 **imitate** v. copy, follow, mimic, mock, ape, parody.

I30 **immaculate** adj. spotless, pure, clean, stainless (U84).

I31 **immature** adj. 1. undeveloped, unformed, unripe, green, raw 2. youthful, simple, inexperienced (A61, M83, M109, R268).

I32 **immediate** adj. 1. instant, prompt, present, instantaneous 2. next, close, near, proximate.

I33 **immediately** adv. at once, directly, instantly, now, forthwith.

I34 **immense** adj. vast, enormous, stupendous, huge, colossal (M161).

I35 **immerse** v. dip, plunge, submerge, douse.

I36 **imminent** adj. close, impending, approaching, forthcoming (R160).

I37 **immobile** adj. fixed, motionless, immovable, stationary (M200) n. **immobility** (M246).

I38 **immoderate** adj. excessive, extravagant, unreasonable (M205, T52).

I39 **immodest** adj. indelicate, shameless, gross, coarse (M105, M207).

I40 **immoral** adj. wrong, wicked, sinful, corrupt, bad (M231, P479, R260).

I41 **immortal** adj. everliving, eternal, undying, endless (M240).

I42 **immune** adj. exempt, protected, invulnerable.

I43 **immunity** n. protection, privilege, liberty, exemption, freedom.

144 **imp** *n.* 1. sprite, hobgoblin, elf, pixie 2. brat, scamp, rascal.

145 **impact** *n.* contact, collision, shock, impulse, impression.

146 **impair** *v.* injure, harm, make worse, damage, weaken (I83).

147 **impartial** *adj.* just, fair, *unbiased,* candid (P60, U38).

148 **impassive** *adj.* unmoved, insensible, indifferent, calm, placid (P75).

149 **impatient** *adj. hasty,* impetuous, restless, testy (P87) *n.* **impatience** (P86).

150 **impede** *v. hinder,* obstruct, stop, thwart, restrain (H102).

151 **impel** *v. drive,* push, urge, incite, compel (D149).

152 **impend** *v.* threaten, hang over, *loom,* menace.

153 **imperative** *adj.* commanding, *compulsory,* authoritative, binding, obligatory.

154 **imperceptible** *adj.* faint, fine, minute, invisible (V72).

155 **imperfect** *adj.* defective, incomplete, faulty, blemished (P135).

156 **imperial** *adj.* regal, royal, queenly, kingly, majestic, grand.

157 **imperious** *adj.* arrogant, haughty, lordly, dictatorial, tyrannical (D273).

158 **impersonate** *v.* imitate, mimic, ape.

159 **impertinent** *adj.* 1. *insolent,* rude, impudent, saucy (P280) 2. irrelevant, inapplicable.

160 **impetuous** *adj.* hasty, passionate, *rash,* impulsive (H56).

161 **implement** 1. *n.* instrument, tool, utensil 2. *v.* fulfill, execute, complete.

Implements.

162 **implicate** *v. involve,* entangle, include.

163 **implicit** *adj.* 1. implied, understood, tacit (E205) 2. firm, steadfast, certain.

164 **implore** *v.* beseech, *beg,* entreat, crave.

165 **imply** *v. signify,* suggest, hint, mean, indicate.

166 **impolite** *adj. rude,* discourteous, uncivil, boorish (C444, G111, P280, R206).

167 **import** 1. *v.* bring in, take in, admit (E210) 2. *n.* goods, merchandise 3. *n.* sense, drift, spirit, intention; *At last the children grasped the import of his remarks.*

168 **important** *adj.* significant, *serious,* weighty, momentous, pompous, influential (F302, I108, I213, P26, P180, T205, T211).

169 **impose** *v.* put, set, place, prescribe, appoint.

170 **imposing** *adj. grand,* majestic, impressive.

I71 **impossible** *adj.* unattainable, inconceivable, unthinkable, unworkable (F66, P304).

I72 **impostor** *n.* deceiver, pretender, charlatan, quack, impersonator.

I73 **impoverish** *v.* pauperize, *ruin,* make poor, bankrupt (E92).

I74 **impractical** *adj.* unfeasible, unworkable, unrealistic (P304, P323).

I75 **impregnable** *adj.* unassailable, unconquerable, invulnerable (V95).

I76 **impress** *v.* 1. print, stamp, imprint, emboss 2. affect, fix, influence.

I77 **impression** *n.* 1. influence, *effect,* sensation 2. mark, stamp, brand, dent.

I78 **impressive** *adj.* striking, affecting, overpowering.

I79 **imprison** *v.* confine, *jail,* incarcerate, commit (L82, R136) *n.* **imprisonment** (R136).

I80 **improbable** *adj.* unlikely, *doubtful,* uncertain (L92, P393).

I81 **impromptu** *adj.* spontaneous, unrehearsed, improvised.

I82 **improper** *adj.* 1. unsuitable, unfit, inappropriate 2. unseemly, *indecent* (P433) *adv.* **improperly** (P434).

I83 **improve** *v.* better, amend, correct, *rectify* (D72, I46, R131).

I84 **improvident** *adj.* thriftless, imprudent, thoughtless, prodigal, wasteful, spendthrift.

I85 **improvise** *v.* invent, extemporize, *devise,* make up.

I86 **imprudent** *adj. indiscreet,* injudicious, ill-advised, rash, careless (C71, W27) *n.* **imprudence** (F200).

I87 **impudent** *adj. insolent,* impertinent, pert, rude, brazen, forward (R223).

I88 **impulse** *n.* 1. *thrust,* push, urge, force, impetus 2. caprice, whim, fancy, notion.

The impulse of a swimming stroke.

I89 **impulsive** *adj. rash,* hasty, quick, impetuous, emotional.

I90 **impure** *adj.* unclean, dirty, foul, contaminated, polluted (C115, P135, S379).

I91 **inability** *n.* incapacity, impotence, incompetence, ineptitude (A5, P321).

I92 **inaccessible** *adj.* unattainable, unapproachable, unreachable, remote.

I93 **inaccurate** *adj.* incorrect, inexact, erroneous, *wrong* (A36, F22) *n.* **inaccuracy** (F105, P340).

I94 **inactive** *adj.* inert, dormant, immobile, indolent, idle (A45, B186, S391) *n.* **inactivity** (L88).

I95 **inadequate** *adj.* insufficient, unequal, incomplete, defective (A21, A51).

I96 **inadvertent** *adj.* neglectful, negligent, careless, inconsiderate, accidental (C41).

I97 **inane** *adj.* vain, frivolous, puerile, empty, void (S127).

I98 **inanimate** *adj.* lifeless, *dead,* inert, defunct, extinct (A90).

I99 **inappropriate** *adj.* unfit, unsuitable, improper (A134, P167, S556).

I100 **inattentive** *adj.* heedless, unobservant, thoughtless, negligent (O16, S516) *n.* **inattention** (O17).

I101 **inaudible** *adj.* noiseless, indistinct, faint, muffled.

I102 **inaugurate** *v.* install, *begin,* start, originate, launch.

I103 **incapable** *adj.* incompetent, weak, *unable,* unqualified (A6).

I104 **incense** 1. *v. enrage,* inflame, exasperate, anger 2. *n.* perfume, fragrance, aroma.

I105 **incentive** *n.* stimulus, encouragement, *spur,* motive.

I106 **incessant** *adj.* ceaseless, continual, perpetual, constant (S345).

I107 **incident** *n.* event, occurrence, happening, experience.

I108 **incidental** *adj.* minor, casual, accidental (F288).

I109 **incisive** *adj.* sharp, acute, sarcastic, satirical, biting.

I110 **incite** *v.* spur, arouse, provoke, urge.

I111 **inclement** *adj.* severe, rigorous, stormy, rough, harsh (M145).

I112 **inclination** *n.* 1. disposition, bias, *tendency,* leaning (R148) 2. slope, slant, incline.

I113 **incline** 1. *n. slope,* hill,

gradient 2. *v.* slope, slant, lean, tilt 3. *v. tend,* be disposed.

I114 **include** *v.* contain, hold, *comprise,* embrace, involve (D82, E3, E175, O55, O136).

I115 **incognito** *adj. & adv.* disguised, unknown, concealed.

I116 **incoherent** *adj.* unintelligible, confused, rambling, inarticulate (I244).

I117 **income** *n.* profits, revenue, gains, *salary,* wages (O112).

I118 **incomparable** *adj.* matchless, unrivaled, unequaled, unique (O88).

I119 **incompatible** *adj. unsuitable,* inconsistent, unadapted, contrary (C350).

I120 **incompetent** *adj. unfit,* unable, incapable, disqualified (A6, C24, C266).

I121 **incomplete** *adj.* partial, deficient, *imperfect,* faulty, unfinished, lacking (C273, P135).

I122 **incomprehensible** *adj.* unthinkable, inconceivable, perplexing, puzzling, obscure (I244).

I123 **inconceivable** *adj.* unimaginable, unthinkable, incredible (C470).

I124 **inconsiderate** *adj.* thoughtless, careless, heedless, selfish (C348).

I125 **inconsistent** *adj.* contrary, contradictory, unsteady, variable (C350).

I126 **inconvenient** *adj.* 1. inappropriate, *awkward,* cumbersome 2. troublesome, annoying, untimely (C388, H27) *n.* **inconvenience** (A29).

I

I127 **incorrect** *adj.* untrue, inaccurate, erroneous, *false,* wrong (C418, P339).

I128 **increase** 1. *v.* grow, enlarge, *expand,* extend, prolong 2. *n.* expansion, growth, enlargement (A13, D54, D182, F13, F24, L72, L154, R98, S538).

I129 **incredible** *adj.* unbelievable, doubtful, preposterous (C470, P242).

I130 **incriminate** *v. implicate,* involve, prejudice, accuse, charge (C182).

I131 **incur** *v.* acquire, bring, contract, become liable.

I132 **incurable** *adj.* hopeless, not curable, cureless, beyond recovery.

I133 **indebted** *adj.* obliged, beholden, owing, involved.

I134 **indecent** *adj.* improper, immoral, *immodest,* impure, outrageous (D45, U92).

I135 **indeed** *adv.* truly, really, positively, certainly, surely, in fact.

I136 **indefinite** *adj.* vague, *obscure,* indeterminate, confused (D71, E205).

I137 **indelicate** *adj.* unseemly, unbecoming, coarse, rude, immodest (M207).

I138 **independent** *adj. free,* self-reliant, unrestricted, bold (D107).

I139 **index** *n.* list, catalog, file.

I140 **indicate** *v.* show, *denote,* point out, designate.

I141 **indifferent** *adj.* 1. neutral, impartial, unbiased 2. unconcerned, unmoved, heedless (E1, S625, W21) 3. middling, ordinary, mediocre, *n.* **indifference** (C39, E101, I253, P73).

I142 **indignant** *adj.* angry, incensed, *irate,* wrathful (S133).

I143 **indirect** *adj.* roundabout, devious, tortuous, out-of-the-way (D189).

I144 **indiscreet** *adj.* unwise, foolish, *rash,* reckless, imprudent (D221).

I145 **indispensable** *adj.* necessary, *essential,* needed, required (U63).

I146 **indisposed** *adj.* 1. unwilling, *reluctant,* averse (W73) 2. sick, *ill,* unwell (H79).

I147 **indistinct** *adj.* indefinite, obscure, vague, *faint,* dim (D252).

I148 **individual** 1. *adj.* particular, special, separate 2. *n.* person, being, character, somebody (G35).

I149 **indolence** *n.* laziness, sloth, idleness (D178) *adj.* **indolent** (E71).

I150 **induce** *v. influence,* impel, move, urge, incite (F192).

I151 **indulge** *v.* gratify, satisfy, humor (A19).

I152 **industrious** *adj.* diligent, hardworking, *busy,* brisk (L45) *n.* **industry** (I149).

I153 **ineffectual** *adj.* fruitless, useless, powerless, weak (E22, S498).

I154 **inefficient** *adj. incompetent,* incapable, wasteful (E22).

I155 **inept** *adj.* useless, worthless, foolish, *silly,* stupid (C24, C266, S234).

I156 **inert** *adj. inactive,* lifeless, passive, motionless, dull, sluggish, idle (A45).

I157 **inevitable** *adj.* unavoidable, necessary, inescapable, destined (U13).

I158 **inexcusable** *adj.* unpardonable, unforgivable, indefensible.

I159 **inexpensive** *adj. cheap,* reasonable, lowpriced (C426, E197).

I160 **inexperienced** *adj.* untrained, unskilled, fresh, raw, *immature* (P412) *n.* **inexperience** (E198).

I161 **inexplicable** *adj.* unexplainable, *mysterious,* strange, incomprehensible (E155).

I162 **infallible** *adj.* unerring, certain, *sure,* unfailing.

I163 **infamous** *adj.* base, detestable, disgraceful, disreputable, shameful, wicked (H154).

I164 **infantile** *adj.* childish, babylike, immature, weak (A61).

I165 **infatuated** *adj.* besotted, deluded, misled, fascinated.

I166 **infect** *v. contaminate,* pollute, corrupt, affect (P482).

I167 **infectious** *adj.* catching, *contagious,* contaminating (H46).

I168 **infer** *v.* conclude, gather, *presume,* deduce, suppose (K24).

I169 **inferior** *adj.* lower, poor, indifferent, secondary, mean (F123, G116, P44, P383, S119, S568, S573) *n.* **inferiority** (P334).

I170 **infernal** *adj.* hellish, fiendish, damnable.

I171 **infest** *v.* overrun, throng, plague, molest, worry.

I172 **infinite** *adj.* boundless, unlimited, immense, enormous, absolute.

I173 **infirm** *adj.* weak, feeble, *frail,* sickly, ill (H79).

I174 **inflame** *v.* excite, *arouse,* animate, incite, provoke (P3).

I175 **inflate** *v.* blow up, *swell,* distend, expand.

I176 **inflexible** *adj.* stiff, *rigid,* firm, dogged, stubborn, unbending (E27, P255, S578).

I177 **inflict** *v. impose,* apply, give, deal.

I178 **influence** 1. *n.* power, sway, control, authority 2. *v.* control, direct, modify, *persuade.*

I179 **inform** *v.* advise, tell, *notify,* acquaint, relate, enlighten (C291).

I180 **informal** *adj.* unconventional, unceremonious, free, easy (F209, O44, P339, P381).

I181 **information** *n.* intelligence, knowledge, news, instruction, facts.

I182 **infrequent** *adj.* uncommon, rare, unusual, *seldom,* occasional (F251, P373).

I183 **infringe** *v.* break, disobey, encroach, violate (O18).

I184 **infuriate** *v. enrage,* anger, madden, annoy (C15).

I185 **ingenious** *adj.* inventive, skillful, *clever,* dexterous (U80).

I186 **ingenuous** *adj.* artless, *naïve,* innocent, candid, unsophisticated (S323).

I187 **ingredient** *n.* component, part, element, particle.

I

I188 **inhabit** v. occupy, abide, *reside,* live in adj. **inhabited** (U64).

I189 **inhale** v. breathe in, sniff, draw in, inspire (E49, E184).

I190 **inheritance** n. heritage, legacy, bequest, patrimony.

I191 **inhuman** adj. barbarous, brutal, *savage,* cruel, merciless (M127).

I192 **iniquity** n. injustice, sin, crime, offense, wickedness (J45).

I193 **initial** adj. *first,* beginning, commencing, primary (F121, L29).

I194 **initiate** v. 1. begin, commence, *inaugurate,* open 2. instruct, teach, educate (E62).

I195 **inject** v. inoculate, vaccinate, *insert,* fill (E224).

I196 **injure** v. harm, *hurt,* damage, impair, maltreat (H78) adj. **injurious** (H46).

I197 **inkling** n. *hint,* whisper, intimation, suggestion.

I198 **inmate** n. *occupant,* dweller, denizen, tenant.

I199 **inn** n. hotel, tavern, motel, pub, hostelry.   IN

I200 **innocent** adj. 1. guiltless, sinless, faultless, blameless 2. *harmless,* inoffensive, naïve (G168, M83).

I201 **innumerable** adj. countless, *infinite,* many, unlimited (F99).

I202 **inoffensive** adj. harmless, innocuous, *innocent* (O41).

I203 **inquire** v. ask, question, investigate, interrogate (A116).

I204 **inquisitive** adj. *curious,* inquiring, prying, questioning, snooping.

I205 **insane** adj. demented, deranged, crazy, *mad,* lunatic (R40, S24).

I206 **inscribe** v. *write,* engrave, imprint, address (E120).

I207 **insecure** adj. *uncertain,* unsure, unsafe, dangerous (S6).

I208 **insensible** adj. 1. dull, stupid, unfeeling, apathetic 2. unconscious, numb (C340).

I209 **inseparable** adj. joined, indivisible, intimate (S130).

I210 **insert** v. introduce, put in, place, inject (E224).

I211 **inside** 1. n. inner part, *interior* 2. adj. interior, inner, internal, intimate (O121).

I212 **insight** n. discernment, penetration, *judgment,* perception, vision.

I213 **insignificant** adj. paltry, petty, *trivial,* trifling, unimportant (I68, M225, P422) n. **insignificance** (E51, M214).

I214 **insincere** adj. false, faithless, dishonest, hypocritical, two-faced (E4, F215, F239, H87, S219).

I215 **insinuate** v. 1. *hint,* suggest, intimate (W86) 2. inject, instill, introduce.

I216 **insipid** adj. flavorless, tasteless, stale, flat, lifeless, dull (T34).

I217 **insist** v. *urge,* demand, press, contend, stress (W8).

I218 **insolent** adj. impertinent, *impudent,* saucy, pert, rude, disrespectful, insulting (P280).

I219 **insoluble** adj. 1. indissolvable, not to be melted 2. insolvable, inexplicable, unexplainable.

I220 **inspect** *v. examine,* scrutinize, investigate, study.

I221 **inspector** *n.* examiner, superintendent, overseer.

I222 **inspiration** *n.* 1. insight, enthusiasm, *idea,* stimulus, spur 2. breathing in.

I223 **inspire** *v.* encourage, enliven, cheer, *stimulate* (D219) 2. breathe in, inhale.

I224 **install** *v.* introduce, *inaugurate,* set up, establish.

I225 **instance** *n. example,* case, illustration, occasion, circumstance.   INSTANTS

I226 **instant** 1. *n. moment,* second, twinkling, flash, jiffy 2. *adj.* immediate, quick, urgent, prompt.

I227 **instantly** *adv.* forthwith, *immediately,* now, at once.

I228 **instead** *adv.* in lieu, in place of, rather than.

I229 **instill** *v.* implant, introduce, *insinuate,* impress (E119).

I230 **instinct** *n. impulse,* intuition, tendency, natural feeling (R64).

I231 **institute** 1. *n.* school, academy, college, association, institution 2. *v.* establish, found, originate, start.

I232 **instruct** *v.* 1. *teach,* inform, train, educate, enlighten (L53) 2. *command,* direct, order; *He was instructed to remove his car.*

I233 **instrument** *n. device,* tool, implement, utensil.

I234 **insufferable** *adj.* intolerable, *outrageous,* detestable, unbearable.

I235 **insufficient** *adj.* inadequate, *deficient,* lacking, meager (A21, A106, E89, S552).

I236 **insulate** *v.* isolate, disconnect, line, envelop, cover.

I237 **insult** 1. *v.* offend, affront, abuse, humiliate (F142) 2. *n.* offense, outrage, *slander,* insolence (C276).

I238 **insure** *v.* guarantee, warrant, underwrite, indemnify.

I239 **intact** *adj.* unbroken, whole, *entire,* complete, unharmed, untouched.

I240 **integrity** *n.* honesty, *virtue,* goodness, uprightness.

I241 **intellect** *n.* brains, reason, understanding, intelligence, sense, judgment.

I242 **intellectual** *adj.* intelligent, thoughtful, rational, learned, scholarly.

I243 **intelligent** *adj.* astute, quick, alert, *clever,* shrewd, bright (H12, I8, S475, S525, V1) *n.* **intelligence**.

I244 **intelligible** *adj. clear,* comprehensible, plain, distinct (I116).

I245 **intend** *v. mean,* contemplate, propose, plan, expect *adj.* **intended** (H30).

The piano is a musical instrument.

I

1246 **intense** *adj.* 1. severe, *extreme,* exceptional 2. ardent (M205) *v.* **intensify** (M205).

INTENTS

1247 **intent** 1. *n.* aim, design, intention, *object* 2. *adj.* resolute, bent, eager, earnest.

1248 **intention** *n.* design, purpose, aim, object.

1249 **intentional** *adj.* deliberate, intended, designed, arranged, willful, planned (A27).

1250 **inter** *v.* bury, entomb.

1251 **intercept** *v.* *interrupt,* arrest, obstruct, seize, deflect.

1252 **intercourse** *n.* commerce, communication, connection, correspondence.

1253 **interest** 1. *v.* engage, attract, concern (B120) 2. *n.* regard, sympathy, attention 3. *n.* advantage, profit, portion, share; *Jones has a financial interest in that company.*

1254 **interesting** *adj.* engaging, pleasing, entertaining, fascinating, gripping (D329, F141, H198, M221, T47, T129).

1255 **interfere** *v.* *meddle,* interpose, intervene, intrude.

1256 **interior** *n. & adj.* middle, inside, inland (E218, E220).

1257 **intermediate** *adj.* between, middle, intervening, interposed, halfway.

1258 **interminable** *adj.* endless, unending, unlimited, boundless, infinite (B151).

1259 **intermittent** *adj.* spasmodic, periodic, recurrent, irregular (C374, I106, P152, R122).

1260 **internal** *adj.* *interior,* inner, inside, inward (E220).

1261 **international** *adj.* worldwide, universal, cosmopolitan, global.

1262 **interpret** *v.* *explain,* define, translate, construe, decipher, decode, clarify.

1263 **interrogate** *v.* *question,* examine, ask, inquire of, catechize, cross-examine.

1264 **interrupt** *v.* stop, disconnect, *disturb,* cut, sever, hinder, interfere, intrude (C375).

1265 **interval** *n.* interruption, interlude, break, gap, pause, period.

1266 **intervene** *v.* interfere, come between, interrupt, mediate.

1267 **interview** *n.* meeting, conference, talk, consultation.

1268 **intimate (int-***u-met***)** 1. *adj.* close, confidential, *familiar,* friendly, personal 2. **(int-***u-mate***)** *v.* suggest, hint, insinuate, allude; *Sam intimated that he would soon retire.*

1269 **intimidate** *v.* frighten, alarm, scare, daunt, dismay, threaten, bully, browbeat, menace (E60).

1270 **intolerable** *adj.* unbearable, *insufferable,* unendurable (B39).

1271 **intolerant** *adj.* overbearing, dictatorial, bigoted, *arrogant* (S625).

1272 **intoxicated** *adj.* drunk, inebriated, tipsy, drunken (S304).

1273 **intrepid** *adj.* bold, fearless, dauntless, *valiant,* heroic (C451).

I274 **intricate** *adj.* complicated, involved, *complex,* perplexing (S215).

I275 **intrigue** 1. *n.* plot, conspiracy, *ruse,* scheme 2. *v.* charm, fascinate, beguile, enthral.

I276 **intriguing** *adj.* 1. cunning, crafty, sly, wily 2. tantalizing, fascinating, absorbing.

I277 **introduce** *v.* 1. present, acquaint (W86) 2. inaugurate, commence, start.

I278 **introduction** *n.* presentation, preface, foreword, preamble.

I279 **intrude** *v.* infringe, *trespass,* encroach, interfere.

I280 **inundate** *v. flood,* deluge, submerge, overflow, drown.

I281 **invade** *v.* attack, overrun, assault, *encroach,* raid.

INVEIGHED

I282 **invalid (in-***vul-ud*) 1. *n.* sick person, patient, sufferer 2. *(in-***val**-*ud) adj.* without value, void, null (V7).

I283 **invaluable** *adj.* priceless, precious, costly, very valuable (W105).

I284 **invasion** *n.* assault, attack, raid, aggression.

I285 **invent** *v.* originate, *create,* conceive, concoct, devise.

I286 **invention** *n.* contrivance, fabrication, design, gadget.

I287 **invert** *v.* turn upside down, *reverse,* overturn, upset.

I288 **invest** *v.* endow, venture, lay out, buy shares.

I289 **investigate** *v.* examine, scrutinize, inspect, study, *probe n.* **investigation**.

I290 **invisible** *adj.* unseen, undiscernible, imperceptible, hidden (V72).

I291 **invite** *v.* request, ask, prevail upon, entice, summon (R172).

I292 **inviting** *adj.* alluring, attractive, pleasing, engaging (R172).

I293 **invoice** *n.* bill, check, account, statement, reckoning.

I294 **involuntary** *adj.* 1. unintentional, automatic, *spontaneous,* instinctive (I249) 2. unwilling, reluctant, forced (V87).

I295 **involve** *v.* 1. *implicate,* concern, affect 2. confuse, complicate, entangle, confound.

I296 **inward** *adj.* interior, internal, inner, inside (O124).

I297 **irate** *adj.* angry, annoyed, enraged, exasperated.

I298 **irksome** *adj. tedious,* annoying, boring, tiresome (A82).

The internal combustion engine—a great invention of our times.

85

I299 **irony** *n.* mockery, *satire,* sarcasm, banter.

I300 **irregular** *adj.* 1. abnormal, unnatural, unusual, exceptional 2. *uneven,* unequal, unsymmetrical (C355, I106, R122, U49).

I301 **irrelevant** *adj.* inappropriate, unfitting, inapplicable, unimportant (A134, R139).

I302 **irresistible** *adj.* overpowering, compelling, overwhelming.

I303 **irresolute** *adj.* weak, undetermined, wavering, hesitant, unsure (I249, R200).

I304 **irreverent** *adj.* impious, *profane,* disrespectful, impudent, impolite, sacrilegious (R145).

I305 **irritable** *adj.* peevish, *testy,* snappish, peppery, touchy (A82).

I306 **irritate** *v.* 1. chafe, stimulate, pain, make sore 2. provoke, exasperate, enrage, *vex* (A126) *adj.* **irritating** (P250).

I307 **isolate** *v. separate,* detach, insulate, set apart, seclude, quarantine (U53).

I308 **issue** 1. *v.* deliver, send out, publish, distribute 2. *v.* flow, come out, appear, emerge 3. *n.* edition, copy, number, publication 4. *n.* question, problem, matter; *Protecting wild animals is an important issue everywhere.*

I309 **itch** *n.* 1. tingle, irritation, sensation 2. craving, desire, hankering.

I310 **item** *n.* detail, entry, part.

J   j

J1 **jab** *v.* poke, prod, thrust, push.

J2 **jabber** *v.* chatter, prattle, gabble.

J3 **jacket** *n.* coat, jerkin, covering.

J4 **jade** 1. *v.* tire, weary, fatigue 2. *n.* precious stone.

J5 **jagged** *adj.* ragged, notched, indented, uneven (E145).

J6 **jail** *n.* prison, lockup *v.* **jail** (L82).

J7 **jam** 1. *v.* press, crowd, squeeze, ram 2. *n.* conserve, preserve.   JAMB

J8 **jar** 1. *n.* pot, urn, crock, vase, bottle 2. *v.* vibrate, jolt, shake, agitate 3. *v.* bicker, argue, clash, quarrel.

J9 **jaunt** *n.* ramble, excursion, trip, tour.

J10 **jealous** (**jel-***us*) *adj.* envious, covetous, resentful *n.* **jealousy**.

J11 **jeer** *v.* sneer, mock, *scoff,* gibe, taunt.

J12 **jerk** *v. & n.* jolt, pull, twitch, flip, shake.

J13 **jest** *n.* joke, quip, jape.

J14 **jetty** *n.* pier, landing, stage.

J15 **jewel** *n.* gem, brilliant ornament, precious stone.

J16 **jiffy** *n.* instant, moment, twinkling, flash.

J17 **jingle** 1. *v.* tinkle, ring, jangle, clink 2. *n.* advertising commercial tune.

J18 **job** *n.* work, employment, profession, calling, *task*.

J19 **jockey** 1. *n.* rider 2. *v.* maneuver, twist, turn.

J20 **jog** *v.* 1. *run,* trot, sprint 2. push, shake, jerk.

J21 **join** *v. connect,* couple, link, unite, assemble (S130, S142, S373) *adj.* **joined** (S130).

J22 **joint** 1. *n.* union, juncture, *connection* (S130) 2. *adj.* combined, concerted, united.

J23 **joke** *n. prank,* jest, quip, quirk, game, anecdote.

J24 **joker** *n.* 1. jester, clown, humorist 2. playing card.

J25 **jolly** *adj. merry,* joyous, cheerful, pleasant, jovial, funny, glad (M108).

J26 **jolt** *n. & v.* shake, *jar,* bump, shock.

J27 **jostle** *v.* crowd, jolt, hustle, press, push.

J28 **jot** 1. *n.* grain, particle, atom, scrap, tittle 2. *v.* record, scribble, note.

J29 **journal** *n.* 1. newspaper, periodical 2. diary, register, log, account book.

J30 **journey** *n.* tour, excursion, *trip,* voyage, expedition, jaunt, outing.

J31 **jovial** *adj. merry,* joyous, joyful, mirthful, jolly (G87, M108).

J32 **joy** *n. delight,* glee, ecstasy, pleasure, happiness (G134, M174, P13, W102) *adj.* **joyful** (D138, M108, M173, M257) *adj.* **joyous** (S4).

J33 **jubilant** *adj.* rejoicing, exulting, triumphant, overjoyed (D138, M108).

J34 **judge** 1. *n.* justice, magistrate 2. *n.* referee, umpire, adjudicator 3. *n.* critic, expert, connoisseur 4. *v.* try, condemn, pass sentence 5. *v.* consider, regard, appreciate.

J35 **judgment** *n.* 1. decision, conclusion, opinion, estimate 2. discernment, understanding, intelligence.

J36 **jug** *n.* pitcher, ewer, flagon, flask, jar.

J37 **juggle** *v.* conjure, shuffle, perform tricks.

J38 **juice** *n.* fluid, liquid, sap, moisture.

J39 **jumble** *n.* mixture, disorder, muddle.

J40 **jump** *v. leap,* spring, bound, skip, hop, vault.

J41 **junction** *n.* 1. connection, joint 2. crossover, crossroads, rail center.

Jewels.

A key in a lock.

J42 **jungle** *n*. thicket, forest, bush.

J43 **junk** *n*. 1. rubbish, debris, salvage, scrap 2. Chinese ship.

J44 **just** 1. *adj*. right, fair, lawful, reasonable, impartial (U38, U56) 2. *adv*. exactly, precisely.

J45 **justice** *n*. fairness, impartiality, equity (I192).

J46 **justify** *v*. vindicate, defend, absolve, exonerate, acquit.

J47 **jut** *v*. project, stick out, protrude.

J48 **juvenile** *adj*. young, youthful, childish, puerile.

K   k

K1 **keen** *adj*. 1. eager, zealous, ardent, earnest, enthusiastic 2. sharp, acute (D333).

K2 **keep** 1. *v*. retain, detain, hold, maintain (D206) 2. *v*. continue; *The river keeps flowing on.* 3. *v*. preserve, save (A9); *I'm going to keep this magazine.* 4. *v*. observe, obey; *God asked us to keep his commandments.* 5. *v*. support, sustain (Y7); *Mary lives at home and keeps her old mother.* 6. *n*. stronghold, dungeon.

K3 **key** *n*. 1. lock opener 2. clue, guide, solution 3. pitch, tone, note.   QUAY

K4 **kick** *v*. strike (with foot), boot.

K5 **kidnap** *v*. abduct, carry off, steal off with.

K6 **kill** *v*. *murder,* slay, execute, destroy, annihilate, slaughter.

K7 **kin** *n*. family, relations, relatives, kinsmen.

K8 **kind** 1. *adj*. gentle, friendly, benign, amiable, *generous,* warm (H86, M92, P226, R194, T92) 2. *n*. sort, manner, description, type *adj*. **kindly** (P226) *n*. **kindness** (M27).

K9 **kindle** *v*. 1. light, *ignite,* fire (E222) 2. arouse, excite, provoke, incite.

K10 **king** *n*. ruler, sovereign, monarch, emperor.

K11 **kingdom** *n*. monarchy, dominion, empire, realm.

K12 **kink** *n*. twist, knot, bend, curl, loop.

K13 **kiss** *v*. salute, caress with lips, embrace, buss.

K14 **kit** *n*. outfit, tools, collection, equipment, apparatus.

K15 **knack** *n*. adroitness, skill, talent, dexterity.

K16 **knave** *n*. 1. villain, rascal, scoundrel, rogue 2. (playing cards) jack.   NAVE

K17 **knead** *v*. work, pound, pulverize, mold.   NEED

L l

Knights jousting.

K18 **knight** *n.* cavalier, champion, partisan.   NIGHT

K19 **knife** *n.* blade, edge, cutter.

K20 **knob** *n.* stud, boss, handle, protuberance, bunch, bump.

K21 **knock** *v. & n.* rap, hit, strike, bang, thump, tap.

K22 **knoll** *n.* hillock, mound, hill.

K23 **knot** *v.* splice, tie, join, connect.   NOT

K24 **know** *v. understand,* comprehend, perceive, recognize, discriminate (I168). NO

K25 **knowledge** *n.* learning, understanding, wisdom, judgment, education, information.

Lamps.

L1 **label** *n.* tag, ticket, docket, stamp, name, sticker, mark.

L2 **labor** 1. *n.* toil, *work,* exertion, effort 2. *v.* work, strive, toil (R210).

L3 **laborious** *adj.* difficult, *arduous,* tiresome, irksome (E7).

L4 **lack** 1. *v.* want, *need,* require 2. *n.* need, shortage, scarcity, dearth (P254).

L5 **lad** *n. boy,* youngster, youth, stripling (L28).

L6 **laden** *adj.* loaded, weighed down, charged, hampered.

L7 **ladle** *n.* dipper, bail, scoop, spoon.

L8 **lady** *n. woman,* mistress, gentlewoman, matron, dame, dowager.

L9 **lag** *v.* loiter, *linger,* dawdle, tarry, fall behind (H210).

L10 **lair** *n.* den, burrow, hole.

L11 **lame** *adj.* crippled, hobbling, limping, disabled.

L12 **lament** *v.* mourn, *grieve,* weep, sorrow, moan (R130).

L13 **lance** 1. *n.* spear, javelin 2. *v.* cut, pierce 3. *v.* fling, toss, hurl, throw.

L14 **lamp** *n. light,* lantern, torch.

L15 **land** 1. *n.* ground, soil, earth, country, district 2. *v.* disembark, go ashore, touch down, arrive.

L16 **landlord** *n.* owner, proprietor, host, innkeeper.

L17 **landscape** *n.* view, scene, prospect.

L

L18 lane *n.* alley, passage, court, mews. LAIN

L19 language *n.* speech, tongue, dialect, jargon, talk.

L20 languid *adj.* weak, drooping, languishing, *inactive,* slow, feeble (E71).

L21 lank *adj.* thin, lean, *slender,* skinny, gaunt (S474).

L22 lap 1. *v.* fold, turn, wrap, cover 2. *v.* lick, lick up, drink 3. *n.* knees and thighs 4. *n.* round, orbit, circuit.

L23 lapse *v.* decline, fail, end, sink, weaken (P155). LAPS

L24 lard *n.* grease, fat.

L25 larder *n.* pantry, buttery, cellar, storage.

L26 large *adj.* big, great, huge, vast, bulky, broad, massive (L111, M155, M161, S276, T125, W45).

L27 lash 1. *n.* thong, whip, cane, scourge 2. *v. flog,* whip, strike, scourge.

L28 lass *n.* girl, maiden, damsel, miss (L5).

L29 last 1. *adj.* latest, hindmost, *final,* ultimate (F129, I193) 2. *v.* endure, remain, continue (F13) *adj.* **lasting** (F150).

L30 late *adj.* slow, *tardy,* behind, delayed (E2, P353, P425, S321) *adj.* **later** (I33, I227, P375, P388).

L31 lately *adv.* recently, latterly, not long ago (S321).

L32 lather *n.* foam, froth, bubbles, suds.

L33 latitude *n.* 1. *extent,* range, scope 2. freedom, liberty, laxity.

L34 latter *adj. last,* latest, recent (F210).

L35 laugh *n.* & *v.* chuckle, giggle, titter, guffaw (C503) *adj.* **laughable** (P85).

L36 launch *(lawnch)* 1. *v. start,* begin, inaugurate, dispatch 2. *n.* tug, tender, boat.

L37 lavatory *n.* latrine, toilet, gents, ladies, privy, washroom.

L38 lavish 1. *adj. generous,* liberal, plentiful, extravagant 2. *v.* waste, squander, bestow (E13, S468).

L39 law *n.* rule, statute, regulation, decree, *order.*

L40 lawful *adj. legal,* legitimate, proper (I15).

L41 lawyer *n.* counsel, advocate, solicitor, barrister, attorney.

L42 lax *adj.* loose, *slack,* relaxed, negligent, lenient (E52). LACKS

L43 lay 1. *v.* put, place, deposit 2. *v.* charge, impute, attribute; *Responsibility for the deal lay with Johnson.* 3. *v.* bet, hazard, wager 4. *adj.* amateur, nonprofessional; *Charles is a lay preacher at the church.* 5. *n.* song, ballad, poem.

L44 layer *n.* seam, bed, row, stratum, coating.

L45 lazy *adj. idle,* slack, indolent, slothful, inactive (A45, B186, D178, E71, I152) *v.* **laze** (L2).

L46 lead *v.* guide, conduct, direct, command (F183).

L47 leader *n. guide,* director, chief, commander, ruler (D209).

L48 leaf *n.* blade, foliage, thin sheet. LIEF

L49 league *(leeg) n.* 1. alliance, union, combination 2. *society*

3. about three miles.

L50 **leak** *v.* drip, dribble, percolate, ooze. LEEK

L51 **lean** 1. *v. incline,* slant, tilt, slope, recline 2. *adj.* thin, gaunt, slim, skinny (F51). LIEN

L52 **leap** *v. & n. jump,* spring, bound, vault, hop, caper.

Leaping on a bull's back—an ancient Cretan sport.

L53 **learn** *v.* acquire, ascertain, master, memorize, discover (I232, T41).

L54 **learned** *adj.* scholarly, erudite, knowledgeable, literate, educated (I18).

L55 **least** *adj.* 1. smallest, tiniest, minutest 2. feeblest, slightest (F129, M243, S584). LEASED

L56 **leave** 1. *v.* abandon, vacate, *depart,* quit, desert (C237, E98, R150, S446) 2. *v.* bequeath, promise, will 3. *n.* liberty, vacation, holiday 4. *n.* permission, consent; *Today I had leave to go home early.*

L57 **lecture** 1. *n.* lesson, *talk,* address 2. *v.* speak, talk, address, teach.

L58 **ledge** *n.* shelf, ridge, edge.

L59 **legacy** *n.* bequest, gift.

L60 **legal** *adj. lawful,* legitimate, proper, allowable, honest (I15).

L61 **legend** *n.* fable, myth, fiction, tale, story (H133).

L62 **legendary** *adj.* mythical, *fabulous,* fictitious, romantic, celebrated.

L63 **legible** *adj.* readable, plain, *clear,* apparent, decipherable (I16).

L64 **legion** *n.* army, host, military force, association.

L65 **legitimate** *adj.* legal, lawful, *genuine,* allowable, rightful (I15, I17).

L66 **leisure** *n.* freedom, spare time, rest, ease.

L67 **lend** *v. loan,* give, advance (B121).

L68 **length** *n.* extent, measure, span, reach, distance.

L69 **lengthen** *v.* elongate, *extend,* stretch, prolong (A3, S185) *adj.* lengthy (B151, S184).

L70 **lenient** *adj.* mild, tolerant, lax, gentle, merciful (R262, S144, S458, S462, S501).

L71 **less** *adj.* smaller, inferior, minor, lesser (M235).

L72 **lessen** *v. diminish,* decrease, reduce, shrink (M268). LESSON

L73 **lesson** *n.* exercise, lecture, teaching, instruction, example. LESSEN

L74 **let** *v.* 1. allow, *permit,* consent, grant (D104) 2. lease, hire, rent.

L75 **letter** *n.* 1. epistle, note, message, communication 2. alphabetical character.

L76 level 1. *adj. even,* flat, smooth, horizontal, alongside (U36) 2. *v.* flatten, smooth 3. *v.* point, aim 4. *v.* demolish, destroy, raze 5. *n.* degree, grade, step.

L77 lever *n.* crowbar, handle.

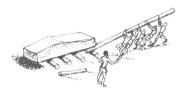

Levering a huge stone.

L78 liable *adj.* answerable, accountable, responsible *n.* **liability** (I43).

L79 liar *n.* fibber, prevaricator, perjurer, cheat. LYRE

L80 libel *v. slander,* defame, lampoon.

L81 liberal *adj. generous,* bountiful, unselfish, kind, lavish, tolerant, broad-minded (M92).

L82 liberate *v.* release, *free,* discharge (C7, C35, C66, D284, R216, S583).

L83 liberty *n. freedom,* independence, autonomy.

L84 license 1. *v.* permit, *allow,* consent, authorize, sanction 2. *n.* permit, authorization.

L85 lick *v.* lap, taste.

L86 lid *n.* cover, top, cap, stopper.

L87 lie 1. *n. falsehood,* untruth, prevarication, fib 2. *v.* fib, tell a lie, prevaricate 3. *v.*

lie down, couch, recline, remain, repose (S427) 4. *v.* be situated, be located.   LYE

L88 life *n.* existence, being, animation, energy, spirit (D35, D40).

L89 lift 1. *v. raise,* lift up, elevate (L154) 2. *n.* elevator.

L90 light 1. *n.* radiance, illumination, brilliance (D21, G78, S149) 2. *n.* candle, taper, match, lamp, torch 3. *v.* kindle, ignite, burn 4. *adj.* bright, clear 5. *adj.* buoyant, flimsy, airy (H93, M70, O56, O75) *v.* **lighten** (D22) *n.* **lightness** (W48).

L91 like 1. *adj.* alike, similar, resembling, equal (O72) 2. *v.* esteem, *admire,* approve, relish, enjoy, *love* (D234, H60) *adj.* **likeable** (H61) *n.* **liking** (D229, H62).

L92 likely *adj.* probable, credible, suitable, possible (I71, U60).

L93 likeness *n.* resemblance, similarity, copy, image, picture, portrait.

L94 lime *n.* 1. quicklime 2. linden tree, fruit.

L95 limit 1. *n.* boundary, frontier, *end* 2. *n.* restraint, check, hindrance 3. *v.* restrain, restrict, hinder, confine *adj.* **limited** (E66, I172, I258).

L96 limp 1. *adj.* flexible, drooping, sagging, flimsy, *supple* (F128, S462) 2. *v. hobble,* walk lame, stagger.

L97 line *n.* 1. stripe, strip, stroke, mark 2. row, rank, file, sequence 3. thread, cord, string, rope, cable, track.

L98 **linger** *v.* loiter, delay, *tarry,* stay, lag (H210, R2, R330).

L99 **link** 1. *v. connect,* join, unite, fasten (S142) 2. *n.* connection, bond, tie.

L100 **lip** *n.* edge, border, rim, brim.

L101 **liquefy** *v.* melt, dissolve, fuse.

L102 **liquid** *adj. & n.* fluid, liquor (S315).

L103 **list** *n.* 1. register, roll, catalog, inventory, series 2. leaning, inclination.

L104 **listen** *v.* hear, harken, attend, heed (D246).

L105 **listless** *adj.* indifferent, heedless, inattentive, languid, apathetic (A45, A87) *n.* **listlessness** (P130).

L106 **literally** *adv.* really, actually, exactly, precisely.

L107 **literate** *adj.* learned, lettered, scholarly, cultured (I18).

L108 **literature** *n.* writings, works, books, plays.

L109 **lithe** *adj.* flexible, pliant, supple, bending (R261).

L110 **litter** *n.* 1. rubbish, refuse, waste 2. bedding, couch.

L111 **little** *adj. small,* tiny, minute, diminutive, brief, short, slight (B70, L26, M70, M261).

L112 **live** 1. (rhymes with *give*) *v.* exist, be, continue, endure (D167) 2. *v.* dwell, abide, reside 3. (rhymes with *hive*) *adj.* alive, living, breathing, active.

L113 **lively** *adj. active,* agile, nimble, supple, brisk, alert (S271).

L114 **livid** *adj.* 1. angry, furious, enraged 2. grayish, pale, purple.

L115 **living** *n.* livelihood, maintenance, support.

L116 **load** *n.* burden, cargo, freight, weight. LODE LOWED

L117 **loaf** 1. *v.* loiter, idle, lounge 2. *n.* bread.

L118 **loan** *v.* lend, advance, entrust (B121). LONE

L119 **loathe** *v.* abhor, *detest,* hate, abominate (A55, A59, L151) *n.* **loathing** (A69) *adj.* **loathesome** (D85).

L120 **lobby** *n.* foyer, vestibule, entrance.

L121 **local** *adj.* regional, district, provincial (I261, U55).

L122 **locate** *v.* 1. fix, place, situate 2. discover, *find.*

L123 **lock** 1. *n.* fastening, padlock, bolt, latch 2. *n.* ringlet, tuft, tress, plait 3. *n.* sluice, weir, floodgate 4. *v.* fasten, latch, bolt (O63).

L124 **lodge** 1. *n.* cottage, cabin, chalet 2. *v.* place, fix, settle 3. *v.* live, abide, stay.

L125 **lofty** *adj.* 1. high, *tall,* elevated (L153) 2. proud, haughty, exalted.

L126 **log** *n.* 1. timber, tree stump, firewood 2. record, register, diary.

L127 **logical** *adj. reasonable,* sound, sensible, rational.

L128 **loiter** *v. linger,* saunter, dawdle, tarry.

L129 **loll** *v.* lounge, recline, lean, sprawl, droop (T131).

L130 **lone** *adj.* solitary, lonely, isolated, single. LOAN

L131 lonely *adj.* apart, *solitary,* desolate, secluded, dreary, friendless.

L132 long 1. *adj.* lengthy, protracted, extensive, extended 2. *v.* covet, crave, desire (S184).

L133 look 1. *v.* watch, regard, behold, see, observe 2. *v.* appear, seem 3. *n.* gaze, glance, appearance.

L134 loom 1. *v.* appear, threaten, menace 2. *n.* weaving machine.

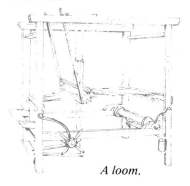

A loom.

L135 loop *n.* noose, coil, circle, ring.

L136 loose *adj.* 1. untied, unfastened, *free,* unattached (F49, S106, T37, T113) 2. vague, indefinite 3. slack, relaxed.

L137 loosen *v.* untie, slacken, relax, release, free (B73, F50, T112).

L138 loot 1. *v. plunder,* ransack, rifle, rob, steal 2. *n.* booty, plunder, spoils.   LUTE

L139 lop *v.* cut, chop, dock, sever, detach.

L140 lope *v.* sprint, run, bound, race.

L141 lord *n.* master, ruler, nobleman, peer, governor, prince (S137).

L142 lose *v. mislay,* fail, forfeit, miss (A41, F122, G4, H66, O24, P413, R219, R227, T210, W76) *n.* **loser** (C96, V55).

L143 loss 1. detriment, damage, defeat, destruction 2. deprivation, want, waste (G4, P413).

L144 lost *adj.* missing, forfeited, wasted, mislaid (F224).

L145 lot *n.* 1. destiny, doom, chance, hazard 2. portion, parcel, division 3. quantity, plenty, abundance (F99).

L146 lotion *n.* salve, cream, ointment, liniment.

L147 lottery *n.* drawing, game of chance.

L148 loud *adj.* 1. noisy, boisterous, blaring, deafening (I101, Q28) 2. flashy, showy, vulgar.

L149 lounge 1. *v.* recline, loll, laze, idle 2. *n.* sitting room, den.

L150 lout *n.* boor, yokel, bumpkin, ruffian, hooligan.

L151 love 1. *v. adore,* esteem, worship, cherish, delight (D151, H60, L119) 2. *n.* affection, tenderness, adoration, warmth, friendliness (E87, H62, L174, M27) *adj.* **lovable** (A10, H61).

L152 lovely *adj.* attractive, *beautiful,* pleasing, delightful, charming, enchanting, sweet, adorable (U1).

L153 low *adj.* 1. sunken, shallow, *deep,* subsided (H120, L125, T14) 2. base, degraded, ignoble, vulgar 3. humble,

poor, meek (M21) 4. cheap, inexpensive, moderate *adj.*
lowly (L125, M21, S532) *adj.*
lowest (S584).   LO

L154 **lower** *v.* 1. drop, sink, let down (E33, H142, L89) 2. degrade, disgrace, reduce 3. diminish, lessen; *You have lowered yourself in my estimation.*

L155 **loyal** *adj. faithful,* true, devoted, constant (T186, U85) *n.*
loyalist (R67, R164).

L156 **loyalty** *n.* fidelity, faithfulness, allegiance, patriotism (T188).

L157 **lucid** *adj.* 1. *clear,* transparent, light 2. intelligible, clear, rational (M4, O15).

L158 **luck** *n.* fortune, chance, hazard, fate, fluke (M175).

L159 **lucky** *adj. fortunate,* happy, favored, successful (A65, H31, U43, U61).

L160 **ludicrous** *adj.* ridiculous, *absurd,* farcical, funny (S135).

L161 **lug** *v.* pull, heave, tug, haul.

L162 **luggage** *n.* baggage, traps, bags, suitcases.

L163 **lull** 1. *v. calm,* still, quiet, hush, tranquilize 2. *n.* quiet, calmness, cessation, stillness.

L164 **lumber** *n.* 1. timber 2. rubbish, junk, trash.

L165 **luminous** *adj.* shining, radiant, lucid, fluorescent.

L166 **lump** *n.* chunk, piece, bump, swelling.

L167 **lunatic** *n.* maniac.

L168 **lunge** *v.* pass, thrust, attack, push.

L169 **lurch** *v.* roll, sway, topple, tumble.

L170 **lure** *v. entice,* allure, attract, decoy, tempt (R172).

L171 **lurid** *adj.* sensational, startling, glaring, terrible, shocking.

L172 **lurk** *v.* skulk, prowl, slink, sneak, snoop, creep.

L173 **luscious** *adj. delicious,* delightful, juicy, palatable (S332).

L174 **lust** 1. *n. desire,* longing, passion, craving 2. *v.* covet, desire, long for, crave.

L175 **luster** *n.* brightness, brilliance, radiance, sheen, gloss, gleam.

L176 **lusty** *adj.* vigorous, sturdy, *robust* (W37).

L177 **luxurious** *adj.* extravagant, *lavish,* splendid, opulent, rich (P234).

M   m

M1 **macabre** *adj.* ghastly, gruesome, *grim,* horrible.

M2 **mace** *n.* 1. club, truncheon, staff 2. nutmeg spice.

M3 **machine** *n. engine,* tool, instrument, device, contrivance.

M4 **mad** *adj.* 1. *insane,* crazy, deranged, demented, idiotic (S24) 2. angry, wrathful, furious (S133).

M5 **madden** *v.* irritate, enrage, infuriate, provoke (S322).

M6 **magazine** *n.* 1. periodical, paper, publication, journal, review 2. warehouse, storehouse, arsenal.

M

M

M7 **magic** *n.* sorcery, witchcraft, wizardry *adj.* **magical**.

M8 **magician** *n.* wizard, sorcerer, conjurer, juggler.

M9 **magistrate** *n.* judge, justice.

M10 **magnate** *n.* bigwig, personage, VIP, tycoon, aristocrat. MAGNET

M11 **magnetic** *adj.* attractive, drawing, alluring *n.* **magnet**.

M12 **magnificent** *adj.* grand, *splendid,* majestic, imposing, gorgeous, superb, luxurious (S215).

M13 **magnify** *v.* 1. *enlarge,* amplify, increase, exaggerate (R98) 2. praise, glorify.

M14 **magnitude** *n.* size, bulk, volume, extent, mass dimension, importance.

M15 **maid** *n.* 1. *servant,* housemaid 2. girl, lass, maiden, damsel. MADE

M16 **mail** *n.* 1. *post,* letters, correspondence 2. armor. MALE

M17 **maim** *v.* cripple, mutilate, disable, injure.

M18 **main** *adj.* chief, principal, leading, important, foremost (M158). MANE

M19 **maintain** *v.* 1. support, keep, uphold, sustain, preserve (R146, W86) 2. assert, allege, declare, hold an opinion.

M20 **maintenance** *n. support,* upkeep, preservation.

M21 **majestic** *adj. imposing,* dignified, stately, regal, royal, splendid, magnificent (L153, M29).

M22 **major** *adj.* greater, chief, larger (M158, S259, S276).

M23 **majority** *n.* greater number, most, mass.

M24 **make** 1. *v.* form, fashion, mold, shape, produce, construct (D143) 2. *v.* perform, do, execute, practice; *Mary made an attempt to break the swimming record.* 3. *v.* compel, force, require 4. *v.* earn, get, secure, gain 5. *v.* appoint, select; *Arthur was made chairman.* 6. *v.* add up to 7. *n.* brand, type.

M25 **malady** *n. illness,* sickness, disease, ailment.

M26 **male** 1. *n.* male animal 2. *adj.* masculine, manly (F82). MAIL

M27 **malice** *n. spite,* hate, rancor, resentment, enmity *adj.* **malicious** (L151).

M28 **malign** *v.* slander, abuse, defame, disparage (P325).

M29 **mammoth** 1. *n.* extinct elephant 2. *adj.* gigantic, huge, enormous, colossal (T125).

M30 **man** 1. *n.* mankind, humanity 2. *n.* male person, adult male, husband (W94) 3. *n.* servant, attendant, workman (M72) 4. *v.* operate, support, crew.

M31 **manage** *v.* 1. *supervise,* administer, guide, handle, conduct, superintend (B177) 2. succeed, maneuver, arrange *adj.* **manageable** (U88).

M32 **manager** *n.* director, superintendent, overseer, supervisor, boss.

M33 **mandate** *n.* command,

order, commission, requirement.
M34 **maneuver** (*man*-**oo**-*ver*) 1.
n. plan, scheme, plot, tactics 2.
v. contrive, manage, intrigue.
M35 **mangle** *v.* mutilate,
destroy, lacerate, maim.

M46 **manuscript** *n.* copy,
document, writing.
M47 **many** *adj.* numerous,
various, frequent, abundant,
diverse (F99).
M48 **map** *n.* chart, plan.

*Mollweide's map
projection.*

M36 **mania** *n.* madness,
insanity, craze, obsession.
M37 **manifest** 1. *v.* show,
exhibit, *reveal,* declare, display
2. *adj.* apparent, open,
obvious, plain, evident (O15).
M38 **manipulate** *v. operate,*
handle, conduct, work.
M39 **manly** *adj.* brave, bold,
courageous, firm, dignified.
M40 **manner** *n.* 1. method,
mode, fashion, way, style 2.
behavior, aspect, appearance.
MANOR
M41 **manor** *n.* estate, mansion,
hall.   MANNER
M42 **mansion** *n.* dwelling, seat,
residence, manor.
M43 **mantle** *n.* cloak, cover,
covering, robe, wrap. MANTEL
M44 **manual** 1. *adj.* by hand,
physical 2. *n.* handbook.
M45 **manufacture** 1. *v.* make,
fabricate, assemble 2. *n.*
production, construction.

M49 **mar** *v. spoil,* ruin, harm,
impair (A60).
M50 **march** 1. *v.* parade, walk,
proceed 2. *n.* parade,
procession, walk, military tune.
M51 **margin** *n.* border, edge,
rim, limit.
M52 **marine** *adj.* maritime,
naval, nautical, oceanic,
seafaring.
M53 **mariner** *n.* sailor, seaman,
seafarer, navigator.
M54 **mark** 1. *n.* sign, token,
symbol, trace, imprint, stamp,
emblem 2. *v.* stamp, brand,
imprint, indicate, distinguish 3.
v. note, observe, heed.
M55 **market** 1. *n.* mart, store,
shop 2. *v.* sell, vend, put on
sale.
M56 **marriage** *n.* wedding,
nuptials, matrimony, wedlock
(D269) *adj.* **married** (S223).
M57 **marry** *v.* wed, unite, join,
espouse, betroth (D269).

M

M58 **marsh** *n.* fen, bog, swamp, morass, quagmire.

M59 **marshal** 1. *v.* arrange, range, array, draw up, organize 2. *n.* general (military). MARTIAL

M60 **mart** *n.* market, store.

M61 **martial** *adj.* warlike, military, belligerent, militant (P99). MARSHAL

M62 **martyr** *n. victim,* sufferer, sacrifice, scapegoat.

M63 **marvel** 1. *n.* wonder, miracle, phenomenon 2. *v.* wonder, admire, be awestruck.

M64 **marvelous** *adj. wonderful,* amazing, stupendous, astonishing, miraculous, incredible (C252).

M65 **masculine** *adj. male,* manly, virile, robust (F82).

M66 **mask** 1. *n.* face covering, cloak, screen, disguise 2. *v.* hide, conceal, disguise, veil.

M67 **mass** 1. *n.* lump, bulk, size, pile 2. *n.* church service 3. *v.* gather, collect, assemble.

M68 **massacre** 1. *n.* butchery, slaughter, carnage, extermination 2. *v.* slay, kill, butcher, murder, slaughter.

M69 **massage** *v.* rub, knead, stroke, stimulate.

M70 **massive** *adj.* 1. *huge,* immense, gigantic (L111) 2. heavy, bulky, weighty.

M71 **mast** *n.* spar, pole, pylon.

M72 **master** 1. *n.* ruler, director, governor, manager, captain, commander, teacher, expert (M30, S137) 2. *v.* overpower, conquer 3. *v.* acquire, learn thoroughly, grasp.

M73 **masterly** *adj.* skillful, clever, expert, adroit (A186).

M74 **mat** *n.* rug, carpet, cover, covering.

M75 **match** 1. *n.* competition, game, contest, trial 2. *v.* equal, harmonize, resemble.

M76 **mate** 1. *n.* associate, companion, fellow, pal 2. *v.* marry, match, breed.

M77 **material** 1. *n.* matter, substance, stuff, fabric, textile 2. *adj.* real, physical, tangible (S367).

M78 **maternal** *adj.* motherly, motherlike, matronly.

M79 **mathematical** *adj.* precise, accurate, strict, rigid.

M80 **matrimony** *n.* marriage, wedlock, union.

M81 **matron** *n.* 1. wife, dame, elderly woman 2. female officer.

M82 **matter** 1. *n.* substance, body, material 2. *n.* topic, subject, affair 3. *n.* trouble, difficulty 4. *v.* signify, import, mean.

M83 **mature** 1. *adj.* ripe, complete, full, mellow 2. *adj.* adult, grown-up (I31, I164) 3. *v.* ripen, age, mellow.

M84 **maul** *v.* beat, bruise, wound, disfigure, injure.

M85 **maxim** *n.* proverb, saying, axiom, rule.

M86 **maximum** *adj.* greatest, largest, highest, most (M156).

M87 **maybe** *adv. perhaps,* possibly, probably.

M88 **maze** *n.* labyrinth, network, warren, intricacy. MAIZE

M89 **meadow** *n. field,* mead,

turf, grassland, pasture, lea, sward.

M90 **meager** *adj.* 1. *scanty,* poor, frugal (E170, P415) 2. gaunt, hungry, lank, lean.

M91 **meal** *n.* 1. repast, collation, spread, snack 2. flour, grain.

M92 **mean** 1. *adj. stingy,* selfish, miserly, mercenary (C108, G38, L38, L81) 2. *adj.* shabby, beggarly, servile, poor (S436) 3. *adj.* average, middle, medium; *His income was below the national mean.* 4. *adj.* unkind, cruel (M127) 5. *v.* intend, signify, indicate, denote. MIEN

M93 **meaning** *n.* 1. intention, purpose, design, aim, object 2. significance, sense, explanation.

M94 **means** *n.* 1. revenue, income, resources, wealth 2. expedient, method, mode, way; *It was a means to an end.*

M95 **measure** 1. *n.* size, gauge, rule, extent, dimension 2. *v.* estimate, rule, appraise, gauge.

M96 **meat** *n.* food, flesh, viands, victuals. MEET

M97 **mechanic** *n.* artisan, craftsman, operative, machinist.

M98 **medal** *n.* award, decoration, trophy, reward, medallion. MEDDLE

M99 **meddle** *v.* interfere, intrude, pry, intercede. MEDAL

M100 **medicine** *n.* drug, physic, medicament, remedy, potion, cure.

M101 **mediocre** *adj.* average, inferior, commonplace, medium (G116, S573).

M102 **meditate** *v. contemplate,* ruminate, reflect, dwell upon, ponder.

M103 **medium** 1. *adj.* middle, mean, average, mediocre 2. *n.* means, agency, instrument; *A medium of communication is the international language, Esperanto.* 3. **media** *n. pl.* newspapers, radio, television.

M104 **medley** *n.* mixture, jumble, hodgepodge, variety.

M105 **meek** *adj.* humble, lowly, submissive, *mild,* modest, docile (U21).

M106 **meet** 1. *v. encounter,* assemble, collect, converge (A182, E143) 2. *v.* comply, discharge, fulfill 3. *adj.* fit, proper, suitable 4. *n.* meeting, contest, match. MEAT METE

M107 **meeting** *n.* assembly, gathering, congregation (P64).

M108 **melancholy** 1. *n.* sadness, dejection, depression, gloom (G68, H33) 2. *adj.* dejected, depressed, sad, sorrowful, *unhappy,* gloomy, glum (J25).

A medal issued by Queen Elizabeth I of England.

M109 **mellow** *adj*. 1. *ripe,* mature 2. soft, smooth, silver toned, sweet, melodious.

M110 **melodious** *adj*. tuneful, musical, dulcet, harmonious (H53, H137).

M111 **melody** *n*. tune, song, air, theme, music.

M112 **melt** *v*. liquefy, dissolve, thaw, soften (F248).

M113 **member** *n*. 1. fellow, associate, partner 2. limb, leg, arm, component.

M114 **memento** *n*. souvenir, memorial.

M115 **memoir** *n*. biography, record, diary, narrative.

M116 **memorable** *adj*. *remarkable,* famous, great, historic, unforgettable.

M117 **memorize** *v*. learn, remember.

M118 **memory** *n*. recollection, remembrance, recall.

M119 **menace** 1. *n*. threat 2. *v*. *threaten,* alarm, frighten, intimidate (E60).

M120 **mend** *v*. *repair,* restore, fix, refit, improve, recover, heal (B147).

M121 **menial** 1. *adj*. servile, low, common 2. *n*. servant, domestic, waiter, valet.

M122 **mental** *adj*. thinking, intellectual, reasoning, rational (P191).

M123 **mention** 1. *v*. declare, name, tell, state, speak of, refer to 2. *n*. allusion, reference, remark.

M124 **mercenary** *adj*. 1. covetous, miserly, avaricious, sordid, selfish 2. hired, paid.

M125 **merchandise** 1. *n*. goods, wares, stocks, commodities 2. *v*. sell, market, promote.

M126 **merchant** *n*. trader, tradesman, dealer, shopkeeper, importer, exporter, retailer.

M127 **merciful** *adj*. lenient, forgiving, gracious, compassionate, kind, humane (I191, M128, R334).

M128 **merciless** *adj*. *pitiless,* cruel, unfeeling, relentless, hardhearted, severe, ruthless (M127).

M129 **mercy** *n*. 1. pity, *compassion,* grace, pardon, forgiveness, sympathy, clemency (C497) 2. descretion, disposal; *He was at the mercy of his enemy.*

M130 **mere** *adj*. simple, bare sheer.

M131 **merely** *adv*. simply, purely, only, solely, barely, hardly.

M132 **merge** *v*. combine, unite, join, mingle, submerge.

M133 **merit** 1. *n*. excellence, credit, worth, *value,* quality (F58) 2. *v*. deserve, earn, have a right to.

M134 **merry** *adj*. happy, blithe, *cheerful,* lively, jolly, jovial (G79).

M135 **mesh** *n*. net, screen, web, network.

M136 **mess** 1. *n*. *muddle,* confusion, jumble, disorder, untidiness (O86) 2. *n*. predicament, *plight,* difficulty 3. *n*. dining hall 4. *v*. jumble, confuse, dirty.

M137 **message** *n*.

M

communication, letter, missive, note, dispatch, information.

M138 **messenger** n. bearer, carrier, courier, envoy.

M139 **meter** n. 1. measure, gauge, recorder 2. rhythm, verse, measure.

M140 **method** n. way, mode, *manner,* process, course, means, system.

M141 **meticulous** adj. careful, precise, demanding.

M142 **middle** 1. adj. *center,* halfway, intermediate, mean 2. n. center, midst, central (E15).

M143 **might** 1. n. *power,* strength, force, potency 2. v. be possible, allow, permit.   MITE

M144 **mighty** adj. *strong,* powerful, robust, sturdy, potent, enormous (W37).

M145 **mild** adj. tender, kind, gentle, soft, *bland,* placid, meek (I109, I111, P271, P473, S144, T32, T233).

M146 **militant** adj. fighting, contending, belligerent, aggressive (P99).

M147 **military** adj. martial, soldierly, warlike (C165).

M148 **mill** 1. n. factory, works 2. v. grind, pulverize, powder.

A hand worked mill.

M149 **mimic** 1. v. impersonate, imitate, mime 2. n. impersonator, impressionist.

M150 **mince** v. chop, grind, cut up, crush.   MINTS

M151 **mind** 1. v. regard, mark, care 2. v. pay attention to, obey 3. v. attend, watch, observe 4. n. soul, spirit, intellect, intelligence adj. **mindful** (R118).

M152 **mine** 1. n. excavation, colliery, pit, quarry, shaft 2. v. dig, excavate, quarry 3. *pron.* belonging to me.

M153 **mineral** n. rocks, ore, metal, stone.

M154 **mingle** v. *mix,* combine, join, blend (S130).

M155 **miniature** 1. n. portrait, small collectible 2. adj. *little,* small, diminutive, wee, tiny (H192).

M156 **minimum** adj. least, lowest, smallest, least part (M86) v. **minimize** (E159).

M157 **minister** n. 1. clergyman, priest, parson, pastor, vicar, cleric 2. administrator, ambassador, official.

M158 **minor** 1. adj. smaller, lesser, inferior, small unimportant (C129, G130, M18, M22, S123) 2. n. child, youth. n. **minority** (M23).   MINER

M159 **minstrel** n. singer, musician, bard.

M160 **mint** 1. n. coin factory 2. v. coin, stamp, forge, fashion, punch, strike 3. adj. fresh, new untouched.

M161 **minute** 1. (**min**-it) n. sixty seconds 2. n. jiffy, instant 3. (*my*-**nute**) adj. little, *tiny,* small, wee, microscopic (G54, H192, V22).

M162 miracle *n. marvel,* wonder, prodigy.

M163 miraculous *adj. supernatural,* wonderful, extraordinary, incredible (C252).

M164 mire *n.* mud, ooze, slime.

M165 mirror 1. *n.* looking glass, reflector 2. *v.* reflect.

A mirror or looking glass.

M166 mirth *n.* merriment, jollity, laughter, joy, fun (G78).

M167 misbehavior *n.* misconduct, naughtiness, rudeness.

M168 miscellaneous *adj.* diversified, *various,* mixed, mingled, diverse.

M169 mischief *n.* 1. evil, harm, injury, damage 2. naughtiness, devilment, roguery, prankishness.

M170 mischievous *adj. naughty,* playful, troublesome (G98).

M171 miscreant *n.* villain, *scoundrel,* knave, rascal, rogue.

M172 miser *n.* skinflint, niggard, tightwad, meanie, hoarder.

M173 miserable *adj.* unhappy, wretched, distressed, forlorn, poor (H34) 2. worthless, valueless.

M174 misery *n. distress,* woe, unhappiness, suffering, grief, sorrow (B93, E14, J32, R33).

M175 misfortune *n. disaster,* calamity, blow, adversity, mishap, bad luck (F77, L158, W51).

M176 misgiving *n. doubt,* mistrust, suspicion, hesitation (T220).

M177 mishap *n. accident,* mischance, misadventure.

M178 misjudge *v.* mistake, miscalculate, misunderstand.

M179 mislay *v. lose,* miss, misplace (F122).

M180 mislead *v. deceive,* misguide, delude, misdirect, trick (G166).

M181 misplace *v.* miss, lose.

M182 miss 1. *v. fail,* lose, forfeit, mistake 2. *v.* want, need, yearn, wish 3. *n.* blunder, slip, failure, fault (H134) 4. *n.* damsel, girl, maiden, maid.

M183 missile *n.* projectile, weapon, rocket.

M184 mission *n.* 1. duty, trust, business, errand, job 2. legation, embassy, ministry.

M185 missionary *n.* evangelist, apostle, preacher, minister.

M186 mist *n. fog,* haze, cloud, steam, vapor, blur.   MISSED.

M187 mistake 1. *n.* error, *blunder,* fault, oversight 2. *v.*

misunderstand, misjudge, confound.

M188 **mistaken** *adj. wrong,* erroneous, incorrect (C418).

M189 **mistress** *n.* governess, teacher, matron, dame.

M190 **mistrust** *v.* distrust, doubt, *suspect,* question (C318, T220).

M191 **misunderstand** *v.* mistake, misinterpret, misconceive (C281, R59, U26).

M192 **misuse** 1. *v. abuse,* maltreat, waste, squander (U99) 2. *n.* abuse, ill treatment.

M193 **mite** *n.* 1. particle, atom, molecule, scrap 2. insect.

MIGHT

M194 **mitigate** *v.* 1. appease, soothe, mollify, allay (A77) 2. *moderate,* abate, lessen, relieve.

M195 **mix** 1. *v.* mingle, *blend,* compound, combine (S130) 2. *n.* mixture.

M196 **mixture** *n.* medley, hodgepodge, variety, miscellany, *blend.*

M197 **moan** *v.* grieve, mourn, *lament,* wail, cry (R130)

MOWN

M198 **moat** *n.* ditch, fosse.

MOTE

M199 **mob** *n. rabble,* crowd, riffraff, throng, swarm.

M200 **mobile** *adj.* movable, portable, changeable, on wheels (I37, S440, S465).

M201 **mock** 1. *v. mimic,* ape, imitate 2. *v.* deride, *ridicule,* jeer, taunt, gibe 3. *adj.* false, counterfeit, imitation, sham (G43).

M202 **mockery** *n.* 1. ridicule,

derision, *scorn* (P325) 2. counterfeit, show, sham, pretense.

M203 **mode** *n.* way, *method,* manner, style, fashion.

MOWED

M204 **model** 1. *n.* pattern, prototype, original 2. *n.* copy, imitation, representation, replica 3. *n.* version, type 4. *n.* mannequin 5. *v.* mold, form, shape, plan.

M205 **moderate** 1. *adj.* temperate, reasonable, *fair,* mild (D303, E171, E227, I38, I246) 2. *v.* soothe, allay, *appease,* quiet, lessen 3. *v.* control, govern, judge.

M206 **modern** *adj.* recent, late, new, novel, fresh, present (A110, O19).

M207 **modest** *adj.* 1. *meek,* unassuming, humble (A148, B105, C293, F221, H63, O100, P452, S286) 2. *chaste,* pure, virtuous (I137, S157, W17) 3. moderate, reasonable (E227).

M208 **modesty** *n.* meekness, humility, simplicity, shyness (V15).

M209 **modify** *v.* shape, alter, change, vary, adjust, qualify, fix.

M210 **moist** *adj.* damp, humid, dank, *wet,* muggy (D329).

M211 **moisten** *v.* dampen, wet, splash (D329).

M212 **moisture** *n.* dampness, humidity, wetness, dankness.

M213 **mold** 1. *n.* earth, loam, 2. *n.* mustiness, mildew, blight, decay 3. *n.* & *v.* form, shape, cast *adj.* **moldy.**

M214 **moment** *n.* 1. instant, second, jiffy, twinkling 2. significance, import, weight, consequence.

M215 **momentous** *adj. important,* serious, weighty, grave (T211, U50).

M216 **monarch** ("*ch*" like "*k*") *n.* queen, king, sovereign, ruler, chief, autocrat.

M217 **money** *n.* wealth, riches, coin, cash, currency, funds.

M218 **mongrel** *n. & adj.* crossbreed, hybrid.

M219 **monitor** *n.* overseer, supervisor, adviser.

M220 **monopolize** *v.* control, *dominate,* hog, absorb, corner.

M221 **monotonous** *adj.* uniform, unvaried, *tedious,* boring, repetitious, humdrum (I254).

M222 **monster** *n.* brute, fiend, villain, demon.

M223 **monstrous** *adj.* 1. huge, *enormous,* vast, colossal 2. shocking, *horrible,* frightful, hideous, outrageous.

M224 **monument** *n.* tomb, gravestone, cenotaph, memorial, pillar, statue.

M225 **monumental** *adj.* important, weighty, stupendous, huge, exceptional.

M226 **mood** *n.* temper, *humor,* disposition, vein.

M227 **moody** *adj.* morose, sullen, sulky, glum, pettish, ill tempered, temperamental (C124).

M228 **moor** 1. *n.* heath, common, bog 2. *v.* fasten, secure, fix.

M229 **mop** *v.* wipe, swab, clean, wash.

M230 **mope** *v.* be sad, be gloomy, grieve, sulk, despair.

M231 **moral** *adj. virtuous,* good, just, upright, honest (I40, I163, U76).

M232 **morale** *n.* spirit, enthusiasm, confidence.

M233 **morass** *n.* bog, *swamp,* marsh, fen.

M234 **morbid** *adj.* 1. sick, unsound, diseased, unhealthy (H79) 2. depressed, gloomy, pessimistic (G79).

M235 **more** *adj.* extra, greater, in addition (L71).

M236 **moreover** *conj. & adv.* besides, further, also, likewise.

M237 **morning** *n.* dawn, daybreak, sunrise, forenoon (E146). MOURNING

M238 **morose** *adj. sullen,* churlish, sour, sulky, moody, gloomy, (C124, G60, S565).

M239 **morsel** *n.* bite, mouthful, *fragment,* piece, tidbit.

M240 **mortal** *adj.* 1. deadly, fatal, destructive, lethal 2. human, destined to die (I41).

M241 **mortar** *n.* cement.

M242 **mortify** *v.* 1. displease, vex, *upset,* annoy, depress (G124) 2. fester, corrupt, putrefy.

M243 **most** 1. *n.* greatest part, greatest number 2. *adj.* greatest extreme, maximum, nearly all (L55).

M244 **mostly** *adv.* mainly, chiefly, generally, principally (S118).

M245 **mother** 1. *n.* female

parent, mama 2. *v.* care for, look after, nurse.

M246 **motion** *n.* 1. movement, action, passage, change 2. proposal, gesture, impulse, suggestion.

M247 **motive** *n.* cause, reason, purpose, spur, incentive, stimulus.

M248 **motley** *adj.* dappled, speckled, mottled, mixed, mingled.

M249 **motor** *n.* engine, machine, car.

M250 **motorist** *n.* driver, automobile traveler.

M251 **motto** *n.* maxim, phrase, proverb, saying, *slogan,* catchword.

M252 **mound** *n.* knoll, hillock, hill, *pile,* heap.

M253 **mount** 1. *n.* mountain, hill 2. *n.* horse, steed 3. *v.* rise, ascend, increase (D123) 4. *v.* climb, scale, go up.

M254 **mountain** *n.* mount, peak, height.

M255 **mountebank** *n.* pretender, charlatan, quack, impostor, cheat.

M256 **mourn** *v.* grieve, lament, deplore, bewail, sorrow (R130).

M257 **mournful** *adj.* sad, distressing, *melancholy,* unhappy (F91).

M258 **mouth** *n.* 1. jaws 2. opening, aperture, entrance.

M259 **move** 1. *v.* go, proceed, walk, march, advance 2. *v.* propel, push, stir, drive 3. *v.* rouse, excite, affect, touch 4. *n.* movement, motion, proceeding *adj.* **moving** (I37).

M260 **movement** *n.* 1. motion, move, change, action 2. party, faction, group 3. melody, rhythmic passage.

M261 **much** 1. *adj.* abundant, plentiful, a great deal of, quantity (L111) 2. *adv.* often, long, frequently, nearly, almost.

M262 **muck** *n.* dirt, filth, refuse, mire, slime.

M263 **mud** *n.* mire, dirt, marsh, swamp.

M264 **muddle** 1. *n.* confusion, disorder, *mess,* plight 2. *v.* confuse, spoil, mix up, jumble.

M265 **muff** 1. *v.* spoil, miss, muddle, bungle 2. *n.* glove.

M266 **muffle** *v.* 1. wrap, cover, shroud, envelop 2. silence, dull, soften, deaden, mute.

M267 **muggy** *adj.* wet, damp, moist, stuffy, close, dank.

M268 **multiply** *v.* 1. increase, advance, gain, grow (L72) 2. reproduce, procreate.

M269 **multitude** *n.* host, legion, throng, assembly, crowd, swarm.

M270 **mum** 1. *adj.* silent, mute, speechless, dumb 2. *n.* (colloq.) mother.

M271 **mumble** *v. mutter,* murmur, speak indistinctly.

M272 **munch** *v. chew,* eat, nibble, crunch, bite.

M273 **murder** 1. *n.* homicide, killing, death 2. *v. kill,* slay, assassinate, massacre, slaughter.

M274 **murky** *adj.* dark, gloomy, obscure, *dim,* cloudy.

M275 **murmur** *n. & v.* 1. mutter, mumble, whisper, whimper 2. whisper, whimper, grumble, hum.

M276 **muscular** *adj.* sinewy, *brawny,* strong, stalwart, powerful (F134).

M277 **music** *n.* melody, harmony, symphony, tune.

M278 **musical** *adj.* melodious, harmonious, tuneful, dulcet.

M279 **must** 1. *v.* should, ought to, be obliged to 2. *n.* grape juice 3. *n.* mold, sourness.

M280 **muster** *v.* assemble, collect, gather, congregate.

M281 **musty** *adj.* moldy, sour, stale, fusty.

M282 **mute** *adj. dumb,* silent, speechless.

M283 **mutilate** *v.* disfigure, maim, cripple, injure, mangle, tear, lacerate.

M284 **mutiny** 1. *v. rebel,* revolt, rise up 2. *n.* revolt, rebellion, uprising, riot.

M285 **mutter** *v.* grumble, *murmur,* complain, whisper.

M286 **mutual** *adj.* reciprocal, joint, alternate, common.

M287 **mysterious** *adj.* unknown, obscure, hidden, *secret,* puzzling, (O26).

M288 **mystery** *n.* secret, enigma, riddle, puzzle.

M289 **mystify** *v. perplex,* puzzle, bewilder, confuse.

M290 **myth** *n.* fable, legend, tradition, tale.

M291 **mythical** *adj.* fabulous, fanciful, fictitious, legendary.

N n

N1 **nab** *v.* arrest, seize, *catch,* grasp, snatch, clutch.

N2 **nag** 1. *v.* hector, annoy, *pester,* worry, vex (A126) 2. *n.* horse, pony.

N3 **nail** *n.* spike, brad, claw, talon.

N4 **naïve** *adj. ingenuous,* unsophisticated, simple, unaffected, artless, innocent (A149, A166, C513, M83).

N5 **naked** *adj.* 1. *nude,* bare, uncovered, unclothed, undressed 2. manifest, unconcealed, evident, open, simple.

N6 **name** 1. *n.* title, appellation, designation 2. *n.* reputation, repute, character 3. *v.* christen, call, entitle, term, baptize.

N7 **nap** *n.* doze, slumber, sleep, siesta, snooze.

N8 **narrate** *v. relate,* recite, recount, tell, detail, describe.

N9 **narrative** *n.* tale, story, account, description, history.

N10 **narrow** *adj.* 1. slender, thin, confined, close, tight (B159, E216, S338, W68) 2. mean, avaricious, ungenerous.

N11 **nasty** *adj.* 1. filthy, foul, unclean, impure, dirty, unpalatable (P21, S611) 2. disagreeable, annoying, troublesome.

N12 **nation** *n.* state, country, people, population, realm.

N13 **national** *adj*. public, general, civil (I261).

N14 **native** 1. *adj*. natural, aboriginal, local, genuine, indigenous, original (A88, F197, O110) 2. *n*. citizen, original inhabitant, resident.

N15 **natty** *adj*. neat, spruce, tidy, smart, jaunty, trim.

N16 **natural** *adj*. 1. normal, ordinary, legitimate, regular (O29, U62, W49) 2. natal, native, inbred, hereditary.

N17 **naturally** *adv*. 1. consequently, because of, necessarily, customarily, usually 2. normally, simply, freely.

N18 **nature** *n*. 1. creation, the world, universe, earth 2. character, species, type, sort 3. disposition, humor, temper.

N19 **naughty** *adj*. mischievous, perverse, bad, worthless, disobedient, unruly, sinful (G98).

N20 **nausea** *n*. sickness, disgust, squeamishness, queasiness, *adj*. **nauseous** (L173).

N21 **nautical** *adj*. maritime, marine, naval.

N22 **navigate** *v*. sail, cruise, steer, direct, pilot.

N23 **navy** *n*. ships, vessels, shipping, fleet.

N24 **near** *adj*. nigh, *close,* nearby, adjacent, adjoining, neighboring (F41, R160).

N25 **nearly** *adv*. almost, approximately, closely.

N26 **neat** *adj*. 1. spruce, trim, clean, *tidy,* orderly (D231, S269, U84) 2. clever, expert, handy 3.

unmixed, pure, straight, unadulterated.

N27 **necessary** *adj*. unavoidable, *essential,* indispensable, needed, obligatory (O77).

N28 **necessity** *n*. requirement, requisite, urgency, essential.

N29 **need** 1. *n*. necessity, want, urgency, *lack* 2. *n*. poverty, penury, distress, need, want (P254) 3. *v*. want, require, lack, miss.   KNEAD

N30 **needless** *adj*. unnecessary, useless, superfluous (N27).

N31 **needy** *adj*. poor, destitute, poverty-stricken, penniless.

N32 **neglect** 1. *v*. omit, leave out, overlook, disregard, ignore (C39, P27) 2. *n*. failure, default, omission, disregard, negligence (O17).

N33 **negligent** *adj*. careless, forgetful, heedless, indifferent, neglectful, thoughtless (V58).

N34 **negotiate** *v*. bargain, arrange, discuss, settle.

N35 **neighbor** *n*. fellow townsman or woman, countryman, compatriot.

N36 **neighborhood** *n*. district, locality, vicinity, nearness.

N37 **nerve** *n*. 1. *courage,* strength, power, force, pluck, bravery (C451) 2. cheek, sauciness, effrontery, impertinence (C445).

N38 **nervous** *adj*. *timid,* fearful, weak, apprehensive, agitated, tense, strained, jittery (C319).

N39 **nestle** *v*. snuggle, cuddle, nuzzle, huddle.

N40 **net** 1. *n.* snare, *trap,* mesh, web 2. *v.* gain, earn, obtain, clear.

N41 **nettle** 1. *v.* fret, chafe, irritate, vex, tease (S322) 2. *n.* plant.

N42 **neutral** *adj.* 1. *impartial,* uninvolved, neuter 2. dull, drab, mediocre.

N43 **new** *adj.* novel, latest, fresh, recent, modern, unused (A110, O19, O52, S421). GNU KNEW

N44 **newcomer** *n.* visitor, caller, entrant, beginner, novice (V47).

N45 **news** *n.* tidings, intelligence, information, word, data, report.

N46 **next** *adj.* 1. nearest, adjacent, closest, beside 2. following, after, subsequent (P375).

N47 **nibble** *v.* gnaw, bite, chew, nip.

N48 **nice** *adj.* 1. pleasant, agreeable, delightful, delicious, good (D197, N11) 2. exact, accurate, precise; *Lawyers are used to working out nice legal points.*

N49 **niche** *n.* cranny, nook, recess, corner.

N50 **nick** *n. & v.* notch, cut, dent, score.

N51 **niggardly** *adj. stingy,* mean, close, mercenary, miserly (H26, H171).

N52 **nigh** *adj. close,* adjacent, adjoining, near (D251).

N53 **night** *n.* darkness, obscurity, dusk, evening (D32). KNIGHT

Nimble play at the net.

N54 **nimble** *adj.* agile, lively, brisk, active, spry (A186).

N55 **nip** 1. *v.* pinch, squeeze, bite, clip, chill 2. *n.* pinch, bite 3. *n.* dram, sip, drink.

N56 **no** 1. *adv.* nay, not at all, in no way 2. *adj.* none, not any, not one. KNOW

N57 **noble** *adj.* 1. great, dignified, *superior,* upright, generous, magnanimous 2. grand, stately, lordly, aristocratic (A10).

N58 **nod** *v.* 1. bow, assent, agree 2. nap, sleep.

N59 **noise** *n. din,* clamor, uproar, tumult, racket (Q28, S211) *adj.* **noisy** (Q28, S465).

N60 **nominate** *v. appoint,* choose, designate, name, propose.

N61 **nonchalant** *adj.* unconcerned, indifferent, careless, *cool.*

N62 **nondescript** *adj.* odd, indescribable, abnormal.

N63 **none** *pron.* not one, not any, not a part. NUN

N64 **nonsense** *n.* folly, absurdity, *trash,* twaddle, balderdash (S126).

N65 **nook** *n.* recess, niche, corner.

N66 **noose** *n.* hitch, knot, loop, rope, lasso.

N67 **normal** *adj.* regular, *usual,* natural, typical, customary (A7, E10).

N68 **nostalgia** *n.* homesickness, memoirs, memorabilia, recollections.

N69 **notable** *adj. remarkable,* memorable, extraordinary, noted, unusual, famous, distinguished (C252).

N70 **notch** *n. & v.* nick, cut, dent, gash.

N71 **note** 1. *n.* comment, report, *notice,* memo 2. *n.* repute, fame, renown, importance 3. *n.* bank note, bill 4. *v.* notice, remark, heed, record (O136).

N72 **noted** *adj.* celebrated, *famous,* eminent, notable (U58).

N73 **nothing** *n.* 1. no thing, no part, nonexistence 2. trifle, small matter 3. nought, zero, cipher.

N74 **notice** *n.* 1. note, observation, heed 2. advertisement, poster, sign 3. warning, intimation, intelligence *v.* **notice** (I13).

N75 **notify** *v.* declare, announce, acquaint, advise, inform.

N76 **notion** *n. idea,* opinion, fancy, view, belief, conception, impression.

N77 **notorious** *adj.* 1. *infamous,* disreputable, nefarious 2. celebrated, famous, famed, well-known.

N78 **nought** (*naut*) *n.* nil, zero, nothing.

N79 **nourish** *v.* feed, nurture, support, cherish, nurse.

N80 **nourishment** *n.* food, sustenance, diet, nutriment.

N81 **novel** 1. *adj.* new, strange, *unusual,* modern, recent 2. *n.* tale, romance, story, narrative, book.

N82 **novice** *n.* beginner, learner, tyro (E201).

N83 **now** *adv.* at this time, at present, at once, right away.

N84 **nude** *adj.* bare, *naked,* unclothed.

N85 **nudge** *v.* jog, poke, push, dig.

N86 **nuisance** *n.* annoyance, *bother,* bore, trouble, irritation (D86).

N87 **null** *adj.* void, *invalid,* useless.

N88 **nullify** *v.* annul, invalidate, *cancel,* repeal, abolish.

N89 **numb** *adj.* dull, insensible, dead, paralyzed.

N90 **number** 1. *n.* figure, numeral, digit 2. *n.* multitude, collection, horde, quantity 3. *v.* count, reckon, compute, total.

N91 **numeral** *n.* figure, number, digit.

N92 **numerous** *adj. many,* numberless, abundant (F99).

N93 **nurse** 1. *v.* nourish, take care of, nurture, feed, suckle 2. *n.* matron, hospital worker.

N94 **nurture** *v.* feed, *nourish,* support, train, educate.

N95 **nutritious** *adj.* nourishing, strengthening, wholesome.

N96 **nymph** *n.* damsel, *girl,* maiden, maid, lass.

O o

O1 **oaf** *n.* blockhead, simpleton, lummox, ruffian.

O2 **oath** *n.* 1. *vow,* pledge, promise 2. *curse,* profanity, blasphemy.

O3 **obedient** *adj.* respectful, dutiful, yielding, subservient (P171, U74, W36).

O4 **obey** *v.* yield, submit, comply, follow, keep (C241, D238, I183, R67, T178).

O5 **object (ob-***ject***)** 1. *n. thing,* article, fact 2. *n.* target, aim, goal, end, objective 3. (*ob-***ject**) *n.* oppose, refuse, protest (A81).

O6 **objection** *n.* doubt, *protest,* opposition, scruple, disapproval.

O7 **obligation** *n.* 1. *duty,* requirement, responsibility 2. agreement, bond, contract, stipulation *adj.* **obligatory** (O77).

O8 **oblige** *v.* 1. please, favor, gratify, serve (A115) 2. compel, force, coerce, require.

O9 **obliging** *adj.* polite, friendly, accommodating, kind.

O10 **oblique** *adj.* 1. inclined, aslant, slanting, sloping 2. devious, indirect.

O11 **obliterate** *v. erase,* cancel, rub out, delete, destroy.

O12 **oblivious** *adj.* forgetful, mindless, heedless, careless.

O13 **obnoxious** *adj.* hateful, unpleasant, blameworthy, disagreeable, odious (P13).

O14 **obscene** *adj.* indecent, impure, gross, coarse, dirty, smutty, filthy, offensive (D45).

O15 **obscure** 1. *adj.* dark, gloomy, dusky, murky, shadowy, indistinct, illegible (D252, L63) 2. *adj.* vague, incomprehensible, doubtful (M37, O26) 3. *adj.* humble, undistinguished, unknown (D254) 4. *v.* darken, hide, disguise, conceal (I20) *n.* **obscurity** (R167).

O16 **observant** *adj.* attentive, watchful, alert, vigilant.

O17 **observation** *n.* 1. remark, comment, note 2. notice, attention, observance, study.

O18 **observe** *v.* 1. notice, remark, note, watch, see, behold, detect 2. utter, express, mention, say 3. celebration, keep up, honor; *Christmas is a holiday which is observed all over the world.* 4. fulfill, obey, comply with; *It is important to observe the law.* (I183).

Instruments which help us to observe.

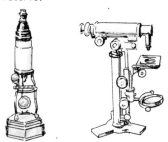

O19 **obsolete** *adj.* antiquated, disused, neglected, old-fashioned (C520).

O20 **obstacle** *n. hindrance,* obstruction, check, barrier (A83).

O21 **obstinate** *adj. stubborn,* dogged, perverse, pigheaded, unyielding, headstrong (D273).

O22 **obstruct** *v.* hinder, *impede,* oppose, stop, prevent, block (A56, A83).

O23 **obstruction** *n.* hindrance, obstacle, impediment, *barrier.*

O24 **obtain** *v. procure,* get, acquire, achieve, gain (L142).

O25 **obtuse** *adj.* blunt, *dull,* stupid, doltish, slow-witted (A47, K1).

O26 **obvious** *adj.* open, exposed, plain, *evident,* clear, visible, unmistakable (I161, M287, O15, S449).

O27 **occasion** *n.* 1. occurrence, incident, event, happening 2. opportunity, suitable time, juncture.

O28 **occasional** *adj.* infrequent, *casual,* rare (F251).

O29 **occult** *adj.* hidden, secret, mystical, supernatural, magical (N16).

O30 **occupant** *n.* possessor, occupier, holder, resident, tenant.

O31 **occupation** *n.* 1. employment, business, calling, vocation, trade, craft, *job,* profession 2. possession, ownership 3. pastime, handiwork.

O32 **occupy** *v.* 1. possess, take up, employ, use; *It is a good thing to occupy the mind with reading.* 2. inhabit, own (E142) 3. capture, invade, seize *adj.* **occupied** (I9, U34, U64, V1).

O33 **occur** *v.* appear, arise, *happen,* befall, come about.

O34 **occurrence** *n. incident,* event, happening, affair.

O35 **ocean** *n.* sea, main, deep.

O36 **odd** *adj.* 1. uneven, 2. unmatched, single 3. singular, unusual, extraordinary, strange (R122, T244).

O37 **odious** *adj. hateful,* detestable, invidious, disagreeable.

O38 **odor** *n.* smell, aroma, scent, perfume, fragrance, bouquet.

O39 **offend** *v.* 1. displease, vex, annoy, *irritate,* mortify (F142, P249) 2. sin, err, transgress.

O40 **offense** *n.* 1. *attack,* assault, aggression 2. displeasure, anger, indignation; *Mary takes offense very easily.* (D86) 3. misdeed, crime, sin, fault, wrong.

O41 **offensive** 1. *adj.* impertinent, rude, unpleasant, insolent (I202) 2. *adj.* disagreeable, revolting, disgusting 3. *adj.* aggressive, attacking 4. *n.* attack, assault.

O42 **offer** 1. *v.* proffer, put forward, present, *tender,* submit (R73) 2. *n.* proposal, proposition, suggestion.

O43 **office** *n.* 1. place of business, room bureau 2. post, situation, position, duty.

O44 **official** 1. *adj.* formal, authoritative, authorized (I180) 2. *n.* officer, officeholder, bureaucrat.

O45 **officious** *adj.* meddlesome, interfering, obtrusive.

O

O46 **offset** 1. *v.* counterbalance, set off, compensate 2. *n.* offset lithography (printing process).

O47 **offshoot** *n.* branch, shoot, addition, by-product.

O48 **offspring** *n.* children, *child,* descendant, young.

O49 **often** *adv.* frequently, repeatedly, many times, regularly (S118, S320).

O50 **ogre** *n.* monster, goblin, fiend, giant.

O51 **oil** *n.* grease, fat, lubricant, petroleum.

O52 **old** *adj.* 1. aged, elderly, mature, (Y9) 2. ancient, antique, old-fashioned (R74) 3. decaying, worn out.

O53 **omen** *n. sign,* warning.

O54 **ominous** *adj.* unfavorable, threatening, *sinister,* foreboding.

O55 **omit** *v.* leave out, neglect, *miss,* disregard, ignore (I114).

O56 **onerous** *adj.* heavy, weighty, difficult, burdensome (L90).

O57 **only** 1. *adj.* sole, solitary, alone, single 2. *adv.* merely, barely, simply, solely.

O58 **onset** *n.* 1. assault, attack, charge (R226) 2. beginning, start, opening, outset (E62).

O59 **onslaught** *n.* attack, assault, charge, storm.

O60 **onward** *adv.* forward, in advance, ahead (B5).

O61 **ooze** 1. *v.* filter, percolate, drain, leak 2. *n.* mud, mire, slime.

O62 **opaque** *adj.* obscure, clouded (T181).

O63 **open** 1. *adj.* unclosed, uncovered (S199) 2. *adj.* frank, candid, fair, honest, sincere (M287, S104, A449, U24) 3. *adj.* clear, unobstructed 4. *v.* begin, commence 5. *v.* unlock, unseal, uncover (C200, L123).

O64 **opening** *n.* 1. *aperture,* hole, gap 2. beginning, commencement 3. opportunity, chance, vacancy.

An opening to a tomb.

O65 **openly** *adv.* candidly, frankly, plainly, freely, sincerely.

O66 **operate** *v.* work, act, *function,* manage, perform, use.

O67 **operation** *n.* 1. performance, process, function, working 2. surgical process.

O68 **opinion** *n.* belief, estimation, idea, impression, viewpoint.

O69 **opponent** *n. rival,* adversary, competitor, enemy, foe, antagonist (A31, A93, C227, F255).

O70 **opportunity** *n. chance,* convenience, occasion, time.

O71 **oppose** *v. resist,* withstand, confront, thwart,

combat, contradict (C404, E67, S581).

O72 **opposite** *adj.* 1. contrary, diverse, unlike, *adverse,* opposed, hostile 2. facing, fronting.

O73 **opposition** *n.* hostility, antagonism, difference, obstruction, resistance, defiance.

O74 **oppress** *v.* burden, crush, overwhelm, persecute, maltreat, torment (R143).

O75 **oppressive** *adj.* 1. heavy, overwhelming, overpowering, hard 2. close, stifling, muggy, sultry.

O76 **optimistic** *adj.* hopeful, confident, cheerful (P173).

O77 **optional** *adj.* discretional, voluntary, elective (C286).

O78 **opulent** *adj.* wealthy, rich, affluent, flush, well off (P287).

O79 **oracle** *n.* sage, prophet, wise man, seer.

O80 **oral** *adj.* spoken, verbal, vocal, uttered, said.

O81 **oration** *n.* discourse, address, speech, lecture.

O82 **orb** *n.* globe, sphere, ball.

O83 **orbit** *n.* path, course, track, circuit, revolution.

O84 **ordain** *v.* 1. appoint, call, elect, consecrate, destine 2. decree, enact, order, prescribe.

O85 **ordeal** *n.* *trial,* test, experience, scrutiny, proof, tribulation.

O86 **order** 1. *n.* regulation, *rule,* law 2. *n.* command, mandate, direction, instruction 3. *n.* requirement, shipment, consignment; *Your order of machine parts has just arrived.* 4. *n.* arrangement, method, plan (C101, E239, M136); *Do not get those books out of order.* 5. *v.* decree, direct, instruct 6. *v.* purchase, request, demand 7. *v.* arrange, classify.

O87 **orderly** 1. *adj.* methodical *neat* (U74) 2. *adj.* well-behaved, quiet, peaceable 3. *n.* servant, attendant.

O88 **ordinary** *adj.* 1. customary, established, *normal,* regular, usual (S348) 2. average, commonplace, mediocre, common (E48, E169, E176, E225, F3, I118, M64, M163, O36, P103, Q17, R34, R153, S371, S490, S524, T194, U16, U52, U86, W96) *adv.* **ordinarily** (E131).

O89 **organization** *n.* 1. system, arrangement, structure, constitution 2. establishment, institute, association, management, group.

O90 **organize** *v.* arrange, establish, order, construct, form (R320).

O91 **orgy** *n.* carousal, revelry, debauchery.

O92 **orifice** *n.* hole, aperture, perforation, mouth.

O93 **origin** *n.* *source,* spring, fountain, beginning, birth, foundation, derivation, root (E62).

O94 **original** *adj.* 1. primitive, aboriginal, primary, first 2. creative, novel, fresh, new (H4, T209).

O95 **originate** *v.* 1. create, discover, invent, produce (E62) 2. arise, begin, *start.*

O

O96 **ornament** 1. *n*. decoration, adornment 2. *v*. decorate, embellish, beautify.

O97 **ornate** *adj*. ornamented, embellished, decorated, adorned (P234, S215, U6).

O98 **orthodox** *adj*. conventional, correct, normal, sound, true.

O99 **ostensible** *adj*. shown, declared, apparent, manifest, superficial.

O100 **ostentatious** *adj*. boastful, vain, showy, pompous, pretentious (M207).

O101 **oust** *v*. eject, expel, dislodge, evict, deprive (A56).

O102 **outbreak** *n*. 1. eruption, explosion, outburst 2. brawl, fray, conflict, revolt, riot.

O103 **outburst** *n*. outbreak, eruption, torrent.

O104 **outcast** *n*. *exile,* castaway, vagabond, wretch.

O105 **outcome** *n*. issue, *result,* consequence.

O106 **outcry** *n*. cry, scream, clamor, hue and cry, uproar.

O107 **outdo** *v*. excel, *surpass,* exceed, beat.

O108 **outfit** *n*. equipment, gear, kit, clothing, rig.

O109 **outing** *n*. excursion, expedition, holiday, trip.

O110 **outlandish** *adj*. foreign, *strange,* exotic, alien, barbarous, uncouth.

O111 **outlaw** *n*. robber, bandit, brigand, freebooter, highwayman, criminal, fugitive.

O112 **outlay** *n*. expenditure, costs, expenses (I117).

O113 **outlet** *n*. *exit,* egress, way out, opening, break, vent (E106).

O114 **outline** 1. *n*. contour, drawing, sketch, plan, draft 2. *n*. silhouette, shape 3. *v*. sketch, draw, draft.

An outline or silhouette.

O115 **outlook** *n*. 1. prospect, view, scene 2. viewpoint, attitude 3. future, chance, prospect.

O116 **output** *n*. yield, production, proceeds.

O117 **outrage** 1. *n*. insult, affront, indignity, abuse, offense 2. *v*. insult, abuse, offend, shock (C276).

O118 **outrageous** *adj*. atrocious, exorbitant, monstrous, villainous, excessive, extravagant (P461).

O119 **outright** *adv*. completely, utterly, entirely, wholly, altogether.

O120 **outset** *n*. *beginning,* commencement, opening, start (E62).

O121 **outside** 1. *n*. *exterior,* surface 2. *n*. utmost, limit 3. *adj*. exterior, external, outer (I211).

O122 **outspoken** *adj*. *frank,* candid, plain, bold, blunt.

O123 **outstanding** *adj*. 1. unsettled, unpaid, owing, due 2. conspicuous, distinguished, eminent.

O124 **outward** *adj. external,* exterior, outer, outside (I296).

O125 **outwit** *v. cheat,* deceive, defraud, confuse, baffle, trick.

O126 **overall** *adj.* comprehensive, sweeping, complete.

O127 **overawe** *v.* alarm, *intimidate,* frighten, cow (E60).

O128 **overbearing** *adj.* oppressive, overpowering, domineering, *arrogant,* imperious (H196).

O129 **overcast** *adj.* cloudy, murky, hazy, obscure (S565).

O130 **overcome** *v. subdue,* conquer, vanquish, overwhelm, defeat, crush (S534).

O131 **overdue** *adj.* delayed, late.

O132 **overflow** *v.* run over, flood, cascade, inundate.

O133 **overhaul** *v.* 1. overtake, gain upon, pass 2. examine, check, repair.

O134 **overhear** *v.* eavesdrop, *listen,* learn.

O135 **overjoyed** *adj.* delighted, rapturous, ecstatic, jubilant.

O136 **overlook** *v.* 1. disregard, neglect, miss 2. *excuse,* forgive, pardon 3. rise above, look down upon (O18).

O137 **overpower** *v. subdue,* overwhelm, overcome, vanquish (S593).

O138 **overrule** *v.* 1. control, direct, govern (A92) 2. annul, cancel, revoke, rescind, repeal.

O139 **overseer** *n.* superintendent, inspector, foreman.

O140 **oversight** *n.* 1. control, direction, management 2. error, blunder, *mistake,* neglect, fault.

O141 **overtake** *v.* pass, catch, overhaul.

O142 **overthrow** *v. vanquish,* conquer, defeat, beat, destroy.

O143 **overture** *n.* 1. invitation, offer, proposal 2. (music) introduction, prelude, opening.

O144 **overwhelm** *v.* 1. *defeat,* conquer, overpower 2. submerge, sink, drown, flood, swallow up.

O145 **owe** *v.* be indebted to, be due, be owing.

O146 **own** *v.* 1. *possess,* hold, have 2. admit, allow, confess, avow.

O147 **owner** *n. proprietor,* possessor, holder, landlord.

P   p

P1 **pace** 1. *n. step,* walk, amble, stride 2. *n.* rate, speed 3. *v.* walk, move, go, stride.

P2 **pacific** *adj.* appeasing, mild, *peaceful,* calm, gentle, unruffled (T233).

P3 **pacify** *v.* appease, tranquilize, calm, lull (D261, I174, M5, U94).

P4 **pack** 1. *n.* bundle, package, parcel, bale, burden 2. *n.* band, clan, crew, gang, herd, mob 3. *v.* compress, stow, store, cram.

P5 **package** *n.* bundle, parcel, pack, packet, box.

P6 **packet** *n.* 1. package, bundle, parcel 2. ship.

P7 **pact** *n.* contract, agreement, treaty, bargain, bond.   PACKED

P8 **pad** 1. *n.* cushion, pillow, wadding 2. *n.* notebook, blotter 3. *v.* protect, stuff.

P9 **paddle** 1. *n.* oar, scull 2. *v.* wade, bathe, dip.

P10 **pagan** *adj. & n.* heathen.

P11 **page** 1. *n.* boy servant, attendant 2. *n.* paper, leaf, *sheet* 3. *v.* find by calling name.

P12 **pageant** *n.* show, spectacle, display.

P13 **pain** 1. *n.* suffering, distress, discomfort, *ache,* pang, agony (C239) 2. *n.* misery, sorrow, grief, heartache (E6, J32, P251) 3. *v.* torment, torture 4. *v.* disquiet, trouble, grieve.
PANE

P14 **painful** *adj.* distressing, agonizing, sore, aching.

P15 **painstaking** *adj. careful,* assiduous, hardworking, exacting (C42).

P16 **paint** 1. *v.* sketch, portray, picture, draw, cover 2. *n.* pigment, color.

P17 **painting** *n.* picture, sketch, composition, portrait.

P18 **pair** *n.* two, couple.
PARE PEAR

P19 **pal** *n.* chum, friend, companion, *fellow* (E70).

P20 **palace** *n.* castle, mansion, stately home (H181).

P21 **palatable** *adj.* savory, delicious, enjoyable, *tasty.*

P22 **pale** 1. *adj.* white, pallid, wan, ashen (D21) 2. *adj.* dim, obscure, faint (B152) 3. *n.* picket, stake, fence, paling.
PAIL

P23 **pall** 1. *v.* dispirit, depress, discourage 2. *n.* cloak, cover, shroud.

P24 **palm** *n.* 1. hand 2. palm tree.

P25 **palpitate** *v. throb,* flutter, tremble, quiver.

P26 **paltry** *adj.* small, little, *trifling,* insignificant, petty (I68).

P27 **pamper** *v. spoil,* fondle, favor, coddle (S75).

Panes of glass.

P28 **pamphlet** *n.* booklet, brochure, leaflet.

P29 **pan** *n.* pot, vessel, kettle, skillet, cauldron.

P30 **pander** *v. please,* gratify, provide.

P31 **panel** *n.* 1. partition, wall board 2. team, group, committee, forum.

P32 **pang** *n.* pain, *throb,* twinge, grip, hurt.

P33 **panic** 1. *n.* fright, *alarm,* terror, dread 2. *v.* terrify, frighten, stampede (C15).

P34 **pant** *v.* puff, gasp, blow, wheeze.

P35 **pantry** *n.* larder, buttery.

P36 **paper** *n.* 1. writing material 2. document, writing, record 3. article, essay, dissertation, report; *Professor Jones has just written a paper on garden flowers.* 4. journal, newspaper.

P37 **par** *n.* equality, average, normal.

P38 **parade** 1. *n.* display, ceremony, *show,* pageant 2. *v.* display, show off, flaunt, strut.

P39 **paradise** *n.* Eden, Elysium, heaven, utopia.

P40 **paradox** *n.* absurdity, reversal, ambivalence, contradiction, enigma, mystery.

P41 **paragraph** *n.* passage, clause, section, sentence, item.

P42 **parallel** 1. *adj.* like, similar, resembling 2. *n.* resemblance, counterpart, equal 3. *v.* resemble, match, equal.

P43 **paralyze** *v.* deaden, unnerve, numb, benumb, transfix.

P44 **paramount** *adj.* supreme, superior, principal, chief, eminent (I169).

P45 **paraphernalia** *n.* trappings, equipment, baggage, belongings, ornaments.

P46 **parasite** *n.* toady, flatterer, sycophant, hanger-on, leech.

P47 **parcel** *n.* bundle, package, collection, lot.

P48 **parch** *v. dry,* shrivel, scorch, brown.

P49 **parched** *adj. thirsty,* dry, arid, withered, scorched (M210, W53).

P50 **pardon** 1. *v. forgive,* absolve, excuse, discharge, release, clear (A180, C309, R220) 2. *n.* forgiveness, remission, absolution, grace, mercy, acquittal *adj.* **pardonable** (I158).

P51 **pare** *v.* 1. *peel,* cut, shave, clip, skin 2. diminish, reduce, lessen.   PAIR PEAR.

P52 **parentage** *n.* extraction, birth, descent, lineage, pedigree, origin, ancestry.

P53 **park** 1. *n.* grassland, garden, wood, enclosure, green 2. *v.* settle, place, station, post, leave, put.

P54 **parley** *v.* talk, converse, discourse, discuss.

P55 **parody** 1. *n.* travesty, burlesque, imitation, *satire* 2. *v.* imitate, caricature.

P56 **parry** *v.* ward off, turn aside, prevent, avert, avoid.

P57 **parsimonious** *adj.* stingy, *mean,* close, avaricious, miserly, closefisted (G38).

P58 **parson** *n.* clergyman, minister, *priest,* rector, pastor, vicar.

P59 **part** 1. *n. piece,* portion, fragment, section 2. *n.* character, role (W65) 3. *n.* component, division, element 4. *v.* break, divide, sever, split (U53) *adv.* **partly** (A99, O119).

P60 **partial** *adj.* incomplete, imperfect, limited (A17, C282, E104, W65) 2. biased, prejudiced, unjust (I47, J44).

P61 **participate** *v.* partake, share, take part in.

P62 **particle** *n. bit,* piece, scrap, speck, grain, spot.

P

P

P63 **particular** 1. *adj.* especial, special, specific (G35, U55) 2. *adj.* distinctive, exceptional, unusual 3. *adj.* precise, careful, fastidious 4. *n.* feature, detail, circumstance.

P64 **parting** 1. *n.* farewell, leave-taking (M107) 2. *n.* separation, breaking, division 3. *adj.* departing, declining.

P65 **partisan** 1. *n.* follower, supporter, disciple 2. *adj.* biased, prejudiced.

P66 **partition** 1. *n.* division, separation 2. *n.* barrier, wall, screen 3. *v.* apportion, share, divide.

P67 **partner** *n.* 1. associate, *colleague,* partaker 2. spouse, companion, consort, husband, wife.

P68 **partnership** *n.* union, connection, company, association, alliance.

P69 **party** *n.* 1. set, circle, ring, league, alliance 2. group, *company,* assembly, crowd 3. person, individual; *When Joan and Mary met, Tom was the third party.* 4. gathering, social, get-together.

P70 **pass** 1. *v.* go, move, proceed 2. *v.* elapse, lapse, pass away, cease 3. *v.* experience, suffer, occur; *We passed the time by playing cards.* 4. *v.* convey, deliver, send 5. v. disregard, ignore; *Fred was passed over and not invited.* 6. *v.* exceed, excel, surpass 7. *v.* approve, enact 8. *n.* license, permit 9. *n.* gorge, ravine 10. *n.* avenue, road, way.

P71 **passage** *n.* 1. passing, transit, movement 2. journey, voyage, trip 3. clause, sentence, paragraph 4. gallery, corridor.

P72 **passenger** *n.* traveler, wayfarer, tourist.

P73 **passion** *n.* 1. rapture, fervor, *zeal,* excitement 2. love, affection, fondness, attachment.

P74 **passionate** *adj.* 1. warm, *ardent,* enthusiastic, fervent, zealous 2. excitable, impatient, angry.

P75 **passive** *adj.* inactive, quiet, unresisting, submissive (A45).

P76 **past** 1. *adj.* gone, spent, ended 2. *adj.* former, previous 3. *n.* past time, bygone time (F303). PASSED

P77 **pastime** *n.* amusement, entertainment, sport, hobby (P410).

P78 **pastor** *n.* clergyman, *minister.*

P79 **pastry** *n.* cake, gâteau, tart, confection, sweet, dough.

P80 **pasture** *n.* grassland, herbage, grass, meadow, *field.*

P81 **pat** *v.* & *n.* rap, tap, hit.

P82 **patch** *v.* mend, repair, restore, fix.

P83 **patent** 1. *n.* copyright, invention, protection 2. *adj.* apparent, clear, evident, obvious.

P84 **path** *n. road,* track, trail, way, route, passage, lane.

P85 **pathetic** *adj.* affecting, touching, tender, pitiable.

P86 **patience** *n.* 1. endurance, perseverance, persistence (I49) 2. calmness, composure, courage. PATIENTS

P87 **patient** 1. *adj.* persevering, persistent (I49) 2. *adj.* submissive, uncomplaining, calm 3. *n.* invalid, sufferer.

P88 **patriotic** *adj. loyal,* nationalistic, chauvinistic.

P89 **patrol** 1. *v. guard,* watch, protect 2. *n.* sentry, watchman, guard.

P90 **patronize** *v.* 1. favor, support, assist, help 2. condescend, look down upon, disdain.

P91 **patter** *n.* 1. chat, chatter, jabber, prattle 2. rattle, tapping.

P92 **pattern** *n.* specimen, sample, model, prototype.

P93 **pauper** *n.* poor person.

P94 **pause** 1. *n. stop,* halt, rest, hesitation, break 2. *v.* stop, cease, desist, wait, delay (C375). PAWS

P95 **paw** *n.* foot, claw, talon.

P96 **pawn** *v.* pledge, stake, wager, deposit.

P97 **pay** 1. *v.* discharge, settle, compensate, *reward* 2. *n.* salary, wages, payment.

P98 **peace** *n.* 1. calm, quiet, stillness, serenity 2. harmony, concord (O106, R266, S503, T230). PIECE

P99 **peaceful** *adj.* calm, tranquil, serene, friendly, pacific (M61, M146, R213, T233).

P100 **peak** *n.* top, summit, crest, crown, pinnacle (B29). PIQUE

P101 **peal** *v.* ring, chime, toll, sound, echo, boom. PEEL

P102 **peasant** *n.* countryman, yokel, rustic.

Peasant plowing.

P103 **peculiar** *adj.* 1. *unusual,* uncommon, exceptional, strange, queer (E152) 2. special, particular, individual.

P104 **pedal** *v.* drive, push with foot.

P105 **peddle** *v.* hawk, sell, vend, retail.

P106 **peddler** *n.* salesman, hawker, vendor, trader.

P107 **pedestrian** 1. *n.* foot traveler, walker, hiker 2. *adj.* monotonous, prosy, slow, dull, stodgy, prosaic.

P108 **pedigree** *n.* descent, lineage, ancestry, breed.

P109 **peel** 1. *n.* skin, rind, hull, coat 2. *v. pare,* strip, skin. PEAL

P110 **peep** *n. & v.* 1. peer, look, glimpse 2. cheep, chirp, cry.

P111 **peer** 1. *n.* equal, equivalent, companion 2. *n.* lord, nobleman 3. *v.* peep, examine, pry. PIER

P112 **peevish** *adj.* fretful, irritable, cross, *testy,* petulant (A104).

P113 **peg** *n.* fastening, hanger, stopper, pin.

P

P114 **pell-mell** *adv.* confusedly, disorderly, helter-skelter.

P115 **pelt** 1. *v.* strike, beat, batter, assail, throw 2. *v.* dash, rush, flash, streak 3. *v.* rain, pour, stream 4. *n.* hide, skin, coat, fur.

P127 **pension** *n.* 1. (**pen-**_shun_) allowance, annuity, grant 2. (_pens-_**yone**) boardinghouse, hotel.

P128 **pensive** *adj.* thoughtful, reflective, dreamy, contemplative, wistful.

Pen and nib.

P116 **pen** 1. *n.* writing instrument, quill 2. *n.* enclosure, sty, coop, cage 3. *v.* write, compose, inscribe.

P117 **penalty** *n.* punishment, fine, *forfeit* (R245).

P118 **penance** *n.* punishment, penalty, humiliation.

P119 **pencil** 1. *n.* crayon, brush 2. *v.* depict, draw, sketch, mark.

P120 **pendant** *n.* earring, pennant, chandelier, hanging.

P121 **pending** 1. *adj.* depending, undecided, waiting 2. *prep.* during.

P122 **penetrate** *v.* 1. *pierce,* perforate, bore, enter, permeate (E224) 2. discern, comprehend, understand.

P123 **penetrating** *adj. sharp,* subtle, discerning, acute, keen, shrewd (B101).

P124 **penitence** *n.* repentance, *remorse,* sorrow, contrition, regret.

P125 **pennant** *n.* flag, pendant, streamer, banner.

P126 **penniless** *adj.* destitute, *poor,* needy, poverty-stricken (R249).

P129 **people** 1. *n.* tribe, nation, race, family 2. *n.* population, folk, persons, human beings 3. *v.* populate.

P130 **pep** *n.* vigor, power, vim, punch, guts.

P131 **peppery** *adj.* 1. hot, pungent 2. irritable, irascible, testy, churlish, hasty.

P132 **perceive** *v.* 1. *see,* discover, notice, remark, observe 2. understand, comprehend, grasp (M191).

P133 **perch** *n.* 1. rod, pole, staff 2. roost 3. fish.

P134 **percolate** *v.* filter, ooze, strain, drain *n.* **percolator.**

P135 **perfect** 1. *adj.* faultless, *excellent,* complete, flawless, blameless (D63, F59, F144, I55) 2. *adj.* entire, total 3. *v.* accomplish, finish, complete *n.* **perfection** (F58).

P136 **perforate** *v. pierce,* penetrate, bore, drill, puncture.

P137 **perform** *v.* 1. do, execute, effect, achieve 2. act, play, present.

P138 **performer** *n.* actor, player, musician, entertainer (S354).

P139 **perfume** *n.* fragrance, aroma, smell, scent, odor.

P140 **perhaps** *adv.* perchance, possibly, maybe, conceivably (A17).

P141 **peril** *n. danger,* hazard, jeopardy, risk (S8).

P142 **period** *n.* time, term, era, epoch, age, interval, span, cycle, course.

P143 **periodical** 1. *n.* magazine, journal, review, paper, publication 2. *adj.* recurring regularly, recurrent, intermittent, regular.

P144 **perish** *v.* die, expire, decease, pass away (E69) 2. decay, waste, wither, shrivel *adj.* **perishable** (D341, I41).

P145 **perky** *adj.* pert, trim, jaunty, airy.

P146 **permanent** *adj.* lasting, enduring, durable, stable, steadfast, *perpetual,* constant (F150, T54, T179).

P147 **permission** *n. consent,* leave, license, liberty, authorization.

P148 **permit** 1. *v. allow,* let, tolerate, endure (F191, P418) 2. *n.* permission, license, pass.

P149 **pernicious** *adj.* hurtful, harmful, injurious, mischievous, destructive, fatal, deadly (H46).

P150 **perpendicular** *adj.* vertical, upright (H164).

P151 **perpetrate** *v.* do, commit, perform, execute, achieve.

P152 **perpetual** *adj.* endless, unceasing, everlasting, eternal, ceaseless, continual, permanent (T54).

P153 **perplex** *v.* puzzle, *bewilder,* mystify, confuse, confound (E85).

P154 **persecute** *v.* oppress, *harass,* distress, torment, victimize.

P155 **persevere** *v. persist,* continue, stand firm, endure (L23).

P156 **persist** *v.* continue, remain, last, endure, persevere (R108).

P157 **persistent** *adj.* constant, enduring, determined, dogged, stubborn.

P158 **person** *n.* individual, one, somebody, human being.

P159 **personal** *adj.* individual, private, special, secret, particular (P465).

P160 **personality** *n.* individuality, character, identity.

P161 **perspective** *n.* vista, prospect, view, aspect, outlook.

P162 **perspire** *v.* sweat.

P163 **persuade** (*per*-swade) *v. induce,* influence, entice, convince, urge, coax (E73).

P164 **persuasive** *adj.* convincing, logical, enticing, compelling (D330).

P165 **pert** *adj.* lively, brisk, smart, dapper, sprightly, nimble, flippant, *saucy* (P280).

P166 **pertain** *v.* appertain, befit, belong, concern.

P167 **pertinent** *adj.* fit, *appropriate,* suitable, relevant (I99).

P168 **perturb** *v.* disquiet, trouble, *disturb,* agitate, confuse.

P

P169 **peruse** v. read, study, observe, examine, scrutinize.

P170 **pervade** v. permeate, penetrate, spread, fill.

P171 **perverse** adj. obstinate, stubborn, willful, dogged, contrary (O3).

P172 **pervert** v. distort, falsify, entice, tempt, corrupt.

P173 **pessimistic** adj. unhappy, cheerless, gloomy, doubtful (O76).

P174 **pest** n. 1. plague, pestilence, infection, curse, affliction, nuisance 2. vermin, insect, virus, germ.

P175 **pester** v. annoy, harass, plague, vex, hector, bother, bore, badger.

P176 **pestilence** n. plague, pest, epidemic.

P177 **pet** 1. v. fondle, indulge, caress 2. n. favorite, darling.

P178 **petition** 1. n. request, appeal, application 2. v. entreat, solicit, ask, beg, appeal.

P179 **petrify** v. 1. astonish, amaze, stun, dumbfound 2. change to stone.

P180 **petty** adj. 1. little, small, trifling, trivial, unimportant, slight, insignificant, paltry (I68) 2. mean, stingy, miserly (G38).

P181 **petulant** adj. irritable, fretful, peevish, hasty, touchy.

P182 **phantom** 1. n. specter, apparition, vision, spirit, ghost, spook 2. adj. ghostly, spectral, unreal, imaginary (R57).

P183 **phase** n. appearance, aspect, state, stage, condition. FAZE

P184 **phenomenal** adj. marvelous, miraculous, wondrous (C252).

P185 **phenomenon** (fee-nom-en-on) n. appearance, manifestation, marvel, wonder, happening, occurrence.

P186 **philanthropic** adj. benevolent, kind, gracious, charitable (S120).

P187 **philosophical** adj. wise, unruffled, calm, serene, tranquil.

P188 **phobia** n. fear, aversion, dislike, distaste, hatred, dread.

P189 **photograph** n. photo, picture, snapshot, film.

P190 **phrase** n. expression, idiom, sentence, clause. FRAYS

Pets.

P191 **physical** adj. 1. material, natural, mortal, substantial (M122) 2. bodily, corporeal, sensible.

P192 **pick** 1. v. pluck, gather, choose, select 2. v. steal, pilfer 3. n. pickax, pike, toothpick.

P193 **picket** 1. n. sentinel, guard, sentry 2. v. stand guard, stand watch.

P194 **pickle** n. 1. preserve 2. plight, predicament, quandary.

P195 **picture** 1. n. painting, drawing, engraving, print, photograph, illustration 2. v.

paint, draw, describe, imagine.

P196 **piebald** *adj.* motley, mottled, pied, mongrel.

P197 **piece** *n.* fragment, part, *bit,* scrap, portion, section. PEACE

P198 **pierce** *v.* 1. stab, puncture, *penetrate,* enter, perforate 2. affect, move, thrill, excite.

P199 **pig** *n.* hog, swine.

P200 **pigment** *n.* color, paint, dye, stain.

P201 **pike** *n.* 1. spike, spear, point 2. fish 3. turnpike, highway.

P202 **pile** 1. *n. heap,* mass, collection 2. *v.* collect, gather, heap up.

P203 **pilfer** *v.* steal, purloin, thieve.

P204 **pilgrim** *n.* traveler, wanderer, wayfarer, crusader.

P205 **pilgrimage** *n.* journey, expedition, tour, excursion, trip.

P206 **pill** *n.* tablet, capsule, lozenge, medicine.

P207 **pillage** *v. plunder,* despoil, sack, rifle.

P208 **pillar** *n.* column, post, monument, prop.

P209 **pillow** *n.* cushion, bolster, headrest.

P210 **pilot** 1. *n.* steersman, helmsman, *guide,* aviator 2. *v.* guide, direct, conduct, steer.

P211 **pimple** *n.* blotch, *spot,* eruption, swelling.

P212 **pin** 1. *n.* peg, bolt, fastener, clip, brooch 2. *v.* fasten, fix, transfix.

P213 **pinch** 1. *v. nip,* squeeze, compress, tweak 2. *n.* nip, pang, squeeze 3. *n.* emergency, crisis, difficulty.

P214 **pine** *v.* languish, droop, yearn, lament.

P215 **pinnacle** *n.* turret, minaret, top, *summit,* apex, zenith, peak.

P216 **pious** *adj.* religious, godly, holy, devout, saintly (P408).

P217 **pipe** *n.* 1. tobacco pipe 2. musical instrument, whistle 3. tube, reed, hose.

P218 **piquant** *adj.* pungent, biting, tart, spicy.

P219 **pique** 1. *v.* offend, displease, affront, vex 2. *n.* resentment, grudge, irritation. PEAK

P220 **pirate** 1. *n.* corsair, buccaneer, privateer 2. *v.* plagiarize, copy, annex, appropriate.

P221 **pistol** *n.* firearm, gun, revolver. PISTIL

P222 **pit** *n.* cavity, hollow, hole, well, mine.

P223 **pitch** 1. *v. throw,* cast, fling, hurl, toss 2. *v.* encamp 3. *v.* plunge, fall 4. *n.* slope, slant, angle.

P224 **pitcher** *n.* jug, ewer, jar, pot.

P225 **piteous** *adj.* sorrowful, woeful, pitiable, *miserable.*

P226 **pitiless** *adj.* merciless, ruthless, cruel, unfeeling (G42, K8).

P227 **pity** 1. *n. compassion,* mercy, sympathy, charity (C497) 2. *v.* commiserate, sympathize.

P228 **pivot** *n.* swivel, turn, hinge, fulcrum.

P229 **placard** *n.* poster, bill, handbill, advertisement, notice.

P230 **placate** *v.* conciliate, appease, *pacify.*

P231 **place** 1. *n.* area, district, location, region, site, spot, situation, position 2. *n.* city, town, village 3. *n.* house, home resident, dwelling 4. *n.* post, office, job, employment 5. *v.* put, set, *lay,* seat, locate, deposit, establish.   PLAICE

P232 **placid** *adj.* quiet, tranquil, unruffled, *calm,* peaceful, serene, composed (T51).

P233 **plague** 1. *n.* pestilence, epidemic, contagion, disease 2. *n.* annoyance, vexation, trouble (B116) 3. *v.* annoy, tease, vex, worry, trouble, molest (P249); *The children are constantly plaguing me to go to the zoo.*

P234 **plain** 1. *adj.* even, smooth, level, flat (U36) 2. *adj.* manifest, obvious, clear, certain, understandable 3. *adj.* simple, unadorned, ordinary (F38, G116, L177, M12, O97) 4. *adj.* homely, ugly, unattractive (P372) 5. *adj.* honest, sincere, straightforward, frank 6. *n.* plateau, pampas, savanna, prairie, steppe.   PLANE

P235 **plan** 1. *n.* sketch, draft, plot, map, chart, drawing 2. *n.* scheme, proposal, system, design 3. *v.* devise, contrive, concoct, plot, arrange.

P236 **plane** 1. *adj.* level, flat, even, smooth, plain 2. *n.* airplane, aircraft.   PLAIN

P237 **plant** 1. *n.* shrub, vegetable, herb, bush, flower 2. *n.* factory, mill, works, equipment, machinery 3. *v.* sow, scatter, seed.

P238 **plaster** 1. *n.* mortar, stucco, cement 2. *n.* dressing, bandage, lint, gauze 3. *v.* daub, smear, coat, cover.

P239 **plastic** 1. *n.* polyethylene, polystyrene, celluloid, latex, thermoplastic 2. *adj.* soft, pliable, flexible, malleable.

P240 **plate** 1. *n.* dish, platter, silverware, engraving 2. *v.* laminate, coat, cover.

P241 **platform** *n.* 1. stage, rostrum, podium, pulpit 2. policy, program, plan, principle; *The new party's platform was based on free trade.*

P242 **plausible** *adj.* 1. *glib,* specious, superficial, deceptive (G43) 2. likely, fair, credible, reasonable (I129).

P243 **play** 1. *v.* sport, frolic, skip, frisk, gambol, caper (W100) 2. *v.* toy, trifle, dally; *At this school, pupils are expected to work, not just play.* 3. *v.* act, perform, impersonate, represent 4. *v.* compete, game, gamble, contend 5. *v.* operate, work; *Can you play the harmonica?* 6. *n.* show, drama,

A plane.

comedy, tragedy, melodrama, farce 7. *n.* amusement, sport, game, recreation.

P244 **player** *n.* sportsman, contestant, competitor, actor.

P245 **playful** *adj. frisky,* merry, jolly, humorous, amusing, lively (F86, S135).

P246 **plea** *n.* 1. request, appeal, entreaty 2. defense, excuse, apology, cause.

P247 **plead** *v.* 1. *reason,* argue, dispute, defend (D109) 2. appeal, excuse, beg, entreaty (R114).

P248 **pleasant** *adj. agreeable,* delightful, gratifying, pleasurable, charming, amiable (D197, H166, O13, O41, R187, S332, T65, T71, U65).

P249 **please** 1. *v. gratify,* delight, satisfy, content (A115, V49) 2. *v.* like, prefer, choose, wish 3. *interj.* polite request *adj.* **pleased** (I297, S328).

P250 **pleasing** *adj.* agreeable, welcome, pleasant, charming (F259, H53, O41).

P251 **pleasure** *n.* enjoyment, comfort, *delight,* joy, gladness, happiness (A111, O39).

P252 **pledge** 1. *n. promise,* vow, guarantee, oath 2. *v.* promise, guarantee, agree 3. *v.* pawn, deposit, plight.

P253 **plentiful** *adj. abundant,* ample, full, fruitful, enough (I182, M90, S52).

P254 **plenty** *n.* abundance, sufficiency, enough (F33, I235, L4).

P255 **pliable** *adj. flexible,* pliant, supple, lithe, adaptable (I176, O21, R261).

P256 **plight** *n.* condition, state, situation, dilemma, scrape, *predicament.*

P257 **plod** *v.* jog, trudge, labor, toil.

P258 **plot** 1. *n. scheme,* plan, conspiracy, intrigue 2. *n.* story, fable, outline, theme 3. *n.* patch, allotment, site 4. *v.* plan, scheme, contrive, devise.

P259 **plow** *v.* till, furrow, cultivate, work.

P260 **pluck** 1. *v.* gather, pick, pull, jerk, tug, snatch (P237) 2. *n.* spirit, courage, nerve, boldness, bravery (C451).

P261 **plucky** *adj. brave,* courageous, bold, valiant, heroic (C451).

P262 **plug** 1. *n.* stopper, cork, peg 2. *v.* block, obstruct, caulk 3. *v.* advertise, puff, boost, hype.

P263 **plump** *adj.* stout, portly, fat, *chubby,* round, obese, chunky (L21, M90).

P264 **plunder** 1. *v.* spoil, rob, *rifle,* sack, ravage, loot 2. *n.* robbery, booty, loot, spoils.

P265 **plunge** 1. *v.* immerse, submerge, dive, dip 2. *n. dive,* dip, ducking, jump.

P266 **ply** 1. *v.* practice, employ, use, ask 2. *v.* go, commute, run 3. *n.* film, layer, laminate.

P267 **poach** *v.* 1. cook 2. purloin, steal, filch.

P268 **pocket** 1. *n.* pouch, compartment 2. *v.* steal, take.

P269 **poem** *n.* verse, poetry, lyric, ballad.

P270 **poetry** *n.* rhyme, verse, lyric.

P

P271 **poignant** *adj.* sharp, severe, piercing, distressing, pointed (M145).

P272 **point** 1. *n.* end, tip 2. *n.* spot, place, location, locality 3. *n.* cape, headland 4. *n.* object, end, aim, purpose 5. *n.* moment, instant, period 6. *n.* dot, speck 7. *v.* aim, direct, guide 8. *v.* indicate, show.

P273 **poise** 1. *n. balance,* steadiness 2. *n.* composure, confidence, control, dignity (A186) 3. *v.* balance, hold in place.

P274 **poison** 1. *n.* venom, virus, toxin, taint 2. *v.* infect, taint, contaminate, corrupt, pollute.

P275 **poisonous** *adj.* toxic, lethal, noxious, deadly, baneful (H46).

P276 **poke** *v. thrust,* push, shove, jog, jab.

P277 **pole** *n.* rod, staff, stick, post, column, shaft.

P278 **policy** *n.* stratagem, action, approach, course, plan, system, program, tactics.

P279 **polish** 1. *v.* burnish, furbish, brighten, *shine* (T30) 2. *n.* brightness, sheen, shine, luster 3. *n.* grace, refinement, elegance *adj.* **polished** (D333).

P280 **polite** *adj. courteous,* civil, affable, gracious, well-bred, respectful (B164, C152, I59, I87, I218, P165, R313, S39, V94) *n.* **politeness** (S38).

P281 **poll** 1. *n.* voting, election, survey, questionnaire 2. *n.* head 3. *v.* lop, clip, shear, crop, mow.

P282 **pollute** *v. contaminate,* defile, taint, foul (P481).

P283 **pomp** *n.* ceremony, display, splendor, magnificence, show, pageantry (S215).

P284 **pompous** *adj.* bombastic, boastful, pretentious, grandiose (U9).

P285 **ponder** *v. consider,* contemplate, study, meditate, examine.

P286 **pool** 1. *n.* puddle, lake, mere 2. *v.* contribute, combine.

P287 **poor** *adj.* 1. penniless, impoverished, needy, poverty-stricken, destitute (G116, O78, P445, R246, W38) 2. unsound, faulty, unsatisfactory, inferior (E167, S35) 3. unlucky, unhappy, pitiable, unfortunate.

P288 **pop** *v.* 1. explode, burst, detonate, bang 2. enter, insert; *Pop this card into the envelope.*

P289 **popular** *adj.* 1. *favorite,* well liked, approved, accepted, famous (D234) 2. current, prevailing, common, general.

P290 **population** *n.* people, inhabitants.

P291 **port** *n.* harbor, haven, anchorage, entrance.

P292 **portable** *adj.* movable, light, handy, convenient.

P293 **porter** *n.* doorkeeper, carrier, doorman, caretaker.

P294 **portion** *n. part,* piece, fragment, bit, scrap, morsel (W65).

P295 **portly** *adj.* stout, *plump,* rotund, bulky (S256, S260).

P296 **portrait** *n.* picture, likeness, painting.

P297 **portray** *v.* paint, depict, draw, sketch, represent.

P298 **pose** 1. *v.* sit, model 2. *v.* affect, pretend, feign 3. *v.* puzzle, embarrass, mystify; *Tom's disappearance poses a problem.* 4. *n.* attitude, position, posture.

P299 **poser** *n.* riddle, enigma, mystery.

P300 **position** 1. *n.* station, *situation,* place, locality 2. *n.* attitude, posture, pose 3. *n.* employment, job, post, situation 4. *n.* state, condition, circumstances 5. *v.* place, put, situate.

P301 **positive** *adj.* 1. defined, *precise,* definite, clear, certain (A65) 2. real, actual, substantial.

P302 **possess** *v. own,* have, hold, occupy, control (W16).

Pouring.

P303 **possession** *n.* ownership, occupation, control, property.

P304 **possible** *adj.* likely, feasible, potential, practicable (I71).

P305 **post** 1. *n.* pillar, column, shaft, pole 2. *n.* job, employment, situation, office 3. *n.* station, position, seat 4. *n.* mail, letters, correspondence 5. *v.* mail, send.

P306 **poster** *n.* placard, advertisement, bill.

P307 **posterior** *adj.* hind, back, rear, after (F267).

P308 **postpone** *v. defer,* delay, adjourn, put off.

P309 **posture** *n.* position, pose, attitude, deportment.

P310 **posy** *n.* bouquet, bunch of flowers, nosegay.

P311 **pot** *n.* pan, skillet, saucepan, jar, crock.

P312 **potential** 1. *adj.* possible, likely, latent 2. *n.* capability, capacity, ability *adj.* **potent** (F71).

P313 **pottery** *n.* earthenware, china, ceramics.

P314 **pouch** *n.* bag, sack, pocket.

P315 **pounce** *v.* seize, *attack,* jump on, swoop, bound.

P316 **pound** *v. beat,* strike, bruise, crush, pulverize.

P317 **pour** *v.* flow, emit, issue, stream, discharge. PORE

P318 **pout** *v.* look sullen, *sulk,* fret, frown, scowl.

P319 **poverty** *n.* 1. penury, want, need, necessity, beggary, lack (W38) 2. scarcity, barrenness, sterility (A21).

P320 **powder** *n.* dust, ash filings.

P321 **power** *n.* 1. *ability,* capacity (I91) 2. force, *energy,* strength 3. authority, rule, control, command.

P322 **powerful** *adj.* mighty, potent, *strong,* robust, commanding (F71, W37).

P323 **practical** *adj.* accomplished, *efficient,* qualified, sound, useful, attainable (R288, U80).

P

P324 **practice** 1. *n.* custom, habit, use, usage, tradition 2. *n.* performance, doing, operation 3. *n. & v.* exercise, drill.

P325 **praise** 1. *v. commend,* approve, applaud, admire (D101, G51, M28, P474, R13, R69, R181, R253, S66, S246) 2. *n.* commendation, approval, glorification, compliment (M202, S51). PRAYS PREYS

P326 **prank** *n.* caper, trick, joke, antic.

P327 **prattle** *v. & n.* prate, gabble, chatter.

P328 **pray** *v.* 1. ask, request, entreat, beseech 2. worship, adore, supplicate. PREY

P329 **prayer** *n.* entreaty, request, petition, invocation, worship.

P330 **preach** *v.* teach, urge, discourse, lecture, proclaim.

P331 **precarious** *adj.* hazardous, perilous, unreliable, uncertain, doubtful (S106).

P332 **precaution** *n.* forethought, prudence, providence, wariness, care, safeguard (C42).

P333 **precede** *v.* go before, head, introduce, lead, usher, herald (E95, S544).

P334 **precedence** *n.* priority, lead, supremacy, preference (I169) *adj.* **preceding** (P307, S537).

P335 **precinct** *n.* limit, bound, boundary, district.

P336 **precious** *adj.* 1. costly, priceless, *valuable* (C119) 2. beloved, dear, darling, cherished, prized.

P337 **precipice** *n.* cliff, crag, bluff.

P338 **precipitate** 1. *v.* hurry, hasten, speed, expedite 2. *v.* throw, hurl 3. *adj.* hasty, hurried, rash, reckless, indiscreet.

P339 **precise** *adj.* 1. *exact,* correct, definite, explicit (A136, I127) 2. scrupulous, strict, careful, formal, rigid (I180).

P340 **precision** *n.* exactness, accuracy, correctness.

P341 **preclude** *v. prevent,* hinder, debar, stop, obviate.

P342 **precocious** *adj.* premature, forward, advanced.

P343 **predecessor** *n.* forerunner, ancestor, forefather.

P344 **predicament** *n.* situation, *condition,* state, plight, dilemma.

P345 **predict** *v.* foresee, foretell, prophesy, forecast.

P346 **predominant** *adj.* prevalent, prevailing, dominant, supreme (S103).

P347 **preface** *n.* introduction, preamble, foreword, prologue.

P348 **prefer** *v. favor,* choose, select, fancy, single out (R129).

P349 **preference** *n.* choice, selection, priority.

P350 **pregnant** *adj.* 1. with child, gestant 2. productive, fertile, fruitful 3. meaningful, significant.

P351 **prejudice** 1. *n. bias,* unfairness, partiality 2. *v.* influence, warp *adj.* **prejudiced** (I47).

P352 **preliminary** *adj.* introductory, preparatory.

P353 **premature** *adj.* unseasonable, early, untimely, unexpected (P425).

P354 **premeditated** *adj.* intended, *planned,* deliberate, prearranged, (A27, S376).

P355 **premium** *n.* 1. reward, recompense, bounty, prize, bonus (D218) 2. enhancement, appreciation.

P356 **prepare** *v.* provide, procure, get ready, *arrange,* order *adj.* prepared (I81).

P357 **preposterous** *adj. absurd,* unreasonable, extravagant, ridiculous.

P358 **prescribe** *v.* direct, order, recommend, ordain, decree.

P359 **presence** *n.* 1. attendance, nearness, vicinity, neighborhood (A16) 2. air, appearance, demeanor, bearing.   PRESENTS

P360 **present** 1. (**pres**-*ent*) *n. gift,* donation, offering, gratuity 2. *adj.* existing, extant, instant, current (P76) 3. (*pree-***zent**) *v.* give, bestow, proffer, donate 4. *v.* introduce, show, display, exhibit.

P361 **presently** *adv.* 1. directly, immediately, forthwith 2. soon, shortly.

P362 **preserve** 1. *v. keep,* guard, save, secure, shield (S401) 2. *n.* jam, jelly.

P363 **press** 1. *v.* push 2. *v.* compress, squeeze 3. *v.* smooth, iron 4. *v.* embrace, hug, clasp 5. *v.* compel, force 6. *v.* hasten, hurry 7. *n.* journalism, newspapers 8. *n.* printing machine.

P364 **pressure** *n.* urgency, hurry, force, influence, power.

P365 **prestige** *n.* credit, distinction, importance, influence, reputation.

P366 **presume** *v. suppose,* think, surmise, believe, assume.

P367 **presumption** *n.* 1. belief, supposition, conjecture, guess 2. arrogance, audacity, boldness, effrontery (M208).

P368 **presumptuous** *adj.* arrogant, bold, forward, insolent, impudent.

P369 **pretend** *v.* 1. *feign,* affect, simulate, sham, deceive 2. make believe, act 3. claim, strive for, aspire *adj.* **pretended** (A46).

P370 **pretentious** *adj.* assuming, ostentatious, affected (H196).

P371 **pretext** *n.* appearance, guise, cloak, semblance.

P372 **pretty** *adj. beautiful,* attractive, comely, fair, lovely (P234, U1).

P373 **prevalent** *adj.* prevailing, predominant, common, extensive, customary (U16).

Printing presses.

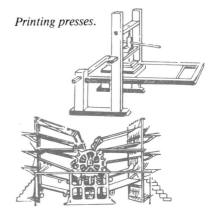

129

P

P374 **prevent** v. obstruct, hinder, impede, thwart, interrupt, slow, keep from, block (E56).

P375 **previous** adj. prior, former, preceding, earlier (S537).

P376 **price** 1. n. cost, value, charge, expense 2. v. value, charge, mark up.

P377 **priceless** adj. invaluable, inestimable, precious (C119).

P378 **prick** 1. v. puncture, perforate, pierce 2. v. sting, wound 3. n. puncture, perforation.

P379 **pride** n. 1. self-esteem, conceit, vanity, haughtiness 2. self-respect, dignity (M208, S156). PRIED

P380 **priest** n. clergyman, minister, pastor, parson.

P381 **prim** adj. formal, stiff, precise, straitlaced, proper (I180).

P382 **primary** adj. 1. primitive, original, first, earliest (S103) 2. chief, principal, main.

P383 **prime** adj. 1. first, original, primary (I169) 2. first-rate, best, excellent.

P384 **primitive** adj. 1. aboriginal, primeval, ancient, simple 2. barbarous, uncivilized, archaic, rough (S323).

P385 **principal** 1. adj. main, leading, foremost, first, essential (S103) 2. n. chief, head, leader. PRINCIPLE

P386 **principle** n. 1. doctrine, tenet, rule, law, standard 2. integrity, rectitude, virtue, honor (D232). PRINCIPAL

P387 **print** 1. v. impress, press, engrave, imprint 2. v. develop (photography) 3. n. mark, stamp 4. n. engraving, lithograph, etching, picture 5. n. printing, typematter adj. **printed** (O80).

P388 **prior** adj. former, preceding, earlier, previous (S537).

P389 **priority** n. superior in rank or order, precedence.

P390 **prison** n. jail, dungeon, lockup.

P391 **private** adj. 1. secluded, solitary, quiet 2. personal, special, individual (P465) 3. confidential, secret, concealed.

P392 **prize** 1. n. reward, premium, bounty, award 2. v. esteem, value, appraise. PRIES

P393 **probable** adj. likely, credible, reasonable, feasible (I71, I80, U60).

P394 **probe** v. investigate, scrutinize, examine, search, explore.

P395 **problem** n. 1. puzzle, riddle, question 2. dilemma, dispute, doubt, difficulty (S317).

P396 **procedure** n. conduct, practice, course, operation, system.

P397 **proceed** v. 1. progress, advance, continue, move ahead (H116) 2. spring, originate, follow, result.

P398 **proceeds** n. product, income, receipts, yield, returns.

P399 **process** 1. n. operation, procedure, method, course 2. v. convert, treat, develop adj.

processed (R48).

P400 **procession** *n.* march, parade, cavalcade.

P401 **proclaim** *v.* announce, declare, advertise, publish.

P402 **procure** *v.* get, *acquire,* obtain, gain, contrive, cause.

P403 **prod** *v.* poke, goad, jab, nudge, push.

P404 **prodigal** *adj.* wasteful, lavish, *extravagant,* profuse (T97).

P405 **produce** 1. *v.* create, originate, make, cause 2. *v.* generate, bring forth, bear 3. *v.* exhibit, show, bring out; *India produces more films than anywhere else in the world.* 4. *n.* product, production.

P406 **product** *n.* produce, yield, result, harvest, goods.

P407 **productive** *adj.* fertile, fruitful, efficient, creative (W29).

P408 **profane** *adj.* 1. irreligious, blasphemous, wicked, impious (F145, H147, P216, S2) 2. worldly, secular.

P409 **profess** *v.* avow, acknowledge, own, confess, affirm, state.

P410 **profession** *n.* 1. declaration, avowal 2. occupation, employment, calling (H140).

P411 **professional** *adj. expert,* competent, businesslike, proficient.

P412 **proficient** *adj.* skilled, *expert,* qualified, practiced, capable (U80).

P413 **profit** 1. *n. gain,* return (S143) 2. *n.* benefit, advantage 3.
v. improve, gain, gain advantage, benefit (S142).

PROPHET

P414 **profound** *adj. deep,* penetrating, thorough, complete, wise, skilled, intellectual (S154).

P415 **profuse** *adj. abundant,* lavish, exuberant, bountiful (M90).

P416 **program** *n.* schedule, record, plan, list, calendar, agenda.

P417 **progress** 1. *n.* advancement, progression 2. *v.* advance, proceed, make headway, improve.

P418 **prohibit** *v. hinder,* prevent, forbid, disallow (A92, L84, P148).

P419 **project** 1. *v.* throw, cast, shoot 2. *v.* protrude, bulge, jut 3. *n.* plan, scheme, proposal, design.

P420 **prolific** *adj.* fruitful, *fertile,* productive, teeming (B26).

P421 **prolong** *v. lengthen,* protract, extend (S185).

P422 **prominent** *adj.* 1. *conspicuous,* obvious, noticeable 2. eminent, celebrated, distinguished, famous (U50).

P423 **promise** 1. *n.* pledge, assurance, word, *vow* 2. *v.* pledge, assure, swear, agree.

P424 **promote** *v.* 1. elevate, raise, exalt, advance (D96) 2. excite, stir up, support, aid.

P425 **prompt** 1. *adj.* ready, quick, alert, active, timely (P353) 2. *v.* stimulate, impel, urge, incite 3. *v.* suggest, hint.

P426 **prone** *adj.* 1. prostrate, recumbent, flat 2. disposed, inclined, tending.

P427 **pronounce** *v. utter,* speak, articulate, declare, affirm.

P428 **pronounced** *adj.* distinct, marked, definite, obvious.

P429 **proof** *n.* 1. test, trial, essay 2. evidence, testimony, confirmation.

P430 **prop** *n. support,* strut, pin, stay, brace.

P431 **propagate** *v.* multiply, increase, continue, spread, diffuse, reproduce.

P432 **propel** *v.* impel, *drive,* push, move, urge (D304).

P433 **proper** *adj.* 1. fit, fitting, *suitable,* appropriate, correct, just (U83, W121) 2. decent, respectable, polite (I82, U77).

P434 **properly** *adv.* suitably, strictly, correctly, accurately.

P435 **property** *n.* 1. quality, feature, characteristic 2. assets, belongings, chattels 3. house, land, estate.

P436 **prophecy** *n.* prediction, foretelling, divination, forecast.

P437 **prophesy** *v.* predict, foretell, divine, forecast.

P438 **proportion** *n.* distribution, adjustment, share, lot, portion, part.

P439 **proposal** *n. offer,* suggestion, scheme, intent.

P440 **propose** *v.* offer, suggest, recommend, intend, mean, offer in marriage.

P441 **proprietor** *n.* possessor, owner.

P442 **prosecute** *v.* 1. sue, *charge,* bring action against 2. pursue, continue, follow out.

P443 **prospect** 1. *n.* view, survey, *scene,* vision, landscape 2. *n.* expectation, anticipation, hope 3. *v.* search, seek, dig.

P444 **prosper** *v. flourish,* thrive, succeed, be successful *n.* **prosperity** (H41).

P445 **prosperous** *adj. successful,* flourishing, fortunate, rich (P287).

P446 **prostrate** *adj.* prone, flat, fallen, stretched out.

P447 **protect** *v.* defend, guard, *shelter,* screen, preserve (E73, V95) *adj.* **protected** (V95).

P448 **protest** 1. (*proh-***test**) *v. object,* dispute, challenge, demur (A135) 2. (**proh-***test*) *n.* complaint, objection.

P449 **prototype** *n.* original, model, archetype.

P450 **protract** *v. prolong,* continue, lengthen, delay (S185).

P451 **protrude** *v.* bulge, extend, jut, project, stick out (R71).

P452 **proud** *adj.* 1. *haughty,* arrogant, supercilious, boastful (M207) 2. grand, stately, noble, lofty, dignified (H196).

P453 **prove** *v.* show, establish, justify, ascertain, verify.

P454 **proverb** *n.* adage, maxim, saying, by-word.

P455 **provide** *v.* procure, get, supply, *furnish,* produce (D116).

P456 **provided** *conj.* if, on condition, supposing.

P457 **province** *n.* 1. territory, region, tract, area, district 2. division, department.

P458 **provoke** *v. excite,* arouse, cause, incite, kindle, enrage (A126).

P459 **prowess** *n.* bravery, valor, courage, daring, skill (C451).

P460 **prowl** *v.* rove, *roam,* sneak, slink, creep.

P461 **prudent** *adj.* discreet, *cautious,* careful, wary, wise (I60, I86, O118, R36) 2. frugal, thrifty, saving (E226).

P462 **prudish** *adj.* coy, *demure,* overly modest, narrow-minded.

P463 **prune** 1. *v.* trim, clip, dock, cut back 2. *n.* dried plum.

P464 **pry** *v. peer,* peep, be inquisitive, meddle.

P465 **public** 1. *adj.* common, general, municipal 2. *n.* persons, people, society, the community (P159, P391, S102, S104).

P466 **publish** *v.* 1. *issue,* emit, distribute, put out 2. proclaim, announce, declare (S583).

P467 **pucker** *v. wrinkle,* crease, crinkle, furrow.

P468 **puff** *v. blow,* swell, inflate, pant, breathe hard.

P469 **pull** *v. & n.* draw, *haul,* tug, drag, pluck (P487).

P470 **punch** *v.* 1. perforate, bore, *pierce,* puncture 2. push, strike, hit.

P471 **punctual** *adj. prompt,* timely, exact, punctilious.

P472 **puncture** *n. hole,* wound, sting, prick.

P473 **pungent** *adj. sharp,* biting, piercing, penetration, piquant, acrid, caustic (B81).

P474 **punish** *v. chastise,* chasten, scold, reprove, penalize, discipline (C312, R245).

P475 **puny** *adj.* weak, feeble, inferior, *little,* small (A167).

P476 **pupil** *n.* 1. student, scholar, beginner 2. opening in iris of the eye.

P477 **puppet** *n.* 1. doll, marionette 2. pawn, vassal, slave.

P478 **purchase** 1. *v. buy,* bargain, obtain, acquire, get (S121) 2. *n.* bargain, acquisition.

P479 **pure** *adj.* 1. *clean,* unsullied, clear, unpolluted (F223, I90, R298) 2. innocent, guiltless, *virtuous* (I39, I134) 3. genuine, real, simple.

P480 **purely** *adv.* absolutely, entirely, completely, merely.

P481 **purge** *v.* 1. cleanse, clear, *purify* (P282) 2. eradicate, eliminate, remove.

P482 **purify** *v.* clean, clear, refine, clarify (I166, P282, R296).

P483 **purloin** *v. steal,* rob, pilfer, thieve, filch.

P484 **purpose** *n.* 1. *aim,* intent, object, end 2. application, usage.

P485 **pursue** *v.* 1. *follow,* chase, hunt, track 2. continue, conduct, persist (A1).

P486 **pursuit** *n.* 1. chase, race, hunt, search 2. undertaking,

Early types of punishment.

133

activity, venture.

P487 **push** v. thrust, *impel,* jostle, shove, force, drive (D304, H64, P469).

P488 **put** v. 1. place, set, lay 2. express, offer, propose 3. inflict, impose, levy 4. oblige, compel, urge; *The farmer put his horse to work.*

P489 **putrid** adj. *rotten,* decayed, corrupt, stinking.

P490 **puzzle** 1. v. *perplex,* embarrass, bewilder, mystify 2. n. riddle, enigma, problem, poser adj. **puzzling** (S215).

P491 **pygmy** adj. & n. dwarf, midget.

Q q

Q1 **quack** n. impostor, pretender, charlatan, humbug.

Q2 **quail** v. cower, *shrink,* flinch, quake, tremble.

Q3 **quaint** adj. strange, odd, unusual, *curious,* uncommon.

Q4 **quake** v. shake, *tremble,* shudder, shiver, quiver.

Q5 **qualification** n. fitness, suitability, capability, *ability,* accomplishment adj. **qualified** (I103, U67).

Q6 **qualify** v. 1. fit, suit, entitle 2. restrict, modify, limit; *He put his case very strongly, but then qualified his remarks.*

Q7 **quality** n. 1. trait, nature, characteristic 2. worth, goodness, soundness, excellence, condition.

Q8 **qualm** n. pang, throe, agony, uneasiness, twinge.

Q9 **quandary** n. difficulty, doubt, *dilemma,* predicament.

Q10 **quantity** n. *amount,* bulk, number, portion, extent.

Q11 **quarrel** 1. n. dispute, difference, disagreement, argument, brawl, tiff (A33) 2. v. wrangle, squabble, bicker, argue adj. **quarrelsome** (A82).

Q12 **quarry** n. 1. pit, diggings 2. prey, victim.

Q13 **quash** v. 1. annul, nullify, *cancel* 2. suppress, repress, crush, quell.

Q14 **quaver** 1. v. tremble, shake, quiver, vibrate 2. n. musical note.

Q15 **quay** n. wharf, jetty, pier, landing. KEY

Q16 **queasy** adj. *sick,* nauseous.

Q17 **queer** adj. *odd,* strange, quaint, unusual, uncommon, peculiar (U102).

Q18 **quell** v. *subdue,* suppress, crush, overcome, restrain, quiet.

Q19 **quench** v. 1. extinguish, put out 2. allay, slake, cool.

Q20 **query** 1. n. *question,* inquiry 2. v. ask, question, inquire, doubt.

Q21 **quest** v. & n. search, hunt.

Q22 **question** 1. n. query, inquiry, debate 2. n. dispute, controversy, doubt 3. v. interrogate, *ask,* inquire (A116, R176, R208, R224).

Q23 **questionable** adj. doubtful, *uncertain,* debatable.

Q24 **queue** 1. n. line, file, procession, retinue 2. v. wait, line up, file. CUE

Q25 **quibble** v. argue, cavil, prevaricate, split hairs.

Q26 **quick** adj. 1. rapid, swift, fast, fleet, speedy (S270, S271, T27) 2. active, nimble, agile, sprightly (O25) 3. skillful, expert 4. hasty, touchy, impatient.

Q27 **quicken** v. hasten, accelerate, hurry.

Q28 **quiet** 1. adj. silent, tranquil, still, calm (L148, T233) 2. n. rest, repose, ease, calm (C169, D184, H187, R266) 3. v. soothe, pacify, lull n. **quietness** (A57).

Q29 **quill** n. pen, feather.

Q30 **quip** n. jest, joke, witticism, gibe.

Q31 **quirk** n. whim, whimsy, fancy, caprice, notion, peculiarity, foible.

Q32 **quit** v. 1. stop, cease, abandon, discontinue 2. resign, renounce, relinquish, leave.

Q33 **quite** adv. 1. completely, entirely, wholly, totally 2. very, considerably, rather.

Q34 **quiver** 1. v. quake, shake, tremble, shiver 2. n. arrow holder.

Q35 **quixotic** adj. imaginative, bizarre, visionary, freakish, fantastic.

Q36 **quiz** 1. n. test, puzzle, riddle, questionnaire 2. v. test, question, interrogate, examine.

Q37 **quota** n. portion, share, proportion.

Q38 **quotation** n. 1. citation, extract, selection, passage, saying 2. estimate.

Q39 **quote** v. cite, repeat, recite, echo, mention.

R r

R1 **rabble** n. mob, crowd, herd, horde, scum.

R2 **race** 1. n. tribe, breed, stock, clan, people, nation 2. n. chase, pursuit, contest, match 3. v. run, hurry, hasten, speed (L98).

R3 **rack** 1. n. frame, holder, bracket, stand 2. v. torture, torment, distress, pain. WRACK

R4 **racket** n. uproar, noise, hubbub, din, fuss (S211).

R5 **racy** adj. strong, vigorous, lively, spirited, sharp.

R6 **radiant** adj. shining, brilliant, beaming, sparkling, luminous (D180).

R7 **radiate** v. shine, gleam, beam, emit.

R8 **radical** 1. adj. fundamental, basic, essential 2. adj. & n. progressive, militant, extremist.

R9 **rag** 1. n. shred, tatter, fragment, bit, cloth 2. n. (slang) newspaper 3. v. bully, needle, jest, lark.

R10 **rage** 1. n. fury, frenzy, wrath, anger (C15) 2. n. fashion, vogue, mode, craze, fad 3. v. rave, storm, ravage, fume.

R11 **ragged** adj. tattered, torn, rent, jagged, rough.

R12 **raid** 1. n. invasion, foray, attack 2. v. attack, assault, invade. RAYED

R13 **rail** 1. n. fence, railing, bar, line 2. v. abuse, scoff, censure, upbraid.

R

R14 **rain** v. & n. drizzle, shower, sprinkle, storm.
REIGN REIN

R15 **raise** v. 1. *lift,* hoist, heave, uplift, advance (L154) 2. excite, rouse, awake, stir up 3. cultivate, bring up, rear.
RAZE

R16 **rake** v. gather, collect, ransack, scour, scrape.

R17 **rally** 1. v. recover, get better, revive, improve 2. v. assemble, gather, meet (D241) 3. n. meeting, gathering.

level, dignity 2. v. class, arrange 3. adj. luxuriant, wild, dense, excessive 4. adj. coarse, foul, rotten, putrid.

R26 **rankle** v. be embittered, inflame, irritate, fester.

R27 **ransack** v. *search,* rummage, plunder, pillage, ravage, sack, rifle.

R28 **ransom** n. *release,* liberation, deliverance, redemption.

R29 **rap** v. & n. knock, thump, whack. WRAP

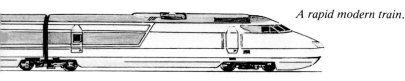

A rapid modern train.

R18 **ram** 1. v. cram, stuff, force 2. v. drive, strike, push, thrust 3. n. male sheep, battering ram.

R19 **ramble** 1. v. *stroll,* rove, wander, range, roam 2. n. excursion, trip, tour, stroll.

R20 **ramp** n. 1. *slope,* gradient 2. fiddle, wangle, racket.

R21 **rancid** adj. rank, musty, sour, tainted, moldy.

R22 **rancor** n. *malice,* malevolence, spite, venom, bitterness, animosity.
RANKER

R23 **random** adj. *chance,* casual, haphazard, fortuitous (D71, S350).

R24 **range** 1. n. rank, row, class, sort, scope, extent 2. v. class, arrange, order 3. v. rove, wander, pass over.

R25 **rank** 1. n. class, grade,

R30 **rape** v. assault, ravish, seduce.

R31 **rapid** adj. swift, *quick,* fast, speedy, hasty (S270).

R32 **rapt** adj. enraptured, charmed, delighted, fascinated.
RAPPED WRAPPED

R33 **rapture** n. ecstasy, *bliss,* joy, delight, exaltation (M174).

R34 **rare** adj. 1. uncommon, *scarce,* infrequent, extraordinary (C251, F251, P253, P373, U102) 2. choice, fine, excellent, exquisite 3. underdone, nearly raw adv. **rarely** (A100, O49).

R35 **rascal** n. *rogue,* knave, villain, scoundrel, scamp.

R36 **rash** 1. adj. *reckless,* headstrong, hasty, impetuous, foolhardy (D221, P461) n. **rashness** (C70).

R37 **rate** 1. n. standard, measure, cost, price, duty, tax

2. *n.* proportion, ratio, speed 3. *v.* assess, price, estimate.

R38 **rather** *adv.* preferably, sooner, more, moderately, somewhat, especially.

R39 **ration** 1. *n.* portion, allowance 2. *v.* apportion, distribute, dole out.

R40 **rational** *adj. reasonable,* just right, sensible, moderate, fair, sane (M4).

R41 **rattle** 1. *n.* clatter, patter 2. *v.* shake, oscillate, vibrate 3. *v.* disturb, upset, unsettle.

R42 **raucous** *adj. hoarse,* husky, rough, harsh, gruff.

R43 **ravage** *v.* despoil, sack, ransack, devastate, pillage.

R44 **rave** *v. rage,* rant, babble, wander, ramble.

R45 **ravenous** *adj.* hungry, famished, starved, greedy, insatiable, rapacious.

R46 **ravine** *n.* gorge, defile, gulch, gully.

R47 **ravishing** *adj. charming,* delightful, captivating, enchanting (R187).

R48 **raw** *adj.* 1. uncooked (C401) 2. inexperienced, unskilled, immature 3. green, unfinished, crude, unripe.

R49 **ray** *n.* beam, gleam, light, flash.

R50 **raze** *v.* overthrow, *demolish,* destroy, ruin, obliterate (R214).   RAISE RAYS

R51 **reach** 1. *v.* extend, stretch 2. *v.* arrive at, come to, get to 3. *n.* range, extent, compass.

R52 **react** *v.* recoil, rebound, respond, answer.

R53 **read** *v.* peruse, interpret, decipher.   REED

R54 **readable** *adj.* 1. *legible,* clear (I16) 2. worth reading, interesting, enjoyable.

R55 **readily** *adv.* quickly, promptly, easily, willingly.

R56 **ready** *adj.* 1. prepared, fitted, arranged (R148) 2. prompt, quick, expert, apt.

R57 **real** *adj. actual,* absolute, certain, genuine, authentic (A150, F3, F23, I25, M201, P182, S155, S393, U69, U70) *adj.* **realistic** (F40, R288).   REEL

R58 **reality** *n. fact,* existence, truth, actuality (D309, H15, I21).

R59 **realize** *v.* 1. comprehend, conceive, *grasp,* appreciate (M191) 2. accomplish, complete, effect, earn, gain.

R60 **really** *adv.* actually, truly, absolutely, certainly.

R61 **realm** *n.* kingdom, province, region, domain.

R62 **reap** *v.* 1. *gather,* gain, obtain, receive 2. *harvest,* gather, garner (S336).

R63 **rear** 1. *n.* back, *end,* tail, behind (F267) 2. *adj.* back, hind, posterior, after (F221) 3. *v.* breed, educate, nurse, foster, cherish, bring up 4. *v.* elevate, hoist, lift, rise; *The bear suddenly reared up before him.*

R64 **reason** 1. *n.* mind, *intellect,* sense, judgment (I230) 2. *n.* principle, motive, cause, aim 3. *v.* argue, debate, dispute, think.

R65 **reasonable** *adj.* 1. right, *fair,* suitable, just 2. tolerable, moderate (A20, E227, I38, O118).

R

R66 **reassure** *v. hearten,* encourage, cheer, comfort, console (F258, I269, S56, T66).

R67 **rebel** 1. *n.* traitor, mutineer, revolutionary 2. *v. revolt,* rise up, defy, disobey (C325) *adj.* **rebellious** (O3).

R68 **rebuff** 1. *n.* repulse, defeat, resistance, snub (A135) 2. *v.* repel, resist, reject, snub (E60).

R69 **rebuke** 1. *n. reprimand,* reproof, censure (P325) 2. *v.* reprove, blame, chide, scold.

R70 **recall** *v.* 1. recollect, *remember* (F205) 2. withdraw, annul, cancel, summon, call back.

R71 **recede** *v. ebb,* retire, go back, return, withdraw, desist (P451).

R72 **receipt** (*re-seet*) *n.* acceptance, admission, voucher, acknowledgment (O112). RESEAT

R73 **receive** (*re-seeve*) *v.* 1. take, accept, obtain, acquire, *get* (S122) 2. entertain, welcome, greet.

R74 **recent** *adj.* new, novel, late, fresh, modern (O52).

R75 **reception** *n.* welcome, entertainment, party.

R76 **recess** *n.* 1. nook, *corner,* niche, cavity, retreat 2. vacation, respite, intermission, break, interval.

R77 **recipe** *n.* prescription, directions, formula.

R78 **recite** *v.* repeat, describe, report, relate.

R79 **reckless** *adj.* careless, heedless, *rash,* negligent, foolhardy (C344, P461).

R80 **reckon** *v.* 1. *count,* number, compute, estimate, guess 2. consider, esteem, infer, regard.

R81 **reclaim** *v.* recover, rescue, restore, improve.

R82 **recline** *v.* lie down, rest, *repose,* lounge.

R83 **recognize** *v.* 1. remember, recollect, know, *identify* 2. admit, own, confess, acknowledge.

R84 **recoil** *v.* rebound, *react,* spring back, shrink, flinch (A62).

R85 **recollect** *v. remember,* recall (F205).

R86 **recommend** *v.* 1. praise, approve, *commend* 2. advise, counsel.

R87 **recompense** *v. reward,* repay, compensate.

R88 **reconcile** *v.* 1. reunite, pacify, appease, harmonize 2. settle, adjust, make up.

R89 **record** 1. *n.* register, account, note, memo, document 2. *n.* disk, recording 3. *n.* supremacy, championship, leadership 4. *v. register,* chronicle, enter, note.

R90 **recount** *v.* 1. describe, *tell,* narrate, report 2. count again.

R91 **recover** *v.* 1. *regain,* reclaim, retrieve, get back 2. heal, cure, revive, get better (C225).

R92 **recreation** *n.* amusement, diversion, entertainment, relaxation, sport (W100).

R93 **recruit** 1. *v.* enlist, sign up, draft 2. *n.* trainee, helper, beginner, learner (V47).

R

R94 **rectify** *v. correct,* amend, improve, straighten, set right (E123).

R95 **recur** *v.* reappear, return, be repeated.

R96 **redeem** *v.* 1. compensate, recompense, make good, recover 2. free, release, deliver, liberate.

R97 **redress** 1. *v.* remedy, repair, amend, set right 2. *n.* compensation, reparation.

R98 **reduce** *v.* 1. contract, *lessen,* decrease, shorten (E84, M13) 2. impoverish, ruin.

R99 **redundant** *adj. superfluous,* unnecessary, excessive, surplus.

R100 **reel** 1. *v.* totter, stagger, falter, waver 2. *n.* fishing rod.

R101 **refer** *v.* 1. *relate,* allude, hint at 2. direct, commit, consign.

R102 **referee** *n.* umpire, judge, arbitrator.

R103 **reference** *n.* 1. allusion, intimation, *hint,* mention 2. respect, regard, relation.

R104 **refine** *v.* 1. *improve,* polish, cultivate 2. cleanse, purify.

R105 **refined** *adj.* 1. purified, clarified (R48) 2. cultivated, polished, elegant, genteel (T39, U14, V94).

Recreation.

R106 **reflect** *v.* 1. mirror, throw back 2. *think,* muse, meditate, deliberate, consider.

R107 **reform** 1. *v.* amend, better, correct, improve 2. *n.* change, amendment, correction.

R108 **refrain** 1. *v.* restrain, withhold, abstain, forbear, desist (P156) 2. *n.* chorus, tune, melody, song.

R109 **refresh** *v.* invigorate, *revive,* enliven (T128).

R110 **refrigerate** *v. cool,* chill, refresh.

R111 **refuge** *n. shelter,* safety, asylum, sanctuary, protection.

R112 **refugee** *n. exile,* deportee, fugitive, emigrant.

R113 **refund** 1. *v.* repay, reimburse, return, restore 2. *n.* repayment, reimbursement.

R114 **refuse** 1. (*ree-***fuse**) *v. deny,* decline, reject, exclude, repel (A25, C277, O42, P247, R190) 2. (**re-***fuse*) *n.* rubbish, garbage, trash, waste, dregs *n.* **refusal** (O42).

R115 **refute** *v.* disprove, invalidate, rebut, *deny,* contradict (A81).

R116 **regal** *adj.* royal, kingly, queenly, majestic, splendid, magnificent.

R117 **regard** 1. *n.* look, view, gaze 2. *n.* care, concern 3. *n.* relation, reference; *I telephoned with regard to your inquiry.* 4. *v.* observe, notice, behold, consider, estimate 5. *v.* esteem, value, respect.

R118 **regardless** *adj.* 1. heedless, careless, indifferent 2. notwithstanding, despite.

R119 **region** *n.* country, territory, area, district, province.

R120 **register** *n.* record, *list,* chronicle, roll, catalog.

R121 **regret** 1. *n.* grief, *sorrow,* concern, remorse 2. *v.* lament, repent, bewail, be sorry for (R130).

R122 **regular** *adj.* 1. *normal,* formal, usual, customary (O36, U86) 2. constant, steady, uniform (I259, I300).

R123 **regulate** *v.* 1. direct, order, manage, govern 2. adjust, correct.

R124 **regulation** *n.* rule, order, law, precept, statute.

R125 **rehearse** *v.* repeat, recite, narrate, practice, prepare.

R126 **reign** (rhymes with *pain*) 1. *v.* rule, govern, prevail 2. *n.* rule, sway, power, sovereignty. RAIN REIN

Reins.

R127 **rein** (rhymes with *cane*) *v.* check, restrain, control, bridle, hold. RAIN REIGN

R128 **reinforce** *v.* strengthen, *fortify,* augment, support.

R129 **reject** *v.* exclude, *discard,* refuse, decline, repel (A25, A28, A56, A58, E29, P348, T10).

R130 **rejoice** *v.* gladden, *cheer,* please, delight, be joyful, celebrate (C270, G136, M197, M256, R121, R173, R315).

R131 **relapse** *v.* fall back, revert, regress, reverse (I83).

R132 **relate** *v.* *tell,* recite, narrate, report, describe 2. connect, compare, concern.

R133 **relation** *n.* 1. connection, relationship, bearing 2. kindred, kinship, kinsman, relative.

R134 **relative** 1. *adj.* referring, respecting, pertaining to, corresponding 2. *n.* relation, kinsman.

R135 **relax** *v.* 1. loosen, slacken, weaken 2. *rest,* ease, repose, recline (S487, T131) *adj.* **relaxed** (T61) **relaxing** (B138).

R136 **release** 1. *v. liberate,* loose, free, extricate, relinquish (A146, C35, C66, C321, I79, S117) 2. *v.* quit, let go (H143) 3. *n.* liberation, discharge, freedom.

R137 **relent** *v. yield,* relax, submit, give in.

R138 **relentless** *adj.* merciless, hard, pitiless, remorseless, *persistent,* steadfast.

R139 **relevant** *adj.* pertinent, *applicable,* fit, suitable, appropriate (I301).

R140 **reliable** *adj.* trustworthy, *dependable,* honest, true (U82).

R141 **relic** *n.* memento, token, souvenir, keepsake, remains, vestige.

R142 **relief** *n.* 1. *help,* assistance, aid, support (D257) 2. comfort, ease.

R143 **relieve** *v.* 1. *ease,* soothe, comfort, cure (A39, H35, O74) 2. change, replace, substitute.

R144 **religion** *n.* creed, faith, piety, virtue.

R145 **religious** *adj.* devout,

holy, pious, faithful, reverent, conscientious.

R146 **relinquish** *v. surrender,* give up, yield, renounce, quit, abandon (M19).

R147 **relish** 1. *n. taste,* flavor, savor 2. *n.* liking, gusto, zest, partiality (D229) 3. *n.* appetizer, sauce 4. *v.* like, enjoy, appreciate (D234).

R148 **reluctant** *adj.* unwilling, loath, averse, disinclined (R56, W73) *n.* **reluctance** (I112).

R149 **rely** *v.* trust in, depend on, count on (D260).

R150 **remain** *v. stay,* continue, abide, last, tarry, linger (F212).

R151 **remainder** *n.* remnant, rest, *surplus,* remains.

R152 **remark** 1. *n. comment,* statement, utterance, saying, observation 2. *v.* note, notice, observe, heed, regard (I13) 3. *v.* express, observe, say, utter.

R153 **remarkable** *adj. extraordinary,* uncommon, unusual, special, strange (C252).

R154 **remedy** 1. *n. cure,* antidote, medicine 2. *n.* solution, answer 3. *v.* cure, heal, relieve, restore.

R155 **remember** *v.* recall, *recollect,* memorize (F205).

R156 **remind** *v.* prompt, bring back, jog the memory.

R157 **remit** *v.* 1. forgive, pardon, excuse, overlook 2. transmit, forward, send, pay.

R158 **remnant** *n.* residue, remainder, remains, rest, scrap, fragment.

R159 **remorse** *n.* penitence, contrition, *sorrow,* regret.

R160 **remote** *adj.* 1. *far,* distant, removed (I36) 2. slight, inconsiderable.

R161 **remove** *v.* displace, transfer, transport, withdraw, extract (A49, R174).

R162 **rend** *v. tear,* break, cleave, split, crack.

R163 **render** *v.* 1. furnish, contribute, submit 2. make, cause to be.

R164 **renegade** *n.* vagabond, deserter, rebel, traitor.

R165 **renew** *v. restore,* renovate, rebuild, revive, refresh.

R166 **renounce** *v.* 1. give up, *relinquish,* abandon, abdicate (A25) 2. repudiate, disclaim, disown.

R167 **renown** *n.* repute, reputation, honor, glory, fame.

R168 **rent** 1. *v. & n.* lease, hire, let 2. *n.* tear, hole, gap, break.

R169 **repair** *v. mend,* patch, restore, make good (B147, H211, S162, S278) 2. *n.* restoration, patch *n.* **reparation** (D8).

R170 **repeal** *v.* revoke, *cancel,* abolish, reverse, set aside (C322).

R171 **repeat** *v.* 1. recite, reiterate, say again (D216) 2. duplicate, reproduce, do again.

R172 **repel** *v.* 1. repulse, drive off, rebuff (A175, C110, E103, F46, L170, T55) 2. reject, refuse, decline (I291) 3. disgust, nauseate, offend *adj.* **repellent** (A176, C111, I292).

R173 **repent** *v.* rue, be sorry for, regret, be penitent, atone.

R174 **replace** *v.* put back, reinstate, return, *restore* (R161).

R175 **replenish** *v. fill,* stock, fill up, supply (E185).

R176 **reply** 1. *v. answer,* respond (A153, Q22) 2. *n.* answer, response, rejoinder.

R177 **report** 1. *v. announce,* declare, mention, tell, relate 2. *n.* account, declaration, statement, description 3. *n.* explosion, noise, sound.

R178 **repose** 1. *v.* lie, *rest,* sleep, recline 2. *n.* relaxation, respite, ease, quiet, sleep.

R179 **represent** *v.* 1. stand for, personate, take the place of 2. portray, reproduce, depict, describe.

R180 **repress** *v. suppress,* subdue, crush, restrain, curb (R240).

R181 **reprimand** *v. reprove,* rebuke, reproach, chide (P325).

R182 **reproach** *v. blame,* reprove, rebuke, reprimand (A135).

R183 **reproduce** *v.* copy, imitate.

R184 **reprove** *v. condemn,* blame, reprimand, chide, rebuke (A135).

R185 **repudiate** *v.* disclaim, disown, deny, reject, renounce (A58).

R186 **repugnant** *adj. offensive,* distasteful, repellent (A82).

R187 **repulsive** *adj.* repellent, forbidding, loathsome, disgusting (R47).

R188 **reputation** *n.* repute, character, name, *fame,* renown, distinction.

R189 **request** 1. *n.* entreaty, *demand,* appeal 2. *v.* ask, solicit, demand, beg. (D104).

R190 **require** *v.* 1. *need,* want (R114) 2. ask, request, demand, direct.

R191 **rescue** 1. *v. liberate,* free, deliver, save, release 2. *n.* liberation, release, salvation.

R192 **research** 1. *n.* investigation, *study,* scrutiny 2. *v.* investigate, study, examine.

R193 **resemblance** *n.* similarity, likeness.

R194 **resentful** *adj.* angry, irritable, revengeful, exasperated.

R195 **reserve** 1. *v. keep,* hold, retain, save 2. *n.* reservation, restriction 3. *n.* shyness, coyness, coldness *adj.* **reserved** (O122).

R196 **reside** *v.* dwell, *live,* inhabit, abide, remain.

R197 **residence** *n.* 1. dwelling, abode, *house,* home 2. stay, sojourn.   RESIDENTS

R198 **resign** (*re-zine*) *v. quit,* give up, forsake, leave, relinquish.

R199 **resist** *v. oppose,* confront, withstand, curb, hinder (A92, O4, S427, S534, S551, S593).

R200 **resolute** *adj.* determined, firm, steady, decided, unwavering (I303).

R201 **resolve** 1. *v.* decide, determine, settle (H116) 2. *v.* interpret, unravel, decipher, solve 3. *n.* intention, resolution, determination.

R202 **resort** 1. *v.* go, repair to, retreat 2. *n.* haunt, refuge, holiday place 3. *n.* recourse, relief.

R203 **resourceful** *adj.* adaptable, flexible, ready, skillful.

R204 **respect** 1. *n.* esteem, regard, admiration, honor (A22, C369) 2. *n.* matter, feature, point, particular; *His idea was good in every respect.* 3. *v.* esteem, honor, venerate (F169, I237, R253, T36).

R205 **respectable** *adj.* reputable, honest, *worthy,* estimable (D247).

R206 **respectful** *adj.* deferential, *courteous,* polite, formal (I59, I87, I218, I304).

R207 **respite** *n.* delay, *pause,* rest, interval.

R208 **respond** *v. answer,* reply, accord, retort, rejoin (Q22).

R209 **responsible** *adj.* 1. answerable, *liable,* accountable 2. reliable, able, trustworthy, capable.

R210 **rest** 1. *n.* repose, quiet, *sleep,* relaxation 2. *n.* pause, stop, stay, cessation 3. *n.* remainder, residue, remnant 4. *v.* repose, relax (L2, W100). WREST

R211 **restaurant** *n.* café, dining room, bistro, buffet.

R212 **restful** *adj. tranquil,* peaceful, relaxing, reposeful (R213).

We retire to bed to rest or repose.

R213 **restless** *adj.* uneasy, disturbed, restive, sleepless, nervous (R212).

R214 **restore** *v.* 1. replace, reinstate, return (E120, O142, R50) 2. renew, recover, mend, renovate (S374).

R215 **restrain** *v. check,* curb, repress, suppress, hold back, prevent (I51) *n.* **restraint.**

R216 **restrict** *v. limit,* bound, confine *adj.* **restricted** (E216).

R217 **result** 1. *n.* end, *effect,* outcome, consequence (C69) 2. *v.* arise, ensue, follow, happen.

R218 **resume** *v.* begin again, recommence, restart, continue (I264).

R219 **retain** *v.* 1. hold, *keep,* withhold, reserve (A1, A9, E24, F212, R161, S78, T177, Y7) 2. engage, hire, employ.

R220 **retaliate** *v.* take revenge, avenge, repay, retort (I13, P50).

R221 **retard** *v.* check, *obstruct,* hinder, delay, defer (A62).

R222 **retire** *v.* 1. *withdraw,* depart, retreat, remove, leave (A62) 2. resign, quit, abdicate, relinquish.

R223 **retiring** *adj.* bashful, *shy,* timid, diffident, modest (O45).

R224 **retort** 1. *n.* repartee, reply, response, answer (Q22) 2. *v. reply,* answer, respond.

R225 **retract** *v.* take back, revoke, rescind, repeal, recant.

R226 **retreat** 1. *v.* withdraw, retire, give way, fall back, *leave* (A62, A169, C107, P397) 2. *n.* departure, withdrawal, retirement 3. *n.* asylum, shelter, refuge.

R

R227 **retrieve** *v.* regain, recover, restore, bring back (L142).

R228 **return** 1. *v.* come back, revisit, go back 2. *v. restore,* give back, repay 3. *n.* account, list, summary, form; *I have just finished filling in my income tax return.*

R229 **reveal** *v. disclose,* discover, divulge, tell, make known (C291, H118).

R230 **revel** 1. *n.* festivity, feast, merrymaking 2. *v.* make merry, celebrate, rejoice.

R231 **revenge** 1. *n.* retaliation, *vengeance,* reprisal 2. *v.* retaliate, avenge, vindicate (F206).

R232 **revenue** *n. income,* receipt, profit, proceeds.

R233 **reverberate** *v.* echo, reflect, resound.

R234 **revere** *v.* venerate, adore, honor, *admire,* idolize (D135).

R235 **reverent** *adj. respectful,* deferential, humble (I304).

R236 **reverse** 1. *v.* invert, overturn, turn, transpose, go back (A62) 2. *adj. opposite,* converse, contrary 3. *n.* contrary, opposite 4. *n.* misfortune, hardship, mishap, setback.

R237 **revert** *v.* return, recur, turn back.

R238 **review** 1. *v.* revise, reconsider 2. *v.* criticize, survey 3. *n. study,* criticism, examination 4. *n.* journal, magazine.   REVUE

R239 **revise** *v.* review, alter, *amend,* update, rewrite.

R240 **revive** *v.* restore, refresh, renovate, *cheer,* recover.

R241 **revoke** *v.* recall, recant, *repeal,* reverse, annul.

R242 **revolt** 1. *v.* repel, *shock,* nauseate, sicken 2. *v.* rebel, mutiny, rise 3. *n.* rebellion, mutiny, uprising, revolution.

R243 **revolution** *n.* 1. revolt, rebellion, overthrow, mutiny 2. rotation, turning, circuit, cycle, orbit.

R244 **revolve** *v.* rotate, *turn,* circle, spin, gyrate, twist.

R245 **reward** 1. *n.* recompense, compensation, bounty, prize (P117) 2. *v.* recompense, compensate, pay.

R246 **rhyme** *n.* poetry, verse, assonance.   RIME

R247 **rhythm** *n.* rhyme, meter, beat, timing, harmony.

R248 **ribald** *adj.* bawdy, base, coarse, gross, smutty.

R249 **rich** *adj.* 1. wealthy, affluent, well-off, opulent (P126, P287) 2. plentiful, abundant, ample 3. nutritious, fruity, full flavored, luscious.

R250 **rid** *v. free,* release, clear, destroy, eliminate.

R251 **riddle** 1. *n.* puzzle, enigma, problem, mystery 2. *v.* perforate, pierce; *The car was riddled with bullet holes.*

R252 **ride** 1. *v.* drive, guide, mount, cycle, motor 2. *n.* journey, spin, voyage, jaunt.

R253 **ridicule** 1. *v.* deride, mock, satirize, *taunt,* jeer 2. *n.* derision, mockery, sarcasm, burlesque (R204).

R254 **ridiculous** *adj.*

preposterous, ludicrous, laughable, *absurd* (S127).

R255 **rife** *adj.* prevalent, prevailing, *common,* abundant (U16).

R256 **rifle** 1. *v.* seize, snatch, rob, plunder, fleece 2. *n.* gun.

R257 **rift** *n.* 1. cleft, fissure, *crack,* rent, breach 2. disagreement, cleavage, divergence, falling-out.

R258 **rig** *v.* dress, clothe, put on outfit, furnish.

R259 **right** 1. *adj.* upright, erect, just, lawful, good, fair 2. *adj.* correct, true, exact, accurate, proper (E126, I127, M188, U83, U85, W121) 3. *n.* fairness, goodness, uprightness, justice (E156) 4. *n.* title, privilege, claim, ownership 5. *adv.* properly, suitably, fairly 6. *adv.* directly, straight.   RITE WRIGHT WRITE

R260 **righteous** *adj.* honest, good, holy, *pious,* virtuous, moral, saintly, religious (I40) *n.* **righteousness** (I192).

R261 **rigid** *adj.* 1. *stiff,* inflexible, unbending (E27, F152, L109, P255) 2. sharp, *severe,* strict, stern (L42, S244, S308).

R262 **rigorous** *adj.* severe, harsh, austere, *stern,* rigid, exact, precise.

R263 **rim** *n.* border, edge, margin, brim, lip.

R264 **rind** *n.* *skin,* peel, bark, hull, shell, crust.

R265 **ring** 1. *n.* circle, hoop, loop, band 2. *n.* arena, stadium, circus 3. *n.* group, clique, crew, set 4. *v.* sound, tinkle, jingle, peal 5. *v.* encircle, surround.   WRING

R266 **riot** 1. *n.* tumult, *brawl,* affray, disorder, disturbance 2. *v.* rebel, revolt, brawl.

R267 **rip** *v.* & *n.* tear, *rent,* slash, slit, break.

R268 **ripe** *adj.* mature, *mellow,* ready, prepared, finished, aged (I31).

R269 **ripple** 1. *v.* *wave,* swell, undulate 2. *n.* wave, undulation.

R270 **rise** 1. *v.* *ascend,* mount, arise, get up (F24, S226, S533, S538) 2. *v.* be advanced, be promoted 3. *n.* advance, increase, addition 4. *n.* ascent, rising, elevation.

R271 **risk** 1. *n.* danger, hazard, *peril,* chance (S8) 2. *v.* endanger, hazard, imperil, gamble *adj.* **risky** (S6).

R272 **ritual** *n.* liturgy, ceremony, custom, formality.

R273 **rival** 1. *n.* competitor, *opponent,* antagonist (P19, P67) 2. *v.* oppose, compete, contest 3. *adj.* competing, opposing.

R274 **river** *n.* stream, water course, brook, bourn, torrent.

R275 **road** *n.* path, way, lane, *street,* route, track.   RODE ROWED

R276 **roam** *v.* ramble, stroll, *wander,* range.

R277 **roar** *v.* & *n.* bellow, bawl, *shout,* yell, howl, cry (W64).

R278 **rob** *v.* *steal,* loot, sack, plunder, strip, fleece, pilfer.

R279 **robber** *n.* *thief,* pirate, plunderer, brigand, bandit.

R280 **robe** *n.* dress, gown, vestment.

R281 **robust** *adj. strong,* stout, brawny, muscular, sturdy (W12).

R282 **rock** 1. *n.* stone, boulder, pebble 2. *v.* sway, swing, totter, reel.

R283 **rod** *n.* stick, *pole,* perch, wand, scepter, cane, staff.

R284 **rogue** *n.* knave, villain, *rascal,* scamp, scoundrel.

R285 **role** *n.* 1. part, character 2. position, function, task, duty.   ROLL

R286 **roll** 1. *v.* turn, revolve, *rotate,* whirl, spin 2. *v.* bind, wrap, swathe 3. *v.* press, level, flatten 4. *n.* scroll, document, list, register 5. *n.* small loaf, bun.   ROLE

R287 **romance** *n.* 1. love affair, engagement, betrothal, idyll 2. novel, tale, story, fable.

R288 **romantic** *adj.* 1. fanciful, imaginative, fictional, idyllic (P323) 2. sentimental, lovelorn.

R289 **romp** *v.* frisk, sport, frolic, *play.*

R290 **roof** *n.* cover, canopy, shelter.

R291 **room** *n.* 1. *chamber,* apartment, accommodation 2. space, extent, expanse.

R292 **rooster** *n. cock,* chanticleer, male fowl.

R293 **root** *n.* bottom, base, cause, origin, radical, stem.

R294 **rope** *n. cord,* cable, string, twine.

R295 **rosy** *adj.* 1. rose-colored, pink 2. blooming, healthy 3. optimistic, promising.

R296 **rot** 1. *v. decay,* decompose, spoil, putrefy 2. *n.* decay, putrefaction.

R297 **rotate** *v.* revolve, *whirl,* turn, spin, turn around.

R298 **rotten** *adj.* putrid, corrupt, moldy, decaying, foul (P479).

R299 **rough** *adj.* 1. uneven, rugged, craggy, unfinished 2. shaggy, hairy, coarse, bristly (S254, S283) 3. rude, uncivil, impolite, churlish 4. tempestuous, stormy (P2) 5. austere, *harsh,* crude *adv.* **roughly** (G56).   RUFF

R300 **round** 1. *adj.* circular, spherical, globular, curved 2. *n.* compass, cycle, circuit, tour.

R301 **roundabout** *adj.* indirect, tortuous, circuitous (D189).

R302 **rouse** *v.* 1. awaken, *wake,* arouse 2. animate, stimulate, stir, excite.

R303 **rout** 1. *v.* defeat, ruin, conquer 2. *n.* defeat, flight, overthrow.

R304 **route** (rhymes with *boot*) *n.* road, way, path, course.   ROOT

R305 **routine** *n.* practice, custom, habit, system, order.

R306 **rove** *v.* wander, roam, ramble, stroll, stray.

R307 **row** (rhymes with *go*) *n.* rank, file, line.   ROE

R308 **row** (rhymes with *cow*) *n. quarrel,* affray, brawl, squabble, noise.

R309 **rowdy** *adj.* rough, disorderly, *boisterous,* noisy.

R310 **royal** *adj.* majestic, regal, kingly, queenly, noble, imperial.

R311 **rub** *v.* wipe, smooth, scour, chafe, scrape, *polish.*

R312 **rubbish** *n*. 1. refuse, litter, trash, garbage, debris 2. nonsense, balderdash, drivel.

R313 **rude** *adj*. 1. impolite, coarse, brusque, impudent, *vulgar* (C444, G111, P280) 2. raw, unpolished, *crude* (R105).
ROOD RUED

R314 **rudimentary** *adj*. elementary, primary, basic, fundamental.

R315 **rue** *v*. deplore, lament, regret, grieve (R130).

R316 **ruffian** *n*. villain, rascal, *scoundrel,* wretch.

R317 **ruffle** *v*. 1. trouble, vex, disturb, torment 2. wrinkle, cockle, pucker.

R318 **rug** *n*. carpet, mat, covering.

R319 **rugged** *adj*. 1. *rough,* uneven, jagged, craggy 2. stalwart, stout, sturdy, hardy, robust.

R320 **ruin** 1. *v*. *destroy,* demolish, overthrow (M120, O90) 2. *v*. impoverish, pauperize, bankrupt 3. *n*. destruction, remains.

R321 **rule** 1. *n*. *command,* control, domination, government 2. *n*. law, precept, order, regulation 3. *v*. *govern,* command, control, manage 4. *v*. settle, establish.

R322 **ruler** *n*. 1. leader, sovereign, governor, monarch, king, queen 2. measure, straightedge.

R323 **rumble** *v*. roar, thunder, roll, boom, drone.

R324 **rummage** *v*. search, examine, hunt, scour, ransack.

R325 **rumor** *n*. *report,* hearsay gossip, scandal, tidings.

R326 **run** 1. *v*. race, speed, hasten, hurry, scamper 2. *v*. flow, glide, stream 3. *v*. proceed, pass, go, operate, work 4. *v*. extend, stretch, lie 5. *n*. trip, excursion 6. *n*. dash, sprint, race.

R327 **rupture** *n*. breach, fracture, break, burst, hernia.

R328 **rural** *adj*. rustic, pastoral, countrified (U95).

R329 **ruse** *n*. trick, artifice, maneuver, deception, dodge.
RUES

R330 **rush** *v*. hasten, speed, *dash,* hurry, scurry, run (T31).

A ruin.

R331 **rustic** *adj*. rural, country, countrified, simple, plain.

R332 **rusty** *adj*. 1. musty, corroded, worn 2. unpracticed, unprepared.

R333 **rut** *n*. 1. *groove,* furrow, track, hollow 2. habit, routine.

R334 **ruthless** *adj*. merciless, pitiless, *cruel,* relentless (M127) *n*. **ruthlessness** (M129).

S s

S1 **sack** 1. *n.* bag, pouch, pack 2. *v.* ravage, despoil, plunder, pillage. SAC

S2 **sacred** *adj. holy,* hallowed, consecrated, divine (P408).

S3 **sacrifice** 1. *n.* offering, atonement 2. *v.* surrender, give up, forego (A25, G4).

S4 **sad** *adj.* melancholy, depressed, dejected, gloomy, mournful, downcast, dismal, tragic (C124, C240, D320, F5, F91, F291, G60, H34, J31, M134) *n.* **sadness** (H33, J32, M166).

S5 **saddle** 1. *n.* pillion, seat 2. *v.* load, burden, encumber.

S6 **safe** 1. *adj.* protected, guarded, secure 2. *adj.* trustworthy, reliable, sure (D16, P331, U75) 3. *n.* coffer, chest, strongbox, vault.

S7 **safeguard** *n.* defense, protection, security, shield.

S8 **safety** *n.* security, preservation, protection (D15, P141, R271).

S9 **sag** *v.* droop, *hang,* dangle.

S10 **sage** 1. *adj. wise,* shrewd, acute, prudent, sensible 2. *n.* wise man, philosopher, savant (F188, I7).

S11 **sail** 1. *v.* voyage, skim, navigate, *cruise,* float 2. *n.* cruise, journey, trip 3. *n.* sheet, sailcloth, canvas. SALE

S12 **sailor** *n.* seaman, mariner, seafarer, tar. SAILER

S13 **sake** *n.* 1. reason, purpose, end 2. account, regard, respect.

S14 **salary** *n. pay,* wages, stipend, allowance, compensation.

S15 **sale** *n.* 1. selling, vending, marketing, disposal 2. clearance, auction. SAIL

S16 **sally** 1. *n.* frolic, escapade, trip, run 2. *n.* raid, attack, sortie 3. *n.* jest, joke, quip 4. *v.* rush out, issue, go forth.

S17 **salute** 1. *v. greet,* hail, address, accost, receive 2. *n.* greeting, address, kiss.

S18 **salve** 1. *n.* ointment, remedy, antidote 2. *v.* rescue, raise, save.

S19 **same** *adj.* identical, similar, like, corresponding, equivalent (O72).

S20 **sample** 1. *n.* specimen, example, pattern, model 2. *v.* taste, try.

S21 **sanction** 1. *n.* confirmation, support, authority, permission 2. *n.* penalty, punishment, embargo 3. *v.* support, authorize, legalize, allow.

S22 **sanctity** *n.* purity, holiness, godliness, piety, grace (S22).

S23 **sanctuary** *n.* 1. asylum, refuge, shelter 2. church, altar, temple, shrine.

The sails of a windmill.

S24 **sane** *adj.* sound, sober, lucid, *rational,* normal (C466, I205, M4) *n.* **sanity** (F250).

S25 **sanguine** *adj.* confident, hopeful, enthusiastic, cheerful.

S26 **sanitary** *adj.* hygienic, clean, sterile, *pure.*

S27 **sap** *v.* mine, undermine, weaken, drain, exhaust.

S28 **sarcastic** *adj.* severe, cutting, taunting, satirical, sardonic, cynical.

S29 **sardonic** *adj.* sarcastic, derisive, ironical.

S30 **sash** *n.* girdle, band, belt, scarf.

S31 **satellite** *n.* 1. moon, planet 2. sputnik, space station, skylab.

S32 **satiate** *v.* satisfy, fill, sate, gorge, glut (S434).

S33 **satire** *n.* *ridicule,* sarcasm, irony, lampoon, burlesque.

S34 **satisfaction** *n.* 1. gratification, contentment, enjoyment, comfort (D200, D215) 2. payment, atonement, discharge, amends.

S35 **satisfactory** *adj.* pleasing, sufficient, adequate.

S36 **satisfy** *v.* 1. please, *gratify,* suffice, content 2. convince, persuade, meet (F276) *adj.* **satisfied** (H205, R45, T87).

S37 **saturate** *v.* drench, soak, steep (D329).

S38 **sauce** *n.* 1. seasoning, relish, condiment, appetizer 2. (colloq.) cheek, impertinence, insolence.

S39 **saucy** *adj.* (colloq.) impertinent, cheeky, insolent, rude, flippant (P280).

S40 **saunter** *v.* loiter, linger, lounge, *stroll,* amble (H210).

S41 **savage** 1. *adj. wild,* rough, uncivilized, crude (C166) 2. *adj.* fierce, ferocious, brutish, inhuman 3. *n.* barbarian, aborigine, native.

S42 **save** *v.* 1. *rescue,* preserve, redeem, deliver, liberate (A1) 2. *keep,* hold, hoard, reserve, store (D205, S360, S401, W29).

S43 **savor** 1. *n. taste,* flavor, relish, odor, smell 2. *v.* taste, enjoy, partake, relish.

S44 **say** *v.* speak, utter, *tell,* declare, express, remark.

S45 **saying** *n.* proverb, maxim, adage, axiom.

S46 **scald** *v.* burn, scorch.

S47 **scale** 1. *n.* flake, lamina, layer, plate 2. *n.* gradation, measure, range; *Our charges are made on a sliding scale.* 3. *v.* climb, ascend, mount.

S48 **scamp** 1. *n.* rascal, rogue, cheat, knave, scoundrel, villain 2. *v.* skimp, neglect, work negligently.

S49 **scamper** *v. run,* rush, tear, scuttle, hurry, scoot (D30).

S50 **scan** *v.* 1. scrutinize, inspect, sift, *examine,* search 2. glance at, browse through, dip into.

S51 **scandal** *n. disgrace,* dishonor, shame, infamy, slander (P325).

S52 **scanty** *adj. meager,* scant, small, sparing, sparse, niggardly (A21, A106, C406, D102, L38, P253, P415).

S53 **scar** *v. & n.* wound, hurt, mark, blemish.

S54 **scarce** *adj.* deficient, wanting, *rare,* uncommon, infrequent, scanty (A21, P253) *n.* **scarcity** (P254).

S55 **scarcely** *adv.* hardly, barely.

S56 **scare** 1. *n.* fright, panic, terror, alarm, *shock* 2. *v.* frighten, terrify, shock, startle (R66).

S57 **scatter** *v.* strew, sprinkle, *disperse,* spread, distribute (F161, G26, H188).

S58 **scene** *n.* spectacle, exhibition, *show,* sight, view. SEEN

S59 **scent** *(sent) n.* odor, *smell,* fragrance, aroma, perfume. CENT SENT

S60 **scepter (sep** ter) *n.* staff, baton, royal emblem.

S61 **schedule (sked-***ule***)** 1. *n.* inventory, list, record, table 2. *v.* plan, list, adjust, time.

S62 **scheme** *(skeem)* 1. *n. plan,* system, theory, design, project 2. *v.* plan, plot, contrive, frame.

S63 **scholar** *n.* 1. pupil, disciple, student, learner 2. savant, professor, academic, don.

S64 **school** *n.* academy, institute, college.

S65 **scintillate** *v.* sparkle, twinkle, shine, gleam, flash.

S66 **scoff** *v.* sneer, gibe, jeer, taunt, deride, ridicule (P325).

S67 **scold** *v.* reprimand, criticize, *chide,* blame, rebuke, reprove (E60).

S68 **scoop** *v.* excavate, hollow out, bail, gouge, ladle.

S69 **scope** *n.* amplitude, room, space, range, extent.

S70 **scorch** *v. burn,* blister, singe, char, roast.

S71 **score** 1. *v.* record, gain, earn, tally 2. *v.* mark, notch, furrow, cut 3. *n.* total, tally.

S72 **scorn** 1. *n. contempt,* disdain, mockery 2. *v.* despise, disdain, spurn (E137).

S73 **scoundrel** *n.* knave, rogue, villain, rascal, scamp.

S74 **scour** *v.* scrub, cleanse, rub, whiten.

S75 **scourge** 1. *v.* whip, lash, punish, chastise, torment (P27) 2. *n.* curse, pest, plague, punishment.

S76 **scowl** *v. & n. frown,* glare, glower (S281).

S77 **scramble** 1. *v.* struggle, climb, clamber, scurry 2. *v.* mix, blend, combine.

S78 **scrap** 1. *n.* fragment, morsel, crumb, bite, bit (W65) 2. *v.* demolish, discard, abandon.

A schoolroom.

S79 **scrape** 1. *v.* rub, grate, rasp, scour, scratch 2. *n.* fix, predicament, trouble; *The children are always getting into scrapes.*

S80 **scratch** *v. & n.* mark, scrape, scribble, score.

S81 **scrawl** *v. scribble,* scratch, write carelessly.

S82 **scream** *v.* & *n.* shriek, screech, yell, shrill, cry.

S83 **screech** *v.* & *n.* scream, yell, shriek.

S84 **screen** 1. *n.* protection, guard, shield 2. *v.* hide, shelter, conceal, protect.

S85 **screw** *v. twist,* force, rotate, turn.

S86 **scribble** *v.* scrawl, scratch.

S87 **scribe** *n.* writer, penman, clerk, notary.

S88 **script** *n.* 1. handwriting, writing 2. alphabet, writing system 3. manuscript, typescript, text; *Mary Green wrote the script for the show.*

S89 **scroll** *n.* parchment, schedule, list.

S90 **scrub** *v.* scour, *clean,* cleanse, rub.

S91 **scrupulous** *adj.* conscientious, strict, vigilant, careful, meticulous (U76).

S92 **scrutinize** *v.* examine, probe, *inspect n.* **scrutiny** (G73).

S93 **scuffle** *v.* struggle, fight, contend, squabble.

S94 **sculpture** 1. *n.* statuary 2. *v.* carve, chisel, sculpt.

S95 **scuttle** *v.* hurry, bustle, run, scamper, dash.

S96 **sea** *n.* ocean, main, the deep waters, billows.

S97 **seal** 1. *n.* stamp, mark, endorsement 2. *n.* sea mammal, sea lion 3. *v.* close, fasten, secure.

S98 **seam** *n.* 1. *hem,* stitching, suture 2. fissure, crevice.
SEEM

S99 **search** 1. *v. examine,* explore, inspect, investigate 2. *n.* examination, exploration, inspection, scrutiny.

S100 **season** 1. *n.* time, period 2. *v.* flavor, spice.

S101 **seat** *n.* 1. place, site, situation 2. chair, stool, bench.

S102 **secluded** *adj. private,* isolated, remote.

S103 **secondary** *adj.* inferior, minor, subordinate, lower (M18, O94, P382, P385).

S104 **secret** 1. *adj.* hidden, concealed, clandestine, private, mysterious 2. *n.* mystery, confidence *v.* **secrete** *adv.* **secretly** (O65).

S105 **section** *n.* division, portion, *part,* segment, piece, slice, partition.

S106 **secure** 1. *v.* fasten, fix, shut, lock 2. *v.* get, acquire, gain, procure; *I secured some shares on the stock exchange.* 3. *v.* protect, guard, defend (E63) 4. *adj.* certain, sure, assured, confident (I207) 5. *adj.* fixed, fast, stable, firm (L136).

S107 **security** *n.* 1. safety, protection, defense, shelter (P141) 2. pledge, pawn, deposit, bond.

S108 **seduce** *v.* decoy, allure, entice, tempt, lead astray.

S109 **see** *v.* 1. behold, perceive, observe, discern, regard, look at (D246) 2. visit, call on 3. attend, escort, wait upon; *May I see you home?* 4. experience, feel, suffer; *Those poor people have seen a lot of hardship.* 5. comprehend, understand.

S110 **seed** *n.* sperm, kernel, embryo, grain.

S111 **seedy** *adj.* old, worn, faded, *shabby,* poor, needy, miserable (S277).

S112 **seek** *v.* search for, look for, solicit, attempt, follow, strive, endeavor (S198).

S113 **seem** *v.* appear, *look.*
SEAM

S114 **seemly** *adj.* becoming, *proper,* suitable, decent (U77).

S115 **seep** *v.* trickle, *ooze,* leak, emit, percolate.

S116 **seethe** *v.* boil, be hot, burn, simmer, be angry.

S117 **seize** *v.* grip, *grasp,* snatch, clutch, catch, capture (R136). SEAS SEES

S118 **seldom** *adj.* rarely, infrequently, scarcely, hardly (M244, O49).

S119 **select** 1. *v. choose,* pick, prefer 2. *adj.* chosen, picked, rare, choice.

S120 **selfish** *adj.* mean, narrow, *greedy,* miserly (G38, L81, P186) *n.* **selfishness** (C109).

S121 **sell** *v.* barter, vend, exchange, trade, peddle (B187, P478).

S122 **send** *v.* dispatch, transmit, forward, post, convey (R73).

S123 **senior** *adj.* older, elder, higher, more advanced, superior (M158).

S124 **sensation** *n.* 1. feeling, sense, perception, *impression* 2. excitement, thrill, surprise.

S125 **sensational** *adj.* exciting, startling, thrilling, spectacular (H198).

S126 **sense** 1. *n.* feeling, sensation, perception 2. *n.* intellect, mind, understanding (F184) 3. *n.* discernment, judgment, conviction 4. *v. feel,* perceive, appreciate, understand.
CENTS SCENTS

S127 **sensible** *adj.* intelligent, rational, *wise,* discreet (F57, F190, I8, I97, I155, M4, O118, R254, S212).

S128 **sentence** *n.* 1. phrase, axiom, maxim 2. doom, condemnation, judgment *v.* **sentence** (A42, P50).

S129 **sentiment** *n.* feeling, sensibility, *emotion,* tenderness *adj.* **sentimental.**

S130 **separate** 1. *v.* part, divide, sever, detach, disconnect (A52, B88, C236, C336, C391, J21, M154, M195, U53) 2. *adj.* detached, disconnected, apart, alone (I209, J22) *n.* **separation** (M56).

S131 **sequel** *n.* continuation, consequence, result.

S132 **sequence** *n.* order, arrangement, series, succession.

S133 **serene** *adj.* calm, quiet, placid, *tranquil,* peaceful (I142, T51) *n.* **serenity** (W110).

S134 **series** *n.* succession, order, sequence, course *adj.* **serial.**

S135 **serious** *adj.* grave, solemn, earnest, important, great (F158, F265, F291, H202, J31, L90, L160, P245) *n.* **seriousness** (M166).

S136 **sermon** *n.* address, talk, homily, lecture, discourse.

S137 **servant** *n.* attendant, employee, help, domestic, drudge, slavey, maid (L141, M72).

S138 **serve** *v.* 1. aid, assist,

help, oblige, wait on 2. satisfy, content.

S139 **service** *n.* 1. employment, aid, assistance, duty 2. ceremony, rite, mass, worship *n.* **servitude** (F247, L83).

S140 **set** 1. *v.* put, place, locate 2. *v.* fix, establish, settle, determine 3. *v.* congeal, harden, solidify 4. *n.* collection, group 5. *n.* scene, backcloth, setting 6. *adj.* normal, regular, standard, firm, unchanging.

S141 **settle** 1. *v.* fix, establish (U78) 2. *v.* pay, discharge, balance, square 3. *v.* dwell, abide, inhabit 4. *n.* bench, seat, stool, settee.

S142 **sever** *v.* part, divide, separate, cut (A52, L99, U53).

S143 **several** *adj.* various, diverse, different, distinct, some, many (S223).

S144 **severe** *adj.* 1. rigid, stern, *strict,* harsh, bitter (C70) 2. simple, plain, unadorned 3. rigorous, hard, intense, violent *n.* **severity** (C185).

S145 **sew** *v.* stitch, seam, work with needle.   SO SOW

S146 **shabby** *adj.* 1. *ragged,* worn, threadbare 2. mean, base, low, despicable.

S147 **shack** *n.* shanty, *hut,* cabin, shed.

S148 **shackle** *v.* & *n.* fetter, chain, manacle, handcuff.

S149 **shade** *n.* 1. darkness, shadow, dusk, gloom (L90) 2. color, hue, tint 3. ghost, phantom.

S150 **shadow** *n.* shade, darkness, gloom.

S151 **shaft** *n.* 1. arrow, missile 2. *handle,* pole, rod.

S152 **shaggy** *adj.* rough, hairy, rugged.

S153 **shake** 1. *v. tremble,* agitate, quiver, shudder, vibrate, jolt 2. *n.* convulsion, jar, jolt, shock, tremor.

S154 **shallow** *adj.* 1. not deep (D60, P414) 2. superficial, silly, slight, foolish.

S155 **sham** *adj.* pretended, false, counterfeit, *mock,* spurious (R57).

S156 **shame** 1. *n.* disgrace, dishonor, ignominy, embarrassment 2. *v.* abash, mortify, humiliate, disgrace, discredit (H153) *adj.* **shameful** (H154).

S157 **shameless** *adj.* impudent, *immodest,* brazen, unashamed, insolent (M207).

S158 **shanty** *n.* hut, shed, cabin.

S159 **shape** 1. *n. form,* outline, figure, pattern 2. *v.* create, make, mold, fashion.

S160 **share** 1. *n.* part, *portion,* interest, dividend (W65) 2. *v.* divide, distribute, portion.

S161 **sharp** *adj.* 1. acute, *keen,* cutting, fine (B101, D333) 2. shrewd, astute, quick, witty (O25) 3. biting, pungent, acrid, sour 4. shrill, piercing.

S162 **shatter** *v.* 1. *break,* burst, smash, destroy 2. despair, upset, shock.

S163 **shave** *v.* trim, clip, smooth, slice, graze.

S164 **shear** *v.* cut, clip, strip, fleece.   SHEER

S165 **shed** 1. *n. hut,* hovel, cabin, shanty 2. *v.* spill, let fall, cast off.

S166 **sheen** *n.* shine, gloss, luster, polish.

S167 **sheer** *adj.* 1. pure, utter, clear, absolute 2. thin, fine, clear, transparent, diaphanous 3. steep, perpendicular, abrupt. SHEAR.

S168 **sheet** *n.* 1. leaf, foil, wafer, plate, page 2. bedclothes, linen, cover.

S169 **shelf** *n.* ledge, rack.

S170 **shell** *n.* case, covering, framework, husk, crust.

S171 **shelter** 1. *v.* screen, hide, protect, defend, shield 2. *n.* asylum, refuge, haven, retreat.

S172 **shield** 1. *n.* protection, defense, guard, shelter 2. defend, *protect,* ward off (B63).

Shields.

S173 **shift** 1. *v.* change, alter, *move,* remove 2. *n.* alteration, move, transfer 3. *n.* turn, stint, stretch, bout, period.

S174 **shifty** *adj.* crafty, sly, furtive, deceitful, foxy (H151).

S175 **shimmer** *v.* glimmer, gleam, *sparkle,* glisten.

S176 **shine** 1. *v.* glisten, sparkle, glow 2. *n.* gloss, glimmer, sheen.

S177 **ship** *n.* vessel, craft, boat, barge, tug, launch.

S178 **shirk** *v.* evade, avoid, *dodge,* shun.

S179 **shiver** 1. *v.* shudder, quake, tremble, *quiver,* shake 2. *n.* tremor, shudder, shake.

S180 **shock** 1. *n. impact,* collision, clash, blow, stroke 2. *v.* offend, upset, disgust, outrage 3. *v.* frighten, dismay, horrify, stun *adj.* **shocking**.

S181 **shoot** 1. *v.* fire, discharge, explode, emit, dart 2. *n.* bud, sprout, twig. CHUTE

S182 **shop** *n.* store, market, workshop, boutique.

S183 **shore** *n.* coast, beach, strand, seaside.

S184 **short** *adj.* 1. *brief,* concise, condensed, pithy 2. terse, curt, severe 3. little, small, puny, not long (L132, T14).

S185 **shorten** *v. abbreviate,* abridge, lessen, reduce, diminish (E36, E215, L69, P421, P450).

S186 **shortly** *adv.* soon, quickly, briefly, tersely.

S187 **shout** *v. & n.* call, cry, yell, roar, bellow.

S188 **shove** *v. & n. push,* jostle, press, thrust, prod.

S189 **show** 1. *v.* exhibit, *display,* present 2. *v.* indicate, point out 3. *v.* disclose, *reveal,* teach (H118) 4. *v.* conduct, guide, usher 5. *n.* spectacle, exhibition, *parade,* performance *adj.* **showy** (M207, U9).

S190 **shred** 1. *n.* fragment, *scrap,* bit, piece 2. *v.* strip, mince, dice, tear.

S

S191 **shrewd** *adj.* 1. artful, cunning, sly, wily, astute 2. clever, sharp, quick, *wise,* ingenious (S525).

S192 **shriek** *v. & n.* scream, *yell,* screech.

S193 **shrill** *adj. acute,* sharp, high-pitched, piercing.

S194 **shrink** *v. shrivel,* contract, dwindle, wither (E84, E192, G15, I128, L69, S500, S612) 2. recoil, flinch, draw back.

S195 **shrivel** *v.* parch, dry up, *wither,* wrinkle.

S196 **shudder** *v. & n.* tremble, shiver, *shake,* quiver.

S197 **shuffle** 1. confuse, jumble, *mix,* disorder 2. falter, crawl, trudge, struggle.

S198 **shun** *v. avoid,* evade, escape, elude, eschew (F4).

S199 **shut** *v. close,* lock, bar, fasten, seal (O63).

S200 **shy** *adj. timid,* coy, bashful, reserved (S286).

S201 **sick** *adj. ill,* unwell, ailing, weak, feeble, unhealthy (H79) *n.* **sickness** (R154).

S202 **side** 1. *n.* verge, margin, edge, border 2. *n.* party, sect, faction, team 3. *adj.* indirect, oblique, secondary 4. *v.* take sides, support, join.   SIGHED

S203 **sieve** *n.* strainer, screen.

S204 **sift** *v.* scrutinize, probe, examine, investigate 2. sort, *filter,* strain.

S205 **sigh** *v.* grieve, mourn, lament, groan, *cry.*

S206 **sight** 1. *vision,* view, look, scene, spectacle 2. seeing, vision, ability to see *adj.* **sighted** (B91).   CITE SITE

S207 **sign** 1. *n.* token, mark, *symbol,* symptom, emblem 2. *n.* indication, hint, manifestation 3. *v.* endorse, initial, subscribe.

S208 **signal** 1. *n.* beacon 2. *n.* mark, sign, indicator 3. *adj.* conspicuous, extraordinary, famous, remarkable.

S209 **significance** *n.* meaning, importance, weight, force, impressiveness *adj.* **significant** (I213, S259).

S210 **signify** *v.* express, *indicate,* denote, mean, imply.

S211 **silence** *n.* calm, *quiet,* peace, stillness, noiselessness (O106) *adj.* **silent** (V81) *adv.* **silently** (A96).

S212 **silly** *adj.* senseless, stupid, *foolish,* simple, weak, frivolous (S127).

S213 **similar** *adj. like,* resembling, uniform (D169, D264, O7) *n.* **similarity** (D168).

S214 **simmer** *v. boil,* seethe, stew, bubble.

S215 **simple** *adj.* 1. *plain,* unadorned, unaffected, natural (E25, F38, M12, P370) 2. clear, unmistakable, intelligible, easy (I274, L2) 3. frank, open, naïve (H63, S323, S542) *n.* **simplicity** (P283) *v.* **simplify** (C275).

S216 **simply** *adv.* plainly, sincerely, truly, merely, barely.

S217 **sin** 1. *n.* trespass, wrong, wickedness, crime, depravity (G100) 2. *v.* trespass, do wrong, transgress, *err,* offend.

S218 **since** 1. *adv.* ago, before this 2. *prep.* after, from the time of.

S219 sincere *adj.* 1. true, real, unfeigned, *genuine* 2. honest, frank, open, candid, direct (I214).

S220 sinful *adj.* wicked, unholy, *wrong,* bad, immoral (H147, M231, U92).

S221 sing *v.* carol, chant, warble, hum, croon.

S222 singe *v. scorch,* burn, sear.

S223 single *adj.* 1. sole, lone, *solitary,* alone (S143) 2. unmarried, unwed, celibate (M57) 3. particular, individual, separate.

S224 singular *adj.* single, individual 2. *unusual,* uncommon, rare, strange, peculiar (C252).

S225 sinister *adj.* unlucky, unfortunate, wrong, bad, evil.

S226 sink *v.* 1. depress, degrade, ruin 2. submerge, submerse, immerse (A141, F160).

S227 sip *v. & n. drink,* taste, swallow.

S228 sit *v.* perch, rest, repose, settle, remain (S427).

A chair to sit in.

S229 site *n. place,* location, position, station.   CITE SIGHT

S230 situation *n.* 1. place, locality, *position* 2. condition, state, plight, predicament 3. employment, job, post, office.

S231 size *n. bulk,* volume, largeness, extent.   SIGHS

S232 skeleton *n.* bones, framework, outline.

S233 sketch 1. *n. drawing,* picture, outline, plan, draft 2. *v.* draw, rough out, design, pencil in.

S234 skill *n.* facility, dexterity, *ability,* aptitude, talent *adj.* **skilled** (I160).

S235 skillful *adj.* skilled, proficient, *competent,* able, clever (A186).

S236 skim *v.* 1. graze, touch, brush, glide, coast, sail 2. browse, scan; *Helen quickly skimmed through the morning paper.*

S237 skin 1. *n.* hide, pelt, husk, hull, peel, rind 2. *v.* husk, peel.

S238 skinny *adj.* lean, *thin,* lank, shrunk, gaunt (P263, P295).

S239 skip *v. & n.* leap, *jump,* bound, spring, *hop,* caper, gambol.

S240 skirmish *n.* conflict, collision, combat, brush, contest, *encounter.*

S241 skirt *n.* 1. petticoat, dress 2. *v.* edge, border, fringe.

S242 skulk *v. lurk,* hide, sneak, slink, prowl.

S243 sky *n.* heavens, firmament, air, atmosphere.

S244 slack *adj.* 1. *loose,* relaxed, hanging, limp (T113) 2. slow, tardy, sluggish 3. idle, inactive, lazy.

S

S245 **slam** *v.* close, bang, shut, push.

S246 **slander** *v.* defame, malign, lie, *libel,* decry, discredit (P325).

S247 **slang** *n.* cant, argot, dialect, jargon, vulgarity.

S248 **slant** *v. & n. slope,* lean, incline.

S249 **slap** *v. & n.* smack, pat, spank.

S250 **slash** *v. & n.* slit, cut, gash.

S251 **slaughter** 1. *n.* massacre, *murder,* carnage, bloodshed, butchery 2. *v.* slay, kill, murder, butcher.

S252 **slave** 1. *n.* vassal, captive, serf 2. *v.* drudge, toil, work *n.* **slavery** (F247, L83).

S253 **slay** *v. kill,* slaughter, murder, massacre.   SLEIGH

S254 **sleek** *adj. smooth,* glossy, silken, silky.

S255 **sleep** *v. & n. slumber,* rest, repose, doze, drowse, nap (W9).

S256 **slender** *adj. slim,* slight, thin, narrow, lean, frail (P295).

S257 **slice** *v.* cut, split, sever, slit.

S258 **slide** *v.* glide, slip, skim, skid.

S259 **slight** 1. *adj. small,* trifling, trivial, petty (I246) 2. *v.* neglect, disregard, snub, ignore.

S260 **slim** *adj.* slender, thin, narrow, lank, gaunt 2. slight, poor, weak, insignificant (C417, P263, P295, T82).

S261 **slime** *n.* mud, ooze, mire, slush, muck.

S262 **sling** 1. *v. throw,* cast, hurl, fling 2. *n.* bandage, dressing, support.

S263 **slink** *v.* sneak, skulk, prowl, steal.

S264 **slip** 1. *v. glide,* slide, skid 2. *v.* mistake, err, blunder 3. *n.* mistake, error, blunder.

S265 **slit** *v. & n.* cut, gash, tear, slash.

S266 **slogan** *n.* phrase, motto, expression, catchword, cry.

S267 **slope** *v. & n.* incline, *slant,* tilt *adj.* **sloping** (S452).

S268 **sloppy** *adj.* 1. careless, slovenly 2. mushy, wet.

S269 **slovenly** *adj.* untidy, disorderly, lazy, slipshod (S277).

S270 **slow** 1. *adj. tardy,* leisurely, slack, sluggish (A87, F49, F149, H56, Q26, R31, S614) 2. *adj.* dull, heavy, tedious (L113) 3. *v.* slacken, retard *n.* **slowness** (S358).

S271 **sluggish** *adj.* idle, lazy, slow, slothful, inactive, drowsy (B157, L113, Q26, R31, S614).

S272 **slumber** *v. & n.* sleep, *doze,* nap, rest, repose.

S273 **slur** 1. *n.* mark, stain, stigma, *disgrace* 2. *v.* discredit, slander, defame 3. *v.* pass over, pass by, skim over.

S274 **sly** *adj.* cunning, artful, craft, wily, subtle.

S275 **smack** *v. & n.* 1. taste, savor, smell 2. buss, kiss 3. hit, slap, whack.

S276 **small** *adj.* 1. *little,* tiny, puny, minute (B70, E88, G130, H192, I34, L26, M29, M70, S338) 2. *petty,* trifling, trivial, unimportant *n.* **smallness** (M14).

S

S277 **smart** 1. *adj.* spruce, fine, trim, *neat,* stylish (D293, S111, S146, U84) 2. *adj.* clever, quick, intelligent (S525) 3. *v.* hurt, pain, ache, sting.

S278 **smash** 1. *v. break,* destroy, shatter, crush (R169) 2. *n.* ruin, destruction, crash.

S279 **smear** *v.* daub, spread, stain, mark, soil.

S280 **smell** 1. *v.* sniff, *scent* 2. *n.* scent, odor, aroma, perfume *adj.* **smelly** (F236).

S281 **smile** *v. & n.* beam, grin, smirk, *laugh* (F271, S76).

S282 **smoke** *n.* fume, mist, vapor, fog.

S283 **smooth** 1. *adj.* even, level, *flat,* sleek (R299, R319) 2. *v.* level, flatten, even.

S284 **smother** *v.* stifle, suffocate, *choke.*

S285 **smudge** *v. smear,* mark, blot, spot.

S286 **smug** *adj.* self-satisfied, *complacent,* conceited (M207).

S287 **smut** *n. dirt,* blemish, blight, smudge.

S288 **snack** *n.* lunch, luncheon, light meal.

S289 **snag** *n.* 1. knot, knob, projection, jag, snare 2. problem, obstacle, handicap.

S290 **snap** *v.* 1. *break,* split, crack, burst 2. bite, seize, snarl.

S291 **snare** 1. *n. trap,* net, hook 2. *v.* catch, ensnare, trap, capture (F246).

S292 **snatch** *v.* grasp, clutch, *grab,* grip, seize.

S293 **sneak** 1. *v.* lurk, skulk, slink 2. *n.* informer, nark, *spy,* snoop.

S294 **sneer** *v. & n. scoff,* jeer, gibe, taunt.

S295 **sniff** *v. inhale,* smell, breathe, snuff.

S296 **snip** *v.* clip, cut, nip.

S297 **snivel** *v.* cry, *whimper,* blubber, weep, whine.

S298 **snobbish** *adj.* vulgar, ostentatious, *pretentious,* assuming, arrogant, haughty.

S299 **snub** 1. *v.* humiliate, put down, *slight,* insult (C276) 2. *n.* insult, slight, humiliation.

S300 **snug** *adj.* comfortable, cozy, close.

S301 **soak** *v. wet,* saturate, steep, drench *adj.* **soaked** (D329).

S302 **soar** *v.* rise, ascend, fly, glide, hover (F24).

S303 **sob** *v. weep,* cry, sigh, lament.

S304 **sober** *adj.* 1. not drunk, temperate, abstemious (I272, T113, T127) 2. calm, *moderate,* steady, collected (H56) 3. grave, solemn, serious, sedate (H201).

S305 **sociable** *adj.* friendly, neighborly, affable, social.

S306 **social** *adj.* 1. civil, civic, fraternal, communal, public, tribal 2. gregarious, sociable, companionable, convivial.

S307 **society** *n.* 1. association, fellowship, company, companionship 2. club, association, organization, group 3. people, humanity, the public.

S308 **soft** *adj.* 1. pliable, flexible, plastic, malleable, smooth (F128, H37, S315) 2. dulcet, smooth, melodious (L148, S193) 3. simple, silly, foolish *v.* **soften** (H38).

S309 **soil** 1. *n.* earth, mold, loam, ground 2. *v.* dirty, stain, sully, begrime.

S310 **sojourn** *v.* abide, stay, remain, *live,* dwell, reside.

S311 **solace** *v. & n.* comfort, cheer.

Shoes have soles.

S312 **sole** *adj. single,* only, individual, unique, exclusive. SOUL.

S313 **solemn** *adj. formal,* ritual, ceremonial, sacred, serious, grave (J31).

S314 **solicit** *v. request,* ask, entreat, beg, implore.

S315 **solid** *adj.* 1. *hard,* firm, compact (H146, L102) 2. substantial, reliable, sound *v.* **solidify** (L101, M112, T77).

S316 **solitary** *adj. lone,* lonely, isolated, remote, only.

S317 **solution** *n.* 1. *answer,* explanation, result (Q22) 2. liquefaction, melting.

S318 **solve** *v.* explain, interpret, answer, make plain.

S319 **somber** *adj.* 1. *dismal,* doleful, mournful, sad (G60, H201, J25) 2. *dark,* dull, gloomy, serious.

S320 **sometimes** *adv.* at times, at intervals, now and then, occasionally (O49).

S321 **soon** *adv.* shortly, presently, before long, early (L31).

S322 **soothe** *v. calm,* quiet, appease, pacify, cajole (A77, A79, A86, A115, A143, C89, H35, H51, I306, M5, P33, T144, T146, U94) *adj.* **soothing** (P14).

S323 **sophisticated** *adj.* worldly wise, experienced, knowing, civilized, urbane (I186, I201, P38, R299, U81).

S324 **sorcery** *n.* witchcraft, wizardry, magic, divination.

S325 **sordid** *adj.* slovenly, *squalid,* low, vile.

S326 **sore** 1. *adj.* painful, *tender,* irritated, aching 2. *adj.* angry 2. *n.* wound, cut, injury, ulcer.

S327 **sorrow** *n. grief,* sadness, misery, trouble, anguish (G68) *adj.* **sorrowful** (H34).

S328 **sorry** *adj.* 1. remorseful, *repentant,* apologetic (G60) 2. *miserable,* wretched, pitiful, shabby.

S329 **sort** 1. *n.* species, kind, variety, *type* 2. *v.* classify, order, arrange, distribute (M154).

S330 **soul** (rhymes with *hole*) *n.* mind, spirit, life, essence. SOLE

S331 **sound** 1. *n. noise,* tone, din, racket 2. *v.* resound, pronounce, utter 3. *adj.* whole, entire, unhurt, *healthy,* secure (U48, U82) 4. *adj.* correct, true, rational, sensible (R254).

S332 **sour** *adj.* 1. acid, *tart,* sharp (L173, S611) 2. cross, morose, surly, harsh.

S333 **source** *n.* origin, spring, beginning, cause, derivation, root.

S334 **souvenir** *n.* memento, keepsake, token, relic.

S335 **sovereign** 1. *n.* monarch, *ruler,* king, queen 2. *adj.* supreme, regal, royal, chief.

S336 **sow** 1. *n.* (rhymes with *how*) female pig, hog, swine 2. *v.* (rhymes with *so*) scatter, strew, propagate, plant (R62) SEW SO

S337 **space** *n.* 1. extent, capacity, room, area 2. cosmos, universe, firmament.

S338 **spacious** *adj.* wide, *extensive,* vast, roomy, broad (N10, S276).

S339 **span** 1. *n.* distance, extent, length, spread 2. *n.* nine inches 3. *v.* reach, stretch, cross.

S340 **spar** 1. *v.* box, fight, wrangle 2. *n.* pole, beam.

S341 **spare** 1. *v.* reserve, *save,* set aside 2. *v.* be merciful, forgive (S253) 3. *adj.* lean, meager, skinny 4. *adj.* superfluous, extra.

S342 **spark** *n.* flash, glitter, sparkle.

S343 **sparkle** 1. *v.* glitter, glisten, twinkle, scintillate 2. *n.* spark, luster, glitter.

S344 **sparse** *adj.* scattered, spread thin, scanty, *meager* (D102, E170).

S345 **spasm** *n.* *twitch,* fit, paroxysm, convulsion.

S346 **speak** *v.* talk, say, discourse, utter, express.

S347 **spear** *n.* lance, javelin.

S348 **special** *adj.* specific, *particular,* unusual, exceptional (O88, S428, U102).

S349 **species** *n.* group, class, collection, kind, sort, type.

S350 **specific** *adj.* peculiar, *particular,* special, definite, precise (R23, V4).

S351 **specimen** *n.* pattern, *sample,* model, copy, example.

S352 **speck** *n.* bit, blemish, mite, atom, particle, spot.

S353 **spectacle** *n.* show, exhibition, *sight,* scene, display.

S354 **spectator** *n.* beholder, witness, observer (P138).

S355 **specter** *n.* ghost, spirit, phantom, apparition.

S356 **speculate** *v.* 1. meditate, *reflect,* ponder, muse 2. *gamble,* risk, hazard, venture.

S357 **speech** *n.* 1. language, words, dialect, talk 2. oration, discourse, address, lecture.

S358 **speed** *n.* *haste,* dispatch, swiftness, velocity.

S359 **spell** 1. *n.* charm, incantation, magic power 2. *n.* season, term, time, period 3. *v.* read, interpret, decipher; *Everyone should learn to spell correctly.*

S360 **spend** *v.* 1. expend, pay out, disburse (E3) 2. consume, exhaust, use up (H136, S480).

S361 **sphere** *n.* 1. globe, orb, ball 2. capacity, department, area, field; *Many women are leaders in the medical sphere.*

S362 **spice** *n.* seasoning, *flavor,* relish, savor.

S363 **spill** *v.* shed, pour out, overflow, drop.

S364 **spin** *v.* 1. twirl, whirl, *rotate,* revolve 2. lengthen, prolong, draw out, twist.

S365 **spine** *n.* 1. backbone, ridge 2. thorn, spike.

S366 **spirit** *n.* 1. soul, life, mind 2. temper, disposition, humor, mood 3. courage, fire, energy, vitality 4. apparition, ghost, specter 5. meaning, significance, intent; *The spirit of the Magna Carta still continues in modern law.*

S367 **spiritual** *adj.* 1. holy, divine, sacred, religious 2. mental, intellectual, moral (M77, P191).

S368 **spite** *n.* malice, *venom,* rancor, ill will, pique.

S369 **spiteful** *adj. malicious,* hateful, vindictive.

S370 **splash** *v.* splatter, dash, wet, sprinkle.

S371 **splendid** *adj.* 1. *magnificent,* gorgeous, sumptuous, superb 2. *remarkable,* brilliant, distinguished (D308, H166, S328).

S372 **splinter** *v.* split, rend, chip, break.

S373 **split** 1. *v.* cleave, burst, rend, splinter, divide (J21) 2. *n.* crack, fissure, break, breach.

S374 **spoil** *v.* 1. injure, harm, mar, *damage,* ruin (E80, M120) 2. decay, corrupt, go bad.

S375 **sponsor** *n.* backer, supporter, patron.

Spinning.

S376 **spontaneous** *adj.* instinctive, natural, unbidden, impulsive (P354).

S377 **sport** *n.* 1. play, diversion, amusement, game, fun, recreation 2. derision, ridicule, mockery; *It is unfair to make sport of people's ignorance.*

S378 **spot** 1. *n.* blemish, speck, blot, stain, flaw 2. *n.* locality, site 3. *v.* recognize, distinguish, identify.

S379 **spotless** *adj.* immaculate, unstained, clean (D193).

S380 **spouse** *n.* husband, wife, married person, mate.

S381 **spout** 1. *n.* nozzle, nose, tube 2. *v.* spurt, *squirt,* gush 3. *v.* declaim, rant, utter.

S382 **sprawl** *v.* spread, extend, *loll,* lounge, relax.

S383 **spray** 1. *v. & n.* sprinkle, splash 2. *n.* twig, shoot, bunch.

S384 **spread** *v.* 1. extend, *expand,* unfold, stretch, disperse, scatter (C377) 2. publish, divulge, circulate, distribute.

S385 **spree** *n.* revel, celebration, fling.

S386 **spring** 1. *v. & n. leap,* bound, jump, vault, hop 2. *v.* arise, issue, emerge, originate 3. *n. fountain,* source, origin 4. *n.* season of the year.

S387 **sprinkle** *v.* scatter, strew, rain.

S388 **sprite** *n.* fairy, pixie, elf, spirit, ghost, specter.

S389 **sprout** *v.* shoot, *grow,* germinate, flourish.

S390 **spruce** *adj. neat,* trim, smart, jaunty, tidy (D293).

S391 **spry** *adj.* active, *lively,* brisk, nimble, alèrt, dapper (I94).

S392 **spur** *v. & n.* urge, goad.

S393 **spurious** *adj.* counterfeit, sham, false, feigned, bogus, fake (G43).

S394 **spurn** *v.* scorn, *despise,* disdain, disregard, reject (A135).

S395 **spurt** *v. & n.* gush, spring, stream, spout, push.

S396 **spy** 1. *n. agent,* scout, informer 2. *v. see,* behold, discern, detect, discover, scrutinize.

S397 **squabble** *v. quarrel,* wrangle, brawl, row (A81).

S398 **squad** *n. gang,* band, set, company.

S399 **squalid** *adj.* dirty, nasty, filthy, *foul,* unclean (G103, M21, S436).

S400 **squall** *n.* 1. *cry,* scream, yell, bawl 2. storm, blast, gust.

S401 **squander** *v.* spend, expend, waste, fritter, dissipate, *lavish* (C345, H136, P362, S42, S341).

S402 **square** 1. *n.* four-sided figure 2. *adj.* true, right, just, honest, exact.

S403 **squash** *v. crush,* press, mash, pulp, squeeze.

S404 **squat** 1. *v.* crouch, cower, settle 2. *adj.* crouching, dumpy, stubby, thickset.

S405 **squeak** *v.* squawk, squeal, yell, cry, creak.

S406 **squeal** *v.* squeak, cry, yell.

S407 **squeeze** *v.* compress, pinch, nip, squash, press.

S408 **squirm** *v. writhe,* wriggle, twist.

S409 **squirt** *v.* spout, emit, expel, spurt, splash.

S410 **stab** *v.* pierce, transfix, gore, spear, *wound.*

S411 **stable** 1. *adj.* fixed, steadfast, solid, *firm,* staunch (F155) 2. *n.* stall, mews.

S412 **stack** *v. & n.* pile, heap, load.

S413 **staff** *n.* 1. stick, rod, pole, *club,* cane 2. personnel, employees, workers, crew.

S414 **stage** 1. *n.* platform, scaffold, theater, playhouse, boards 2. *n.* step, degree, point, period 3. *v.* arrange, produce, present, put on, direct.

A Japanese stage.

S415 **stagger** *v.* 1. *reel,* totter, waver, falter 2. shock, astonish, amaze, surprise 3. alternate, vary; *Working hours are sometimes staggered to avoid traffic congestion.*

S416 **stagnant** *adj.* sluggish, inactive, still, *dormant.*

S417 **staid** *adj. sober,* grave, serious, solumn, sedate (G52). STAYED

S418 **stain** 1. *v.* soil, sully, *tarnish,* blemish, blot (C181) 2. *v.* dye, color, tinge 3. *n.*

disgrace, dishonor, taint (H153)
4. *n.* blemish, spot,
imperfection.

S419 **stair** *n.* step, staircase.
STARE

S420 **stake** *n.* 1. *stick,* post,
pole, rod, peg 2. wager, bet,
risk, hazard 3. share, interest.
STEAK

S421 **stale** *adj.* 1. *old,* dry,
musty, fusty, decayed (F252) 2.
trite, common, uninteresting,
flat, dull.

S422 **stalk** (rhymes with *walk*)
1. *v.* follow, *hunt,* pursue,
walk, track 2. *n.* stem.

S423 **stall** 1. *v.* hesitate,
dawdle, hinder, delay, stop 2.
n. stable, cell, recess, stand,
shop, booth.

S424 **stalwart** *adj.* 1. strong,
robust, brawny, muscular (W37)
2. bold, manly, valiant, daring,
brave.

S425 **stammer** *v.* stutter, falter,
hesitate, pause.

S426 **stamp** 1. *v.* imprint,
impress, print, mark 2. *v.* tread,
crush, pound, trample 3. *n.*
block, seal, mark.

S427 **stand** 1. *v.* stay, rest, stop,
remain (W86) 2. *v. arise,* be
erect, get up (S228) 3. *v.* endure,
sustain, bear 4. *n.* stall, booth,
kiosk 5. *n.* platform, table, rest.

S428 **standard** 1. *n.* flag,
ensign, banner 2. *n.* model,
rule, measure, scale 3. *adj.*
consistent, uniform, normal,
constant (U86).

S429 **staple** 1. *adj.* chief,
principal, *important,* necessary
2. *n.* fastening, clasp, hasp.

S430 **stare** *v. gaze,* gape, look
intently. STAIR

S431 **stark** *adj. sheer,* bare,
downright, entire, absolute.

S432 **start** 1. *v. begin,* initiate,
commence (C74, D216, E62, F126,
H17, S479, T64) 2. *v.* shrink,
flinch, jump, startle 3. *n.*
beginning, outset (D140) 4. *n.*
twitch, spasm, surprise *adj.*
starting (F121).

S433 **startle** *v.* frighten, alarm,
shock.

S434 **starve** *v.* famish, be
hungry (F72, S32).

S435 **state** 1. *n. condition,*
situation, plight 2. *n.* country,
commonwealth, land, nation 3.
v. express, say, narrate, affirm.

S436 **stately** *adj.* majestic,
dignified, magnificent, grand
(S399).

S437 **statement** *n.* 1.
announcement, report,
declaration 2. account, record.

S438 **statesman** *n.* politician,
minister, official.

S439 **station** 1. *n.* place,
location, situation 2. *n.* depot,
halt, stop, terminus 3. *v.* place,
locate, post, fix.

S440 **stationary** *adj.* fixed,
stable, still, motionless, at rest
(M200). STATIONERY

S441 **stationery** *n.* pens, ink,
pencils, paper. STATIONARY

S442 **statue** *n. image,* sculpture,
figure, monument.

S443 **status** *n.* standing, rank,
station, condition, position.

S444 **statute** *n. law,* act,
ordinance, edict, decree,
regulation, rule.

S

S445 **staunch** *adj.* constant, faithful, firm, loyal, steadfast (U39).

S446 **stay** 1. *n.* sojourn, *halt,* rest, repose 2. *n.* check, bar, restraint, stop, halt 3. *n.* support, prop, buttress, brace 4. *v.* dwell, lodge, tarry, abide, remain (M259, S494) 5. *v.* stop, restrain, check, hold.

S447 **steady** *adj.* fixed, *firm,* stable, regular, constant (E125, F101, I125, U78, V85).

S448 **steal** *v.* 1. *purloin,* pilfer, filch, poach, rob 2. prowl, go stealthily, sneak.   STEEL

S449 **stealthy** *adj.* sly, secret, *furtive,* sneaking, skulking (O26).

S450 **steam** *n.* vapor, mist, fume.

S451 **steed** *n. horse,* charger, mount, nag, stallion.

S452 **steep** 1. *adj.* sheer, abrupt, precipitous 2. *v.* soak, drench, immerse, submerge.

S453 **steeple** *n.* spire, tower, turret.

S454 **steer** *v.* direct, *pilot,* guide, conduct, govern.

S455 **stem** 1. *n.* branch, *trunk,* stock, shoot, stalk 2. *v.* stop, check, oppose 3. *v.* arise, originate, emanate.

S456 **step** 1. *n.* pace, gait, walk, *stride* 2. *n.* grade, degree, stage 3. *n.* means, measure, expedient 4. *n.* stair, rung, tread 5. *v.* walk.   STEPPE

S457 **sterilize** *v. disinfect,* decontaminate, cleanse *adj.* **sterile** (F88).

S458 **stern** *adj.* austere, *severe,* forbidding, harsh, strict (L70).

S459 **stew** 1. *v.* boil, seethe, simmer 2. *n.* stewed meat, casserole, ragout.

S460 **stick** 1. *v.* pierce, penetrate, *stab,* spear 2. *v.* attach, glue, cement, adhere 3. *v.* remain, abide, cleave, cling 4. *n.* rod, switch, club, cudgel, cane, staff.

S461 **sticky** *adj.* adhesive, glutinous, gluey.

S462 **stiff** *adj.* 1. *rigid,* unbending, inflexible, firm, solid (S244, S578) 2. severe, rigorous, strict, austere 3. difficult, formidable, laborious.

S463 **stifle** *v.* 1. smother, choke, *suffocate* 2. repress, check, stop, hush, still (E60).

S464 **stigma** *n.* stain, blot, disgrace, blemish, mark.

S465 **still** 1. *adj.* motionless, inert, stationary 2. *adj.* quiet, *tranquil,* placid, serene 3. *conj.* yet, till now, however, nevertheless 4. *adv.* always, ever, continually 5. *v.* silence, stifle, muffle, calm, quiet *n.* **stillness** (M246).

S466 **stimulate** *v.* incite, excite, animate, provoke, encourage, *urge* (F276).

S467 **sting** *v.* prick, wound, pain, afflict.

S468 **stingy** *adj. mean,* miserly, close, niggardly, tightfisted (G38, L38, L81).

S469 **stink** *v. & n.* smell, reek.

S470 **stint** 1. *v.* limit, bound, restrain, stop, cease 2. *n.* task, job, chore.

S

S471 **stir** *v*. 1. churn, agitate, shake, whisk, beat, mix 2. disturb, arouse, stimulate, prompt 3. move, budge, go.

S472 **stitch** *v*. sew, needle.

S473 **stock** *v*. & *n*. store, supply, hoard, reserve.

S474 **stocky** *adj*. stout, stubby, short and thick (L21).

S475 **stolid** *adj*. stupid, *dull,* slow, foolish (I243).

S476 **stone** *n*. rock, pebble, boulder, gem, jewel.

S477 **stool** *n*. seat, chair.

S478 **stoop** 1. *v*. bend, lean, crouch, *squat,* bow 2. *n*. doorsteps, porch, veranda.

S479 **stop** 1. *v*. cease, desist, *end,* finish, halt, terminate (C243, C375, M259, P155, P156, R218) 2. *v*. hinder, impede, check, obstruct, close 3. *n. pause,* rest, halt.

S480 **store** 1. *n*. warehouse, depot, shop, market 2. *n*. stock, supply, hoard, provision 3. *v*. provide, keep, reserve, stock.

S481 **storehouse** *n*. warehouse, repository.

S482 **storm** 1. *n*. tempest, gale, hurricane, tornado, squall (C15) 2. *v*. rage, fume, rant 3. *v*. attack, assault (R172) *adj*. **stormy** (F19, M145).

S483 **story** *n*. 1. tale, legend, fiction, narrative, romance 2. falsehood, lie, fib 3. floor, level, stage, tier.

S484 **stout** *adj*. 1. strong, brawny, robust, *sturdy* (F234, F237) 2. brave, valiant, bold, intrepid 3. plump, fat, chubby, portly.

S485 **stow** *v*. pack, stuff, store, load.

S486 **straight** 1. *adj*. direct, undeviating, unswerving (C488) 2. *adj. honest,* fair, honorable, upright 3. *adj*. faultless, perfect, right 4. *adv*. directly, immediately, at once *v*. **straighten** (B58, C376, D255). STRAIT

S487 **strain** 1. *v. stretch,* tighten, pull (R135) 2. *v*. wrench, injure, sprain 3. *v*. filter, purify, percolate 4. *n*. effort, exertion 5. *n*. melody, music, tune.

S488 **strait** *n*. 1. passage, channel, narrows 2. difficulty, distress, hardship; *After losing our money, we found ourselves in serious straits.* STRAIGHT

S489 **strand** 1. *n*. beach, shore, coast 2. *n*. thread, string, line 3. *v*. wreck, castaway, abandon.

S490 **strange** *adj*. 1. *uncommon,* odd, singular, peculiar (F31) 2. foreign, outlandish, *alien.*

S491 **stranger** *n*. alien, visitor, foreigner, outsider (F255).

S492 **strangle** *v*. throttle, choke, suffocate.

S493 **strap** *n*. thong, band, *belt,* strip.

A store, shop or supermarket.

S494 **stray** 1. *v. wander,* rove, roam, straggle, swerve 2. *adj.* lost.

S495 **stream** 1. *n.* river, rivulet, brook, current 2. *v.* flow, rush, pour, issue, spout.

S496 **street** *n.* road, highway, avenue, lane.

S497 **strength** *n.* 1. power, might, *force,* vigor 2. fortitude, courage, spirit 3. sturdiness, soundness, solidity *v.* **strengthen** (F135).

S498 **strenuous** *adj.* determined, energetic, ardent, strong, *vigorous.*

S499 **stress** 1. *v.* emphasize, underline, accentuate 2. *n.* force, strain, pressure 3. *n.* emphasis, accent, weight.

S500 **stretch** *v.* 1. *extend,* lengthen, elongate (C377) 2. exaggerate.

S501 **strict** *adj.* 1. *severe,* rigorous, stern, austere (L70) 2. exact, precise, accurate.

S502 **stride** 1. *n.* step, gait, pace 2. *v. walk,* march, pace.

S503 **strife** *n.* conflict, contest, quarrel, *discord,* animosity (P98).

S504 **strike** 1. *v.* smite, *hit,* beat, knock, pound 2. *n.* walkout, lockout, revolt, boycott 3. *n.* attack, *assault,* offensive.

S505 **string** *n.* cord, line, twine, thread.

S506 **strip** 1. *v.* uncover, take off, divest, remove (A60) 2. *n.* piece, slip, band, ribbon.

S507 **stripe** *n.* stroke, line, chevron, streak, belt.

S508 **strive** *v.* toil, struggle, aim, *attempt,* endeavor.

S509 **stroke** 1. *n. blow,* knock, rap, tap 2. *n.* feat, effort, accomplishment 3. *n.* attack, shock, seizure 4. *v.* rub, caress, smooth, massage.

S510 **stroll** *v. & n.* walk, ramble, saunter, amble.

S511 **strong** *adj.* 1. robust, sturdy, *brawny,* sinewy, hardy (F71, F155, F234, F237, H104, I173, W37) 2. firm, solid, compact, *secure* 3. *pungent,* piquant, sharp, spicy.

S512 **structure** *n.* 1. building, edifice, erection 2. construction, form, arrangement.

S513 **struggle** 1. *n.* conflict, *fight,* contest 2. *n.* labor, exertion, effort 3. *v. strive,* fight, content (Y7).

S514 **stubborn** *adj. obstinate,* perverse, headstrong, willful, rigid (F152).

S515 **student** *n.* pupil, learner, scholar.

S516 **studious** *adj.* diligent, eager, zealous, learned, scholarly (I100).

S517 **study** 1. *n.* research, inquiry, investigation 2. *n.* studio, office, sanctum, den 3. *v.* meditate, muse, *learn,* examine, consider.

Bowstring.

S518 **stuff** 1. *n.* material, matter, substance 2. *n.* cloth, textile, fabric 3. *n.* nonsense, twaddle, balderdash 4. *v.* stow, pack, fill, cram, ram.

S519 **stuffy** *adj.* 1. musty, *close,* confined 2. pompous, prudish, prim, staid.

S520 **stumble** *v. trip,* fall, flounder, falter.

S521 **stun** *v.* 1. stupefy, bewilder, overcome, astonish, amaze 2. render unconscious.

S522 **stunt** 1. *v.* shorten, dwarf 2. *n.* performance, feat, exploit.

S523 **stupefy** *v.* dull, make stupid, deaden, stun.

S524 **stupendous** *adj.* astonishing, surprising, amazing, *wonderful* (O88).

S525 **stupid** *adj. foolish,* dull, senseless, brutish, silly (A87, B152, C188, I243, K1, S10, S191, S277).

S526 **sturdy** *adj.* strong, lusty, robust, stout, *stalwart,* firm (F234, F237).

S527 **stutter** *v.* stammer, stumble, falter, hesitate.

S528 **style** 1. *n.* manner, method, way, *mode* 2. *n.* kind, sort, type 3. *n.* elegance, chic, *fashion* 4. *n.* diction, phraseology 5. *v.* title, name; *He styles himself "Mr."* STILE

S529 **suave** *adj.* affable, agreeable, polite, *sophisticated,* urbane (R299, U19).

S530 **subdue** *v.* conquer, overcome, vanquish, beat, quell, soften (Y7).

S531 **subject** 1. *n. topic,* theme, point, matter 2. *n.* dependent, subordinate 3. *adj.* subordinate, obedient (I138) 4. *v.* subdue, control, expose.

S532 **sublime** *adj.* high, grand, exalted, *noble,* magnificent.

S533 **submerge** *v. immerse,* plunge, sink, submerse, drown (R270).

S534 **submit** *v.* 1. yield, *surrender,* resign (F112, O130, R199) 2. refer, tender, offer; *The engineer has submitted his report. adj.* **submissive** (D67).

S535 **subordinate** *adj.* inferior, subservient, subject (S573).

S536 **subscribe** *v.* 1. contribute, *support,* donate to 2. agree, consent, approve.

S537 **subsequent** *adj.* after, following, succeeding, (P375, P388).

S538 **subside** *v. sink,* settle, lower, descend, diminish (R270).

S539 **substance** *n.* 1. *matter,* material, texture, stuff 2. meaning, import, gist, essence.

S540 **substantial** *adj.* 1. *real,* actual (U50) 2. strong, firm, solid, sound (F155) 3. wealthy, affluent.

S541 **substitute** 1. *n.* makeshift, replacement, proxy 2. *v. exchange,* change, replace.

S542 **subtle (sut-***tul***)** *adj.* 1. deep, delicate, ingenious, fine, suggestive (B101, O26) 2. cunning, artful, crafty, tricky.

S543 **subtract** *v. deduct,* withdraw, take, take away, reduce (A49, S579).

S544 **succeed** *v.* 1. *prosper,* flourish, *thrive* (F15, L142, M182) 2. follow, ensue, come after (P333).

S545 **success** *n.* prosperity, *luck,* good fortune, accomplishment (F16, F17, R236).

S546 **successful** *adj.* prosperous, fortunate, lucky.

S547 **succession** *n.* sequence, series, course, order.

S548 **suck** *v.* imbibe, absorb, swallow up, engulf.

S549 **sudden** *adj.* unexpected, abrupt, hasty, rapid, unusual (G113).

S550 **sue** *v. prosecute,* litigate, take action against.

S551 **suffer** *v.* 1. undergo, *feel,* endure, sustain, *tolerate,* bear 2. permit, allow, admit, let (R199).

S552 **sufficient** *adj.* adequate, ample, *enough,* satisfactory (I95, I235, S54).

S553 **suffocate** *v.* stifle, choke, *smother,* strangle.

S554 **suggest** *v.* hint, *intimate,* propose, indicate, advise.

S555 **suit** 1. *v. fit,* adapt, adjust, become, befit 2. *n.* costume, outfit, habit, dress 3. *n.* action, case, trial.

S556 **suitable** *adj.* fit, proper, apt, *appropriate,* applicable (I82, I99, I155, U40, U77, U83).

S557 **sulk** *v.* fret, scowl, *mope,* glower *adj.* **sulky.**

S558 **sullen** *adj.* cross, *morose,* sulky, sour, moody, gloomy, dismal, somber (C124).

S559 **sum** *n.* amount, total, whole. SOME

S560 **summary** *n.* synopsis, digest, abstract, precis, outline.

S561 **summit** *n. top,* apex, acme, peak, pinnacle, zenith (B29).

S562 **summon** *v. call,* cite, invite, send for, request (D237).

S563 **sumptuous** *adj.* magnificent, *costly,* splendid, gorgeous, rich.

S564 **sundry** *adj. several,* diverse, various, miscellaneous.

S565 **sunny** *adj. bright,* cheerful, shining, brilliant, clear, happy (F223, G79, O129).

S566 **sunrise** *n.* dawn, daybreak, morning (E146, S567).

S567 **sunset** *n.* evening, sundown, nightfall, dusk (S566).

S568 **superb** *adj. splendid,* elegant, exquisite, marvelous, excellent (I169).

S569 **supercilious** *adj.* haughty, arrogant, overbearing, proud, disdainful (H196).

S570 **superficial** *adj.* 1. *trivial,* shallow, slight, cursory (M240, P414) 2. external, exterior, outer.

S571 **superfluous** *adj.* excessive, redundant, *unnecessary,* needless (E134).

S572 **superintendent** *n.* overseer, supervisor, manager, warden.

S573 **superior** 1. *adj. better,* greater, higher, upper (I169, M101, O88, S103) 2. *n.* chief, principal, boss (S531, S535).

S574 **supernatural** *adj.* miraculous, *abnormal,* mysterious.

S575 **supersede** *v.* displace, supplant, *succeed.*

S576 **superstition** *n.* false belief, folklore.

S577 **supervise** *v. direct,* regulate, manage, oversee.

S578 **supple** *adj.* pliant, yielding, flexible, *lithe* (I176, S462).

S579 supplement 1. *n.* addition, extra, appendix, sequel 2. *v.* add, supply, extend, complement.

S580 supply 1. *v. provide,* furnish, stock, store (W88) 2. *n.* reserve, store, *stock,* hoard.

S581 support 1. *v. sustain,* uphold, bear 2. *v.* maintain, cherish, provide for 3. *v.* assist, aid, *help,* patronize (O71, O73, R180) 4. *v.* substantiate, confirm; *His opinion was supported by the chairman.* 5. *n.* prop, supporter, brace 6. *n.* aid, help, assistance (H128).

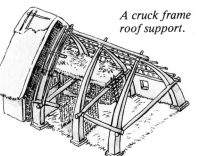

A cruck frame roof support.

S582 suppose *v.* 1. presume, conceive, imagine, *assume* 2. think, believe, surmise.

S583 suppress *v.* crush, overpower, subdue, *stifle* (A114, P466).

S584 supreme *adj.* highest, greatest, principal, *chief,* best (L55).

S585 sure *adj.* 1. *certain,* confident, positive, convinced (D292, U13) 2. safe, secure, stable, firm 3. unfailing, infallible, indisputable.

S586 surface *n.* outside, exterior, face, covering *v.*

surface (S533).

S587 surge 1. *n.* billow, wave, breaker, roller 2. *v.* gush, swell, flow, *heave* (D182).   SERGE

S588 surly *adj. morose,* cross, testy, touchy, peevish (G39).

S589 surmise 1. *v.* imagine, suspect, suppose, *guess,* presume 2. *n.* conjecture, guess, supposition.

S590 surpass *v.* excel, *exceed,* outdo, pass (F15).

S591 surplus *n.* excess, residue, *remainder.*

S592 surprise 1. *v.* astonish, amaze, startle, *astound* 2. *n.* wonder, astonishment, amazement.

S593 surrender *v. yield,* give up, relinquish, renounce (C337, C370, D62, O137, R199).

S594 surround *v.* encircle, encompass, *enclose,* circle.

S595 survey 1 *n.* view, observe, scan, *contemplate,* inspect 2. *n.* inspection, scrutiny, review.

S596 survive *v.* remain, outlive, *endure,* persist (P144).

S597 susceptible *adj. sensitive,* impressionable, responsive (I48).

S598 suspect *v.* 1. distrust, *doubt,* mistrust 2. surmise, imagine, fancy, believe.

S599 suspend *v.* 1. *hang,* sling, dangle 2. discontinue, break off, postpone (C375).

S600 suspense *n.* uncertainty, doubt, anxiety, fear, concern.

S601 suspicion *n.* doubt, mistrust, *distrust* (T220).

S602 sustain *v.* 1. bear, *support,* uphold, maintain,

keep 2. suffer, undergo, endure (F156).

S603 **swagger** *v.* bluster, bully, strut, parade, boast.

S604 **swallow** 1. *v. devour,* eat, engulf, gulp 2. *v.* believe, credit, accept 3. *n.* mouthful, gulp 4. *n.* bird.

S605 **swamp** 1. *n.* bog, marsh, fen, quagmire 2. *v.* engulf, overwhelm, deluge, capsize.

S606 **swarm** 1. *n.* multitude, *crowd,* throng, flock 2. *v.* collect, crowd, throng.

S607 **sway** *v.* 1. move, swing, *wave,* turn, bend 2. control, influence, direct.

S608 **swear** *v.* 1. *vow,* declare, affirm, assert 2. blaspheme, curse, utter an oath.

S609 **sweat** 1. *v.* perspire 2. *n.* perspiration.

S610 **sweep** *v.* brush, clean, clear, remove.

S611 **sweet** *adj.* 1. sugary, honeyed, luscious (B78, S332, T32) 2. soft, melodious, harmonious, tuneful 3. pleasant, charming, agreeable 4. pure, fresh, clean (R298).

S612 **swell** *v.* dilate, expand, distend, increase, *enlarge* (L72, S194).

S613 **swerve** *v.* deviate, diverge, *swing,* veer.

S614 **swift** *adj. fast,* quick, fleet, rapid, speedy (S270).

S615 **swim** *v. bathe,* float, glide, skim, paddle.

S616 **swindle** 1. *v. cheat,* deceive, trick, defraud 2. *n.* cheat, fraud, deception, trickery.

S617 **swine** *n.* hog, pig.

S618 **swing** *v.* vibrate, wave, dangle, *sway.*

S619 **swirl** *v.* eddy, whirl, gyrate, spin, reel.

S620 **switch** 1. *v.* change, turn, *shift,* replace 2. *n.* control, push-button.

S621 **swoon** *v. faint,* pass out.

S622 **swoop** *v. dive,* pounce, seize, plummet.

The foil (left) and epée—two types of sword.

S623 **sword** *n.* blade, saber, cutlass, rapier.   SOARED

S624 **symbol** *n.* emblem, sign, device, token, figure.
CYMBAL

S625 **sympathetic** *adj.* compassionate, tender, kind, understanding, *considerate* (I141).

S626 **sympathy** *n.* 1. understanding, feeling, *compassion,* tenderness 2. *harmony,* agreement, concord.

S627 **symptom** *n.* indication, sign, mark.

S628 **synthetic** *adj.* artificial, manufactured.

S629 **system** *n.* scheme, plan, *method,* arrangement, order, procedure.

T t

T1 **table** *n.* 1. slab, tablet, board 2. index, list, statement.

T2 **tablet** *n.* 1. table, slab 2. lozenge, pill.

T3 **taboo** *v.* forbid, prohibit, ban.

T4 **tack** *v.* 1. fasten, attach, nail, pin 2. (nautical) go about, change course.

T5 **tackle** *v.* 1. *seize,* grab, attack 2. undertake, attempt.

T6 **tact** *n.* discrimination, *judgment,* skill, diplomacy *adj.* **tactful** (I144).   TACKED

T7 **tactics** *n.* strategy, diplomacy, method, plan.

T8 **tag** *n.* label, card, ticket, sticker.

T9 **taint** *v.* infect, corrupt, pollute, *contaminate.*

T10 **take** *v.* 1. receive, accept (G59) 2. seize, grab, clasp, grasp 3. capture, catch 4. choose, *select,* pick 5. conduct, lead 6. understand, interpret; *I take it that you will visit us on Sunday.* 7. demand, require; *It takes too long to explain!*

T11 **tale** *n. story,* account, fable, legend.   TAIL

T12 **talent** *n.* gift, skill, ability, aptitude.

T13 **talk** 1. *v. speak,* converse 2. *v.* confer, reason 3. *n.* conversation, parley 4. *n.* lecture, discourse.

T14 **tall** *adj.* lofty, *high,* big (L111).

T15 **tally** *v.* 1. *match,* agree, conform 2. count, calculate.

T16 **tame** 1. *adj. docile,* domesticated, mild (F110, S41, W70) 2. *adj.* dull, flat, tedious 3. *v.* domesticate, make tame.

T17 **tamper** *v. meddle,* dabble, tinker.

T18 **tang** *n. flavor,* taste, quality.

T19 **tangible** *adj. real,* certain, substantial, material (V4).

T20 **tangle** *v. & n.* knot, *muddle,* twist (U68).

T21 **tank** *n.* 1. cistern, reservoir 2. armored vehicle.

T22 **tantalize** *v.* torment, irritate, *frustrate* (A126).

T23 **tantrum** *n.* whim, fit, outburst, temper.

T24 **tap** 1. *v. & n.* strike, rap, hit, knock 2. *n.* plug, stopper, valve, faucet.

T25 **tape** 1. *n.* strip, ribbon, strap 2. *v.* wrap, tie, bind 3. *v.* record.

T26 **taper** *v.* narrow, contract, lessen.

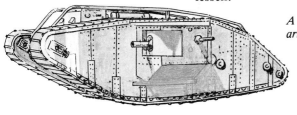

A tank is an armored vehicle.

T27 **tardy** *adj. slow,* late, slack (Q26, R31).

T28 **target** *n.* object, aim, end, goal.

T29 **tariff** *n.* duty, tax, schedule, levy.

T30 **tarnish** *v. & n.* soil, *stain,* spot, blemish (P279).

T31 **tarry** *v.* wait, linger, delay, loiter, *stay,* remain (H210, R330).

T32 **tart** 1. *adj.* sour, acid, *sharp,* bitter (S611) 2. *n.* pie, flan.

T33 **task** *n.* work, labor, *job,* undertaking, chore.

T34 **taste** 1. *n. flavor,* relish, savor 2. *n.* discernment, judgment 3. *v.* savor, try, sample, experience *adj.* **tasty,** **tasteful** (I216).

T35 **tattle** *v.* chatter, prattle, chat, babble.

T36 **taunt** *v. & n.* ridicule, reproach, insult, *jeer* (R204).

T37 **taut** *adj.* stretched, tense, *tight,* strained (S244).
TAUGHT

T38 **tavern** *n. inn,* hostelry, bar, pub.

T39 **tawdry** *adj.* showy, *gaudy,* flashy (R105).

T40 **tax** 1. *n.* duty, levy, excise 2. *v.* assess, burden, load.
TACKS

T41 **teach** *v. instruct,* educate, inform, train, drill.

T42 **teacher** *n.* instructor, tutor, master, mistress, lecturer, coach.

T43 **team** *n.* crew, group, band, company, gang, party.
TEEM

T44 **tear** 1. *v. rend,* pull, rip, split 2. *n.* rip, split, rent, fissure. TARE

T45 **tease** *v.* vex, tantalize, badger, *pester,* provoke (P3).
TEAS TEES

T46 **technique** *n.* system, method, procedure.

T47 **tedious** *adj.* wearisome, irksome, *tiresome,* boring (I78, I254).

T48 **teem** *v.* abound, be prolific, swarm. TEAM

T49 **tell** *v.* 1. *relate,* narrate, describe 2. reveal, divulge 3. discern, discover 4. command, bid, order.

T50 **temper** 1. *n.* disposition, humor, mood 2. *n. anger,* passion, irritation (C15) 3. *v.* soften, moderate 4. *v.* anneal, harden.

T51 **temperamental** *adj.* irritable, moody, touchy, sensitive (P232, S133).

T52 **temperate** *adj.* moderate, calm, dispassionate, restrained, calm (E227, I38).

T53 **tempest** *n.* storm, hurricane, gale, violence.

T54 **temporary** *adj.* short-lived, passing, momentary, transient (E140, E150, P146, P152).

T55 **tempt** *v. lure,* persuade, induce, seduce, attract (R172).

A team.

T56 **tenacious** *adj.* stubborn, obstinate, persevering, diligent, *steadfast.*

T57 **tenant** *n.* occupier, *resident,* dweller.

T58 **tend** *v.* 1. watch, guard, protect 2. incline, lean, verge.

T59 **tendency** *n. inclination,* bias, trend, susceptibility.

T60 **tender** 1. *adj. soft,* delicate 2. *adj.* compassionate, *kind,* gentle, loving (C14, H37, H39, H86, T152, U57) 3. *adj.* sensitive, painful 4. *v. & n.* offer, bid.

T61 **tense** *adj. tight,* stretched, strained, rigid (R135).   TENTS

T62 **tenuous** *adj.* thin, *slender,* small, fragile (S511).

T63 **term** *n.* 1. time, season, period, interval 2. word, expression, phrase, name.

T64 **terminate** *v. end,* conclude, close, finish, stop, cease (I102) *adj.* **terminal** (I193).

T65 **terrible** *adj. frightful,* horrible, dreadful, fearful, horrid.

T66 **terrify** *v. frighten,* alarm, scare, horrify, shock (R66).

T67 **territory** *n.* district, area, quarter, country, region.

T68 **terror** *n.* fright, alarm, panic, horror, *dread,* fear.

T69 **terse** *adj.* concise, brief, *curt,* laconic (F172).

T70 **test** 1. *n. experiment,* trial, proof, quiz 2. *v.* examine, question, try.

T71 **testy** *adj.* peevish, fretful, touchy, *cross,* snappish (P248).

T72 **text** *n.* 1. passage, sentence, clause, verse 2. topic, theme, subject.

T73 **textile** *n. cloth,* material, fabric.

T74 **texture** *n.* grain, surface, pattern.

T75 **thank** *v.* acknowledge, give thanks, be grateful, appreciate.

T76 **thankful** *adj. grateful,* obliged, indebted, beholden (U46).

T77 **thaw** *v. melt,* defrost, liquefy, dissolve (F248).

T78 **theft** *n.* larceny, robbery, stealing, pilfering.

T79 **theme** *n.* subject, *topic,* text, thesis.

T80 **theory** *n.* conjecture, speculation, hypothesis, opinion.

T81 **therefore** 1. *adv.* consequently, accordingly, thus 2. *conj.* thence, then, for that reason.

T82 **thick** *adj.* 1. dense, gross, bulky, solid, squat, dumpy 2. viscous, gummy, gooey, syrupy, stodgy (T84).

T83 **thief** *n.* robber, burglar, pilferer, crook.

T84 **thin** *adj.* 1. slender, slim, lean, skinny, lank, meager, narrow (F51, P263, P295, S484, W68) 2. diluted, watery, weak (T82).

T85 **thing** *n.* being, creature, object, body, substance.

T86 **think** *v.* 1. *reflect,* meditate, muse, speculate 2. conclude, suppose, believe, fancy, consider.

T87 **thirsty** *adj.* dry, parched, arid.

T88 **thorn** *n.* spine, prickle, barb, bramble.

T89 **thorough** *adj.* complete, *entire,* total, perfect (H30).

T90 **thought** *n.* 1. reflection, meditation, *notion,* idea, fancy 2. judgment, conclusion.

T91 **thoughtful** *adj.* 1. mindful, *considerate,* prudent, attentive, kind (M92, R36, T92) 2. reflective, *pensive,* studious.

T92 **thoughtless** *adj.* heedless, regardless, *careless,* neglectful (C348, T91).

T93 **thrash** *v. beat,* flog, punish, whip.

T94 **thread** *n.* fiber, filament, *cord,* string.

T95 **threaten** *v.* 1. *menace,* denounce, intimidate 2. impend, loom, forebode.

T96 **threshold** *n.* 1. entrance, gate, door 2. *beginning,* outset, verge, start (E62).

T97 **thrifty** *adj. frugal,* sparing, careful, saving (E226, I84, P404).

T98 **thrill** 1. *v. excite,* agitate, stimulate 2. *n.* excitement, joy, kick.

T99 **thrive** *v. prosper,* succeed, grow, increase, flourish (E202) *adj.* **thriving** (S111).

T100 **throb** *v. & n. beat,* pulse, pound, thump.

T101 **throng** 1. *n.* crowd, multitude, horde, host 2. *v.* swarm, crowd, flock.

T102 **throttle** *v. choke,* strangle, suffocate, stifle.

T103 **throw** *v. & n. toss,* pitch, thrust, fling.   THROE

T104 **thrust** *v. & n.* push, shove, pass, stab, assault, attack.

Timepieces tell the time.

T105 **thump** *v. & n.* rap, beat, knock, *strike,* punch, whack.

T106 **thwart** *v.* hinder, oppose, obstruct, contravene, *frustrate* (A161, E60).

T107 **ticket** *n.* pass, permit, label, slip, note, sticker.

T108 **tickle** *v.* 1. titillate, touch, stroke 2. please, amuse, delight.

T109 **tide** *n. current,* stream, ebb, flow.   TIED

T110 **tidings** *n. news,* information, advice, word.

T111 **tidy** *adj. neat,* orderly, trim (D231, S269, U84).

T112 **tie** 1. *v.* bind, *fasten,* knot, connect, link 2. *n.* knot, bond, link 3. *n.* cravat, necktie.

T113 **tight** *adj.* 1. close, *firm,* taut, secure, closefitting (L136) 2. (colloq.) drunk, befuddled, boozy, tipsy (S304) 3. stingy, closefisted, mean (G38) *v.* **tighten** (L137, R135).

T114 **till** 1. *v.* cultivate, plow 2. *n.* money drawer, cash register.

T115 **tilt** *v. & n.* slope, incline, *slant.*

T116 **timber** *n.* wood, planks, logs, lumber.

T117 **time** 1. *n. period,* spell, age, interval, term 2. *n.* measure, tempo, beat, meter 3. *v.* regulate, measure.   THYME

T118 **timely** *adj.* opportune, early, punctual, prompt, convenient (I126).

T119 **timid** *adj.* diffident, bashful, coy, shrinking, *shy,* fearful (B110, C319, F65, H115).

T120 **tinge** *v. & n.* dye, stain, color, tint.

T121 **tingle** *v. & n.* sting, prickle, itch.

T122 **tinker** *v. mend,* patch, cobble, repair, fix.

T123 **tinkle** *v. & n.* jingle, clink, ring, jangle.

T124 **tint** *v. & n. color,* tinge, dye, stain.

T125 **tiny** *adj.* little, wee, *small,* puny (B70, C233, E88, H192, I34, L26, M29, M70, M223, M225).

T126 **tip** 1. *n.* end, *point,* extremity, top, peak (B126) 2. *n.* gift, gratuity, reward 3. *n.* advice, information, hint, clue 4. *v.* lean, incline, tilt.

T127 **tipsy** *adj.* drunk, befuddled.

T128 **tire** *v. fatigue,* weary, exhaust, weaken (R109) *adj.* **tired.**

T129 **tiresome** *adj.* arduous, annoying, boring, dull, exhausting (I254).

T130 **title** *n.* 1. name, designation, heading 2. claim, right, deed.

T131 **toil** 1. *v. labor,* work, drudge (R135) 2. *n.* labor, work, drudgery, exertion.

T132 **token** *n.* sample, mark, symbol, souvenir.

T133 **tolerate** *v.* permit, allow, admit, suffer, *endure* (D219) *adj.* **tolerable** (I234, I270) **tolerant.** (I271).

T134 **toll** 1. *v. peal,* ring, chime 2. *n. tax,* duty.

T135 **tomb** (rhymes with *room*) *n.* vault, crypt, grave, sepulcher.

T136 **tone** *n.* 1. sound, note, noise 2. accent, intonation, expression 3. color, shade, hue.

T137 **tongue** *n.* language, speech, dialect.

T138 **tonic** *n.* 1. medicine, refresher 2. key, scale.

T139 **tool** *n.* instrument, implement, utensil.   TULLE

T140 **top** *n.* 1. *peak,* summit, acme, pinnacle (B126) 2. surface, upper side 3. cap, tip, stopper, lid 4. spinning toy.

T141 **topic** *n.* theme, *subject,* question, matter.

T142 **topple** *v.* fall, tumble, overturn.

T143 **torch** *n.* lamp, light, lantern.

T144 **torment** 1. *v.* torture, *distress,* pain, annoy, pester (S322) 2. *n.* torture, agony, pain.

T145 **torrent** *n.* downpour, *flood,* deluge, stream.

T146 **torture** 1. *n. anguish,* agony, torment, pain 2. *v.* agonize, distress, pain (C239, S322).

T147 **toss** *v.* throw, *pitch,* cast, hurl, heave, fling.

T148 **total** 1. *n.* whole, *amount,* sum (P59) 2. *adj.* complete, full, entire.

T149 **totter** *v. stagger,* reel, falter.

T150 **touch** 1. *v.* feel, grope, finger, handle 2. *v.* enjoy, suffer, experience; *The radio touched on something I remembered.* 3. *v.* affect, impress, move; *The sad plight of the wounded stag touched our hearts.* 4. *n.* feeling, contact 5. *n.* taste 6. *n.* power, ability, skill; *The painting shows a touch of genius.*

T151 **touchy** *adj. peevish,* cross, snappy, testy, irascible (A82).

T152 **tough** *adj.* strong, firm, *hardy,* leathery, severe, sturdy, durable (T60).

T153 **tour** *n.* journey, excursion, *trip,* expedition, visit.

T154 **tourist** *n.* traveler, pilgrim, sightseer, visitor.

T155 **tournament** *n.* contest, game, match.

T156 **tow** *v.* draw, *haul,* drag, pull, tug. TOE

T157 **tower** *n.* turret, minaret, spire, steeple, belfry.

T158 **town** *n.* place, city, municipality, metropolis (C438).

T159 **toy** 1. *n.* plaything, bauble, trinket 2. *v.* trifle, play, dally.

T160 **trace** 1. *n. mark,* sign, vestige, remains 2. *v.* follow, track, trail 3. *v.* draw, sketch, delineate.

T161 **track** 1. *n. trail,* trace, footprint 2. *n.* course, way, road, path 3. *v.* follow, trace, trail, pursue.

T162 **tract** *n.* area, region, district, quarter. TRACKED

T163 **trade** *n.* 1. traffic, commerce, business, barter 2. occupation, employment, craft.

T164 **tradition** *n. custom,* usage, folklore, convention.

T165 **traffic** *n.* 1. trade, commerce, exchange, sale 2. movement of vehicles.

T166 **tragedy** *n. calamity,* disaster, catastrophe (C238, F42).

T167 **tragic** *adj.* shocking, dreadful, sad, miserable, unfortunate (C240).

T168 **trail** 1. *v.* trace, track, *follow,* hunt 2. *v.* draw, drag, pull 3. *n.* track, scent, path.

T169 **train** 1. *n.* followers, staff, retinue 2. *n.* series, chain, succession 3. *v.* educate, drill, instruct.

T170 **trait** *n.* feature, characteristic, peculiarity.

T171 **traitor** *n.* betrayer, *renegade,* rebel, deserter, spy.

T172 **tramp** 1. *v.* journey, walk, march 2. *n.* vagabond, vagrant, loafer, hobo.

Toys are playthings.

T173 tranquil *adj.* calm, still, quiet, *serene,* peaceful (F240, R213, U94) *n.* **tranquility** (A57, S503) *v.* **tranquilize** (P33).

T174 transaction *n.* deal, business, negotiation.

T175 transcend *v.* exceed, pass, surmount, surpass, excel.

T176 transfer 1. *v.* carry, move, convey, transmit 2. *v.* consign, make over, confer, assign 3. *n.* change, removal, shift.

T177 transform *v.* change, convert, alter (R219).

T178 transgress *v.* err, sin, offend, infringe, disobey (O4).

T179 transient *adj.* passing, fleeting, temporary, brief (P146).

T180 transmit *v.* send, remit, forward, transfer, dispatch.

T181 transparent *adj.* 1. *clear,* lucid, diaphanous (O62) 2. evident, obvious.

T182 transport 1. *v.* carry, fetch, convey, bear 2. *n.* conveyance, carriage, transportation.

T183 trap 1. *n. snare,* ambush, pitfall 2. *v.* ensnare, catch.

T184 trash *n. rubbish,* junk, refuse, waste, garbage.

T185 travel 1. *v.* journey, ramble, voyage 2. *n.* journeying, touring.

T186 treacherous *adj.* traitorous, unfaithful, *disloyal,* false *n.* **treachery** (L156).

T187 tread 1. *v.* & *n.* walk, step, tramp 2. *n.* tire surface.

T188 treason *n.* treachery, disloyalty, betrayal (L156).

T189 treasure 1. *n.* money, wealth, cash, riches 2. *v.*

cherish, value, prize.

T190 treat 1. *v.* use, *handle,* manage 2. *v.* entertain, feast 3. *v.* nurse, doctor, minister to 4. *n.* pleasure, entertainment.

T191 treatment *n.* usage, handling, management.

T192 treaty *n.* agreement, *pact,* alliance, negotiation.

T193 tremble *v. quake,* shake, shudder, quiver.

T194 tremendous *adj.* 1. *enormous,* huge, immense, vast 2. terrible, fearful, horrid, awful 3. remarkable, superb (O88).

T195 tremor *n.* trembling, shaking, agitation, quivering.

T196 trench *n.* ditch, channel, trough, moat, gully.

T197 trend *n.* tendency, inclination, direction, *fashion.*

T198 trespass 1. *v.* transgress, sin, *offend* 2. *v.* infringe, intrude 3. *n.* crime, fault, sin.

T199 trial *n.* 1. test, *ordeal,* examination, action 2. suffering, trouble, affliction.

T200 tribe *n.* family, clan, race, set, group.

T201 tribute *n.* 1. donation, subscription, *payment,* tax 2. compliment, praise, admiration.

T202 trick 1. *n.* deceit, deception, fraud, trickery, wile 2. *n.* antic, caper, jest 3. *v. cheat,* defraud, deceive, dupe.

T203 trickle *v.* & *n.* drip, drop, flow, dribble, *leak.*

T204 trifle 1. *n.* small amount, bauble, plaything, nothing 2. *n.* dessert 3. *v.* dally, play, toy.

T205 **trifling** *adj. trivial,* petty, frivolous, worthless, slight (M215).

T206 **trim** 1. *adj.* snug, *neat,* compact, tidy (U84) 2. *v.* clip, lop, *prune* 3. *v.* decorate, ornament, adorn.

T207 **trinket** *n.* trifle, bauble, toy.

T208 **trip** 1. *v.* skip, hop, dance 2. *v. stumble,* stagger 3. *n.* jaunt, excursion, tour, voyage.

T209 **trite** *adj.* common, dull, ordinary, banal, *stale,* corny (U16).

T210 **triumph** 1. *n. victory,* success, conquest 2. *v.* win, succeed, prevail (D62).

T211 **trivial** *adj.* trifling, *petty,* small, slight, paltry, unimportant (G126, G130, I68, M215, S135, S540).

T212 **troop** 1. *n. band,* company, squad, throng 2. *v.* throng, collect, march.

TROUPE

T213 **trophy** *n.* prize, award, memento, souvenir.

T214 **trot** *v.* run, canter, sprint, jog, amble.

Horses trotting.

T215 **trouble** 1. *v.* disturb, disorder, *distress,* annoy, pester, vex (A126) 2. *v.* inconvenience, bother 3. *n.* annoyance, distress, adversity, difficulty (H33).

T216 **truce** *n.* armistice, cessation, *respite,* peace.

T217 **true** *adj.* 1. *real,* genuine, actual, valid (E126, F27, U85) 2. honest, upright, faithful, steady.

T218 **trunk** *n.* 1. stem, stalk, body, stock 2. snout, proboscis 3. box, chest, case.

T219 **truss** *v. bind,* pack, bundle, cramp.

T220 **trust** 1. *n. confidence,* reliance, faith, hope, belief (D260, D291, M176, M190, S601) 2. *v.* believe, rely on, credit.

TRUSSED

T221 **trusty** *adj.* trustworthy, strong, firm, reliable.

T222 **truth** *n. fact,* reality, veracity, honesty, sincerity (F25, F28, F101) *adj.* **truthful.**

T223 **try** 1. *v.* test, examine, prove 2. *v. attempt,* endeavor, strive, aim 3. *n.* attempt, experiment, trial.

T224 **trying** *adj. irksome,* wearisome, difficult, troublesome.

T225 **tube** *n. pipe,* hose, channel.

T226 **tuck** *v.* pack, stow, fold, press together.

T227 **tuft** *n.* knot, bunch, cluster, crest.

T228 **tug** *v. pull,* draw, haul, drag.

T229 **tumble** *v. fall,* stumble,

sprawl, topple, plunge.

T230 **tumult** *n.* uproar, affray, row, disturbance, *commotion* (P98).

T231 **tune** *n.* melody, refrain, strain, song.

T232 **tunnel** *n.* passage, cave, cavern, channel, shaft.

T233 **turbulent** *adj. wild,* violent, disorderly, unruly, riotous (M145, P2, S133).

T234 **turn** 1. *v.* revolve, spin, rotate 2. *v.* reverse, alter, change, divert; *Turn right at the next street.* 3. *v.* bend, curve, twist 4. *v.* change, alter, transform; *In autumn, the leaves turn to gold.* 5. spoil, go sour 6. *n.* revolution, rotation 7. *n.* chance, spell, stint; *It's my turn to walk the dog.* TERN

T235 **tussle** *v. & n. scuffle,* struggle, conflict.

T236 **tutor** *n. teacher,* instructor.

T237 **twaddle** *n. nonsense,* balderdash, prattle, chatter.

T238 **twinge** *n. pain,* pang, gripe, ache.

T239 **twinkle** *v.* sparkle, wink, *flash,* glitter.

T240 **twirl** *v.* whirl, revolve, turn.

T241 **twist** 1. *v.* twine, wind, encircle, interweave 2. *v.* contort, distort, writhe 3. *n.* bend, curve *adj.* **twisted** (S486).

T242 **twitch** *v. & n. jerk,* snatch, shudder, shake.

T243 **type** 1. *n.* sort, *kind,* class, group, brand 2. *n.* printing character 3. *v.* typewrite.

T244 **typical** *adj. characteristic,* symbolic, distinctive, representative (O36).

T245 **tyrant** *n.* despot, autocrat, oppressor, dictator.

U u

U1 **ugly** *adj.* 1. *plain,* unsightly, frightful, hideous (B43, B113, G103, H26, L152, P372) 2. nasty, unwelcome, beastly, unpleasant.

U2 **ultimate** *adj.* last, *final,* eventual, extreme (F129).

U3 **umpire** *v. & n.* referee, judge.

U4 **unable** *adj. incapable,* incompetent, powerless (A6).

U5 **unaccustomed** *adj.* unused, new, unfamiliar (A38).

U6 **unadorned** *adj.* simple, *plain,* unembellished (F38, O97).

U7 **unaffected** *adj.* simple, plain, *natural,* artless, naïve (H63).

U8 **unanimous** *adj.* agreeing, united, harmonious.

U9 **unassuming** *adj. modest,* humble, unpretentious, (P284, V5).

U10 **unaware** *adj.* heedless, ignorant, insensible, *oblivious* (A184, C340).

U11 **unbiased** *adj.* impartial, neutral, *fair,* disinterested (B68).

U12 **uncanny** *adj. strange,* mysterious, creepy, weird.

U13 **uncertain** *adj.* unsure, doubtful, *dubious,* unreliable (C86, I157, S585).

U

U14 **uncivilized** *adj.* barbarous, savage, *wild,* brutal (C166).

U15 **uncomfortable** *adj.* displeasing, distressing, upset, troubled (C239).

U16 **uncommon** *adj. rare,* unusual, odd, strange, queer, singular (O88, P373, R255, T209).

U17 **unconscious** *adj.* 1. insensible, senseless 2. ignorant, unaware (C340).

U18 **unconventional** *adj.* informal, unusual, odd, *eccentric* (O98).

U19 **uncouth** *adj.* boorish, loutish, clumsy, unrefined, awkward, rude, *vulgar,* coarse (G41).

U20 **uncover** *v. disclose,* reveal, unmask, expose (O15).

U21 **undaunted** *adj. bold,* intrepid, fearless, brave, courageous (F64).

U22 **under** *prep. beneath,* below, underneath (A12).

U23 **undergo** *v.* bear, *suffer,* endure, sustain, experience.

U24 **underhand** *adj.* secret, *sly,* unfair, fraudulent, dishonest (H151).

U25 **underneath** *adj.* under, beneath, below (A12).

U26 **understand** *v.* discern, see, *comprehend,* know, learn, hear (M191) *adj.* **understandable** (I122).

U27 **undertake** *v. attempt,* set about, try, venture.

U28 **undesirable** *adj.* unwelcome, objectionable, unacceptable, unpleasant (P248).

U29 **undo** *v.* unfasten, loosen, untie, open, dismantle (A157).

U30 **undress** *v.* disrobe, *strip,* divest (D312).

U31 **unearth** *v.* uncover, find, *discover,* disclose.

U32 **unearthly** *adj. weird,* strange, eerie, supernatural.

U33 **uneasy** *adj.* restless, disturbed, worried, anxious (C239).

U34 **unemployed** *adj.* unoccupied, out of work, *idle,* inactive, jobless (E53, O32).

U35 **unequal** *adj.* uneven, disproportionate, irregular, inadequate (E114, E117).

U36 **uneven** *adj.* rough, jagged, odd, irregular (E145, F141, L76, S283).

U37 **unexpected** *adj. sudden,* abrupt, surprising, unforeseen, chance (A117).

U38 **unfair** *adj.* unjust, partial, unequal, biased (F19, I47, J44).

U39 **unfaithful** *adj. faithless,* treacherous, false, deceitful (D160, F22, S445).

U40 **unfit** *adj. unsuitable,* incapable, unqualified, incompetent (F131).

U41 **unfold** *v.* open, *reveal,* unroll, disclose, decipher, clarify (F182).

U42 **unforeseen** *adj.* unexpected, *sudden,* unanticipated (A117).

U43 **unfortunate** *adj.* luckless, unsuccessful, *unhappy,* hapless (F219, L159).

U44 **unfriendly** *adj.* unkind, *hostile,* malevolent (F256, H171).

U45 **ungainly** *adj.* clumsy, *awkward,* uncouth, gawky, loutish (G110).

U46 **ungrateful** *adj. thankless, selfish* (G123, T76).

U47 **unhappy** *adj.* wretched, *miserable,* distressed, sad, melancholy (G60, H34) *n.* **unhappiness** (J32).

U48 **unhealthy** *adj.* sickly, unwell, *infirm,* ill (H79, S331, W66).

U49 **uniform** 1. *adj.* regular, unchanging, constant, alike (I300) 2. *n.* costume, outfit.

U50 **unimportant** *adj.* unsignificant, *trivial,* trifling, slight, petty (G126, M215, P422, S540, U98).

U51 **union** *n.* 1. alliance, league, association 2. combination, junction, agreement, concord.

U52 **unique** *adj.* rare, exceptional, single, sole, unprecedented (C251).

U53 **unite** *v.* join, *combine,* connect, attach, associate (D266, I307, P59, S130).

U54 **unity** *n.* oneness, singleness, *concord,* harmony, agreement (D217).

U55 **universal** *adj.* unlimited, general, total, whole, entire, all, international (L121).

U56 **unjust** *adj.* merciless, ruthless, biased, unfair (J44, M127).

U57 **unkind** *adj.* heartless, mean, unfeeling, pitiless, *cruel* (K8, T60).

U58 **unknown** *adj.* unexplored, mysterious, mystic, hidden, obscure (F35).

U59 **unlike** *adj. different,* dissimilar, opposite (A89).

U60 **unlikely** *adj.* impossible, *improbable,* implausible (L92, P393).

U61 **unlucky** *adj.* unfortunate, unsuccessful, disastrous (F219, L159).

U62 **unnatural** *adj.* 1. *unusual,* uncommon, irregular, abnormal 2. forced, strained, artificial, stilted (N16).

U63 **unnecessary** *adj.* useless, needless, *superfluous,* pointless (I145).

U64 **unoccupied** *adj.* vacant, *empty,* uninhabited (O32).

U65 **unpleasant** *adj.* horrible, *obnoxious,* offensive, repulsive, sour, unpleasing (P248).

U66 **unprincipled** *adj.* wicked, vicious, *dishonest,* villainous, tricky (H151).

U67 **unqualified** *adj.* 1. incapable, incompetent, unfit (E34) 2. downright, absolute, unconditional, utter; *The new play was an unqualified success.*

U68 **unravel** *v.* disentangle, extricate, unfold, decipher, interpret (T20).

U69 **unreal** *adj.* imaginary, *false,* mock, spurious, artificial, fake, sham, phantom, fantastic (A46).

U70 **unreasonable** *adj.* irrational, foolish, unwise, absurd, extreme, immoderate, outrageous, illogical, senseless, excessive (R65).

U71 **unrest** *n.* disquiet, trouble, stir, disturbance, *turmoil* (C15).

U72 **unrivaled** *adj.* unequaled, *peerless,* matchless, incomparable.

U

U

U73 **unruffled** *adj.* calm, *tranquil,* quiet, placid, peaceful, serene (T51).

U74 **unruly** *adj.* turbulent, disobedient, mutinous, riotous, *wild* (O87) *n.* **unruliness** (D210).

U75 **unsafe** *adj.* dangerous, perilous, *hazardous,* insecure (S6).

U76 **unscrupulous** *adj.* unprincipled, ruthless, reckless, corrupt (H151, S91).

U77 **unseemly** *adj.* improper, unbecoming, *unfit,* indecent, vulgar (S114).

U78 **unsettle** *v.* derange, *disturb,* disconcert, confuse, unhinge (S141).

U79 **unsightly** *adj.* ugly, deformed, *disagreeable,* hideous (A176).

U80 **unskilled** *adj.* inexperienced, inexpert, awkward, *inept* (E201, I185, P323, P412).

U81 **unsophisticated** *adj.* naïve, natural, *simple,* inexperienced, raw (S323).

U82 **unsound** *adj.* 1. *defective,* imperfect, decayed 2. diseased, sickly, poorly 3. *wrong,* false, incorrect 4. thin, weak, feeble, flimsy (S331).

U83 **unsuitable** *adj.* inappropriate, inept, *unfit,* improper (P433, R259, S556).

U84 **untidy** *adj.* disheveled, *slovenly,* unkempt, sloppy (I30, S277, T111, T206).

U85 **untrue** *adj.* 1. false, *wrong,* erroneous, incorrect 2. unfaithful, disloyal, treacherous (T217).

U86 **unusual** *adj. rare,* special, uncommon, abnormal, extraordinary, queer (C251, C252, E152, O88, R122, S428, U102).

U87 **unwary** *adj. imprudent,* hasty, careless, heedless, rash.

U88 **unwieldy** *adj.* unmanageable, *ponderous,* bulky, heavy, clumsy.

U89 **unwilling** *adj.* reluctant, opposed, averse, loath (R56, W73) *adv.* **unwillingly** (R55).

U90 **uphold** *v.* support, *sustain,* maintain, defend, aid, back.

U91 **upkeep** *n. support,* maintenance, provision.

U92 **upright** *adj.* 1. *erect,* perpendicular, vertical (H164) 2. *honest,* just, honorable, virtuous, good (B29, C423, I134, S220) *n.* **uprightness** (I112).

U93 **uproar** *n.* tumult, disturbance, *commotion,* racket, din.

U94 **upset** *v.* 1. overturn, *capsize,* invert, overthrow 2. disconcert, *perturb,* startle, bother (C15, P3, S322, T173).

U95 **urban** *adj.* metropolitan, suburban, civic, municipal (R328).

U96 **urbane** *adj.* polite, civil, *courteous,* elegant, polished.

U97 **urge** 1. *v.* push, press, impel, drive, force, incite, spur, *stimulate* (D219) 2. *v.* beg, plead, *entreat,* beseech 3. *n.* impulse, desire.

U98 **urgent** *adj.* pressing, imperative, *important,* immediate, insistent, persistent (U50).

A vacuum cleaner.

U99 **use** 1. *v.* employ, apply, utilize (M192) 2. *v.* practice, exercise 3. *v.* expend, consume, exhaust 4. *n.* employment, application 5. *n.* advantage, benefit, utility 6. *n.* usage, custom, habit.

U100 **useful** *adj. helpful,* beneficial, serviceable, handy (U101).

U101 **useless** *adj.* unserviceable, valueless, fruitless, *futile* (H103, U100).

U102 **usual** *adj.* customary, common, familiar, *normal,* frequent, habitual, regular (A7, E225, Q17, R34, S348).

U103 **usurp** *v. seize,* take over, appropriate, assume, take control (A4).

U104 **utensil** *n.* implement, tool, instrument, appliance.

U105 **utmost** *adj.* extreme, farthest, last, uttermost, ultimate.

U106 **utter** 1. *adj.* total, complete, *entire,* absolute 2. *v.* speak, articulate, say, express.

V v

V1 **vacant** *adj.* 1. empty, void, unfilled, *unoccupied* (F281) 2. thoughtless, unthinking, stupid.

V2 **vacuum** *n.* void, empty space.

V3 **vagabond** *n.* vagrant, outcast, beggar, *tramp,* hobo.

V4 **vague** *adj. uncertain,* dim, doubtful, obscure, indefinite (D252, S350, T19).

V5 **vain** *adj.* 1. *conceited,* arrogant, self-opinionated (H196, U9) 2. useless, unavailing, futile, worthless.   VANE VEIN

V6 **valiant** *adj. brave,* courageous, intrepid, gallant, heroic, daring, fearless (F64).

V7 **valid** *adj. sound,* weighty, good, effective, real, genuine (I282, V84).

V8 **valley** *n.* dale, dell, dingle, vale, ravine, glen (H125).

V9 **valor** *n.* bravery, courage, boldness, *daring,* heroism (C451).

V10 **valuable** *adj.* 1. *precious,* costly, expensive (W105) 2. worthy, estimable, important.

V11 **value** *n.* 1. *worth,* importance, merit 2. price, cost.

V12 **van** *n.* truck, lorry, wagon.

V13 **vandal** *n.* barbarian, savage, destroyer, wrecker.

V14 **vanish** *v. disappear,* dissolve, fade, evaporate (A125).

V15 **vanity** *n. conceit,* pride, arrogance (M208).

V16 vanquish *v.* conquer, *defeat,* overcome, subdue, beat (Y7).

V17 vapor *n. steam,* fume, fog, mist, haze.

V18 variable *adj.* changeable, shifting, inconstant, unsteady (C355).

V19 variety *n.* 1. assortment, diversity, difference 2. kind, species, class, sort, type.

V20 various *adj.* diverse, different, *several,* numerous, many.

V21 vary *v.* change, *alter,* deviate, differ (C375).

V22 vast *adj.* huge, *enormous,* immense, colossal, measureless, wide (M161).

V23 vault 1. *v.* & *n.* leap, bound, jump 2. *n.* tomb, crypt, catacomb 3. *n.* safe, coffer, deposit.

V24 veer *v. shift,* turn, change, swerve.

**V25 vehement (vee-*a-ment*) ** *adj.* impetuous, passionate, hot, ardent, eager, enthusiastic (C402).

V26 vehicle *n.* carriage, conveyance.

V27 veil 1. *n.* screen, shade, curtain, gauze 2. *v.* cover, hide, mask.

A veil.

V28 vein *n.* 1. course, current, seam, streak; *The diggers had struck a new vein of gold.* 2. bent, character, mood, humor; *Their conversation was in a light and humorous vein.* 3. blood vessel.   VAIN VANE

V29 velocity *n. speed,* swiftness, quickness.

V30 venerate *v.* reverence, respect, *honor* (D227).

V31 vengeance *n. revenge,* retaliation, reprisal.

V32 venom *n.* 1. poison, virus, toxin 2. malice, *spite,* rancor, grudge, acrimony.

V33 vent 1. *n.* opening, hole, outlet 2. *v.* emit, pour out, utter, discharge.

V34 ventilate *v.* 1. air, fan, winnow, aerate 2. discuss, examine.

V35 venture *v.* & *n.* hazard, risk, chance, gamble, undertaking, experiment.

V36 verbal *adj. oral,* spoken, unwritten.

V37 verdict *n.* decision, finding, *judgment,* opinion, sentence.

V38 verge 1. *n.* edge, rim, *brink,* margin 2. *v.* tend, incline, lean.

V39 verify *v. prove,* authenticate, attest, confirm.

V40 versatile *adj.* adaptable, many-sided, capable, *flexible* (I176).

V41 verse *n.* poetry, rhyme.

V42 version *n.* translation, rendering, interpretation.

V43 vertical *adj.* perpendicular, *upright,* plumb, erect (H164).

V44 **very** *adv.* highly, extremely, excessively.

V45 **vessel** *n.* 1. utensil, container, receptacle 2. ship, boat, craft.

V46 **vestige** *n.* evidence, indication, hint, residue, sign.

V47 **veteran** *n.* old soldier, expert, adept, master (R93).

V48 **veto** 1. *v. prohibit,* forbid, deny, refuse (A135) 2. *n.* prohibition, denial, refusal.

V49 **vex** *v.* tease, torment, harass, worry, *annoy,* pester (P249).

V50 **vibrate** *v.* oscillate, quiver, *shake,* quake, tremble.

V51 **vice** 1. *n.* wickedness, sin, evil, corruption (V70) 2. *n.* clamp, cramp, wrench 3. *adj.* deputizing, representing, substitute; *Smith has been elected vice-chairman.*

V52 **vicinity** *n.* nearness, proximity, neighborhood (D251).

V53 **vicious** *adj.* wicked, mischievous, immoral, sinful, corrupt (V71) 2. *cruel,* ruthless, brutal, savage.

V54 **victim** *n.* sufferer, prey, dupe, loser, scapegoat, butt.

V55 **victor** *n.* conqueror, vanquisher, *winner.*

V56 **victory** *n.* conquest, *triumph*, success (D62).

V57 **view** 1. *n.* sight, survey, vision 2. *n.* prospect, *scene,* vista 3. *n.* opinion, judgment, belief 4. *v.* survey, scan, see, witness, *behold.*

V58 **vigilant** *adj.* watchful, careful, wakeful, *alert* (N33).

V59 **vigor** *n.* strength, *energy,* force, might, power, vitality *adj.* **vigorous** (L20, W37).

V60 **vile** *adj. wicked,* sinful, base, mean, offensive, obnoxious, disgusting (W106).

V61 **villain** *n.* rascal, rogue, knave, *scoundrel* (H114).

V62 **vim** *n.* vitality, vigor, pep, punch (W37).

V63 **vindicate** *v.* defend, *justify,* uphold, acquit, free (D101).

V64 **vindictive** *adj.* revengeful, unforgiving, *malicious,* spiteful (C108).

V65 **violate** *v.* 1. infringe, break, trespass, transgress 2. *abuse,* outrage, defile.

V66 **violent** *adj.* passionate, raging, furious, fiery, *turbulent* (M145).

V67 **virgin** 1. *n.* maiden, girl, maid, lass, damsel 2. *adj.* chaste, pure, untouched, fresh.

V68 **virile** *adj.* manly, male, masculine, *robust,* forceful (F82).

V69 **virtual** *adj.* implicit, implied, essential, substantial.

V70 **virtue** *n. goodness,* uprightness, morality, integrity, excellence, distinction (F58, V51).

V71 **virtuous** *adj.* upright, honest, good, *righteous,* excellent, chaste (V53, W67).

V72 **visible** *adj.* perceptible, discernible, apparent, evident, clear (I54, I290).

V73 **vision** *n.* 1. sight, seeing 2. appearance, apparition, ghost 3. perception, foresight; *The king was a man of some vision, and was able to avert war.*

V

V74 **visit** *v. & n.* call, stay, stop.

V75 **visitor** *n.* guest, caller, habitué.

V76 **vital** *adj. essential,* indispensable, necessary, critical (U50).

V77 **vivacious** *adj.* lively, sprightly, *cheerful,* merry, pleasant, attractive (D333).

V78 **vivid** *adj.* clear, bright, lucid, *brilliant,* intense (D333).

V79 **vocal** *adj.* spoken, uttered, said, oral, outspoken.

V80 **vocation** *n.* occupation, employment, *career,* profession.

V81 **vociferous** *adj. noisy,* clamorous, loud, blatant (S211).

V82 **vogue** *n. fashion,* mode, custom, style.

V83 **voice** *n.* articulation, language, words, tone, speech, utterance.

V84 **void** 1. *adj.* empty, vacant, unoccupied (F281) 2. *adj.* null, invalid, ineffectual, useless (V7) 3. *n.* space, vacuum, emptiness.

V85 **volatile** *adj.* 1. evaporable, gaseous 2. airy, lively, buoyant (D102) 3. fickle, changeable, flighty.

V86 **volume** *n.* 1. book, tome 2. contents, capacity, dimensions, bulk, amount.

V87 **voluntary** *adj.* unforced, free, gratuitous, optional (C286, I294).

V88 **vomit** *v.* be sick, retch, disgorge, puke, emit, belch.

V89 **vote** 1. *n.* suffrage, ballot, election, choice 2 *v.* choose, elect, select.

V90 **vouch** *v. affirm,* declare, guarantee, attest.

V91 **voucher** *n.* receipt, coupon, certificate.

V92 **vow** 1. *n.* promise, *pledge,* guarantee 2. *v.* dedicate, pledge, swear, assert.

V93 **voyage** *n. journey,* cruise, trip, tour.

V94 **vulgar** *adj. common,* rude, coarse, rustic, unrefined, ordinary (E31).

V95 **vulnerable** *adj.* defenseless, exposed, sensitive, susceptible (I75, P447, T152).

W　W

W1 **wad** *n.* bunch, batch, bundle, packet, pack, wedge, plug.

W2 **wag** 1. *v.* vibrate, shake, wave, flap 2. *n.* humorist, wit, joker.

W3 **wage** 1. *v.* undertake, conduct, engage in; *Many countries waged war during the last conflict.* 2. *v.* bet, stake, pledge *n.* **wager** 3. *n.* wages, salary, pay, earnings.

W4 **wagon** *n.* vehicle, carriage, truck.

W5 **wail** *v. & n.* lament, moan, cry, *howl.*

W6 **wait** 1. *v. stay,* tarry, delay, remain, linger (D105) 2. *v.* attend, serve 3. *n.* delay, hold up. WEIGHT

W7 **waiter** *n.* attendant, servant, steward.

W

W8 **waive** v. relinquish, *renounce,* forego, defer (C167). WAVE

W9 **wake** v. awaken, rouse, stir (S255).

W10 **walk** 1. *n. step,* gait, carriage 2. *n.* stroll, promenade 3. *n.* avenue, path, way 4. *v.* step, tread, go, march, hike stroll.

W11 **wallow** v. flounder, roll, grovel.

W12 **wan** adj. pale, pallid, ashen, haggard (R281).

W13 **wand** n. rod, stick, truncheon, baton, mace, scepter.

W14 **wander** v. ramble, *roam,* . rove, deviate, swerve, stray.

W15 **wane** v. decrease, diminish, lessen (E84, S587, W34). WAIN

W16 **want** 1. *v.* require, *need,* desire, wish, crave 2. *n.* desire, need, necessity, requirement (P254) 3. *n.* poverty, need, penury.

W17 **wanton** adj, 1. reckless, needless, careless (H96) 2. immoral, lustful, unchaste (C115) 3. sportive, playful, frisky; *The wanton lambs will skip and play.*

W18 **war** n. hostility, conflict, *battle,* combat (P98). WORE

W19 **ward** n. 1. pupil, minor, dependent 2. division, district, quarter 3. room, apartment. WARRED

W20 **wardrobe** n. 1. closet, *cupboard* 2. clothes, clothing.

W21 **warm** 1. *adj. hot,* tepid, heated, sunny (C132, C224, C402, F260, F269) 2. *adj. friendly,* cordial, hearty 3. *v.* heat, cook.

W22 **warn** v. *caution,* inform, admonish, give warning. WORN

W23 **warning** n. caution, notice, advice.

W24 **warp** v. twist, bend, contort.

W25 **warrant** 1. *v. guarantee,* assure, attest 2. *n.* authority, commission, permit, voucher.

W26 **warrior** n. *soldier,* fighter, champion, hero.

W27 **wary** adj. *cautious,* careful, watchful, chary (U87).

W28 **wash** 1. *v. clean,* cleanse, scrub, launder 2. *n.* washing, bathing, cleansing.

Washing.

W29 **waste** 1. *v. squander,* dissipate, misuse, lavish, spend (P362) 2. *v.* dwindle, wither, pine, perish 3. *n.* refuse, rubbish, garbage 4. *n.* loss, consumption, wasting *adj.* **wasteful** (E13, P407, T97). WAIST

W30 **watch** 1. *n.* vigil, guard, patrol 2. *n.* timepiece 3. *v. observe,* regard, view, look at.

W31 **water** v. shed water, irrigate, moisten, wet, sprinkle *adj.* **watery** (T82).

W32 **wave** 1. *v.* brandish, *flourish,* motion, flicker 2. *n.* undulation, billow, surge, ripple.   WAIVE

W33 **waver** *v. hesitate,* doubt, fluctuate, flicker, quiver *adj.* **wavering** (R200).

W34 **wax** 1. *n.* mastic, resin 2. *v.* increase, gain, grow, swell (D347, E9, W15).

W35 **way** *n.* 1. *road,* path, route, track 2. method, *manner,* mode, style.   WEIGH

W36 **wayward** *adj. perverse,* willful, contrary, disobedient, naughty (O3).

W37 **weak** *adj.* 1. *feeble,* sickly, infirm, delicate, not strong (E71, H10, H42, H87, L176, M38, M144, M276, P322, R281, R319, S424, S511, T152) 2. irresolute, undecided (R200) 3. unsound, unsafe, frail (S6) 4. thin, watery, diluted (S511) *n.* **weakness** (F218, I178, P321, S497, V59, V62) *v.* **weaken** (D179).

W38 **wealth** *n.* abundance, affluence, *fortune,* treasure, riches (P319) *adj.* **wealthy** (D142, P126, P287).

W39 **wear** *v.* 1. impair, rub, waste, use, consume, corrode 2. dress in, bear, don, have on. WARE

W40 **weary** 1. *adj.* fatigued, *tired,* exhausted 2. *v.* fatigue, tire, exhaust (I253).

W41 **weather** *n.* climate, the elements.   WHETHER

W42 **weave** *v.* interlace, plait, braid.

W43 **web** *n.* membrane, cobweb, tissue, textile, netting.

W44 **wed** *v.* marry, espouse, unite (D269).

W45 **wee** *adj. little,* small, diminutive, tiny (L26).   WE

W46 **weep** *v. cry,* sob, shed tears, lament.

W47 **weigh** *v.* 1. balance, measure 2. deliberate, consider, ponder.   WAY

W48 **weight** *n.* 1. heaviness, gravity, burden, load 2. importance, influence, power. WAIT

A well with a weighted pole.

W49 **weird** *adj.* supernatural, unearthly, strange, *eerie,* uncanny (N16).

W50 **welcome** 1. *v. greet,* receive (B20, B22) 2. *n.* greetings, salutation, reception.

W51 **welfare** *n.* happiness, success, advantage, benefit, profit.

Weaving and spinning.

W52 **well** 1. *adv.* rightly, justly, satisfactorily 2. *adv.* amply, fully, thoroughly, certainly 3. *adj.* healthy, hale, hearty, fortunate (I14, I146, S201, U48) 4. *n.* fountain, spring, source.

W53 **wet** 1. *adj. damp,* moist, humid, rainy (D329, P49) 2. *v.* moisten, dampen, soak.

W54 **whack** *v. & n.* bang, beat, strike, rap, slap.

W55 **wharf** *n.* pier, quay.

W56 **wheedle** *v.* coax, *cajole,* flatter, persuade.

W57 **whet** *v.* sharpen, stimulate, excite, rouse.

W58 **whiff** *n.* puff, blast, aroma, odor, *smell,* perfume.

W59 **whim** *n.* fancy, caprice, *quirk,* humor.

W60 **whine** *v. & n. cry,* whimper, moan, groan.

W61 **whip** 1. *v. lash,* strike, beat, flog 2. *n.* lash, strap, scourge.

W62 **whirl** *v.* rotate, *twist,* revolve, spin.

W63 **whisk** *v.* rush, speed, hasten, *brush.*

W64 **whisper** *v. & n. murmur,* mutter, mumble (R277).

W65 **whole** *adj.* total, *entire,* complete, undivided (F232, F235, P59, P294, S78, S160). HOLE

W66 **wholesome** *adj. healthy,* beneficial, nourishing, nutritious (U48).

W67 **wicked** *adj. bad,* evil, villainous, sinful, depraved, immoral (V71).

W68 **wide** *adj. broad,* vast, ample, extensive, spacious (N10, T84).

W69 **wield** *v.* handle, brandish, *use,* control, manipulate.

W70 **wild** *adj.* 1. untamed, undomesticated, *savage* (D282, T16) 2. turbulent, disorderly, *violent* 3. reckless, harebrained.

W71 **will** 1. *n.* determination, decision, resolution 2. *n.* testament, legacy 3. *v.* desire, choose, elect, wish.

W72 **willfull** *adj.* obstinate, *stubborn,* perverse (I294).

W73 **willing** *adj.* disposed, inclined, *ready,* agreeable (I294, U89).

W74 **wilt,** *v.* wither, *droop,* sag.

W75 **wily** *adj.* artful, cunning, *sly,* crafty, subtle, canny, shrewd (S215).

W76 **win** *v. gain,* procure, acquire, achieve, succeed, triumph (L142).

W77 **wind** 1. (rhymes with *sinned*) *n.* air, breeze, draft 2. *v.* (rhymes with *kind*) coil, twine, twist, turn.   WINED

W78 **wink** *v.* blink, squint.

W79 **wipe** *v. rub,* clean, stroke, mop.

W80 **wire** *n.* 1. electric cable 2. telegraph, telegram, cablegram.

W81 **wise** *adj. sensible,* sage, intelligent, erudite, learned (I112) *n.* **wisdom** (F184).

W82 **wish** 1. *v.* desire, hanker, want, long for, crave 2. *v.* bid, direct, mean, express; *I wish you well on your journey.* 3. *n.* intention, desire, will.

W83 **wistful** *adj.* reflective, thoughtful, longing, yearning, hankering, nostalgic.

W

W

W84 **wit** *n*. 1. *humor,* fun, sparkle 2. humorist, wag, comedian 3. intelligence, understanding; *She had the wit to move quickly.*

W85 **witch** *n*. sorceress, enchantress, hag (W92).

W86 **withdraw** *v*. 1. *retire,* retreat, recede, abandon (A62, A169, I277, P397) 2. take away, take back (A49, D110, I215) 3. disavow, recant, recall (I215, S554); *I must ask you to withdraw that remark!*

W87 **wither** *v*. *shrivel,* dry, wilt, fade, droop (B95).

W88 **withhold** *v*. *retain,* suppress, keep back, restrain (A91, G59, S580, U41).

W89 **withstand** *v*. *resist,* oppose, confront, thwart (Y7).

W90 **witness** 1. *n*. beholder, collaborator, *spectator* 2. *v*. attest, observe, see, notice.

W91 **witty** *adj*. humorous, amusing, droll, *funny,* sprightly, alert.

W92 **wizard** *n*. conjurer, sorcerer, magician, diviner (W85).

W93 **woe** *n*. *sorrow,* grief, distress, agony, torture, trouble (H33).

W94 **woman** *n*. lady, female, wife, girl (M30) *adj*. womanly (M26).

W95 **wonder** 1. *n*. amazement, astonishment, awe 2. *n*. curiosity, phenomenon, spectacle 3. *v*. *marvel,* stare 4. *v*. ponder, meditate, question.

W96 **wonderful** *adj*. astonishing, astounding, amazing, startling, *marvelous,* miraculous (H166).

W97 **woo** *v*. court, make love.

W98 **wood** *n*. 1. forest, grove, copse, thicket 2. timber, lumber, stick, log.   WOULD

W99 **word** *n*. 1. term, utterance, phrase, statement 2. pledge, promise 3. report, tidings, news.

W100 **work** 1. *n*. toil, *labor,* effort (P243, R92) 2. *n*. employment, job 3. *n*. performance, achievement, production; *Tomorrow, the school will hold an exhibition of the children's work.* 4. *v*. act, labor, toil, drudge 5. *v*. run, operate, function.

W101 **world** *n*. earth, globe, planet *adj*. **worldly** (S367).

W102 **worry** 1. *v*. tease, vex, harass, annoy, bother 2. *v*. *grieve,* chafe, fret 3. *n*. anxiety, vexation, trouble (C239).

W103 **worship** 1. *v*. *adore,* revere, idolize, venerate, respect (D151) 2. *n*. adoration, reverence, homage.

W104 **worth** *n*. value, merit, virtue, integrity, cost.

W105 **worthless** *adj*. useless, valueless, futile, unworthy, trifling, paltry (I283, V10, W106) *n*. **worthlessness** (W104).

W106 **worthy** *adj*. deserving, meritorious, *excellent,* honest (V60, W105).

W107 **wound** 1. *v*. hurt, *injure,* damage, harm (H78) 2. *n*. hurt, injury, damage, harm.

W108 **wrangle** *v*. & *n*. quarrel, squabble, tiff, brawl, dispute.

W109 **wrap** *v.* envelop, *enclose,* enfold, cover. RAP

W110 **wrath** *n. anger,* ire, fury.

W111 **wreck** 1. *v.* strand, founder, destroy, shatter 2. *n.* destruction, *ruin,* desolation.

W112 **wrench** 1. *v.* twist, tug, jerk, strain 2. *n.* tool.

W113 **wrestle** *v.* strive, *fight,* struggle, battle.

W114 **wretched** *adj.* unhappy, forlorn, distressed, *miserable* (F219).

W115 **wriggle** *v. squirm,* writhe, twist, turn.

W116 **wring** *v.* twist, *squeeze,* wrest. RING

W117 **wrinkle** *v. & n.* furrow, *crease,* pucker, twist.

W118 **write** *v.* inscribe, scrawl, scribble, pen, record *adj.* **written** (O80, V36). RIGHT RITE WRIGHT

A ROOF (MIEN)

ABUNDANT (FENG)

A SHADOW (YING)

Two types of writing: Chinese (above) and Arabic.

W119 **writer** *n.* author, scribe, penman, clerk, secretary, composer.

W120 **writhe** *v.* twist, contort, squirm.

W121 **wrong** 1. *adj.* unjust, unfair 2. *adj.* incorrect, inaccurate, false (A36, C418, R259) 3. *adj.* bad, wicked, improper, sinful (R259) 4. *adv.* falsely, improperly 5. *n.* injustice, unfairness 6. *n. sin,* wickedness, evil 7. *v.* injure, abuse, maltreat.

W122 **wry** *adj.* askew, contorted, crooked, twisted. RYE

Y y

Y1 **yap** *v.* yelp, bark, cry.

Y2 **yard** *n.* 1. three feet, thirty-six inches 2. court, enclosure, compound, square.

Y3 **yarn** *n.* 1. thread, fiber, wool 2. story, tale.

Y4 **yawn** *v.* gape, open wide.

Y5 **yearn** *v.* long for, hanker, desire, *crave.*

Y6 **yell** *v. & n.* screech, *shout,* shriek, scream.

Y7 **yield** 1. *v.* produce, bear, confer, impart 2. *v.* surrender, abandon, relinquish, give way (C337, D75, I217, O130, R199, S513, S530, V16, W89) 3. *n.* product, crop, harvest *adj.* **yielding** (O21, S514).

191

Z

Y8 **yoke** *n.* bond, chain, link, bondage, servitude.   YOLK

Y9 **young** *adj.* youthful, juvenile, immature (A75, M83, O52).

Y10 **youth** *n.* 1. *boy,* stripling, lad, youngster 2. youthfulness, adolescence, immaturity *adj.* **youthful** (A75, O52).

Z   z

Z1 **zany** *adj. foolish,* clownish, droll, funny.

Z2 **zeal** *n.* ardor, fervor, devotion, *enthusiasm,* passion *adj.* **zealous.**

Z3 **zenith** *n. summit,* peak, top, apex, acme.

Z4 **zero** *n.* nought, nothing, nil.

Z5 **zest** *n. relish,* gusto, appetite, savor, delight.

Z6 **zone** *n. region,* climate, area, belt, district.

A yoke makes burdens easier to carry.